T0103579

JAMIE SUMMER
WALKER

JAMIE SUMMER WALKER

VAISHALI BHARGAVA

PARTRIDGE
A Penguin Random House Company

Copyright © 2015 by Vaishali Bhargava.

ISBN: Hardcover   978-1-4828-5227-1
             Softcover   978-1-4828-5226-4
             eBook   978-1-4828-5225-7

All rights reserved. No part of this book may be used or reproduced by any means, graphic, electronic, or mechanical, including photocopying, recording, taping or by any information storage retrieval system without the written permission of the publisher except in the case of brief quotations embodied in critical articles and reviews.

This is work of fiction, characters and situations do not bear resemblance to anyone.

Because of the dynamic nature of the Internet, any web addresses or links contained in this book may have changed since publication and may no longer be valid. The views expressed in this work are solely those of the author and do not necessarily reflect the views of the publisher, and the publisher hereby disclaims any responsibility for them.

Print information available on the last page.

To order additional copies of this book, contact
Partridge India
000 800 10062 62
orders.india@partridgepublishing.com

www.partridgepublishing.com/india

My hands are always held tight,

Whether there's darkness or light,

Thank you Father for being my root,

Thank you Mother for being my stem,

Thank you Brother for being the shade…

Acknowledgements

Writing is a way to express yourself but what are expressions when you don't have people teaching you how to do the same.

To my father, for always being there no matter what the disaster as someone who inspires me to keep faith in myself whatever the circumstance. To my mother, for encouraging me to think out of the box every time so as to let me give full justice to my writing.

Thank you to the first publishers – **'Partridge Company'** for providing a platform to relieve my passion. It would have been impossible without your expertise and patience.

To my best friend Appurv Mehra, for being the rock solid support that gets a smile on my face every time I break down. Yes, you shall get your signed copy.

I'd like to thank Inge for always getting super excited every time I came up with a crazy idea for Romance and

Jamie to deal with. Your reactions have always made worth telling you the whole story.

To the director and staff off Symbiosis School of Liberal Arts, Pune for giving me an opportunity to polish my talent more by providing me the gift of education

To all those who I couldn't mention here but have always been there encouraging me to write and believing in my talent . . .

Thank you to you for picking this book up and giving it a chance to enthral you and take you into some other world for a little while.

And finally to someone who would know between the lines that it's for you. The inspiration and love that you've given will always be the reason I got through this as smoothly as I could. Thank you for being there.

Jamie Summer Walker

What was it about the magic of love that drove a billion people on the verge of even committing suicide? Just recently I had grappled with the theory of Maslow's Hierarchy of needs but failed to understand the classification of love being the third priority when actually the whole thing revolved around love or as I liked to say - that four letter *bull*.

For a guy dealing with the whole stereotypical theory of being one, I did live a tough life. Even if watching some sentimental, cheesy, romantic nonsense brought the inevitable emotions in me; I had to strive for the contrary. That was what my testosterone infatuated childhood had taught.

I gazed as the blood oozed out from the paper cut. My thoughts were running wild and hence I couldn't even act towards cleaning the wound.

My brothers and father practised the art of being a man to their full extents.

My oldest brother, Grover, deserved the honours of making me a true fan of blood and gore. Be it from gibbering zombies to satanic monsters, I revelled in the scenes of human flesh being torn ruthlessly apart.

"Dad's calling you downstairs, Kitty."

Breaking from my reveries, I chucked a cushion at my youngest brother Luke. He knew how to rattle my nerves anytime.

According to one of my dead mom's monotonous traditions, the whole family had to sit at the table for any sort of meal. All five of us loathed that but father loved her enough to keep following it ardently. Recently though, Mr Winter had started going away for work. We hardly saw him around the house. Thus, the tradition was almost broken.

Rules were just another of those things binding you in a circle and teaching you to be a slave.

I was greeted with the usual 'There comes the girl of our house' or 'Hey puberty, why art thou give him smaller boobs' and even obscene ones ranging from my inadequate height to whether I was yet in that time of the month or not.

I ignored them.

Human nature was adamant on being envious of perfection.

If you're thinking that I'm in any way driving on the other side of the road . . . then no. I was as straight as any straight object on this planet. In fact, I had had a wide range of girlfriends but none matched the expectations I held.

That was . . . except Kitty Somers.

"If Kitty be the love of our Romeo, let there be no music in life."

I spread a thick amount of jam on my bread.

"Want to bet that he'd be getting a cat next week introducing it as our future sister-in law?"

"Or it could be a donkey with the taste he has!"

"I'd say it would probably be in the next ten years when he gets a girl but by then the oil prices would have sky rocketed for robots to be fed . . ."

I placed my headphones and notched the volume high. 'Beatles' blared in my ears sort of calming the anger down. Mother had always defended me unlike father who I knew would be laughing at the meagre attempts of my brothers to degrade me. However, it had been ten years or so since mom had passed away and by now I was used to being ill treated.

Kitty was the epitome of perfection. She had thick blonde hair that always flew ever so gently in the wind. The expanse of her blue eyes stretched like the wide spreading ocean. Her nose gently curved towards the end so you could nuzzle it and hear the cute little piggy giggles she made. Her full lips bloomed like that rose reaching its maturity, a crimson one to expand on that. The long blonde eyelashes blinked coyly beckoning you forward with all the force of attraction. Her body would put any woman to shame, such luscious features.

Kitty had been my sole girlfriend from a long time now, the one that still continued to be so.

To say I loved her was insulting the word.

The whole day I tried my best to maintain a dignified distance from all the men. At night, I slept after my usual time spent with Kitty.

She was perfect in every way. I was sure no one would ever be able to meet her standards.

Hence, I was humbly surprised the next day in school when out of nowhere a new person had been added to the already overflowing class of twenty making us a formidable twenty one.

Life is full of vile yet beautiful surprises and Jamie Summer Walker was one for me.

The First Time I Met Jamie

Akin my daily routine I strolled towards the classroom, bobbing my head inconspicuously to Beatles. A few guys greeted me with a pat and I returned a nod. Even though, I wished dearly to mingle with the walls rather than be under the tube light, human regulations of social norms demanded that I be friendly to at least a few.

I ignored my second elder brother Parsley making obscene faces at me and entered the class assigned. That's when a strawberry scent hit me.

I don't pride on having a photogenic memory but I believed in using one's acquired skills from the start. Hence, the alien odour had me alerted about a new possible danger. Rightfully so, the minute I stepped inside my eyes out of habit travelled towards the last bench on the left corner which I usually habited.

There was someone sitting there.

My male classmates specialized in trying to prove their strengths now and then but no one dared to test my patience as a challenge. Not that I was some bulky hunk who would beat the stars out of them but because I used my brains and eventually landed them more hurt than they intent to inflict on me. So to say that some guy had decided to sit on my seat was a thing to be debated upon. The sudden hush in the class was a signal enough.

Nineteen pair of eyes travelled with every step I took. They expected a dramatic scene and unfortunately so did me.

I cleared my throat while popping the headphones out. The seat stealer did not glance at me. I tapped the shoulder after failing in thrice of attention-seeking, clearing throat gestures.

A pair of light brown eyes gazed at me. They were shaped like almonds outlined by kohl. A certain magic lay underneath the gothic colour which immediately entranced me. I detested the hue with my whole heart so finding this attractive was a shock to my little heart. With all my inner strength and a bull load of internal screaming, I still couldn't manage to look away. Why was I falling for a guy? Wait till the clan backs hears of this. I might need a year to live that humiliation down.

"Please vacate this seat immediately as this is where I sit," I said confidently, even surprising myself.

Was the darkness comparable to the inside of your body or maybe the deepest cave where sunshine hasn't visited for years?

"Excuse me?" I tried again.

"Does this 'usual seat' of yours hold a patent on your name?"

I stared at him in astonishment. I hadn't ever thought of scribbling my name on the school furniture. That was utterly out of question.

"My apologies but you see I can't sit anywhere but here. It's against my universal rules." I tried to explain with exasperation. This was a tedious task.

Why were his lips so . . . womanish?

"Then today Mr OCD, you'll be sitting somewhere else," he said shrugging.

"For a good amount of my senior year I have occupied this space and that's what I'll continue to do so. Either you get up on your own free will or there will be circumstances in which you might acquire injury."

"Why are you so uptight? It's like talking to a classic novel character."

My temper was boiling inside. The anger management classes had made me learn how to be in control so I just let out a slow breath.

Wait, breasts? Why was I seeing a bust on a guy? It was that time of the year when my brain started hallucinating maybe.

"I don't have OCD," I growled suddenly understanding what had been spoken before. That certainly didn't cease my anger.

"Good morning sunshine. I see you process things at the speed of a snail."

"Listen here Mister . . ."

"Miss Jamie Summer Walker."

Oh, that explained a lot of things.

"Miss Jamie Summer Walker. You have to establish some rules if you want to stay peacefully with me for I can be vile when I wish to. I have particulars that I follow strictly and no foreign particle can disturb that equilibrium. This is not OCD but mere human nature so please vacate my seat immediately."

"Oh did you stop the boring lecture," she yawned. Then with a brilliant smile that took my breath away, she shifted sideways.

We didn't have separate tables but bench-kinds. I had always sat alone but this was new.

"So Mr Upright, what are you waiting for? Christmas?" she smiled at me.

Those white things should remain in their cage for they have the power to make a heart beat miles ahead of the usual. Sighing with defeat I slid in. I ignored the gasps. Even though I wanted to argue about the ownership of this place, I had to admit with shame that my mild curiosity about Jamie Summer Walker had won the battle.

"What brand of underwear do you wear?" she asked me.

"What?" I retorted shocked. What sort of a person asked such obscene questions. "Why do you want to know that?"

"Do I have to answer every question of mine with your own question now?"

"But this information is personal."

"You're acting as if I asked about the size."

"In social decorum no one has the right to ask . . ."

"Oh please! Decorum my derriere, I'll ask what I desire."

They said curiosity kills the cat. I was literally being slaughtered by this barbarian the whole class. So I made a list of everything she did that annoyed me.

1. Chewing bubblegum incessantly.
2. Sitting with one leg crossing the other from top.

3. Hitting me with that leg frequently but without knowledge.
4. Humming.
5. Scribbling nonsense and wasting paper.

The list went on to like twenty things and then I felt a sense of relief. At least all the things I wanted to say were expressed somewhere though I detested writing. Anger management classes do help somehow.

Unfortunately for the peace of my mind, Jamie Summer Walker snatched the paper out of my hand and read my untidy scrawl. God knows how she made sense of what was my unruly writing. I tried snatching it away but she had been pricking her nose a while back and I couldn't stand the thought of germs.

I sat cross armed and with a scowl clearly trying to show my disapproval which definitely didn't work with this woman. I knew what was coming next - the typical girl drama with a lot of crying.

That's just what I needed for a perfect day.

And then she laughed. She chortled so much that her pudgy face became pink. She fell down chuckling from the other side of the bench. It took a while for her to calm down but by then we were the centre of attention.

Hopefully, I wasn't blushing. Thanks mom for giving me you easy-blush gene.

"I have a crooked nose? What is this, she blinks a lot? How am I supposed to stop my reflexes?"

I did not have an answer for that.

"I scratch my boobs inappropriately? What do I do if it itches?"

Or that

Okay, I admit some of the points were silly but then I had been distracted getting over some weird feelings.

"You know Xerkis Moon, for a typical teenage guy you do have a lot of issues. Don't worry honey bun. Jamie Summer Walker will teach you how to be alive. I'll make you realize the power of each little cell in your body. Your heart will finally learn how to beat," she rambled on.

And you know what?

Maybe it was the blackness of the eyes or the pouty shape of the lips.

But my heart did start beating inappropriately.

Wait.

How did she know my name?

The Day Jamie Pinched My Cheeks

It had been a week and somehow Jamie had inculcated herself into my life without prior permission. It wasn't the fact that I despised extra company but the thought of having to behave normally terrified me.

Only Jamie Summer Walker was far from normal.

The day after our first meet, I heard a honking outside my house at the break of dawn.

There she was – clad in a grey baggy hoodie with the words 'Devil's rule me' sprawled across the expanse of the chest. Her boyish fingers tapped the steering wheel and her mouth sprayed out a wide range of beats. I stumbled into the convertible.

And just like that it became a daily routine.

Every morning I would be greeted by some obscene beat boxing and every afternoon I'd be dropped in the same manner. We hardly spoke but were always together. Jamie Summer had most of her classes similar to mine.

"Kitty . . ."

I suppressed my groan as Grover walked towards me. On the way he made sure to keep his *coolness* intact as conversing with me would rub it down. Finally after charming our school's most popular girl Crystal Meth (don't even ask) as much as plausible, he stopped in front of me with an annoyed expression.

"What is this rumour I receive little brother?" he asked.

I shrugged. There had been uncountable gossips flying around all targeted at me. I had long ago stooped to a level of not caring.

"You've started hanging out with riff-ruffs? Who is this Gayme Monsoon Stalker?" He provided some more details.

Now I know Jamie Summer Walker wasn't exactly the perfect *girl* but giving her such a title was plain inhuman. The anger I had learned to press down somehow resurfaced. I clenched my fists in a tight round and tried to even my breathing. Why was I getting so affected by this? For God sakes it wasn't even related to me.

"You know I don't like to be ignored Kitty," Grover spoke to me sternly.

"She's a perfectly moulded human. There is nothing wrong in hanging out with a girl like that. Her name by the way is Jamie Summer Walker which sounds like the immense pleasure you get when you come out of an extremely cold area to a tepid one with sunshine. Also, it doesn't concern you who I hang out with even if it turns out to be a gorilla. Stay away."

That was a long speech that had me and Grover shocked. I never defended myself the way I had done for a stranger today. He seemed baffled enough to reply witty. I did the only thing I could.

I fled.

Jogging upstairs to the alley which was frequented by jobless humans constituting me, I stopped in a corner and huffed. This girl was twisting my thoughts in inappropriate ways. I had to keep distance.

"That was something."

Despite my rules of not groaning in public due to it being against good mannerism, I did. The moment my mind made up to stay away that voice made my heart put up the strongest fight ever.

"Do you always sound so defensive?"

I ignored her pretending to concentrate on the non-existent bird flying outside.

"Xerkis Moon?"

I put up my Skulls and started humming the tune.

"Romance Winters?"

They gazed at each other happily. The baby was their third child. The couple couldn't have asked for more. He would someday break hearts.

"Let's name him Mat," the man said.

"What?" the woman asked shocked. "People would make fun of that. Wipe your feet, Mat is here."

"My grandfather was named Mat," the man argued.

"Honey . . ."

He sighed. There was nothing he loved more than his family and wife.

"We'll name him . . ." she began.

"Romance Winters, isn't it?"

I had despised that name ever since the knowledge of reading embellished in my mind. Romance Winters, who would name their child that? Didn't they think that of all the amount of bullying possible on this Earth would be directed at me? Mom was understandable, she was an affectionate woman but someone else agreeing to this atrocity seemed nothing less than foolish.

Keeping all that aside, I glared at her.

"How did you know my name?"

It wasn't much of a known fact that my real name wasn't Xerkis Moon.

"I know a lot about you Romance Winters."

Maybe she *was* Gayme Monsoon *Stalker*.

There was something about the nonchalance in her that riled me up further. Pulling the headphones down roughly, I moved towards the wall, pinning her. She seemed unfazed by the close proximity.

"You better start talking woman," I spat at her.

"Did you know Casey Hayes of Geography got a boob job done?"

No wonder her bust practically spilled out off every shirt she wore. Not to forget the number of boys currently pinning behind getting those artificial pieces laid.

"Jamie Summer Walker"

"Romance Hunter Winters"

"Don't call me that," I growled at her.

"I'll call you what I desire to. No one can control my mouth."

The moment she spoke about that organ my gaze was fixated on the pink, pouted lips. Now I had a good share of females lips but *her* lips compelled, beckoned me like a siren's song.

I shook my head to get rid of the absurd thoughts.

"How did you find out about my name," I tried again though calmly.

"See, everything works with being polite. If Hitler had been polite to the Jews, we would have had a different history."

"But if Hitler hadn't done the massacre, no one would have understood the degraded level humans can stoop down to."

"Point noted. Let's get down to business now. Why did you defend me?"

"How did you . . .?"

"It was on Facebook," she replied rolling her brown orbs. They were almost black if not for the light reflecting off. "Now, it's your turn to answer."

Ah! that accursed social media. That must be Parsley's handiwork. Creating my fake id and gaining me much more popularity than I required.

"If you don't mind I really don't like people crossing my personal space so would you be a gentleman enough and step back?"

I looked at her amused expressions. Shaking my shoulders in weariness, I took some steps back. Placing the Skulls back on, I distanced myself from that annoying midget and the world.

Yes, she was stout and short. Not the perfect girl as I mentioned earlier.

"Gone back to your dark paradise Romance Winters?"

"Shut up. Don't call me that."

"Why would you name yourself Xerkis Moon? That's seriously the dumbest thing I've heard in all my lifetime and I'm saying that after spending so much time with you."

She started chuckling. For once in my life, I didn't mind being teased as much. Her laughter sounded like the flute music I listened to at random times - so serenely melodious.

"So why did you defend me?" she asked again persistently.

I ignored her for there was something else I had to defend first. There was no way I would be unselfish when it involved her.

"If you must know than Xerkis Moon is one of the most . . ."

"Romance Winters. Now that sounds like the name of a guy I would do."

I stifled my gasp. Talk about being straightforward. Before I could reply to that, Jamie Summer Walker pinched my cheeks making some sort of cooing sounds and then walked away.

More like pulled her hood up and trudged away like some gangster.

No one, not even my parents had dared to pull my cheeks like that after I gained sense reading about germs when I was seven. The mere thought of foreign particles inside my hygienic body was cringe worthy. For the first time, I was more concerned about how I felt than running away to get my skin sanitized.

Jamie Summer Walker was giving me a lot of first things.

The Day Jamie Winked At Me

"She's too shallow . . . nah too obese . . . too gothic . . ."
I nodded with the music from the radio as the rant went on. Grover and Parsley were doing their daily chore of rating woman. I had made the grave mistake of turning in late at night and thus ended up having to resort to asking my brothers for lift. I regret this a tad bit for my attention had been caught up last night in replying to Jamie Summer Walker's horrendous questions.

I had no clue as to how she acquired my number but I wasn't going to complain.

Unknown: *Knock! Knock!*

I had been cleaning my desk at the usual time when the screen of my Blackberry lit up. I scrunched up my eyebrows in consternation at the unknown number.

Me: *What is the use of this exaggeration when I don't know who you are?*

I thought my reply was decent enough considering I did not know the stranger.

Unknown: *<insert roll eyes smiley> Are you kidding me here? You just had to say who's there?*

Well I didn't think of that but then why would I want to know who it was as otherwise I would have taken their number on my own accord.

Me: *I don't really believe in wasting my time talking to strangers when I could be instead doing something productive with my time. So unless you like to state who you are, I will henceforth terminate this conversation.*

There was no reply for fifteen minutes. I smiled with triumph. That is how it is done. After that, I busied myself in colour-coding the washed laundry so that they could be placed into appropriate shelves. Just when I thought of going downtown for a cup of coffee, my phone vibrated.

Unknown: *Oh bummer! You seriously need to have a life. I'm sorry but it took me all this time to even make sense of the weird way you converse in. So, do you work out? I can't make out if you have muscles underneath those baggy clothes. I like hunky boys, you know.*

I sighed. I thought I'd got rid of that person but some people are persistent and stubborn.

Me: *What do you want Jamie Summer?*

The moment that first text had lit my screen, I'd guessed it was her. No one texted me like that.

Walker: *So you knew it was me? Why the show?*

Me: *I repeat what do you want?*

Walker: *You . . .*

My eyes widened in shock. I could feel my face scrunching up in displeasure. This was more than I had bargained for. What does she mean by violating my privacy like that? I could just bash her head into . . .

Walker: *Don't get that unknown branded underwear into a twist. I sent that by mistake. I was just asking whether you'd like to hang out tomorrow evening.*

I let out a slow, relieved breath. Not that the prospect of *hanging* out with Jamie Summer Walker was appropriate than what was happening but the fact that she wasn't being serious before was reprieving.

However, I was stuck in turmoil. If I said yes, I would betray Kitty who had a date with me then. If I denied then Jamie Summer would probably storm inside my room and create havoc in my already annoying family. Kitty had always been there for me, I couldn't break her heart.

Jamie: *I'm not an immortal and nor are you.*

She was getting impatient. I know I was wasting time which I usually didn't but this was something I couldn't just do. I couldn't betray Kitty. I wouldn't. That was against my norms.

Jamie: *. . . ?*

Me: *Alright. I'll hang out with you.*

I sincerely apologized to Kitty. I made sure to make it up for her later by giving her a lesson on quantum physics, something she had always wanted to learn about.

Jamie: *;)*

I dropped my phone. No one had ever winked at me. Even though it was a text, it still sent my heart into frenzy. I remembered I had to act cool as I was the guy. So, I started rummaging through my clothes again with a manly grunt.

*   *   *

Coming back to the drive towards school, I swatted Parsley's hand away as he was trying to ruffle my hair.

"What kind of shampoo do you use? Your hairs are softer than my girlfriend's," he chuckled.

I admit I did pick out one of the shampoos based for women but then I wanted to take care of myself and that seemed the most appropriate thing.

"Mind your own business Parse," I said without looking at him.

"Or you'll claw me kitty?" he smirked.

"Or he'll give you a lap dance at night like Brittany did," Grover howled from the front.

"Or he'll give you a behind fu . . ." Luke said.

Even though the two elder brothers hated me, we still had something in common - fixing Luke and his obsession with slangs. Before that kid could finish whatever we all inevitably guessed, Grover turned around and smacked his head before gripping the wheel of the jeep again, Parsley punched him on his shoulder and as he was sitting next to me, I kicked him towards the side making him slide further down the seat.

"Hey ars- . . ."

That gained him another round of beating until he shut up and scowled, glaring at all of us.

There was nothing in this world that would cease me from correcting my younger brother.

Ten minutes later we reached but not before Parsley and Grover had discussed the geography of half the girls in the senior year.

"Hey, wait for me lover boy."

I groaned and quickened my pace only to be stopped by Parsley who had grabbed my collar. Grover had that look of a hunter; more like let's-get-Romance's-life-more-twisted-than-it-already-was.

"It looks like someone is cheating on their imaginary girlfriend with a real woman eh?" Luke sniggered.

The only reason he didn't really say what he wanted to was that the other two including me would have shooed him away making him miss the golden opportunity of seeing me uncomfortable which frankly was his life ambition. But now as I was outnumbered, I could only await my impending doom.

"Hello?" she said happily.

"So you are Gayme Stalker, eh?" Parsley said making me groan.

"Oh what a sweet name that is. Did your bisexual girlfriend give it to me when I kissed the daylights out of her yesterday," Jamie retorted making me and Parsley gasp.

"Burn mate," Grover laughed.

My family were British but we had moved a long time ago to America so sometimes our roots came back to us. Otherwise, we were quite American.

"How dare you . . .?" Parsley growled. "Yasmine is perfectly straight."

"A line is straighter than that woman. She was also saying something about your uh . . . inappropriate size," Jamie replied nonchalantly, her gaze moving down Parsley's body making him go crimson.

Grover and Luke were laughing so hard that I feared they might rip something a.k.a. their clothes. They had this weird thing with laughter. Grover had some day, in one of the good times where he was in a happier mood, said to me that he just felt like having his body liberated from the cage (clothes) whenever he wanted to laugh heartedly. Of course, Luke ardently followed his idol in all his beliefs. Parsley was gaping at Jamie with his mouth opening and closing akin a fish's. I was trying to debate whether to stand there like a moron or vacate the area pretending I didn't know anybody. However, the way Parsley was being beaten down was worth watching.

"Listen dude, why don't you go check out the mirror to see how ugly you look before throwing bull like my girlfriend snogging you."

"You have a dirty mouth don't you?"

"That's what your mother said," Parsley smirked triumphantly as his eyes raked the anger that instantly flared into Jamie Walker's eyes.

That's when I came in between.

"That's more than enough Parse. Let it be," I said calmly.

"Oh look at that," Grover grinned. "Now what will happen to poor Kitty? Her smashing boyfriend has found someone new."

Then all my idiotic brothers started making these girly, sobbing sounds. I ignored them, taking hold of Walker's wrist and pulling her roughly towards the direction of my first period.

They were going to be horrendous at home especially Parsley since he had never been insulted that bad but that was something I had to endure later. Now, Jamie Summer was equal to all of them together.

"How do you feel?" she asked.

I scowled while continuing to walk. I didn't turn back to look at her into those deep brown eyes that always entangled my thoughts. This inquiry about my feelings was something new that she'd started. The whole day even if she didn't speak a word, she'd make sure to at least ask me this unnecessary question once.

As usual I ignored her.

"Romance, Romance, leave me . . . I don't have Arts remember? My first period is AP biology. I'll be late if you don't let go."

I let her go.

"So, how do you feel?" she asked giggling for some absurd reason.

That got more on to my nerves, those giggles, though they sounded like a brook bubbling on a glorious, sunny day.

"I feel," I started. My clear anger directed at her very pointedly was blatantly ignored while a small smile replaced those annoying chuckles. "I feel nothing."

"Oh, then you soon will," she said, smiling wider. She started walking backwards, still staring at me as my face loosened up and I almost smiled at how cute she looked with her boyish hair-cut and the bangs falling into those eyes I happened to admire.

Wait, what did I just ponder upon?

As I was trying to recall my jumbled up thoughts, she gave me the flirtiest wink and turned around hitching up her bag higher.

Well, who would have thought that an actual wink would be more lethal than a texted one?

The Day Jamie Rolled
Her Eyes at Me

'*Radioactive*' blared from the speakers in my room. I ignored the frequent banging on my door of the people who habituated the house. The moment I had entered, they had made life hell and as I had predicted Parsley leading the troop. So, I trudged inside my room, locked the door and blasted the music on to full volume.

Frankly, I didn't care if they even broke the door down.

I was exhausted from too much of Jamie Walker in school and her 'How-are-you' questions.

There was a tapping on my window. Thinking it's one of the birds coming early for the daily food I provided, I blatantly ignored the sound. The constant knocking though was annoying so I threw the pillow I'd kept on my face to diminish the light and with an angry glare turned towards the window.

There was that silly bird. I had half a mind to punish all their species today and devoid them off lunch.

The creature or rather the pigeon struck its beak on the glass and then twisted its head in the usual way their kinds are characterized for doing, as if implying just open the stymie and feed me already.

I sighed in defeat and picked up the bird feed from the side table.

Throwing the window open in an exaggerated sigh of frustration, I scattered the amount that my curved palm could hold and then started moving back.

"Ack!" I gulped moving my hand back. Seeing the blood oozing out of the little wound made my head start aching. I wasn't a phobic but the memories that came along with this liquid were more than I could bear to think presently. I scurried towards my medical drawer and quickly brought out a swab of cotton, antiseptic and a bandage. Dabbing my hand quickly, I ignored the burn and placed the bandage on top.

That's when I realized that twat was perched on my shoulder, again ticking its head.

I might rethink on the whole doing something good for the birds' outlook agenda.

The thing that astonished me was the fact that the bird just wouldn't leave. If I pushed it away it would come right back. The amount of germs I was being subjected to was driving my mind insane. I might have to cleanse myself for an hour at this speed.

That's when I noticed a note tied up on its leg.

Are you kidding me?

Out of curiosity, I gently took out the note and the monster decided to fly and sit on top of my head –so much for not having a head bath today.

Jamie Summer Walker

Come downstairs at your door in five minutes.
- J.S.W

I should have known something to this level of craziness would belong to someone as retarded as her. That oath of never breaking up promises was going to eat me alive someday.

I did promise to go out in the evening.

Shrugging, I walked towards my closet to change but then switched my direction angrily, realizing that the silly pigeon had pooped on my head.

Curse the day they made a girl like Jamie Summer Walker and her bloody good for nothing pet.

*　　*　　*

I opened the door trying in vain to dry my wet brown hair. Though with water mingled it seemed more blackish than dirty-muddy. Unconsciously I leaned my arm against the ledge and tried to ruffle the droplets away.

I wasn't this untidy but nor was I non-punctual. Five minutes was the target after all.

"Ahem, I . . ."

A nervous voice vibrated in my ears. That was a shocker. Jamie Summer Walker was anxious?

I gazed up as bangs of my wet hair fell onto my forehead annoying me further more. My eyes bore into those dark shadowy ones. I travelled my gaze and with a shock realized that she was blushing. A smirk crept up on my face even though I wasn't used to being so egoistic but there was something about her being shy that drove my insides into molten lava.

Gosh! I needed a breather.

"I umm . . . hmm," she stumbled upon words but managed incorrigible sounds.

"If you are going to just waste time then I'd rather go upstairs and commence my school work as the project is due next week. There are lot of things I could be doing right now Jamie Summer Walker than standing here and watching you be affected by my presence," I rambled.

I watched as her eyes ignited with the all too familiar look. Before she could burst on me with the whole Summer fire however I turned to flee the wrath.

"It's just that I never thought you'd look so good with the wet hair dripping like that and the black leather jacket makes you look all gangster kind which frankly Romance I never thought you could be. You're just so high and mighty with those fancy words and unbelievable non-emotions that you carry around. You just look so . . . sexy," she huffed in a breath.

I had stopped with my back facing her. Even though the words shook me up in the nicest way possible I still didn't like the fact that someone would like me. It was well-known that I preferred a single, care-free life and a girl stomping on my morals was never a good sight or bearable for that matter.

Turning around I walked forward until I was towering over her. I admit she looked cute with the two ponies, face void of make-up except a light-pink lip balm, the skirt with the netted stocking and the shirt tied up baring her midriff for all but for now my mission was something else than appreciating.

"Listen to me very distinctly Jamie Summer. There's only one thing that infuriates me more than dirty shoes or socks worn upturned and that is being subjected to cheesy bull like that. At no angle do I look *sexy* and in no way do I prefer being called that. If you can't handle keeping that inside then please leave. I have no interest in girly brewed spatter," I said finishing with my nose almost touching hers. "And also my name is Xerkis and that's what you'll call me."

"Don't get over your head. I was just trying to annoy you," she grinned cheekily.

I should have known.

"You look like a swine rolling in wet, muddy areas. C'mon let's go, we're getting late. Plus, I have an appointment with the dentist tonight . . ."

That was the Jamie Walker I knew.

"Are you listening to me . . . Romance?"

No matter what evil eye I threw at her, she just winked doing that annoyingly adorable eye exercise and took hold of my hand pulling me.

"We'll have a complete no having mushy feelings towards each other bond okay? A no strings-attached relationship?" she said as we walked on the front path towards the gate.

I nodded. What I was going to be subjected to next took some time to register as shock slowly took over my body.

"What in the name of sweet Mary is this?" I inhaled deeply.

"Our means of transport," she replied nonchalantly.

"Are you kidding me?"

"It's quite an effective way; we don't even pollute the environment and save loads of bucks which we can use to eat instead of waste away in diesel."

I looked at her. She was more deranged than I had predicted. In front of us stood a bright blue tandem cycle gleaming as the sun hit the metal. What did she have in mind – both of us riding together while the birds twittered a melodic song with the *Disney* tune playing from the radio and the sun shining high with the wind gently blowing the grass on the side as people smiled and waved us by?

That was some horrific picture I tell you.

"C'mon kiddo, hop on the magic carpet," she purred happily.

"Why don't I just go, disguise as a female and come back to flirt with some passerby for a lift?" I grumbled.

"Okay pal, let's see you do that shall we? God knows how long it has been since I've actually laughed like those clutch your tummy and wipe your tears sorts," she chuckled.

Then that predator of my hand egoistically flew and sat on the handle of the bike, cooing.

"Look at little Turkey, Romance Winter. It's not scared of a little bike ride are you, you sweet cupcake?"

I don't know whether it was the jealousy that something as meagre as a pigeon was getting her attention or the condescending look of the bird that got me riled up and on the seat in front.

"Ah! I see you learnt to follow the easy way Romance Winter," she said, smudginess lining her voice.

"It's Xerkis Moon," I grumbled.

"Roger that Mr. Grumpy."

I scowled as I started to peddle. After a while, the sun shining, the birds (Turkey) cooing and the wind blowing didn't seem too bad.

"Why would you name a pigeon *Turkey?*" I asked just to make conversations.

"Take a left from the next turn. Well because I named my turkey *Pigeon,*" she replied.

She was so weird. Who kept a turkey as a pet?

"Turkey?"

"Yes, Pigeon is a very chirpy little thing. I saved it from the clutches of death itself one Thanksgiving night. Poor thing was trembling all over with fright."

I kept silent. Whatever she was, there was something sweet about it.

"We're there," she said after fifteen minutes as we stopped in front of a cottage. It looked as if the most tranquil, decent place to visit. There were neat bushes with a clean area around. The roof was brick red while the white walls painted serenity. The windows were lined with open curtains that seemed of the softest fabric. The brown door contained a hung up sign with *Home is where the heart is* splattered across it. A smile lit up my face. It was the first time I felt elated to have come out with Jamie Summer Walker this evening.

We strolled up to the front. A waft of apple pie hit my senses making my stomach rumble. It smelled exquisite.

She neatly knocked on the door. Turkey decided to make way to his favourite spot a.k.a. my head and I stumbled backwards trying to get that vile creature away.

"Turkey," Walker whistled.

To my disbelief it flew and settled on her arm giving me that look again. Those gaze of triumph.

After five minutes we both heard voices and the door was thrown open.

A plump woman with haphazard dress, ginger coloured hair tied up in a messy bun, cheeks full of blood and piercing blue eyes looked at both of us. The scowl she was holding turned into a full blown smile.

"Ah Jamie boo," she said cheerfully hugging Jamie Summer.

I clenched my fists as her attention turned towards me and a heavy mass of meat engulfed my body.

"Who's this fellow you've brought to old Amy?" she asked.

"This is Roman- . . ."

"Xerkis . . ."

"Xerkis Moon," Jamie Walker said rolling her eyes at me. "He's a pal of mine."

"Oh, welcome to my humble abode. I'm Amy Howl," she said. "Whenever you're down-y, howl for Amy."

I hid my horror in respect of polite mannerism. This woman looked as dicey in spite of how homely I felt the moment I entered her aura.

We entered the place which was as unruly as the woman. The clothes were strewn everywhere and food was just lying around. The smell of incense infatuated the place. Sunlight poured in through the various windows that lined the wall here and there. I tried to move as cautiously as possible.

"Isn't this great?" Walker whispered to me.

"Yes, it's like I'm at Bill Gates hub. Very immaculate for human habitation I must say," I retorted.

She gave me a stern look and then shook her head in defeat following a rambling Amy towards what I could only presume the kitchen.

"So you have my stash ready?" Walker asked Amy.

"Yes Jams, I have all the order in place. Your payment has been covered by Turkey here so don't worry your pretty little head over that darling."

As I was wondering how a place with a neat front yard could turn out to be such a dump, I was offered a piece of that delicious smelling pie. Distracted, I took up the part forgetting momentarily about not accepting anything from strangers especially people like Amy.

"Mmm . . ." I expressed. "This is nice. What is it made up of other than the usual? There's a different taste to it."

"Marijuana," Amy replied.

I nodded and took a huge bite.

Wait what?

I spat the whole thing out and started coughing badly as some pieces got stuck into my throat. Jamie Summer quickly handed me a glass of water and I chugged it down. They both looked at me with concern.

"You mean . . . weed?" I asked breathless.

They both relaxed and Amy even laughed. Then ignoring me they started chatting. I finally looked around and what met my sight almost gave me a heart attack.

The walls were lined with jars of what I could only presume the secret ingredient of the apple pie. There were so many that I forgot the need to count. On the side, there were few windows lined together with the sun pouring in and a number of plants which again I didn't have to guess of what, lining the area. No wonder there were so many windows. Now that I thought of it, the light pouring in was usually subjected to some sort of pot or something.

I was stunned beyond belief. I couldn't even join in the conversation of the two females or try to comprehend their chatter. I didn't even realize that Turkey was sitting on top of my head.

"Let's go grumpy."

Some voice was calling out. I was too mesmerized to speak.

"Ouch," I said and rubbed my shoulder where the burn yelled pain. "Why are you injuring me?"

"I'm sorry delicate darling," Jamie Summer rolled her eyes. She seemed to do that a lot today. Didn't she know it was cute? "We have to go now. Amy is expecting uh . . . guests."

I shrugged and walked away.

I didn't get annoyed when Amy hugged me more like just ignored the fact that I was in this universe for now my mind was into oblivion. I couldn't actually feel anything. It was too hard. This was the worst situation I could ever fall into.

"You okay grumpy?" Jamie Summer Walker asked shaking me gently.

Everything suddenly became clear as I felt her warm hand cupping my cold cheek.

"Goodness Romance! You're sweating and yet your skin is so icy. What is wrong?"

"Can we get out of here?" I asked her frantically. "I really do need to get out!"

"What's the matter though?"

"Just get on the bike Walker," I snapped.

She jumped startled but got on the vehicle. I started pedalling like a maniac away from that disastrous dump. Nothing seemed to make sense anymore. I didn't care as long as I was miles away from the place.

I stopped finally as my mind began to cool. My senses told me that we were safe. I got down from the bike and turned around with my hand on the handle and the other on the seat looking down at the ground.

"Better?" Jamie Walker asked after a while.

I looked up at her and felt anger boiling inside me.

She had paper rolled up and was clearly smoking that vile stuff. I took hold of the cig and threw it away with force.

"Hey that's not cheap you as- . . ." she stopped probably looking at my expression. "What is *wrong* Romance Winter?"

That was followed by a long silence.

"I just hate smoking," I said gritting my teeth. "I loathe it. I despise it."

Then followed more silence.

"I will slap you the next time I see that in your mouth. My mother died because of that."

With that I got up on the bike and started pedalling.

Jamie Summer Walker did not say anything but I did hear a sniff. When I got down at my place, I walked away without acknowledging her. I turned around as I reached my garden gate to see her throwing a brown packet in a dustbin some distance away and cycling on.

That sniff had broken my heart.

The Day Jamie Broke
My Finger

I dreaded going to school.

The very fact that I had to because some ingenious, powerful personality had structured a rule on ninety percent attendance was annoying.

I refused to.

It wasn't because Grover had again put some dye in my shampoo rendering my hair mauve.

It wasn't due to Parsley who had cut drawn a disgusting figure on my forehead again.

It wasn't to be blamed on Luke either who could have repeated the nail-polish, make-up fiasco.

Jamie Summer Walker?

Oh no! I didn't even remember that name or what had occurred yesterday.

The reason was solely based on procrastination and extreme levels of laziness. In human words, I wasn't ready to get out of bed. Why were the sheets so warm? The pillows were beckoning me with the cushiony feel. Sleep was calling out to me like a long lost lover.

"Dude, I swear I'll drop Basket's poop on you," Grover warned me as he passed my room.

Somehow, I had again managed to be late something which never happened. Thanks to Jamie Summer Walker and her horrendous emotions, I was behind schedule.

"Kitty . . ."

I heard Grover again and quickly got up. Well, it wasn't the first time he would be dropping our neighbour's dog's crap on me. He wasn't a big fan of lying about threats.

The usual bickering occurred in the jeep. I pulled up my hoodie and pumped up the volume to listen to '*Black Veil Brides*.' To deal with life circumstance all you really needed was a good, eclectic taste in music.

The moment I got down something felt wrong. It was just one of those intuitions you get about certain stuff. For one, Jamie Summer Walker didn't bound towards me asking the usual *How-are-you-feeling* nonsense. It didn't matter much but I guess it had become a usual routine.

However, by lunch when I hadn't spotted her worry instilled its virus in me. What could have happened to her? The only thing that I could now depend upon was our English class that we had together. If she wasn't there then maybe she hadn't come at all.

That shouldn't have disturbed me yet it did.

I was the reason after all.

I had made her sob yesterday.

There was some monster inside that curled up in shame. I hadn't felt that since years after mother's death until the feelings had eventually subsided and I didn't want to accept *emotions.* But it was back. I felt horrible.

The gnawing continued even after the school time finished. I decided to walk home as a punishment or rather a way to pent up my anger. I kept trudging without actually noticing where I was as memories flooded my brain.

Funny thing those figments of past are, don't you think? The more you try to erase them, the more they haunt you. It's better to let them invade and satiate themselves than keeping them caged.

I kicked some can that was lying idle on the path. The silence was only broken by the rattling sound of the metal.

"Why so serious, grumpy?"

I looked up in shock. What was she doing here?

"Are you stalking me now, Summer?" I inquired.

"I do have better things to do then waste my time. There's school homework I need to commence," she said smugly.

Only later I realized she was mimicking me.

"Why weren't you at school today," I said, finally breaking the dull silence.

"Looks like someone missed me, eh?" she smirked.

I shook my head. "You wish I did."

"I do wish you did Romance."

"Xerkis Moon."

"Kipisi Star."

I looked at her with an incredulous expression.

"Anyone can make up names babe," she replied shrugging.

I hated her at the moment.

Just as I was about to walk away, leaving her to whatever she had been doing in the deserted street, there was a bang.

A gun shot.

That's when I looked around properly. My heart crawled towards my throat. This was the most erroneous place I could have ever landed into. The walls were full of graffiti. There were broken cars with tyres missing. Here and there you could spot marks of gun shots. There were even splashes of dried blood.

This was the thug street of our city.

"C'mon, we need to walk away from here," I said frantically.

"You do fret a lot. Keep calm and take the name of Jamie Summer Walker. I'm telling you Romance, one day your blood pressure will skyrocket and then I'll have to nurse you back to health. Your heart might burst and I'd have to give mine."

I stared at her with a blank look. What was her deal? Here, possible gangsters were running to claim us as their victims and all she cared about was humour. That girl would be my death someday. No actually, this very day.

"Did you ever wonder Romance Winters as to why people chose the occupation to thug?" she asked.

We were still standing there and I could hear the footsteps coming closer. I didn't want to leave but her nonchalance was giving me no option.

Still, had to be the guy and wait for the girlish insanity she was portraying to get over.

"Maybe they had difficult families. It could be the parents who ill-treated, abused and finally led them to the path as extreme as this. It may be the thirst for revenge.

In fact, how about guilt ridding? Some people are forced to think that they are the reason for something and then boom . . . they perceive themselves bad and become bad," she rambled on.

I stopped. Whatever she spoke next I barely heard. My fists clenched, eyebrows scrunched in and the unusual shivering occurred, the kind of trembling when I tried to control my wrath. It had been ages since I had let out the fury and I didn't want the hard work of a year going down the drain. Taking in deep breaths and trying to sooth the beast inside, I gazed at Jamie Summer Walker but it was too late.

I saw their menacing faces looming forward. The way their eyes raked down her body. That girl sure knew how to dress for the occasion. Out of all the days today was the one she decided to wear mini-shorts with a cut tee showing off her stomach. Their vile eyes followed the contours of her curvy body and mentally violated the short, black haired girl.

"Why are you looking grumpier? Jesus Christ! Learn to live a little will you?" she groaned. "Fine, let's move."

She walked towards me but my eyes were trained on them- how their pupils dilated and the vile smiles widened.

"Romance?" she looked at me curiously.

"Get back," I muttered.

"What? Are you okay? How are you feeling?"

If it hadn't been for the situation we were facing, I would have yelled at her like a maniac. Why wasn't she a normal, freaking teenage girl?

I grabbed her arm roughly and pulled her back. I heard a little yelp of pain and then a gasp when she realized why I did so. Well, at least now she'd shut up and listen to me.

"Ah! There's a pretty girl Shark. What do you say we shag her?"

One of the imbeciles said smiling with most of his teeth missing. I cringed imagining the germs I'd acquire fighting all of them. The way they were looking, merely their gazes were enough to fuel me. How dare they even look at Jamie Summer Walker?

How dare I protect her like that when I should have nothing towards her?

"Yo Brick! Would you see this piece of popsicle defending her like that?" some douche said loudly making all of the others chuckle.

Oh, we'll surely see in time who was going to be the real casualty. I had seen enough movies to know what to do even though the prospect of fighting wasn't appealing to me. I removed my baggy hoodie to show them just how menacing I could be as well.

Their laughter rang out loudly.

"Oh look at the little thing trying to show off," the guy who had been called Shark said.

There were five of them, one of me. It wouldn't be that tough a deal.

"Let's beat him into a pulp and then do his girlfriend in front of him," Shark said.

"Or better, let's hold him and make him watch the scene before beating," Brick said.

"I want a go at the bitch first," one of the guys yelled.

"Oh but I saw her."

"I called dibs."

They were arguing as if she was a piece of meat. With all the strength I could muster to keep calm and not let my wrath overpower rationality, I spoke to Walker.

"Don't worry. I got your back."

They all had ceased arguing and were now casually strolling towards us. One of them was swinging a chain. They were all throwing obscene comments towards Walker making me cringe at the harshness. They were going to pay for each dirty word.

"Just stay behind me and I will protect you. There's nothing to fear. I won't let them touch a hair on your body. Trust me. I'll make sure each one of them regrets the day they were born, okay?" I whispered to her. "Okay, Walker? Okay? Bloody hell! Answer me. Walk- . . ."

I turned around only to meet with an empty street ahead. Panicking, I looked around just as a woman cried loudly.

Oh. My. God.

What happened next shocked me so much that even when Luke had kept the other deal of the bet and went to school dressed up as girl seemed a lot more less astonishing than this.

Before I could finish saying her name, she had beaten all the men down towards the ground. Every one of them had been punched and kicked roughly. It was like watching an action movie scene only done much realistically. By the end of it, Shark was supporting a bleeding lip, Brick had a black eye and the others were just limping or moaning in pain. She finished the last guy, I think his name was Stone and then clapped her hands together as if dusting dirt.

Was it just me or that fight scene had actually been a turn on?

I needed pills to get sane.

"Look guys," she said standing in the middle of bruised humans. "No one in this world is bad or good. It's how they chose to be. A flower cannot choose to bloom nor can a river opt to drain into a different ocean but we as humans, we're way luckier. The path to a happy life isn't full of thorns but perceived ones. If you think positive and just trudge along greeting your helpers instead of shooting them, believe me you'll be much better off. Killing, stealing, breaking and so on is just what losers do. I know there are reasons you blame yourselves but the sun never blamed itself when it perished the dinosaurs. The Tsunami never claimed the guilt after its massacre. We already have these finishing us, we don't need each other. Let's just do a simple thing and make each other smile. Let's just do another simple thing and love because that takes much less of you than hating. That is more life than death."

There was a silence so acute that I could hear my heart beat, hear my thoughts whirring. I presumed that we would be beaten up black and blue pretty soon. But as now-a-days I was running low on being correct, the unbelievable occurred.

There was a loud applause and cheering. Brick with more of his teeth missing was grinning with full force. She smiled and bowed at them. Then blowing away kisses, she ran away only to return with a cycle. The basket contained a box of first-aid kit which she used to clean up their wounds and bandage them.

I was stunned.

A girl had taken up five guys against one when all I'd ever thought of females was the one needing protection, just chock full of vulnerability. Then she had melted their hearts with her words – the cold-blooded murderers, the monsters, the ones who no one crossed, the gangsters, the thugs and maybe even the ones who had probably just finished their sentences in jail.

If this wasn't the outright definition of crazy, I didn't know what was.

"Let's go have some ice-cream guys," she said jovially.

Well, I had my answer.

"Romance, you coming?" she asked politely. Her eyes were gleaming with this hidden energy or something I couldn't figure out.

I nodded. "It's Xerkis Moon."

"Yes, boss!" She saluted me.

All the men chose their flavours. I didn't really like ice-creams so I was sitting on a bench watching Jamie Summer Walker joke around.

"You don't want this paradise?" she asked surprised as I shook my head.

"I don't like sweet."

Her jaw fell down as the coffee brown eyes widened. "Really, that's absurd. It's more astonishing than your name."

I wanted to glare at her but somehow I ended up chuckling which in turn made her giggle.

I liked that sound.

She was about to sit next to me when I saw this lady bug and yelled pushing her away. I let the creature crawl on my finger as she stumbled forward from my jerk. She turned around with anger as her ice-cream had slipped and she hadn't known the reason of my outburst.

"Hey, there's a creature on your finger," she screamed suddenly.

The next thing I knew was that the poor thing I almost lost my voice to save was crushed along with my finger.

*   *   *

"I'm so sorry," she said for the hundredth time.

"It's okay," I replied for the hundredth time.

We were walking back from the hospital.

"You're such a noble guy you know? You were trying to save a lady bug!"

I looked at her in confusion. "So?"

"Well, she was a lady you know? That's so gentlemanly of you. I'm so impressed Romance."

I shrugged. I'd just dived in the hope of saving a life; she was just exaggerating it as if I had done something huge.

"I'm so sorry," she mumbled.

"It's okay," I mumbled back.

"Those thugs would be laughing at me right? I gave them such a silly monologue. I mean, when I think back it was just so stupid," she said blushing.

I liked the way her cheeks coloured.

Oh God! Save me from all these likes. It was Facebook all over again. Just liking and commenting about her little things being that creepy stalker who waited for another picture upload.

"Are you kidding me? I thought you made Shark cry. He was this Hulk of a man who was sobbing on other bulky guy's shoulder. That monologue was more emotional than a funeral's speech," I muttered.

She gave me this genial smile. The kinds I would want to frame and hang on top of my bed or probably keep it as a wallpaper on my phone so that every day I woke up to it.

We reached my place. I gave her a curt nod and started walking towards the front porch.

"Romance Winters?"

I sighed. It wasn't because she stopped me but the name. She never got it right.

"What?" I asked defeated.

"I think you have the best muscles I've ever seen. I knew you were hiding some good stuff under those hoodies. I like you. After all, I do like hunky boys," she said and winked at.

And you know what?

I winked back.

The Day Jamie Wanted
A Piggy Back Ride.

The place looked familiar. I had been here before but it wasn't something I was proud of. My head dissented with my senses. I felt woozy as if somehow I had gotten drunk. Everything seemed to be spinning in and out of view.

"Romance . . . you okay?"

A voice tried to reach to me. I knew that familiar tone. The one I wanted to record and listen to for a long time.

I hated her but the more I did that the more attractive she became.

"Romance, answer me?"

The distant voice was becoming much clearer through the haze. A pair of cold hands touched my heated face. That felt so soothing. So when those sources of warmth tried to pull away I covered them with mine and nuzzled in smelling the strawberry smell they diffused. That could only belong to one person.

It was Kitty Somers.

"You were insane inside. What happened to you?"

The girl chuckled.

The scent of strawberries wafted around.

No Jamie Summer Walker.

None could ever beat the cute sound that little mouth made. The dizziness seemed to reside as I looked into the most beautiful face in this galaxy.

The brown orbs shone with amusement as the pink lips stretched into a gorgeous smile. Her well defined cheek bones stretched making her face look less stout as the black bangs fell into her eyes. I gently pushed back the loose hair on the side of her face behind her ears and in that process ended up cupping her face as she was mine.

It started to snow.

We were surrounded by a concrete jungle but the dim light above us give in the romantic ambience I desired. A couple of flakes resided on her hair making it look simply breathtaking as her cheeks tinged pink. A dimple formed on her chin.

I don't know what it was – the way she looked, the gorgeous smile, the snow, the beat of hearts, the sudden confidence I had coursing through my veins or merely the fact that I've wanted to do this for a long time.

I kissed her.

The soft plump of her lips mingling with mine brought something alive inside me, that raging feeling of the monstrous emotion to cherish, to satiate my hunger. Her small body trembled so I wrapped my arms around her and pulled her closer. She might have been having a tic-tac for the kiss tasted minty. Her breaths mixed with mine as ying with yang, somehow together yet separated. I could feel my heart beat racing as her teeth bit my lower lip. I didn't like it but nor did I hate that primal thirst. She pulled away and I trailed kissed down her throat just to show her who was the boss. She called out my name and I took possession of her lips. Now mad with desire, I pinned her towards the tree bark ignoring the cold. Her hands encircled around my neck as mine moved under her hoodie, beneath her jacket . . .

"Ouch," I yelled rubbing my back. "What is your problem?"

Parsley laughed. "You were blushing."

"I wasn't," I mumbled.

"Were you having a wet dream of Kitty?"

"Shut up." I threw my pillow at his annoying face. That did nothing but fuel up his fire.

"I bet she wore one of those lacy things Grover keeps asking Crystal to buy . . . oh no wait it must have been that Jamie Stalker. Am I right or am I right?"

I got up and without a word strolled out of my room. The only way these imbeciles left me alone was if ignored or boxed. The latter was something I'd only do if I had a death wish.

That really had been a dream? I looked at myself in the mirror. The skin was weary and pale. My hair was sticking out in odd angles. There were frown lines painted on my forehead. Everything seemed haywire but my eyes, the grey seemed to be coming out. The black specs in the iris looked prominent, they were gleaming.

If it had been a fluke why was I so jovial? Why could I still feel the touch of her lips on mine? Just that thought had me going frenzied. This wasn't right for my health and yet it felt so right. So perfect!

"Dude, it's been fifteen minutes now. Get out. I have a . . ."

He said something so outrageous that I threw him a dirty look.

"What?" Grover said innocently. "Every guy has that problem not that you would understand considering how you aren't one."

Only, I did. Today out of all the days, I did.

Reluctantly, I put on my hoodie. Even if the weather was a tad bit hot I didn't really care. Sometimes you have too much to hide and that's why you do certain things you're uncomfortable with.

"Hey handsome," Walker smiled at me.

I shrugged and started walking forward ignoring her.

"Okay, so we're again back to being grumpy. What happened? Did those *Homo Erectus* specie you call brothers trouble you?"

I didn't look at her.

"Romeo, answer me?"

Not only was she terming me as Romeo now which did not help my anger but she was also repeating the dialogues from my horrific dream.

This was the actual nightmare.

"What is it with you, seriously? I'm just trying to be nice here? Fine, don't talk to me. It's not like I want to. It's not like I'm this beautiful girl with perfect features that you crave. I'll just walk away, okay?"

If only she knew. It was taking all of me to just keep walking and not push her towards something hard and drink the lusciousness of those kissable lips. Didn't she know I was this close to making her mine there and then?

Okay, maybe that was getting too exaggerated. I wouldn't be so animalistic.

She started walking away faster. I couldn't help but smile as her behind ticked from side to side. Our school was far away but it wasn't like we couldn't walk. I wanted to, presuming it as a good excuse to stay away from disaster and clear up my muddled mind but I didn't think Jamie Walker would follow.

After a while, I decided to be noble. Taking long strides I reached her quickly. She turned her face away from my side and kept walking forward.

I chuckled.

"Hey Summer," I began only to be cut short by her singing. Deciding it was useless to tackle me politely she had chosen the path of obscenity that was serenading at the top of her lungs and none less that *Eminem*. So I gave a shrug and started beat boxing.

I saw the side of her face lightly scrunch up. It wasn't long before the muscles relaxed. Funnily enough, at least for the passerby who saw a tom boyish girl in trunks rapping while an unusual guy with spikes – booming and bobbing his head while moving like a rapper, we started to actually enjoy. Even though she did not look at me, it was still worth it.

"You know we make a good team," I said but she didn't reply.

I guess I wasn't completely forgiven.

"Okay, let's make a deal Walker. I'll buy you an ice cream?" I tried making amends.

"Four," she retorted.

I pushed my hands inside my pocket to check if I had enough bucks.

"Five," I smiled.

"Three and I will not bargain further," she snapped finally looking at me only to blush realizing that she'd tricked herself.

I started laughing. She swatted my arm playfully as we stood near the ice cream stall.

"I want vanilla pop . . . no the chocolate bar but the orange ice is so good," she started debating.

I took my chance to gaze at her. I observed how she blinked her eyes continuously while trying to think and how her hands kept making their way to my chest to grab my attention which frankly was already directed at her.

I didn't believe in miracles before.

She ate three ice-creams so fast that I dreaded I had missed getting a record noted.

Now after watching that happen, I did.

"You want to have?" she asked me.

I shook my head. "I hate them, remember?"

She rolled her eyes but just as soon as the brown balls had disappeared they made their way back only widening in excitement.

The sort of look her face held, that filled my heart with dread of what was to follow ahead.

"Let's bunk the school."

I knew it.

"No way are we doing anything of that sort."

"Please Romance," she stretched her voice making it shrilly.

I closed my ears and started walking ahead. We only had ten minutes to reach school and I wasn't breaking my good-boy record.

"Why are you so boring?" she growled stamping her foot. "I'm going to go whether you come or not."

I waved her a farewell. There were some things' I could do such as waste money on unfruitful but going out of the social norms I had set for myself was much more than I could deal with. I wasn't a rebel and nor would she turn me into one.

Five minutes shy of the school properties; I heard her voice yelling at me from behind. I turned to watch her running towards me, waving her hands like a maniac.

Smirking, I grinned at her in triumph.

I admit a part of me wanted her to have followed me badly because the thought of not seeing her in school was troublesome.

It was only when my silly thoughts cleared that sense embedded itself.

Jamie Summer Walker wasn't waving a white flag but she was running away from a bunch of dogs that were coming directly towards . . .

I yelped and started running as well. She joined me as we huffed our way away from the dogs, away from the school building. I scornfully gazed at her.

"What the hell did you do?" I yelled at her.

"I was just trying to see what provokes them," she yelled back.

"Are you out of your mind? Why would you do that?"

"Well, I heard that men are like dogs so if I found out how they get provoked I could do the same with you.

Apparently, poking them with a pointed stick in the balls is what riles them up . . ."

If the dogs wouldn't have been barking behind me I would have been hitting my head on the wall. What was wrong with this girl? We fled into the local park. Even the rough terrain didn't have the canines leave our track.

"If I get away alive from this fiasco, I swear on Jesus I'll make you pay," I huffed.

"If I get away alive I swear on you I'll poke you with a stick," she chuckled breathlessly.

Somehow she couldn't stop giggling imagining god knows what insane picture. I looked backwards and sighed in relief. We had lost the dogs thankfully. Only the chuckles reminded me of what would be the result. I blanched.

Well to gain something I have to lose something.

"Walker," I said looking forward. We were a running with a formidable gap in between. "Hey! Would you listen . . .?"

"I could try it with that brother of yours . . ."

"Jamie Summer li- . . ."

". . . What was his name again? Parcel? Prickly? Peni . . ."

"You have to listen to . . ."

". . . and then I could put chillies in that bottle he drinks from. He'll never know what hit . . ."

Bam!

Just as I yelled her name in vain, she'd already smashed her head on the bark of the tree. Who talk-giggles without looking forward while running? It isn't her fault her eyes squeezed into tiny slits when she laughed but doing that while running is plain dense.

I jogged towards her and bent down, worry lining my aura.

"Are you alright?"

She was covering her nose while I saw water dribble from her eyes. It wasn't a nice sight.

It was gut-wrenching.

I gently took hold of her hands and pulled them down. Her nose had a gash which was bleeding. Quickly taking out my emergency kit from the bag, I followed the procedure of sanitizing the wound.

"Thank you Nurse Romance," she giggled after the pain must have subsided.

I didn't reply.

"I'm sorry," she said sadly.

"It's okay," I replied back immediately.

"It's because of me you missed school. I'm so sorry Romance."

"Xerkis Moon."

"Romance Winters."

I sighed. "Let's go to some hospital. I think we should check for concussions."

"Or we could go to Burger King and check out our tummy rats," she smiled.

I shook my head in defiance. "Hospital it is."

"Burger King . . ."

"Shut up!"

"How much?" she looked at me innocently. "How much do you want me to pull my shirt up?"

"All of it. Just freaking remove it if that's the case," I played along.

"Eager for a taste of Summer are we now Romance?" she said smugly.

"Well if you ask the bee how much honey it desires it won't say no to a whole hive. C'mon let's go. I promise the doctor first and then the cashier of junk."

She nodded happily and got only to start swaying dangerously.

"You okay?"

"I feel so woozy," she said, holding her temples.

I made her sit down again and then bent on my knees with my back facing her. "Hop on."

She seemed to hesitate for a while but then her arms slung around my neck and I held onto her legs. Her tiny body pushed towards my back was enough to send electric shocks through my veins. She was quite light to hold.

Her breath fanned my ears as I felt her nose nuzzle into my hair.

"You smell heaven," she whispered into my ears.

I almost dropped us there. Almost.

If it hadn't been for the nagging worry of her hit head, I would have never made it to any medical building forget a hospital. It was too hard having her body so close to mine. I had never despised wearing a hoodie before as much as I did then.

The results were positive.

I breathed a sigh of relief as we left the hospital.

As we were walking towards no destination as such she stopped me suddenly and ran towards a stall on the pavement. Buying some food, she ran away.

I followed her only to find her feeding some canines.

The same monsters that had made us run like *Usain Bolt*, the very same creatures that had given her a scar on the nose. Did I mention she had two stitches there?

Only Jamie Summer Walker could be as sweetly sour as that.

The Day Jamie Bit
Her Lower Lip

"So now that you've fed the dogs would you like me to call up Parse so that you can apologize?" I asked her sarcastically.

She looked at me with interest. "Why would I want to say sorry to that *guy*?"

"Well, let's just say you stamped on his ego hard. The boys at home are teasing him continuously about his bisexual girlfriend. I bet he's hatching a plan to overthrow you."

I thought she would giggle at my use of terms but then again I could never fathom Jamie Summer Walker's reactions.

"He's . . . hurt?" she asked me appalled.

"You didn't know that? He's more than bruised if you ask me."

"Oh gosh, do call him Romance. I want to say sorry."

I just shrugged and started walking ahead whistling a random tune. I could feel her presence behind me but for once the silence was what rendered us more comfortable. The sun overhead decided to grace us a little darkness by hiding behind the clouds.

We were walking towards a mall when Jamie gripped my arm and pulled me back. I could see her cheeks flushed and eyes shining which only yelled trouble ahead, figuratively of course.

"No," I adamantly said even before she opened up her mouth to blabber gibberish.

"You haven't even heard me," she pouted.

I wanted to roll my eyes at her but that would be rude so I counted backwards and tried to soothe myself.

10 . . . 9 . . .

"Romance, we should totally steal that police car in front."

8 . . . 7 . . . 6

"We could ride it around town pretending to be officers on duty."

5 . . . 4

"Also, the red light on top blaring plus oh my god *donuts*"

3 . . . 2

"Then we can stash it someplace no one would care to look at."

1

"You need to learn how to be a good citizen Jamie Summer," I spoke calmly.

"And thus spoke the goody two shoes," she chuckled. "C'mon, we have a job to do."

There was something in that expectant look of hers that made me follow. I didn't know whether I was looking for the adrenaline rush of danger I craved or pleasing the girl who I wanted. But whatever the reason, once we were sitting inside the car, all my worries flew out of the window.

"What would the officer say to his fellow mate?" Jamie Summer asked me sitting shotgun.

"Why are kids in this generation so retarded?" I answered.

She groaned but shrugged and continued. "No, that's not what they'd say."

After the silence became unbearable I sighed. "So?"

"Dude, where's my car?" She burst into a bout of giggles although I had no idea what was so hilarious.

Apparently my non-laughing self did not deter her sense of humour.

I put the car in third gear and settled down to drive trying to look unaffected. The fact that there had been a police car lying around with the gates open and the keys in ignition only implied one thing. There had been an urgent case the officers had been too mugged up to solve and thus trusting the citizens left the car as it was.

Boy, were we screwed.

"Oh gosh, Romance look!"

I momentarily gazed sideways at her after making sure there was no one in front only to yell and try to hold the balance of the car.

"Are you stupid? Why the hell would you point that thing at me," I shouted at her as the car again started moving in the right way.

I wasn't a terrible driver but I always kept my speed around the limit. A law-abiding good citizen should never try to endanger people around. Apparently for Walker though placing a gun right in front of my eye level was funny.

"Relax, it wasn't as if I was about to shoot," she rolled her eyes.

"Oh that's great news. So let's all point guns at Romance while he's driving because of course he doesn't need to concentrate on the road," I fumed.

She did not give me back a sassy Jamie Walker reply. I had to look on the side to see if she was even there for it had gone awfully quite.

"What?" I asked her irritated.

"You just called yourself Romance," she said breathless.

"Whatever."

But the deal was that I indeed had. This was getting more complicated than I could handle.

"You did," she giggled.

"Shut up. I'm Xerkis Moon."

"Time out buddy, what's done is done. Golden words are never to be taken back."

"It is golden words are never repeated."

"Who cares? You called yourself Romance. I'm the queen of hearts."

I quit arguing. She was just being childish now and it didn't give grace to my identity to be the same. I focused on the important task that was driving oh but not before I had snatched the gun out of her hand as she'd been aiming at an elderly woman. What was her fetish with being abnormal was beyond me.

It was as we were driving towards the highway that my eyes fell upon the screen of her phone on which she had been scrolling mindlessly through. Actually, the cooing sounds she had silently made had reached me and I wanted to see what had got her excited.

What I saw shocked me to the core. I smashed my foot on the break jerking us both forward as the rule of inertia went.

"What are you doing?" she scowled while rubbing her head.

"How . . . who . . . why do you have t-that?"

"What?"

I didn't care if she was annoyed. I needed an answer no matter what.

"That picture," I whispered.

She gave me a confused look, the kinds I usually threw at her, the are-you-sure-you-weren't-hit-in-the-head-as-a-baby look.

"This?" She brandished the picture on my face and I cringed. Where in the world would she have got this click? The hand was obscuring most of the face which was already hid behind the hood of the black jacket. The only thing that could be made out was that there was a guy – a person who had the potential of darkening the whole room if he wanted to, a boy that mostly had gone around ruining as many lives as he could. He was known for the street fights, the break-ins, the thefts, the drug abuse and what not.

He went by the name of Dark Joker.

Funny . . .

I don't think so.

"He's my idol," she swooned. "I love him so much that I can't even breathe . . ."

She was turning pink and so was I, though my pink was more a shade of red. Out of all the people she could fantasize about this one was the only human she found?

"Where did you get this picture?" I grumbled.

"You're so annoying Romance," she pouted.

God! Why did you make pouting the most adorable gesture in the world?

"Xerki- . . ."

"Blah, blah, blah . . . and before you ask again, I'll answer the real question. It was during the time he put crackers under the stage in the 'Ghetto' band's concert . . ."

He shook his head in vain at the four people who had once been his friends. They had promised that they'd change his life that all of them would stick with one another like family but all it had taken was a girl and a fight to throw him out. It wasn't as if he was trying to steal her. He had just wanted to warn Yen of the kind of person she was.

No one had heard a thing.

And now when she had robbed the guy emotionally and physically, they still blamed him.

He wanted just one thing out of those four now – the sweet taste of revenge. He smiled malignantly as they stepped on the stage. The plan was just to scare them not to kill.

And petrified they were.

Just as they started the second song which he had composed and written but never got the credit for, the fireworks went off. What followed next was havoc and pure bliss for him. He saw Yen's hand get slightly burned a smirk crept on his face.

Later when the police handcuffed him, he gave a condescending smile to his ex band mates who were eyeing him wearily. Pleased that they were pissed he willingly walked towards the police car.

"Why?" Officer Kent asked him. "It's the ninth time this week I'm taking you to the prison for something. I know you get out in a day or so as the crimes aren't huge but why kiddo? Lead a good, clean life instead of spoiling your record like that. If you don't want that then at least be subtle. You always own up the moment you're successful."

"That's the fun Sir," he said gruffly. "I don't want to feel as if I wasn't punished for being bad."

Just as they were about to reach the car, a girl called out from behind. He quickly pulled up his hoodie and the handkerchief that had been tied up around his lower mouth before being pulled down by the police.

"Oh my God, is that you?"

He wanted to see who it was but kept looking down lest he be recognized by someone known.

"Dark Joker, I'm so excited to meet you. I can't believe it's you. I'm you're biggest fan ever. So sorry about this awfully embarrassing fan-girling but I'm so super excited to meet you . . ."

She rambled on for five minutes listing off everything she approved off. If it hadn't been for the situation he would be feeling jovial instead of tensed.

". . . and that kid you let ride a bike, actually let him drive it. That was the best thing ever I've seen. I love you."

Those three words

The words he'd never heard been spoken for him from a long time. The ones he had stopped caring to think about or want.

Out of shock he looked up.

Two things happened in a second. One he realized what was happening and placed his hand in the front while the hood pulled lower to cover his eyes and two the flash of the camera went off.

". . . and that's how I acquired this epic picture."

I didn't know what to say. The anger bubbling inside for being so stupid wasn't dying down and so I sped.

The speed was way off the limits presently but I didn't care. I could hear Walker yelling at me to slow down or get my senses back. I couldn't deal with the pressure. It wasn't until we were back at the place where the car had been parked that I stepped on the break and we halted.

"I'm not even going to ask," Walker mumbled and stepped outside banging the door close.

My knuckles were white. I had been gripping the wheel harder than I should have trying to repress the urge to throw her phone. It was probably the fact that I had already been nervous about stealing this car that had got me riled up more post seeing that picture.

It was after five minutes that I stepped outside and walked over to where Walker was standing leaning against the wall. The location was an alley between the wall of some sweet shop and a random building.

"Do you think cats are better than dogs?"

That was something I wasn't expecting.

"I'm sorry," I mumbled, ignoring her usual self.

"It's okay," she said automatically.

We stared at each other for a while – she with a blasé look and I with a curious one. My attention started to waver and I moved my gaze from her face to what was happening behind. I don't think looking at her lips would be a big help on controlling desires.

That's when I saw the two blue suited men. They were in a deep conversation while walking towards the car with donuts in their hands. One of them dropped the tissue without noticing. After they had walked a few steps, he noticed the missing thing and turned around.

I gasped.

Officer Kent.

"Hey, where do you think you're going?" Walker asked pulling me towards her.

I tried to get away but it wasn't possible without hurting her.

"I have to apologize."

"To whom?" she asked incredulously. "The only person who deserves that is me and I already told you it's alright."

"Him . . . that guy," I mumbled.

Somehow, I broke free from her grip and started walking towards the men as if in a trance when suddenly my vision was obscured by a girl tiptoeing in front of me trying to reach my height and look intimidating.

"Seriously weirdo, what are you trying here?" she asked while blowing her cute bangs away from her face.

When I didn't answer, she pouted.

Not those things again. I shielded my eyes by placing my arms in front of her face.

"Dude," her muffled voice reached me so I let go. "What the actual heck?"

She gazed at me, followed the direction of my eye sight and then gasped. "No Romance . . ."

I side stepped and started walking again only she pulled me backwards and pinned me against the wall. Her hand clasped my mouth. If it hadn't been for her tiny body all over mine and the hot breath fanning my face, I would have literally pushed her away.

"Are you out of your mind? Do you want both of us to land in jail?" she tried to talk calmly.

"What *you* did would. But if I apologize they will let us go."

"No. You will do no such thing idiot."

"I'm a follower of stringent rules and what we did was extremely out of order. We need the punishment so that the guilt does not nag us later."

"All I heard was blah, blah, blah; I'm an idiot and blah"

"Shut up Walker. I will go and fix this."

"I will break your organ so hard that you'll never have kids."

"Good, I hate kids."

"Romance Hunter Winter"

"It's Xerkis Moon, Jamie Summer Walker"

"No imbecile fool commits a crime and then willingly goes for repercussions. Let's just bloody leave it, okay? Who even does this kind of small crimes without trying to . . .?"

"Dark bloody Joker"

It was too late to take back my words or pretend that I hadn't said anything.

"I never mentioned the name," her gaze narrowed towards me. "I thought you didn't know him?"

Busted

I looked at her blankly.

She pouted.

Enough with the pouts already! I wanted to scream, stomp, yell and just strangle her.

So, I left.

Just walked away

Hoping she took it as a sign that I wasn't just walking away from there but from her life.

The Day Jamie Slapped Me

It hurt.

Not the sting on my cheek.

Or the way her hand had struck my skin.

What pained was like a shock across the expanse of my chest. For once, I deserved it. The agonized look in her eyes was enough to satiate the reason. I saw her lower lip tremble and for once I felt ashamed of the way things went.

*　　*　　*

"Oh c'mon Romance, you've been avoiding me all day," she whined.

I didn't look up from Calculus. The problem I was trying to solve was much easier than what I was facing in real life.

"You have to look up at me."

So I peeked. She was sitting there with black kholed eyes making a funny face with her tongue poking out. I stifled a laugh.

"Fine . . . don't talk. That doesn't ban me from not doing the same. You just stress a lot like an old grandmother worried about everything."

"At least he's not like the octopus that eats itself when it stresses. Don't worry your pretty little head over this loser, doll."

I looked up to glare at him. "Out of your rat nest I see!"

"Well at least I don't live in a dump hole."

"A person is defined by their intellectual not the habitat."

"You are wrong as always Rom-com. A man is delineated with their capability to love and you have no emotion what so ever."

"Who let the leash out of your neck?"

"That's what said the man who was ready to bite this beautiful angel off. I never get it why girls even come after you. You suck!"

"At least I don't suck with them."

"Touché . . ."

We were already standing in a predatory position. He was looking at me calmly as if this was a normal discussion while I was trying to look bored. Of course being a terrible actor I managed to clench my fists and narrow my eyes at him.

Then we laughed out loud, scaring Walker and gave each other a man-hug.

"How have you been, bro?" he asked.

"Like a fish who escapes from being caught," I replied.

"Fish always reminds me of that night."

We both chuckled. He had been drunk out of his mind and had thrown a pet clownfish out of the window shouting 'Go Nemo; find your dad little buddy.'

"Ahem!" Walker cleared her throat.

I returned my attention to Calculus while he turned on his charms. I shook my head as his flirty comments vibrated around. This guy had been my friend since nine years probably and he knew all the latent dirt on me. The moment he'd seen me and Walker interact, he knew that I liked her. That's how well *he* knew me. I was just horrible with guessing and life in general so I hardly could even figure out anything different about him, unless he pointed it out.

"The name is Reed, Alan Reed," he spoke in a deep British accent. He wasn't a Brit but staying around me he'd learnt that girls dug that stuff.

"Walker, Jamie Summer Walker," she replied with the usual blasé attitude of hers which she specially reserved for strangers.

"Is that sunburn or are you always this hot?"

I sighed in exasperation. Half the time Alan surfed the net trying to find methods to charm. I peeked at Walker to see her smiling carelessly.

"Did you invent the plane? You seem Wright for me."

I looked up in alarm. Even Jamie Summer Walker was this free in life? Then again it was *her* we were talking about.

"Do you have a map? I'm getting lost in your eyes," Alan replied enthusiastically.

Well, I wouldn't say no to one either.

"Your body is 65% water and I'm thirsty," she retorted back.

"My doctor says I'm lacking vitamin U."

"Damn, if being sexy was a crime, you'd be guilty as charged."

"Was your dad a boxer? You're such a knockout."

"Was your dad a drug dealer? You're such a dope."

"That reminds me . . . Rom-com, have you recently done . . ." Alan started off.

"Shut up Alan," I snapped in time.

He threw a wide-eyed look and my eyes strayed momentarily towards Jamie Summer Walker. He nodded slightly and mouthed 'later'.

"Oh don't worry about him Alan. He's just a party pooper."

I glared at her.

"Yeah I know. Once we went to Jasmine's birthday party and he actually pooped everywhere because the loos were all occupied."

I turned my stare towards him. He was going to pay later. Jamie Summer started laughing hysterically. It wasn't even that funny.

"We were two years old," I said through gritted teeth.

"That didn't give you the right to go and relieve yourself on Jasmine. No wonder she wrinkled her nose every time you passed-by."

I stood up. The thing was Reed couldn't understand the trouble I was finding with this conversation. He was saying things which Walker should never find out unless I was ready for her to know.

"Oh c'mon Rom-com, I'm sorry man. Sit down. I know you have learnt the social decorum pooperly," he said with a straight face.

"Hey Alan, did you know when Romance wears those black jackets he looks spoopier?"

"Black jackets, you say? I thought he'd left wearing those after they caught . . ."

"That's it!" I yelled at them. Forgetting my rule of never ditching class, I grabbed Walker's arm and pulled her outside. What was a class been missed when I had already dumped school yesterday? See, that was the thing with being a rebel. Once you taste the liberation, you can't get over the hangover.

Walker was trying to talk and free herself at the same time. I didn't care even if this was hurting her. It wasn't the whole teasing that had me riled up. It was the fact that Alan was being so careless with the stuff he should keep secret.

"What is your problem?" she asked clearly annoyed.

I was about to reply when yesterday's event floated in my mind and that reminded of how I wasn't supposed to speak to her. Great! This was just grand.

"Oh so now what will you do Mr. Genius?" she voiced my thoughts.

After a long silence, I did finally speak. "Would you quit with the nicknames?"

She smirked.

And here I thought only guys could look cunning doing that expression.

"Why do they annoy you sweetheart?" she giggled.

"Shut up."

"Or what honey bun?"

I glared into her eyes. They were twinkling like diamonds in coal mines. I slapped my hand on my forehead. Unrealistic thoughts are never good for health.

"Why did you come to this school? Even if you did, why is it me that you're after?" I inquired.

"I think that you're hotter than Ryan Gosling and that's saying something."

"Keep your pick-up lines for Reed. I'm not falling for them."

"Oh, so that's what it is about huh? You're jealous," she teased.

"I'm not."

"So are"

"Shut up"

"How much should I? Admit it you're feeling that green-eyed monster squeezing your heart."

"I don't feel."

"Liar"

I grabbed her hand and pulled her towards me roughly. I didn't care if she felt being man handled but heck I was letting her get away from being rude. That's not how Romance . . . I mean Xerkis rolled.

"I don't care about you," I spat every word at her face. It stabbed her but again the fact was I didn't care.

"Of course you wouldn't. You can't even use pick-up lines. I'm not beautiful like those girls you stare at."

I looked at her incredulously. She seemed sad. Why, though?

"Listen Walker I . . ."

"And the worst part is that you can't even admit that you were envious."

"But you don't . . ."

"I saw your face when he was flirting. It's not like I'm completely blind to being a girl."

"No, it's not like . . ."

"But no. Romance heartless Winter doesn't care to admit he does because his ego is bigger than the length of our intestines."

"What are you crazy? Just let me . . ."

"And then out of all the guys who do not hit on me because they think I'm so well guy-ish there's one who does and all you care about is degrading the memory. You don't even admit you're jealous because you so were. Reed knows and I know . . ."

"I wasn't whatever you think because Reed is the last I would be jealous off in fact he's the last guy anyone would be envious off because he's gay. He's is as gay as anyone could be. He's gay!"

I had been repeating myself but she wasn't ready to listen in the first place. She had cringed when I had started yelling. I liked being in control.

"Thanks Rom-com. The man in the hospital at the end of the road couldn't hear you. Could you be a little louder?"

I shrugged at Alan as he passed by scowling. I felt guilty that my timing had been absolutely horrible. I would apologize to him later. Let's just say he was like the pink jacket Parse had gifted me on my fifteenth which stayed deep inside my closet. I knew that Alan had ushered outside to maintain the storm he knew was brewing inside me but unfortunately tables had turned.

An awkward silence followed.

"Well, that was quite insensitive of you," Walker mumbled.

"Who are you to say that?" I scowled at her.

"That's right," she said in a small, despondent tone. "You don't even think about me. I'm like this minuscule being that doesn't exist in the map of your life. I'm like that broken streetlight nobody cares about. I try my best to make you feel happy and you do the same just making me feel terrible . . ."

The rant went on. I don't know what took control over me. The fact that the ever so confident Jamie Summer Walker was feeling so insecure (which for the first time made me see how much girly she could be) or the fact that she looked so adorable spilling out stuff without realizing how attractive it seemed.

I pulled her towards me.

I bent down.

I took possession of those talkative lips.

I stopped breathing.

It was exactly like the kiss in the dream. The only thing that changed was that it was ten times better. I never knew lips could feel so soft when melded with yours. I couldn't fathom that another person could taste as sweet as nectar to a bee. I didn't know that it was enthralling to have a girl clutch her fingers around your hair tugging you in.

In fact, I was as clueless about smooching as anyone could be.

Not that I hadn't kissed before.

But boy was this different.

She broke apart to breathe but I pushed her back and surrounded her with me. I caged her in with my hands and rained kissed down her jaw. At first Jamie Summer Walker hadn't responded and I had fretted. That had hurt my ego. But once I was lured in, I was a victim.

"Rom . . . Roman . . . we . . . I can't . . ." she was muttering.

Heck! I didn't care. It was her fault at first for being so compelling. She was the one who felt so unattractive and all I ever wanted to do was make her feel how beautiful she was.

"You have to stop," she was whispering. I could barely hear her as my lips moved down the length of her neck.

"Pleas-se Ro-oma-nc-e . . ."

That name again.

That's what brought me back to my senses. That title I despised. I pushed myself against the wall and moved back. Her lower lip was swollen. Her eyes were closed and she was breathing heavily. As they fluttered open like the gentle way butterfly's wings do, I gazed into them.

They looked so sad.

Still.

I loathed myself.

Turning to walk away, I could only think of one thing I wanted to do so badly. The thing I had been craving for ever since she had walked into my life. I stopped.

"Just so you know Jamie Summer Walker. I think about you a lot. In fact, if every time I thought about you and a star fell, the sky would be a pretty darn empty sight."

With that said I walked away.

*   *   *

And that's how I ended up on the roof of the school doing that one thing I'd vowed never to.

And that's how Jamie Summer Walker found me, shock lining every bit of her aura.

Smoking a cigarette, that is.

I knew I had made a scene out of the whole *hang-out* we had some days back. That's why when her hand struck my cheek, I knew I deserved it.

That's when her eyes glazed over with water, I knew I cared.

And that's when she left me standing there like a moron, I knew what I felt.

Broken

The Day Jamie Was Difficult To Please

I crossed my fingers and then slapped myself for face it, all these superstitions were just speculative. The fact on which Jamie Summer Walker would agree to forgive me was based on realism and what I did not achieve crossing fingers.

So that's why I held my breath while peeking from behind the bark of the tree. There she sat. So serene with the wind gently blowing her boyish bangs while Tiara her friend chatted humorously about some guy. Walker wasn't a loner. In fact she had more friends than Grover which is saying something because face it Grover was the most popular senior in school.

While I was seventeen years and just about to complete my junior high, Grover and Parsley were a year apart though – Grover was twenty while Parse was nineteen. We had all started school late except Grover who failed his junior high once. He hardly cared though. Luke was the youngest at fifteen.

I meticulously planned in my mind again before actually carrying out the thing.

It had been a week since Jamie Summer had spoken to me. I knew the fault was mine but which human lived perfectly? It was these imperfections that actually counted when you loved someone because perfection everyone craved. At first, I'd presumed she'd come around but as the days progressed and the aloofness increased, I realized how wrong I actually was. This was no surprise actually.

It was time for action.

I pushed the button and watched as my plan came alive. I wasn't really romantic but after four days this was what could be managed.

Tiara nudged Walker and pointed downwards. Slowly, their eyes widened unanimously.

Pushing the button forward and backward I made the remote controlled car gently poke her legs. She looked around horrified but then shrugged and bent down, her hand enclosing around the handle of the basket I'd taped on top. Tiara bent down and pulled off the tape after which Walker pulled the little basket up and put it into her lap.

"Who is it from?" Tiara asked her breathlessly.

"I don't know."

Walker sure had a lot of guys pinning behind her even after the whole boyish thing she had going on. Even though it was obvious at times, she wasn't ready to believe in her beauty. It was actually the way she was. One smile from her could light up the whole place as if the darkness had been craving to witness something that magnitude of beauty.

I despised them with all my heart.

She removed the cloth from the basket and gasped.

"Is that a ring?" Tiara shrieked probably alarming the whole city.

I cringed. Maybe I should have done this when Walker was sitting alone. Well, every plan possessed some flaws and mine was just being discovered.

"Oh my God Jams! Someone is asking you to marry them?" Tiara yelled jumping up and down.

I could see that she had gone very pale. Her fingers were trembling while her breaths were coming out in gasps.

Wait a minute.

Why was Tiara shouting about marriage ceremonies?

Oh my god! Why was there a bloody ring in the basket?

I started panicking. It felt almost like one of those panic attacks people have. With my luck, I might have that as well. More than that though I was worried about amnesia, I hadn't most definitely placed a ring inside the basket?

Where was the silver pendant shaped like a sun in between a snowflake that I had especially scoured most of the town for?

Trying to control my erratic breathing, I walked forward only to stop at the look on Walker's face.

She was furious would be an understatement.

I could see the red overtaking the white. This was the worst apology anybody could have asked in the world. Someone, specifically called Tiara, was going to burn tonight as I poured kerosene and lit a covering up for murder bonfire. There was something called being quiet and not exaggerating but oh no she was currently done with the bridal shopping and was gibbering about being maid of honour.

Insolent girl!

81

"You can thank me later bro."

I turned around and groaned. Luke and Alan were standing with their arms crossed supporting similar smiles. One was a genuine and another was charlatan.

"You like the idea Rom-com?"

I glared at Alan. "Are you out of your mind? Why would you do this?"

My tone faltered his smile though Luke's widened.

"Is there a problem Rom-com? I was just trying to help."

"You call this help?"

I pointed towards a bouncing with immense happiness female and a simmering with volcanic fury another one. Maybe my anxiety had turned everything hyperbole.

"Um, what is happening?" Alan looked confused until Tiara's words started getting embedded in his senses. He gasped and turned towards Luke who was laughing so hard.

"Oh my god, Romance this guy told me to exchange the gift because rings were more romantic. I didn't know. I mean I believe it because rings are. They are the symbol of pure and undying bond that a human ties . . ."

"Are you serious Alan? I'm not marrying Jamie Summer Walker, you idiot!"

He stopped blabbering and looked at me scared. First he had almost spilled out the fact that I smoked and now he had done worse. I had somehow equated the first with revealing he was gay but this was irreparable.

"Let's go make this right," Alan said with determination.

As if I'd march over there and say I'm the one who gave the ring. Imagine the wrath that would thunder down.

"No way am I ever walking out there."

"Hey girls," Luke screamed. "Won't you like to meet the groom?"

And I punched him in the nose. He howled while clutching it. I saw the bleeding but at present I didn't care if he bled to death. Luke cursed under his breath and took off as I gave him the evil eye for cussing. He knew about the loath for any form of slang.

That's when I saw Jamie Summer Walker marching towards me with clenched fists and Tiara following her like a puppy. If she had a tail she would have wagged but guess the tongue hanging out was good enough.

Okay, I admit it was petrifying.

Though being the guy I showed the strong exterior while Alan was praying next to me. He was literally shivering and calling out to Jesus to save his soul. Though if you ask me we should all pray to Satan to kill Tiara and Luke as thanks to her this dramatic scenario was being painted for otherwise I'd be behind the tree gazing at Summer smiling at my locket.

"I'll fix this," Alan muttered to me.

Now whenever Alan decided it was up to him to save the world, that's when everything went exactly the contrary. So, my sudden worry was justified.

"What is the meaning of this *Xerkis Moon?*"

Okay, I was in deep trouble.

"Listen Jamie it was . . ."

"You shut up Alan," she screeched at him. He widened his eyes in horror. I guess I did too.

"We could have pink birds flying with flower petals and dropping on top of you," Tiara sang.

Yes, she sang that like some Disney character. Where were the curses or poisoned apples when you needed them?

Walker's eyes turned to me. "Will you explain or do you want to fight?"

"I didn't know you'll get this mad," I stammered. "See, I just put a . . ."

That's when I became mute. Not a word escaped my mouth. My brain sure threw in loads of insults at my direction though.

"He's innocent. I'm guilty as charged . . ." Alan stammered.

"You mean to say you gave me the ring?" Walker asked shocked.

"And then we can have champagne. Though white wine would do good . . ." Tiara rambled on.

"Yes, I mean not like in the sense I gave it for Romance to present it to you as a . . ."

"So it was you're absurd idea?" she inquired.

"And then we can have dancers from our ballet group teach you the father-daughter dance because that is as important . . ."

"Well, the idea was actually Luke's. He's Rom-com's youngest brother. The one with beach blonde hair . . ."

"You agreed to this insanity?" Walker questioned looking at me with narrowed eyes.

"It's just that he was nervous . . ."

"Shut up Alan. I asked him."

"The bachelorette party has to be at my place. I can arrange the decorations . . ."

"But he really didn't . . ."

"Stop defending his mistakes Alan . . ."

"With the orchestra which I bet Xerkis's dad can provide . . ."

I was getting a headache because literally everyone was shouting at this point. When I thought all this would be the weirdest thing well I never thought about what happened next. That topped everything even Parsley's phase of shaving even without any facial hair.

It was actually because of Tiara no one could continue sanely so Alan had done what he could do.

He kissed her.

Not only silencing her but all of us.

Well, Walker of course as I was already quiet while those two couldn't speak even if they wanted to. I saw Tiara's arms go around his neck and I saw him cringe. Well, he had sort of sacrificed for me. I could forgive.

That's when I felt the second panic attack building up. I clenched my fist and tried to even my breathing.

Walker was looking from them to me in disbelief. Her mouth was open in slight shock which looked adorable.

My stupid heart needed to be shot for giving insane ideas. That's what Alan said. In case of her, I always thought from my blood-pumping organ.

Alan pulled apart and looked horrified. Tiara looked on top of the world. I wanted to puke or probably die. At least she stopped gibbering.

Jamie Summer Walker breathed hard and then stomped away.

Not before throwing the ring at my face which kind of got my trance induced state active again and I started chasing her. Though what was happening with Alan and Tiara was much more fun to watch. She was cooing, actually singing again while Alan was looking as if he had died a very harsh death and was seeing it happening again after becoming a paranormal spirit.

But as much as that was entertaining I still had a lady to woo.

And a brain to get fixed

And a heart to replace

"Hey," I yelled. That came out kind of feminine. She didn't stop. Instead of shouting I tried another tactic which was twist her arm around and pull her towards me.

In a sense, that was the best thing my heart could think off.

"What?" she scowled.

"It wasn't me."

"I don't care."

"Then why are you mad?"

She just turned her face away. Silence followed us as I peered into her beautiful face. I didn't agree with some guys basing her features similar to a man's whatever the truth is. It wasn't about their opinions though, it was what I felt. For me Walker was perfect.

I was still demented.

"Walker . . ."

I couldn't do it. Say sorry. It was tough this time as it scared me whether she'd forgive or not.

"You know Romance; I don't care about that ring. It started to feel really silly at some point but then when I saw Alan kiss Tee, I just realized that you've done nothing but lie to me."

"I did?" I looked at flabbergasted.

"You made a show of me buying weed for a friend but you smoke. You said Alan was gay but clearly he isn't. You said you weren't jealous. You say you don't care but that kiss? Why? Forget that entire thing heck even your name is a lie. Xerkis Moon isn't who you are. You are Romance Winters!"

And that's when I felt ashamed. More than I had when she'd slapped and walked away. In a way she was right. I did live in a life of denial.

"I'm sorry," I said in a small voice leaving her hands.

She looked at me. "It's okay."

I bent down to kiss her but she moved her head. That hurt.

"I'm sorry but no Romance. We can't."

I nodded. "Umm . . ."

"What the hell?"

Okay, showing her the ring wasn't a brilliant idea. She glared at me the anger returning in her brown eyes.

"You want to marry me?" she asked grumbling.

"What?" I looked at her appalled. "No, no I don't want to. This is not that."

"It clearly looks like that. There's even a diamond."

"Woman that's a . . . this is . . . it's a promise ring," I blurted out closing my eyes. Here comes the slap.

But when I opened them she was no longer glaring but smiling – a genuine heart-tickling one. Squealing she snatched the ring from my hand and placed it into her right hand's index finger. She put it back to admire.

"What are you promising me Romance Winter?"

"Uh . . . I shall quit smoking?"

She seemed satisfied so nodded her head appreciatively.

Grover started calling me. It was probably his tenth one and I was sure he was going to bite my ear off. We had to go home as Parsley had an appointment with the dentist. Having no transport really sucked. Actually, I could have walked but Grover had commanded me to go back with him.

I don't know why.

But you always listen to him or he beats. I don't want that.

"Excuse me Walker. This is urgent," I said.

She looked at me with her eyes twinkling. It was good to have the old Jamie back.

"Hey Winter," she called as I had started moving away.

I turned and looked at curiously.

"Do you have a heart?" she asked.

"Not that I'm aware of."

"Oh goody because mine belongs to you and always will."

The Day Jamie Ate Half of My Toblerone

When Grover had demanded a few minutes ago that I travel with them it wasn't because he had suddenly sprouted a caring heart but he wanted to berate for punching Luke.

In between his yells I tried to subtly explain the fact that Luke asked for it but Grover was driven by fury. I don't know why he hated me so much. It's not like I had stolen his love or even a piece of chocolate but I guess that's how sibling rivalry existed.

So I just muttered a sorry to Luke who grumbled. He didn't even acknowledge me. Whatever, like I cared.

What I did care for was Walker, so I texted her.

Me: I'm sorry

A guilty conscious is never good for the health.

Jamie: It's okay ☺

I smiled at the text.

"What are you smirking at?" Luke asked and peered over my shoulder. "Oh god, you and that girl are going to give me herpes."

That didn't even make sense.

"What girl?" Parsley laughed.

"Jamie Stalker," Luke chuckled.

Parsley scoffed. He rolled his eyes as if this was the last thing he cared about in the world.

"You are still dating her?" Grover asked.

"I never did," I replied.

"Have you snogged her pretty boy face? That almost makes you like Alan. That faggot!"

Parsley turned around. I thought he would pinch me to annoy but he hit Luke who growled. "What's up with all of you? The elders are ganging up against me. I'll tell dad."

"Shut up idiot!" Parsley said. "And stop cursing. Stop saying things you aren't supposed to say. Most of all don't . . . just don't"

All of us were looking at Parsley in shock. Even Grover who was driving and if it hadn't been for Parse retaining his senses and swerving the jeep on time, we would have died today.

"What bit you?" Grover asked.

"Nothing," Parsley shrugged.

"Parse, what do you mean?" I asked.

"You were born in the wrong family. In fact, you may be adopted," Parse sniggered. Grover and Luke laughed.

I just let it be.

Me: Jamie Summer, why didn't you kiss me?

This was the most I'd ever anticipated for any answer. But when no text came back, I realized maybe it was the worst thing to have done. I'd yet again degraded myself to a level Xerkis Moon would be ashamed off.

Somehow, Xerkis Moon seemed like a stranger now. Kitty Sommers, the girl I knew in a past life.

Only thing that I, Romance Winter now cared for was a certain Jamie Walker who would eventually hurt me. Maybe, I was waiting to relish in that hurt. Maybe the hurt was worth every memory made.

Later when I was climbing steps to reach my room, I heard Grover and Parsley talking. It seemed like they were in a heated discussion and I didn't want to be caught red-handed only to be ragged. It was when I stepped on the fifth step that I heard Walker and completely stopped. I didn't care if ten of them came and beat me up now.

"What do you mean?" Grover asked urgently.

"I don't know."

"Will you answer Parse? What's going on? I don't want you hiding anything from me bro. You know we always tell everything."

Somehow that stung. They shared a mutual brotherhood which I'd seen many a time. It was quite agonizing to think that none of them cared to let me join the fun. I wanted to but all they did was insult me which wasn't even friendly banter. It was horrible. I wasn't really that emotional but somewhere their words pierced me.

"Parse if seriously I find out something amiss later mate, I swear you'll regret it."

"Would you just let it go?"

I gasped but thankfully so did Grover. Parsley had shouted at our eldest sibling. Now that was once in a blue moon rarity. It was more like Britney Spears dating Luke. (That guy was absolutely fanatic for her)

"Look," Parse sighed. "Bro, I just . . . it's just Jamie is like my target. She's my victim. I want to be the only one who can revel speaking out profanities attached with her name. You know I've never liked sharing. Plus, Luke is just getting out of hand. It's high time someone fixed that little git."

"Yeah," Grover replied. "I'm just worried, never mind . . . I have some work."

"Sorry man."

I heard the clap of hands on backs and then a door slam shut. That should have been face-smacking clear that Parsley had selfish reasons. Now, I was positive he was going to hatch a plan so vile that Walker would get depressed. I needed to be there for her. I had to warn her.

Only she hadn't yet replied to my text.

I fell on my bed with a relieved sigh and closed my eyes. Memories of the contours of her face floated in, lighting up the darkness.

Tap!

I pulled my pillow and slammed it over my face trying to cover my ears.

Tap!

Those horrible birds never gave me the time to relax. I was going to cease feeding them.

Tap!

I threw my pillow and got up furiously. Picking up the baseball bat which Grover used to play with four years ago,

I marched over to the window and slammed the bat down without looking.

"Are you insane?"

I dropped the bat which fell down on the floor. The familiar tone shocked my inner core.

"Just because I didn't let you eat my face, it doesn't mean you hit me with bats!"

"You can fly?" I asked her stupidly.

"What?"

"How are you . . . oh?"

She had placed a steel ladder that dad used to keep near the garage to clean roofs during winters. Turkey cooed and sat on top of my head. Even though I despised the pigeon, I felt happy seeing him. I could say the same because he pooped on my head.

As always, some things never changed.

"Oops," Jamie Summer giggled. "Turkey, come here boy."

I scowled at the pair and rushed to the bathroom. Though my heart was glad that she had come to meet me my mind still screamed unhygienic. Therefore, I decided to take a shower forgetting that Walker was at my window.

"Oh gosh, you don't . . ."

Startled, I looked at my bed where she was sprawled. Everyday I'd pictured this scenario only it wasn't like this.

"You okay?" I asked moving towards her.

"Please wear clothes," she blushed.

"So . . . what if I don't? Clothes are after all just a basic necessity. I mean, shouldn't we walk around the way our ancestors used to? Showing off all the goodies nature provides. Look at mountains or rivers. They don't dress up to show off. Let's be modest."

She rolled her eyes at me. I could see her flush deepening as those brown orbs travelled around my abs.

I really didn't like muscles but it wasn't as if I could control their building up.

At first, I thought of annoying her by just sitting on my bed with the towel wrapped around me but then I felt better wearing clothes, being more human.

"You have tattoos?"

I stiffened. Well, I'd forgotten about them momentarily. No one knew about it. One was my real name written on my lower back in a beautiful cursive encased in a border of roots which seemed as if it was being trapped between thorns. The other was on my chest.

"They're beautiful."

I felt warm fingers tracing the letters on my back and that made panic attack three occur. Again, I closed my eyes and clenched my fists trying to control the outburst. The feel of her bare skin on mine was like giving water to a plant that had been dying in the sun. It was essential that she didn't get to observe the one on my chest for that could get scandalous. I never wanted that part of my life invaded anymore. In the beginning I'd been unconsciously covering my chest, now it became essential I did.

Moving forward to avoid her touch, I pulled out a tee and quickly adorned it. Picking up a pair of shorts I walked towards the washroom to get changed. She didn't say anything for a while. I dried my hair as much as I could. The last reaction she had when they were unruly and wet

Jamie Summer Walker

was worth gazing at again. However, I had to apologize not insinuate.

It took almost fifteen minutes for both of us to settle down. It wasn't because we were uncomfortable but that crazed bird of hers again sat on my head and I had a dramatic show of shooing it away which made Jamie Summer laugh.

That was worth it.

Finally when the bird was out, we were able to converse properly.

"Walker, sorry," I mumbled.

She put her hands inside her pocket and pulled out something.

There were two things that I loved more than anything in this world. One was watching series related to paranormal or fantasy creatures and the second was hoodies. Today, I added a third and that was eating Toblerones.

"The thing about chocolate you see Romance Winter is that it cures a broken bond. It's like the glue that sticks the molecules back together. Therefore, I brought this for you."

I smiled gratefully and took it from her.

"Let's watch something," she sighed happily.

There went my speech about the irrationalities of a guy and the way I should behave around her. Who cares about a mere kiss when she was asking me do something with her?

I switched on my laptop while she propped the pillows up against the best post. I really liked a lot of support when I slept. Hence, we had enough fluffiness to be cosy.

"No . . . no, nah . . ." she scoured the whole list I had. "Seriously, you watched _Godfather_? How horrendous is that!"

"Well to tell you the truth, that movie is one of the best ever made because hello the political drama and family divisions are just what I . . ."

"Ew . . . *Kill Bill*? That movie gave me nightmares though the woman was sure an inspiration," Jamie rattled on completely ignoring me.

So after she had degraded all the theatre I ever loved, she looked at me with a wrinkled brow. "Where is the romance stuff?"

"What stuff?" I asked her confused.

"Well you know chick-flicks."

I blanched. It wasn't like that genre was new to me but every time I'd decided to sit and watch the horror they called reel love, it baffled my mind. How could anyone deal with the entire unreal situation? The drama was out of the planet. Men in white horses, red rose petals on bed, love letters spewing venom, flirting with each other which weren't really like that and what not.

"I uh . . ."

"Oh my goodness, I found it yes!"

I jumped as she squealed. I hope none of the brothers had heard that.

"You have twilight? I've always wanted to watch twilight."

"You should know that Luke just stays next door. I mean he does have his headphones on most of the time but still . . . wait what?" I looked at her aghast.

"Look, twilight!"

That Alan Reed of a man was going to suffer through a very cold death once I was done with him.

"This is so exciting. Can you get popcorn? Is that a teddy bear? Can I cuddle it?"

I looked at the soft toy which was kept on top of the dresser. It was my mother's. Luke loved playing with it when he had been a baby and well as most things end up in my room, there it was – the only memory of my parent which I had no heart to throw away. I walked towards the thing. It had been years since I cared to pick it up. The moment I touched, her memories flooded me. It was unbearable but I didn't let it show. I gave the thing to her and she cuddled it happily.

As long as she was happy, it was okay.

"I'll get some popcorn," I muttered quickly walking out. Once I was standing near the room door, I leaned against the wall and breathed in and out. The way mum ruffled my hair when I'd bring that thing to her, the smile that lit up the beautiful face like sun shining, the smell of baking cookies which wafted from her skin . . .

"You okay?"

I blinked backed the tears and looked at Parsley. He was giving me a funny look. I started walking away.

"Is she in there? I heard laughter."

I stopped. It wasn't going to help if I lied but the truth would be no aid either. I just nodded without turning back.

"You sure you're alright?"

This was so weird, Parsley pretending to be nice. I knew he was going to do something Parsley-ish.

"I'm fine. It's just . . . mom."

"Oh!"

That's all he said and silence followed us. Mother had always been the tabooed topic in the family. I guess she was the only thing that had kept all of us together. There had been a time when all four of us brothers would be unbreakable. We loved each other like families should and it was perfect. Playing catch with each other, going fishing with dad, yelling at T.V. screens during matches . . .

Well, things change.

"It'll be alright," Parsley whispered. He patted my shoulder and I jumped in alarm. Then, he walked away.

Well, that was awkward.

I shrugged. He must be on drugs. That guy managed to look the most decent human on Earth while inside vileness brewed waiting to erupt.

After I was composed enough, I grabbed some Dr Peppers and a bowl of butter popcorn.

"Hey kitty . . ."

I turned around and Parsley poured Hershey all over me.

"Tell that itch to lick it off," he winked and walked away laughing.

That had to happen. If it hadn't I don't think I'd be able to sleep for a month imagining Parsley sneaking at night to maybe shave my hair off.

"What happened?" Jamie Summer giggled. "Why do you look like you've always been pooped on?"

I shrugged while putting the things I'd got on the side table. It was time for a second shower. I'd manage to finish the water in this world at this rate.

"Umm . . . the chocolate on this is amazing," Jamie Walker mumbled, chewing a piece of popcorn.

Fifteen minutes later, I was sitting next to her watching the worst movie of my life.

Which by the way, Alan had already forced me to see some months back. He must have not deleted the movie hoping we would see it again. That idiot!

"Romance . . . don't you sleep while watching. It's the best part now," Jamie Summer poked me.

I groaned as her sharp elbow possibly fractured my ribs. "Let me nap Walker. I might get diarrhoea watching this."

"Look at Edward, he's so hot," she squealed.

Where was the gangster Walker? I missed her so much. "I'm better than him."

"No you're not. You don't sparkle," she mumbled. "Shut up! Let me watch."

I groaned. She wouldn't let me speak, she wouldn't let me sleep. What was I supposed to do?

I felt my eyes closing up again. It felt so nice having her body nearby, her odour tinged with strawberries entering my senses, her hand now and then brushing some part of my body . . .

"Romance, I can't ever be with you. I think like Edward leaves her in New Moon, I'll have to as well. I won't come back though. I can't. I don't have a choice . . ."

I dozed off thinking that wasn't her but Bella speaking to her shiny vampire.

Also, the last I'd seen her with full sense after being woken up the fourth time was when she was eating half my Toblerone.

They say sharing creates feelings and chocolate creates happiness.

So, she couldn't have said that dialogue.

She just wouldn't have . . . right?

The Day Jamie Ended Up Fractured

"Will she be alright?" I yelled and pulled the doctor's coat towards me. I breathed on his face which made him cringe.

That wasn't a good idea but I was so worried.

"Mr Winter, will you relax? She's perfectly fine," he mumbled.

It wasn't the first time I'd ended up here creating havoc.

"That doesn't seem like fine to me," I scowled at him while waving my hand towards Jamie Summer who was groaning in absolute pain. I let go off his collar as a couple of security people took hold of my arms and pulled me away.

That's why you should cage temper. You are otherwise thrown out of the hospital without getting to know the condition of the person you care for. Luckily for me Dr Hugh, being the family doctor, told the guards to let me be. He was kind enough to even let me stand by Jamie Summer as he tried fixing her leg. I shuddered as her agonized yells filled the room. She had been pretty brave all the way till here but I guess sooner or later pain always triumphs.

"What is it? Is she going to die?" I asked in a strained voice.

He gave me a ludicrous look. "Don't be ridiculous. It's just a fracture. I've stitched her up and the plaster is being currently placed on her foot. She'd have to stay here for a week as there are other minor injuries as well. The important question is . . . what happened exactly?"

"Well it was when . . ."

*   *   *

"Do it!"

I gave her the vilest look I could manage.

"Aw, that's cute. Now do it," she yelled.

I looked at her but my mind was elsewhere. The next day after the movie when I'd woken up, I'd stumbled across a watch. It wouldn't have mattered but the thing was that it belonged to Parsley. That was worrisome enough. What was he doing in my room at night?

The whole day in school that's all I could ponder upon. Afterwards Jamie Summer had wanted to *hang out* so that's how we had ended up in the park.

"Romance, it's just hanging on to the bars and coming to this side. How difficult can that be?"

I groaned. First, she wanted me to walk in a park full of kids and then she wanted me to be one as well. It was easy for her as her height wasn't what mine was. My legs were practically touching the ground.

"Just bend your knees and pretend that they aren't."

I sighed in defeat. There was no use trying to argue so I complied. She started pictures against my wishes.

"He he, that guy is so foolish."

"I think he's pretty cool. He's like Superman."

I shook my head at the kids and glared at them. They gave me a look of fear and scurried away.

"Why do you have to ruin every moment?"

I turned my scowl towards her. She just shrugged and walked away towards the swing. So then I did what my heart thought off.

Walking towards the middle of the park, I stood upon one of the huge boulders placed for kids to climb and yelled at everyone to turn their attention to me.

"So little creatures," I began. I saw Jamie Summer biting her lip to control her smile. Forgetting what I was about to say I stared at the faces looking expectantly at me.

"I err . . . free ice creams?"

And then there was an uproar that almost made me tumble down as various small beings tried to hug me. It wasn't a bad feeling but my god was I petrified. I glimpsed at her laughing. She winked at me and I grinned back at her. Then I walked towards the ice-cream truck with all the kids trailing behind me as if I was God.

"I told you he's cool like Superman."

"Or maybe he could be Batman. I like him more."

"Superman"

"Batman"

"Guys," I came in between the two boys fighting. "If I tell you something, will you keep it a secret?"

They stared at me with awe.

"I'm an elf from the North Pole. Santa sent me here to see who is being a good boy and who's not. I'll give him a report when I go back."

Their eyes widened in astonishment. Quickly they apologized to each other and threw me sheepish grins. I chuckled and patted their heads.

"Will you tell Santa I want that super fast racer car from hot wheels?"

"I want a skating board."

"Sure, I'll tell him what you want."

Then both the boys beamed at me with that heroic gaze still stringent in the eyes and skipped away to get themselves ice-cream.

"Will you tell Santa I want a revealing dress I can wear on some upcoming birthday of mine?"

I shook my head as she winked at me after pinching my behind and walked away to get her share of sugar.

I watched each face light up as they consumed their own drugs but the brightest was Jamie Summer Walker's. That was probably one of the things I would never get over with. I drank in every bit of the perfect emotion that lined her expressions. So engrossed was I that when she strolled towards me, her pink lips shining with the cream, I didn't realize.

"It is like . . . Romance?" She hit my head.

"Yeah, what's wrong?" I muttered stupidly.

"I have to go."

"Don't leave me."

She chuckled as I looked at her bewildered. What was wrong with my senses?

"I wouldn't like to but this is important. I promise I'll be back."

I frowned but nodded at her.

For the next thirty minutes I played around with the kids. I had despised them previously but once you're called a superhero and worshipped reverently, you just can't get over the popularity. So there I was giving plane rides to kids or telling stories. At some point Luke had passed through the park with some girl in tow. When he saw me with a bunch of children sitting around in a circle, he laughed so much I worried he might crack a rib. Well, even if they did tease me later, it was all worth it.

It was dusk by now. I felt the cool breeze warm my heated face. It had been five minutes since all the little angels had rushed back home. She had promised me she'd come back so I sat on the bench.

"Romance . . ."

I looked around flabbergasted. That was her alright. Though she sounded a little . . .

"I'm back for your baby."

"Uh, what baby?" I asked as she literally fell on top of me.

"You know that little kid you produced just a while back."

This was her important work? Get drunk? I mean she looked adorable what with the way her eyes shone and the tinge in her cheeks but this was something I couldn't accept. We were after all in a public place.

"Jamie Summer there is perfectly no reason as to why you exposed your liver to vulnerability of . . ."

"Oh look, there's that expensive car I wanted. It's like I have to get a thousand bucks but I steal a million dollar car for it. GTA I tell you is serious game."

So we weren't in the mood to be sane.

I watched as she spread her arms wide and with a whistling sound ran around the ground. After that she pretended that we were in some Call Duty scenario. It was entertaining to watch her peek out of trees with a hand-made gun or roll on the ground. Sometimes she would even make sounds of bombs dropping.

"Let's go, crazy. Its night time," I finally mustered up the courage to say.

"I want to sleep under you."

Horrified was an understatement to what I felt. "No?"

"I see a glimmer of hope there Winter. You're unsure of this proposition. I say we do it."

"No."

"That doesn't change things."

She moved towards me until she had me pinned against the tree bark. It should have been the other way around as I'd observed in the dream some days ago. It kind of struck on my male ego but currently I was too busy counting the inches between me and her nose. She slowly moved forward as if teasing me, a slight tilt in her smile. Soon, I could feel her strawberry infatuated breath fan my face.

Okay, this wasn't good.

Just when I thought she would grasp my lips with hers she brought her pupils together so that they were looking at the bridge of her nose and poked her tongue out, only twisted.

It took me five minutes to get over all that. In those distracted moments I never realized when and how Walker managed to climb up a tree.

"This is amazing," she screamed standing precariously on one of the branch.

"Where did you get that from?" I yelled back.

Her hands held a bottle of champagne and two glasses. She was currently filling one.

"You should try this," she shouted at me.

I gave her a stop kidding with me look. She shook her head and giggled. It was time to pick her up brutally. Desperate times after all called for desperate measures.

"I will get you," I warned her as she poured some of the drink down.

"You're a little pussy cat. You won't be able to catch a panther like me. I'm super . . ."

And then she fell. The glass shattered on the ground. Her body tumbled down in such a fashion that her right leg managed to fall on to the broken pieces. She screamed in agony.

"Jamie . . ." I gasped. Running towards her, I quickly picked her up and brought her towards the bench. Before doing anything else I dialled for an ambulance. Then crouching low I took out the shard of glass poking out from her bloodied leg.

"I told you not to climb the tree," I scowled at her.

She giggled.

"What's funny?"

"Your voice sounds squeaky like a woman's."

I stared at her baffled. Here she was bleeding the hell out with such a long gash and so many minor bruises which

I could make out and there she was laughing because I sounded . . . feminine? She was crazier than what I'd first presumed.

"You really fell for it? I wasn't drunk."

I shook my head at her in disbelief.

"Seriously Romance. That was fruit champagne. I had just gone to meet Perry and then come across this shop. I thought of making a fool out of you. Guess, I got too carried away."

The paramedics arrived. Jamie Walker was placed in a gurney. I stumbled after her trying to be as cool as possible.

She was bleeding profusely. She hadn't even cried once yet. She wasn't normal. Though she was human and the agony must have been horrible to deal with plus without expressing, I couldn't even imagine.

But the only thing that troubled me was . . .

Who the hell was Perry?

The Day Jamie Bit Me

I hated seeing her lying helpless on the bed but a lunatic she was. Who gets fractured up and then decides to skate?

The next day the doctor had permitted release. Grover had called me for some family stuff which turned out to be the brothers locking me up for an interrogation about Parsley's lost shoes. We ended up fighting with food and also finding the shoes under the couch which Luke upturned when he swore unintentionally and the three of us ran to beat him. Luke put his feet on the head rest and the couch fell forward. I had deserted Jamie Summer at a park with the promise I'd be back soon.

The moment I entered the sights of the park I saw several teens surrounding a girl who was holding her head. For the second time in two days I felt worry eat away my heart.

All this running around to the hospital would soon make me thin if nothing else.

"We have to keep her here for a week not for the fact that she's okay and can go but she seems dangerous outside in the world." I nodded on every word of the doctor.

"Why can't you let your life be a drag instead of spicing it up more than required?" I asked her wearily as I took up a seat next to her bed. A tube injecting blood into her vein was the sole reason she was tied to the bed. Her leg was hanging up with the support while her head was bandaged up meticulously.

"Ah but then what's the use of living. As long as you breathe do something worth remembering. I want people to reminisce me as an epitome of life not a symbol of boredom such as you."

"You're sounding reckless Jamie Summer Walker."

"All I need to save is my heart anyways. That's the thing required."

I just shrugged and changed the topic. My mind was full with what I had to do for her birthday just some days away. Though the plan was well-thought off I still feared failure. It was the most arduous scheme I'd ever designed. There were just too many flaws.

But it was worth everything.

We conversed till the night time. I decided to go out and get us some take away. It was while I was returning from KFC when I stumbled upon a familiar person. I apologized but then gasped as my eyes raked him up.

What was he doing here?

He was very nervous, the signs –

His hand was ruffling his hair.

His eyes weren't meeting mine.

His other hand was clenching and unclenching.

He was biting his lower lip.

"Should I ask?" I enquired.

He shifted on to his other leg. I saw a slight tinge of colour creep into his cheeks. This was freaking me out. Parsley was not even yelling at me for asking him something when I clearly had no right in their eyes.

"I um . . ."

I kept staring at him. That was all I could muster up in courage.

"Parse?"

His dark brown eyes snapped to mine. He'd inherited mother's features while I was more like dad. It was my hard luck that most of them were genetically similar to mother while I was stuck with father. Not that it mattered when it came to loving.

My thoughts then flirted to planning for Jamie Summer's birthday and also to how worried she must be feeling being starving and alone at the moment. I was about to excuse myself when Parsley spoke.

"I have to leave. Don't ask me questions," he snapped.

Well, at least things were normal.

"Sorry, I didn't mean to sound like that."

Or maybe they would never be the same.

He never said sorry that also to me. I dropped my paper brown bag and gaped at him. He shrugged.

Wait a minute.

A hostile thought floated into my brain making my insides crawl up and light in fire.

Jamie Walker was here.

Had Parsley come here to strike? After all, this was the moment of her weakness where he could dominate and show the world that the boss was him. It was totally acceptable and the only reason I could fathom. Maybe he had slipped in poison inside the blood tube inside her room. Worse of worse he could have spiked her water. I blanched.

He picked up the brown bag and handed it out to me. I was fighting between so many emotions that I silently took it.

"Are you here to create havoc in Walker's life because if that be so then man up and combat me," I said gritting my teeth.

He looked astonished. "She's here?"

His face pulled into a void expression making my mind rattle with nervousness. Maybe I had dug a well for myself by confessing bravery.

"Here," he said after quite a while and lifted the right side of his khaki pants. I saw a bandage wrapped tightly around his leg.

"Are you okay?"

Not that I was concerned.

I did care. He was my brother whatever the relation faced.

"Nothing Henrique fell on my leg during practice and you know that mo- I mean that guy is fat so . . ."

He coughed uncomfortable. I looked away and nodded.

"See you later," he muttered and walked away.

I stood there trying to get myself back together. One thing was sure.

Something had changed Parsley. It had to be that blonde, Yasmine Yolander. I'd seen them hanging out together a lot during school. She was an exchange student from Nepal.

I'd spoken to her a couple of times and by the way she held herself, she was a great girl.

If she was the reason then I was the happiest guy today. She was good for Parsley.

Only he wasn't that good for her.

*   *   *

The week was passing by quickly. I'd thought the fractures had been major but the doctor said another week or so and the plaster could be taken off.

"Happy birthday," I yelled jovially.

She jumped up and rubbed her eyes. "Get out you oil on my beautiful fresh water."

"What?"

"You split ends to my beautiful hair."

"Walker it's . . ."

"You malaria to my body . . ."

She kept up the examples while I just stood there, amusement lining my face. I kept the bouquet of yellow roses on her lap and folded my hands to stare at her comfortably.

Her hairs were sticking out as if electrocuted while her skin shone with the light falling on it. She had such a beautiful, ivory skin even though freckles splattered most of her nose. The dark eyes were powdered with sleep. Her left side of the face was pink as she'd been sleeping on her hands which were currently demonstrating her examples.

I smiled at her for there was nothing I wanted to do but that. My heart skipped a beat as she yawned cutely. Her hands went up to her head.

"Is that okay?' I asked concerned.

"Are you kidding me?"

Her eyes widened around in surprise as they travelled around. It had taken up the whole night but luckily the doctor had given her a pain medication for the stringent headache she had yesterday evening which had somehow knocked her off solidly.

The majority of the room was drowning in streamers and balloons. A part of it was covered in a huge banner saying 'Happy Birthday'. Lots of ice cream caricatures lined the walls. I had placed a couple of gifts from her friends in school on her side table which lit up the room more with the bright paper. A separate table had a cake in the shape of a gun with the words 'JSW' scrawled on it.

"Senorita"

We both looked towards the door.

I sighed.

"Alan," Jamie Summer yelled gleefully. He moved towards her in what I almost presumed was cat walk and engulfed her in a hug. She squeezed him tightly.

"Sure *give him a hug*. I'm just the villain here," I grumbled.

"Aw Grumpy, come here!"

I shook my head.

"Get here Winter or else I'll walk there and hug you. After I kick you down below that is."

That sure had me moving.

"I don't think this boy likes me Alan," Walker grumbled.

"What are you saying," Reed inhaled dramatically like she'd said something so unbelievable it was worth dying for. "He doesn't like you?"

"He isn't behaving properly."

I rolled my eyes. Even though this habit was degrading it had become exactly that, a habit.

"There isn't a day he stops talking about you. If I have to hear anything more in your case from this man I swear I will cry so much that people would solve water shortage problems. He's close to loving you more than he loves me. In fact even before you came in his life there was a sign that said you'd come . . . look."

Before I could process anything, Reed had pulled up one side of my shirt. Thankfully, it was the wrong side. I spanked his hand away and glared at him. He shrugged his shoulders innocently as Walker stared at me curiously. I started a random conversation about what we'd done these past days which diverted both their attention.

All three of us talked for a while. Alan animatedly told her about this new guy that had come into our class and according to him was pretty sexy. He was detailing about the boy's features and I looked at both of them appalled.

I'm 'ere

I looked at the screen of my phone.

Alright, I'm coming to get you.

I excused myself and went outside. The smell of tobacco was what pulled me towards his direction. I quickly reprimanded him to snuff that out as the hospital was a no smoking zone. We gave each other mannish hugs and clasped our hands in brotherhood. He ruffled my hair and smirked.

Good old times.

"Yo'r meat in 'ere mate?"

I smirked at him. No matter what happens, some things remain the same.

"She's not mine yet bro."

"Like tha's evr stoped yu b'fore."

I had my arm around him as I manoeuvred him towards Jamie's room. I let go as we neared. He was talking about the party he'd attended yesterday and what I'd missed. I entered the room and stood in astonishment.

Both the fools were trying to flirt profusely with the nurse who looked as if he wanted to stab himself with one of the injections in embarrassment.

"Did I tell you I like brunettes?"

"Did I tell you I like big thumbs?"

I cursed at Alan.

"Did you know you have the best cheek bones in the world?"

"Do you like your bed warm or cold on the side because I can fix either?"

"Hey guys," I interjected. They both spun towards me as I walked in. Jamie Summer's eyes were fixed on mine with enthusiasm while Alan's teasing eyes moved from mine to him. His brownies widened in surprise. The expressions changed from that to bliss.

He did have a huge school going teenage crush on him after all.

I was standing right next to Jamie Summer Walker whose coffee brown eyes travelled behind me and landed on the stranger.

She had been holding my arm to get up for washroom. The next thing I knew, her teeth were drilling holes into my skin.

Jamie Summer Walker had bitten me!

The Day Jamie Hugged Me

"I can't believe it."

I clenched my fists. It was for the sixteenth time in the past five minutes that she had whispered this to me.

Alan on the other hand was already cosy with his old friend. It was tough to stand there and not want to slap both. The place she'd bit me had been stinging all this time. I scowled as Alan winked at me his hand trailing flirtingly over the black jacket.

"Is he really there or are my eyes blind?" Jamie Summer was uncontrollably excited.

Should I be regretting this decision?

"Damn, he's so gorgeous Romance. I love him."

Yes, definitely affirmative.

Sometimes in life you have to do things that make you the unhappiest man in town while it makes your girl the happiest. This was one of those times.

"*Dark Joker . . . Are you really him? The Joker . . . Mr. Joker, I have been your fan since I learnt to spell fan! You are just perfect. I love your beliefs, your stunts, the way you place the foundations of society on a brittle path . . ."*

How did they know it was him? Well, he'd dressed exactly the way he used to with the black clothes. Anyone could recognize the style, that meaning among his fans.

I cowered in a corner as she went on piling praise on praise until every core of my being was loathing my old buddy. I watched on as Jamie and Alan jovially listened to the 'Great Adventures of The Joker.' I rolled my eyes as the exaggeration queued on in the series. The fact that anyone would believe he escaped the jaws of police with the help of his pet alligator was mere appalling.

I mean who keeps an alligator as a pet?

Turkey pecked me on the head. Yes, a pigeon was still a far more believable pet than an alligator. Knowing Hunter, he had to exaggerate.

I couldn't stand the whole 'I love you blah-blah' . . . nonsense, so I walked out.

"Have you been consuming a lot of greens?"

"Go away Alan," I grumbled.

"You know even if Jams is gaga-ing over Hunter, I still wuff you."

I pushed him away as he slung his arm around me and made sloppy kissing sounds. Trust Alan to be gross in any situation. Despite my reluctance, a smile escaped me.

"Uh . . . what are you doing dimwit?" I asked awkwardly as Alan pushed me towards the wall and breathed close to my face. "If this is another of those tactics then please let me go, I swear to God I'm straight as there can be."

"Oh please, don't flatter yourself. I just saw Trion Baxter aka my ex. He needs to understand I have upgraded . . . well hello there darling!"

I rolled my eyes as Alan got distracted and bounded off towards a male nurse who looked right out of a Jockey catalogue. I could hear him talking about being injected in the arse as he suffered from a disease no one had heard off.

Smooth Alan, smooth.

I strolled towards Walker's room. It was just a couple of minutes more for Hunter to go away then I could have my crush to myself. Speaking off my crush, she was missing.

I should have known.

With a poker face I trudged outside feeling no pull to go and even try to find her.

*   *   *

It had been a week since the hospital incident. The exhaustion with being around Walker had me hung up on staying home. I couldn't yet digest the fact that I was fine with missing a week from school. My phone rang loudly. For the millionth time I picked it up in hopes it was Walker but . . .

"And then . . . then he just . . ."

"Al, would you just calm down. Stop sobbing!"

An hour had passed. I was literally half on the floor in my hopes to perish from it cracking up.

"But Rom-com I'm the cutest, fluffy bunny on this planet. Why would anyone reject me?"

"That's because he's a douche."

"A really hot one though"

See that's why I did not require a girlfriend or any other social relationship. Alan Reed took up the responsibility to satisfy every form of relationship I could otherwise have.

"Did you notice his biteable arse and those goddamn lips . . . ?"

Even on the other end of the telephone I could imagine Alan drooling over the phone.

"Err no?"

"Why would you not?"

I held the phone away as the screech rang loudly making the speaker vibrate.

"I don't know how many million times more I'll have to inform you that I'm not gay."

He giggled. "You would look amazing in a tutu with pink feathers around your neck. Don't roll your eyes at me young man. You do remember the glorious childhood days when I dressed you up as a woman for my tea party?"

Hit me amnesia, anytime (now) would be great.

"No I don't. I'd advise you Al my boy that you don't either or I'll soon be fisting your face."

"As long as it's not just my face, fisting is fine."

"Re-Reed, shut your hole."

"You're bringing it on yourself Rom. Hole? Really, I need you to do . . ."

I hung up. I was too scared to even decipher what he was trying to imply. I flipped on my back, took hold of my phone on the side table and looked to check if I had closed the window.

"What the hell?" I gasped falling off my bed in fright. "What are you doing here creeping on me like a supernatural being?"

"I was watching you talk to your boyfriend."

"Shut your hole."

"I would need you for that."

Alan and Summer would make a perfect pair. I had an overdose of both these drugs and believe me one day it would be the death of me. I turned on my stomach and switched on my phone to surf the Internet.

"Aren't you going to ask me how I got up here?"

I was pretty sure she would have barged in through the open door. We were mad inhabiting this dump. The most anyone could steal from us was Luke who anyways would beat them down with his attitude. I'm pretty sure if anyone ever kidnapped Luke, he would be returned back in minutes.

"Why are you giving me the cold shoulder? Is it because I left the hospital without being discharged? I can explain!"

I ignored her pretending to be engrossed in my Galaxy wallpaper. The stars sure shone brighter today.

"I'm sorry Winter but seriously I have a valid reason for leaving the place."

"Oh, as Hunter must be taking you out for the greater good." Despite my strong will to not speak, I couldn't resist a taunt.

"Are you jealous?" she flared up.

"Yes . . . of a man who claims to be '*Dark Joker*' like a character out of a badly rated Batman movie? You think?"

"You're clearly envious of him. I never confessed Romance but your facial expressions are the easiest to decrypt."

"It's . . . Xerkis . . . Moon."

I had thrown away my phone with plans of pinning her towards the wall. I'd all inclinations of making the scene aggressively seductive except for one minor thing.

The stupid roller skate Alan had politely left after his *Ice Princess* auditions. Oh he sure was going to be an iced princess once I was done with him. I slid, smashing against Jamie and pushing her backwards making both of us topple. In my sensitivity to save her leg from permanent damage, I took hold of her bag and the side of my cupboard making her swing towards my bed. I pushed her so that she fell a distance away on my bed. Her plaster had just come off two days ago.

In the process her bag got ripped.

You know the times when you just feel like giving up on life? Yes? No? I clearly do. I would like to terminate my existence on this hopeless planet.

"Oh my God . . ."

"I can explain."

"Oh my Lord . . ."

"Romance you need to calm down."

"Oh my Jesus . . ."

She shook me hard.

I'm not saying I didn't deserve that but when you see a million pregnancy tests lying on your floor then I bet so would you. They were practically mocking my existence.

"Now listen . . ." Walker began.

"I leave you for five minutes . . . five godly minutes with him and you end up what pregnant? How many tests are these?"

"Twenty. That's not the point . . ."

"You are twenty times pregnant?" I screamed a tad bit shrilly. Alan would have swooned.

"That doesn't even make sense. This isn't me . . ."

We stared at each other in silence. She was waiting for me to continue but I flopped on my bed making her jump on it slightly.

"I think I'm developing a migraine," I mumbled to no one in particular.

The phone started ringing.

I picked it up dazed without checking the number.

"How dare you hang up on me? I had to travel all the way to the other end of my room to get reception to yell at you. Do you have anything to say in your defence Mr Romance Winters?"

I couldn't take this anymore. All this drama was much more than the soap operas bargained for. Why was a mere mortal like me being subjected to them?

"I love you Alan but I need some time off . . ."

He dropped the phone. I might have slightly exaggerated the reply while dealing with the migraine. I know I had difficulty expressing that L-word out loud but presently the damage was done. Alan I'll deal with later.

"So . . . are you waiting for the illegitimate kid to be born to explain things?" I asked resigned.

"It isn't me. I mean . . . its Hunter's girlfriend."

"Wait a minute, Hunter's girlfriend is pregnant?" I asked with all the hope in the world.

"Uh . . . she's sort of."

"How can someone be sort of pregnant?"

"It's a long story . . ."

"Is it . . . longer than my manhood?"

Yes, the migraine was worse than I thought. I and Hunter had to have a long heart to heart conversation too one of these days. That man was hiding secrets like mothers hiding Christmas presents places.

"I don't know how long your uh . . . manhood is," Jamie Walker blushed. She looked adorable.

"Hunter and Cameron were drunk. They ended up in Vegas. They somehow ended up married like it happens. Now, they aren't officially partners but plan to be. However there was a thing stopping them which was a baby and now they are having one hence all the pregnancy tests because they didn't believe it for like ten times then Cameron's mother refused to and then all the seven siblings she has. Hunter is quite unpopular among them – no surprise there as duh he's Dark Joker."

I watched as her face went redder and redder. I knew this story well. Hunter was one of my best friends after all.

"Okay."

"Okay?" she looked at me in disbelief. "I ranted for like light years and you say okay?"

"Light years are to measure distance not time."

"Seriously, is that all you got?"

"That's what science says."

"Science is my beautiful posterior."

"Well considering biology is a part of . . ."

"Romance, are you listening to yourself? What do you think this is an audition for a Nobel Prize?"

I wanted to reply to that with an even more snobbish answer. Knowing Walker, it would make her mad to no ends. Hence, I kept shut on that topic.

"Hunter can have as many kids as he wants. I'm not going to do anything except go and punch his sorry, filthy, friend-pact breaking face."

She hugged me.

Yes, ladies and gentleman the little, warm body of a girl which I've hardly ever felt wrapped around my torso was doing exactly that like a red ribbon on a green Christmas present. Her head made up to my chin so that I just had to bend a little to kiss the top of it. I could feel her arms snaked back and fingers entangled into each other. I felt her heart beating fast. Lethargically, I patted her back. I wish this was the moment time stopped moving and Summer stayed in my arms completely shining on my heart. The migraine also seemed to be reducing. She pressed even closer and somehow managed to tiptoe.

I felt her hot breath on my neck. It made me jelly. Yes, a guy can get weak kneed as well. Screw me. Her nose was near my ear and soon her lips substituted.

"I thought you'll panic. I'm so glad you didn't. I'm proud of you."

We stood like that for a long while.

"What do you mean panic? When there is nothing for me to worry about . . ."

"I thought me announcing something like that would. After all I'm pregnant."

Okay, someone get me a chair and lots of cold water.

Time, you two faced devil.

The Day Jamie Stabbed Me

Chopsticks were a fun medium to eat noodles with. I never concentrated so hard on the grace with which I could pick and easily access my food. They could also be used as a weapon to stab someone multiple times till they realized making the girl you love pregnant could come at the cost of death.

Walker sat there with a peaceful smile lighting her beautiful visage. There was no sign of fear or regret. Alan as usual was cracking some insensitive jokes about his mighty self making her laugh out loud in intervals. I was grateful for his presence today.

I relayed the conversation that had occurred a while ago in my head.

"So you are saying he can't have a baby?"

"For the millionth time Romance, yes!"

"Then why is it a valid reason for you to have one? You just met the man for god sake and in a couple of hours you decide it's worthy to give up so much and have a monster?"

"*It's nice to know how well you think of what I can produce.*"

"*Summer, you know I didn't mean it that way. I'm just concerned. How did you even manage to get knocked up so fast?*"

"*Uh . . . haven't you heard of test tube babies? I think it was obvious that's what happened. Wait, what do I have to give up for this?*"

"*Your life can be in danger. Forget that, imagine all the tantrums. The fat you'll be accumulating, the uninvited pain waves, the morning sickness . . . plus test tube babies don't work so fast.*"

"*I love how encouraging you are. You will not understand what it's like to do a good deed anyways and hence I won't waste my time sitting and lecturing you on life.*"

I didn't like arguing with her even a tad bit. She sat there at present, miffed with me. I wanted to kiss her cute face so hard that she would admit to being wrong and assure me about the hallucinations of being pregnant. Alan had handled the situation well and that's why I needed a best friend like him in my sad life.

"Romance is an emotionless mess. Don't listen to a word that man utters. He has no sense of living a life."

Or maybe not . . .

I got up pushing back the chair as slowly as possible to attract less attention. While walking back though my knee hit the edge of the seat hard making the furniture fall. I yelped as the pain shot through my leg. Not just the two but most of the people were looking at me now. I felt like taking a bow for the amazing show. It anyways seemed like everyone was crying here.

"Are you okay?" Walker asked me.

I nodded at her with a small smile. I had no idea why she'd forgiven me without me trying to apologize but I wasn't complaining. It was time I did something to take my mind off reality.

*   *   *

I'd been skating since a while now. The houses were changing from posh to rugged. All the rainbow coloured tiles were switching to one dirty brown colour. The red roofs were nothing but wooden planks falling in now and then from the top. The smell of flowers was long gone and a pungent smell dominated the atmosphere. I covered my mouth by pulling the tee up. The road was more a rubble now. I had to carefully ride it just in case I missed the place.

Miss Wilson had emailed me all the details the instantly I'd shot her a text. She was glad that after so long, I still didn't forget my duty towards the society.

The news Walker had kindly bestowed upon me wasn't easy to digest. Even if I wanted to, I'd never be able to stop thinking about it. It seemed as if majority of my hours were spent just pondering about that woman. Why was love such an annoying pest? More importantly, why was it so essential for her to take such a dramatic approach to the situation. It wasn't as if no other woman was available for Hunter to ask for help.

The building finally came in sight. I hit the ground harder to increase my speed. The pleasure of being in another world was just moments away.

I stood outside with bated breath. It took me some minutes to be ready but when I was, the confident knock vibrated inside the house. The wait was sticking its sharp end on to my brittle patience. Was there anyone even inside?

"Hello Ms. Roxanne? I'm Romance Winter here." I shook her hand politely. She appeared to be a gentle old lady living a life worth breathing for. The wrinkles on her face lit up at the mention of my name.

"They've been waiting for you. It's been quite a while son."

I nodded sadly. The last time I'd visited had been around four months now. Ever since Walker had skipped into my life, it had become a daily routine to focus nowhere else. At first this work had been like the consequence of something bad but soon it became a thing I needed to do to make that bad switch to good.

The walk in the familiar alley felt so good. I still remembered the first day when the same path had seemed so intimidating. I'd forced my legs forward till every step seemed closer to hell. If the officials hadn't been walking behind me, I would have made a run for it.

I gently knocked on the door.

Some girl screamed that it was open. I pushed the obstruction away to enter into a well lit room that had sketches of cartoons painted across the wall. Nothing had changed around here. The tables were still kept haphazardly. The blackboard was still cleaned up to satisfy my hygienic virus. The sun rays still poured in from the huge windows making the room bright and happy. There were still racks of books lining the wall right behind the kid's toy room where carpets still lay strewn with toys. The best part that brought a genuine smile on my face was the kids though. They were divided in groups and encircling all around the various tables. Most of them were drawing whatever was coming to their innocent minds while the others were just being kids. I bit back laughter as one of the boys snatched the pink colour from the girl and she yelled at him to return.

This was all what life was about.

"Romance, you're back," a little girl squealed. She had her hair in pigtails. I couldn't believe how much she'd grown up in such a short time. Her short legs sprinted towards me as fast as they could. She squealed as she hugged me tightly. "I've missed you so much."

All the kids had their attention on me now. There were a lot of chattering and excited yells as they made a beeline to welcome me back.

If I'd known my absence had affected them so badly, I would have just never left. Maybe I should shift in here and spend all day with these angels. Nobody cared for what I felt or thought outside this house anyways. The girl who had greeted me first held my index finger and another one with short brown hair kept neatly by a blue ribbon grabbed my other finger. They both walked with me towards the desk happily.

I sat down in content.

The first class had been horror. They'd all had tantrums. Some fought like cats, some screamed like animals, some bit each other and the others just threw around stuff. I'd almost thought someone would die that day.

Today they all stared at me with admiration.

It had been a long process of gaining trust. The problem at the root was my reluctance to be with them or even understand them. Then I stared discovering each individual, I got more close to them. Giselle was the first one that had touched my heart. She'd always be special to me. Currently, the little girl was sitting in front of me with loving eyes, twirling her pigtails around.

"So, who has been practising numbers?"

All the hands shot up with Giselle in the lead. I was proud of her. There was intelligence sprayed across her face. Those grey eyes shone with diligence. She was as much in love with numbers as I was.

"Romance, I know how to count now," Samantha smiled at me sweetly. "Andrew taught me."

Andrew gave me a cold look. He'd given into listening to what I said but he'd never warmed up to me. The kid had had a hard life on the streets so I understood. I never badgered him much, he didn't bother to rebel. We had a mutual understanding to maintain distance.

They were all of different age groups with Giselle being the youngest at four and Timothy being the eldest at fourteen. None of them had a home to turn to. They'd made this place their life. It was as if the term, home is where the heart is, held real meaning here.

"Let's hear you count then Sammy," I said gently.

The five year old cleared her throat importantly. They were all late in their education but the money was scarce to fix any. I'd agreed to continue doing this after my term on voluntary basis. It benefitted everyone.

"One, two, three, six, five, eight, nine, and ten . . ." She clapped her hands together in glee.

I chuckled. Her arms opened wide asking for a hug so I gave her one.

"Romance, I can count to," Giselle said immediately. She got up from and quickly moved towards me. Before I could do anything she'd settled on my lap. The glare she threw at Samantha should have started a fight but luckily Samantha was busy counting on her fingers.

"We'll listen to you soon okay princess?"

She nodded at me happily.

"Okay, before I start babbling about today's class how about we all catch up on each other's life?"

There was an appreciative response. Only Andrew and Simon walked back to finish their drawings. They wouldn't concentrate unless I started off the real work. It was a task breaking through their tough exterior but I was not going to give up. One day, they'd trust me enough to let me take away the pain.

I heard a lot of chatter, a huge amount of stories. There were so many emotions running through me but the happiness remained constant. Their innocence was so much greater than anything in the world. I couldn't remain grumpy with the silly things they did or said.

"Do you have a girlfriend now Romance?" Giselle asked me seriously.

I'd managed to finish teaching the class some addition. I'd given the different groups their own tasks accordingly. Giselle had refused to leave me even for a second. She'd stood near the blackboard clutching my jeans as if the moment she let go of any part of me I'd disappear.

I felt really bad.

I'd put the little girl through so much pain. That's why there was no point in refusing whatever she wanted.

"No I don't. You're my only girlfriend."

She pecked my cheek. "If I was big Romance I would be so happy to be your girlfriend. I'm you friend silly, almost like a little sister. I mean do you have a real girlfriend?"

I laughed. Even though the girl was four she spoke like she was my mother.

"No, nobody loves me Elle. This world is so cruel."

"Oh stop being a ninny," she rolled her eyes at me. I pinched her cheeks.

"Do you have a boyfriend?"

She blushed.

Oh was I going to be breaking some bones today.

"No, I don't really have one. I just like Enrique."

There was a commotion outside so I excused myself. Giselle followed me quietly. I didn't stop her.

"Is everything okay Ms Roxanne? I heard some talking?"

"Oh it's those usual fools. This is Paulo. He's the youngest in our family. They left him at the door step and ran away. Now this mad couple next door keeps claiming him as theirs. I'm telling you this world is going to the dogs. Such unkindness! I would never let those reckless humans have such a darling. He'd be dead in a day in their hands."

I gazed at the baby in her hands. He had bright brown eyes that shone with glee. I stroked his cheeks and he caught my finger. Before I could pull it away, he started suckling on it making happy sounds.

"Aren't you adorable?"

"Can you believe how horrible his parents must be? Who would even leave such a beautiful creature is beyond me. I just hope I can give him enough happiness around here."

I nodded with a sinking feeling. I'd realized something. People were really horrendous at times carrying out such hideous actions. Then there was my Walker. All she'd tried to be was noble. There were babies like Paulo with no proper home and then there were homes like Hunter's that really needed the echoes of adorable laughter. How could I be so stupid? I'd upset her even after she'd done something worth lifting her up in the air for.

"I'll go back inside now," I said distracted to Ms. Roxanne. Paulo bade me farewell with giggles. "I'll hang out with you in a while little buddy. Let me just check on your brothers and sisters."

They were still working quietly on the sum. If the kids started liking you, they were the best well behaved bunch of children in the world. I gazed at them proudly.

"Kids, I have an errand to run. I'll be back in half an hour. Keep working okay?"

They all screamed a yes in unison.

"Don't leave me," Giselle whimpered.

I kneeled down next to her so that we could see eye to eye. I clutched her tiny hands into mine.

"Hey, I'll come back soon that's a promise. Do you trust me Elle?"

She nodded her pretty head really fast.

"Then believe me. I won't leave you alone for this long ever, okay?"

There was a moment of hesitation however she let go off my hand. I threw a grateful smile at her.

I was just about to leave when I remembered something. "Hey Enrique, I want you to clean up that mess of the toys before I come back okay?"

He gave me thumbs up. I ruffled Giselle's hair affectionately and walked out.

It was time to fix my other mess.

* * *

Alan had texted me that she was in alley 7 of the area. I didn't realize how dark the place was until the darkness started engulfing me. I'd been calling Walker since a while now but she hadn't picked up yet. I picked up my board and started to walk around.

What was she doing in this area? It wasn't safe to be found alone here. Yes, it wasn't the thug street that didn't mean Walker could be so careless.

The evening was slowly fading away. I had to go back before their sleeping time or Giselle would never forgive me. How that smile could light up my life was a mystery to me? That princess had the knowledge of the world stuffed in the pretty little head of hers. It was just as I was turning the corner when someone yelled and attacked me.

We both stared at my tee as it started soaking in blood.

"You stabbed me?" I voiced out in disbelief. "Did you just make a cross on my chest with a knife?"

"Oh my God, it's you Romance. I thought it was some intruder trying to rob me. The baby has me worrying about my safety more you know?"

"You stabbed me?" I mumbled stupidly.

"I'm so sorry. It's not a deep cut. I'll just bandage it c'mon my friend lives nearby."

"But you stabbed me?"

I couldn't get over the fact she did. We managed to get my wound bandaged. Luckily her out of the blue friend turned out to be a practising medic so she knew what to do. This Walker woman was going to be the death of me. All this commotion had cause me to lose precious time.

"I want you to accompany me," I requested Walker as we were finally standing outside. I had an hour and half to make it back now. There was no way I wasn't going back.

"Where are we going?"

"Can you please not ask questions?" I pleaded.

"Okay, cool."

She was back to being formal with me. I hated this tone. It wasn't what mattered for now. I had to apologize to her for being insensitive. We reached the house. She stared at it curiously.

"Let's go," I said moving my hand to hold hers but she moved faster. She was at the door before I could even say anything else.

"Thank god you're back. The kids are going wild Romance. Giselle almost threw a tantrum. You know how difficult she gets after that."

"I'm so sorry Ms. Roxanne. I'll go handle the situation."

Walker followed me inside as I went to the study room. They were all making a lot of noise. Enrique slammed into me as he was chasing another kid.

"What is going on here?" I yelled.

Everyone became silent.

"Romance, you're back," Giselle squealed as she ran to hug me. I kneeled down so that her tiny arms could engulf around my neck.

"I promised you right? You know I never break them"

She snuggled into my neck. The rest of them were surrounding as well. All the eyes were fixed on the stranger though. I could feel their hostility towards her.

"Hey kids, this is my friend Jamie Walker here. All of you be nice now."

At first they were reluctant then they started being friendly with her. It was probably Walker's nature more than the kids who didn't know how to handle such situations. She was so sweet with them that even I would have melted had I been one of them, lost and defensive against an unknown personality in my only comfort zone.

"Is she the girlfriend?" Giselle whispered in my ears. Walker paused as she heard the words as well but she chose to ignore thankfully.

"No Elle, I told you I don't have one."

"She's pretty. I'd let you have her as your girlfriend."

"I'm glad I have your permission. I'll try okay?"

"She won't say no to you. You're an amazing human being. No one would care to give us so much time and love. I really appreciate you Romance."

I patted her head lovingly. Trust Giselle to make everything emotional.

"Kids, it's time for dinner. Scoot all of you to the dining hall. Remember to wash your hands."

"Uh, can we stay till dinner if you don't mind? I promised Elle I'd tuck her in today."

"Will you tuck me in too?" Samantha asked sadly.

"Of course sweetie," I winked at her. I held her hand as she happily skipped towards the hall.

"Yes, I'd be glad to stay as long as you want Winter."

I nodded at her gratefully.

"Walker," I called out. We were sitting on the huge table where all the kids were busy chattering and eating. Giselle was on my one side and Walker on the other. "I'm really sorry for how I reacted. The fact that you had the guts to do something so unselfish is respectable. I will take care of you and the baby as much as I can. That's the only way to redeem myself. Believe me I've learnt how much I should start appreciating you more."

She sniffed.

"Would you like some mashed potatoes Romance?"

I smiled at her. "Sure, hand me some."

It took another forty minutes for everyone to settle down. I'd finally tucked Giselle in with the promise that I would be back soon. She'd slept off happily snuggling with the teddy bear I'd got her as a birthday present a long while back.

I bade farewell to Roxanne promising a visit within the next three days. She patted my back appreciatively. Walker had been playing with Paulo since a while now. It was an adorable scene as she cooed to the baby and the angel responded with contagious giggles. She was smitten by the baby. That's when I was sure she would make a hell of a great mother.

We were walking back towards my home. I'd asked to camp there tonight.

"Those kids simply adore you Romance. Why didn't you take me before?"

"Those orphans are my life Walker. I don't share them with anyone. You're the only person who knows about them now. I can't let anyone hurt them anyhow. You are a different case. I trust you."

"Thank you," she whispered. Her voice was cracking.

That's when she did the most amazing gesture in the whole time I'd known her which made the beat of my heart erratic.

She slipped her hand into mine entwining our fingers as if for some moments she belonged entangled in my destiny.

The Day Jamie Asked Me Out

She smiled at me. You never know what's different about any smile unless you observe it intricately. Summer was the kind of person who constantly put up a facade when it came to expressing herself at the expense of someone else. She was a pro at it though after all this time spent with her I had managed to decipher when it was fake. Hence, it was a surprise to see her actually emoting knowing the fact that her pregnancy was affecting me a lot. No, it wasn't as if she never spoke out what she felt, in fact she was quite verbose about it and made sure I spoke my feelings but it just somehow never felt real.

"What are you thinking?"

Are the summer days hotter or is it just you.

"I'm contemplating on the perks of getting a haircut."

She started giggling. Over the time I'd concluded one thing – romance wasn't exactly my thing. Pun intended.

I gazed at her as she closed her eyes in contentment. It was one of my favourite hobbies involving her. She never seemed to mind. Who was this creature? What was she doing to me? She was pregnant and yet there was not an utter of complaint. It was unusual the absence of frequent morning sickness, unrealistic wants and what not that entails with this situation. There was always a constant radiance on her face. She was my sunshine after all. It was still baffling to see her not grumble or even complaint once about her pains.

"What are you thinking now?"

I wished sometime she would stop these unnecessary questions. The brown eyes were reflecting warmth from the sun rays. I could feel the tingles all over my bones. The trembles of my limbs were real as her pupil pierced my incessant thoughts.

"Romance, are you listening?"

I shrugged out of my trance. "I'm thinking of how you shouldn't be continuously badgering people with questions."

She sighed and closed her eyes again.

"Hey", I held her hand. I wanted to ask her for coffee but my ego was always the master. It caged me inside. Even before the next set of words left my mouth, I felt the immense loss that tags along with defeat.

"What's the matter Rome?" she asked carefully.

I didn't like the sudden change in her tone. I let it pass though. "I think maybe I should leave. I have some work with Greasly . . . I mean Grover."

I let go off her hand and got up to leave. She kept her eyes closed. Inwardly, I cursed myself furiously and started strolling out.

"Rome, would you like to go out for some coffee?" she suddenly mumbled.

I clenched the door handle hard while holding back a smile. Other than the random coincidences we had with certain situations or thoughts, this was one of the other things that amused me. Somehow, she never understood me and then she just did.

"Okay," I said emotionlessly. My whole persona though was doing a fanatic lindy hop.

"Did you know they stopped selling choc-chip in the mart downtown? Have you any idea what the end of life seems like? It's the same."

I chuckled. Her face was scrunched up in panic.

"It's okay. I'll make you some ice cream at home."

"You can make ice cream?" she squealed into my ears. "Why have you been telling me nonsense about everything in the world instead of informing about the most important aspect of your life?"

"I'm sorry I didn't know ice cream making was an art worth categorizing as even essential."

She gasped in horror as a response to my sarcasm. "You really need to prioritize life Romance."

We entered the cafe. It was a local favourite of mine. There was a Marvel corner they'd built which was full of superhero art. I'd sit there excited about every little detail. The first time Walker had come here, she'd become annoyed with my lack of attention span. However, today my concentration was all on her.

"What if some day I told you that there was some disease in me and death will take me in its beautiful clutches?"

"Then I'd tell you to get out of the romance novel this instant because if I get mad at such nonsense, I'll have to get therapy."

She stared at me in disbelief. I shrugged and ordered for some coffee.

"What would you say at my funeral?" she asked. "You know when I die eighty years later . . ."

"How did this woman survive for so long will always be a mystery to me," I chuckled.

"Fine, don't talk to me," she huffed.

I stared at her sitting there with puffed cheeks. I committed the cuteness to my memory.

"Okay, what do you want? A full blown speech about how much irrevocable love I had for you and that got wasted because after all the eighty years I still couldn't have you?"

She stared at me sadly.

"Don't look at me like that," I sighed. "Eighty years of happiness was more refined than a hundred year old wine. There wouldn't be a day I wouldn't miss your laughter. The sun will always shine on me reminding the light you showered brightening my dark days. If there was a way I could exchange, you would be standing here while I lay down underneath all the sand. We were both walking alone in our own thorny paths until destiny fixed one where we got reminded of the roses that accompany the thorns. I'm back as a loner but the roses still bloom from the radiance you left. I love you then when you had soft velvety skin, I loved you then when the wrinkles aged your face and I love you now when nothing but memories stands around me as witness of a story that never ended well but was a happy one."

Her eyes pierced mine seriously. They were shining with unshed tears.

"That was beautiful."

"You're beautiful."

She blushed. I smirked at her.

"It's ironic how non feminine you are though."

"What do you mean?" Her face turned into a frown.

"I mean any other woman would be demanding so much with the pregnancy and everything. I'm not trying to be a sexist but usually the tantrums are accompanied with having a baby. You hardly even complaint of morning sickness."

"That's not normal?"

"I don't know. I've never experienced all this before as well. From what I've seen on television and heard though, the stories are different.

We both sat in silence for a while. The waiter placed the coffee on the table. I took a tentative sip. I wasn't sure if I'd said the right things anymore. She seemed lost in thought. A crease formed on her forehead. I wanted to even out really badly.

"Did you talk to Parsley lately?" Jamie asked me suddenly.

"Who did I talk to?"

"Parsley, don't you remember your second eldest brother?"

I still gave her a confused look.

"The Winter hierarchy for your generation starts with Grover Winter being the eldest followed by Parsley Winter and then you which leaves Luke Winter as the youngest. Do you remember now?"

"Why would I speak to him?" I ignored her previous comment.

"He's been having troubles with his girlfriend Yasmine. He was yelling at her about some medication or something . . ."

"Okay."

She looked at me for more response. I continued sipping on my coffee.

"Is that all you have to say?"

I nodded.

She grumbled in frustration. I put down the mug of coffee and looked at her sternly. I don't know what the matter was today; all I wanted to do was not make Walker see how much she affected me. I was trying my best every second to tell her who was dominating the situation

"I don't care what happy endings you keep making in your head Walker but I won't talk to any of my brothers ever. I hope you understand that it isn't as easy as it looks. They've been like that with me for years. I'm done."

I threw some cash on the table and got up.

"It won't harm to care?"

"I never said I don't care. That doesn't mean I'll go and show that to them directly. I might be selfish in saying this however I still will. I don't want them to think they won in whatever competition of being the best that we all are playing. They can't have the last move. I'll be the one saying check-mate as and when I want."

No matter how sad her eyes looked, I turned away.

It wasn't always right to let the other be happy. Sometime there were things in your life that no one, be it a friend or a lover could fix with words. Those things were all your decisions. Nobody had the right to dictate terms then.

Not even Jamie Summer Walker.

The Day Jamie Slammed Me Down

Jamie Summer Walker was two months pregnant and smiling like a Cheshire cat at a mannequin.

Her face was radiant giving the obvious hint of her supporting another life. The brown eyes were lit with the usual sunshine only brighter. I couldn't settle the fanatic beating of my heart as a beautiful smile stretched from those luscious lips. Her slender fingers were caressing her tummy gently. The black hair was reflecting everything any other woman should be jealous off.

I approached her as slyly as I could such that the trance wasn't broken. She turned towards me. There was an expression of a woman on a mission and I got taken aback. Walker held my wrist tightly and started pulling me away. She pushed me into an alley and suddenly I found myself pinned towards the wall.

"Uh, Summer what's going on?" I asked her confused.

The brown eyes were blinking really fast while looking here and there erratically.

"I have to tell you something grave."

I held my breath as hers fanned my face.

"Romance, I am so scared but it's been so long now. I need to tell you this before it gets worse. I really tried to avoid the situation. The more there is running away involved, the deeper the crisis becomes."

The words were getting slurred. The desperation for understanding the whole problem as quickly as possible was frankly scaring me.

"What are you talking about?" I enquired again more baffled than I ever was.

"I think . . ." she paused dramatically. Her fingers tightened on my shoulders. "Alan Reed has fallen in unconditional love with me."

The words took quite some time to sink in. The moment they did I lost my sanity. The laughter bubbled out in peals. The prospect of making her furious wasn't my aim. However, many a time this woman spewed such nonsense.

"You do know he's gay right?" I chuckled.

"So? He can stop being gay. If he hasn't ceased that I'm pretty sure he has turned bisexual. There's not a day he makes me feel special. He's taking extra care with the baby on board. It's not normal Romance. You are so close to me and yet you don't even care half the time so compare it to the magnitude he does. I'm assuring you he's in reckless love with me. There's no other explanation."

I held back laughter.

"I think your hormones are finally reacting. The pregnancy has rendered you retarded as it does to most women."

As soon as the sentences finished, even I knew how offensive I'd been. Walker's face turned red as slowly as my beats started to decrease. I held my breath anticipating the well-deserved slap across my face. She huffed and stormed away.

I let go off my breath. Now, I had to devise a plan to sort this out. An exhausted sigh left me. Women were such work sometimes.

"Alan," I yelled on the phone.

"Yes, what is it darling? What does my boo want from me?"

I rolled my eyes. "What bloody signals are you throwing at Summer? She just confessed that you're in love with her."

I could make out the confused tone of his voice even over the phone. "Of course, Rom-com I am in love with that woman. She's amazing. I ship you guys so much."

"She thinks you are in actual love with her."

"Like Romeo-Juliet love?"

I nodded forgetting the fact that I was on the phone.

"What?" He started guffawing. "Isn't she well aware how boys make me ding?"

I sighed. This boy will never improve on his vernacularism.

"Listen, fix this Reed or I'll tell you what a ding is."

"I will think about the proposal. Just how hard would the ding be?"

"Reed," I muttered threateningly.

"Okay, okay! I will fix this. You don't worry about a thing. She'll ding-dong you soon."

He cut the call before I could retaliate. Even though I was annoyed, a smile crept on my face. Reed could always make things better. It was the way he spoke that made me light-hearted. I should apologize to him later for being rude.

"Romance," she mumbled. I turned with a smile on my face. Reed sure was fast.

She spanked my head and walked away.

Reed, that sly old peer of mine was as good as dead.

*   *   *

He was giving me a miffed look. I rolled my eyes. The fake mad look did not suit Reed at all. I agree I had over reacted and shouldn't have beaten him black and blue. He shouldn't have pulled off such a frustrating prank too.

We were sitting in Alan's favourite cafe. I was compensating for being rash.

"I said a million times how sorry I am. Stop pouting."

He turned his face away from me. I sighed and secretly ordered for his favourite sizzling brownie.

"It's not even my fault," he said in a small voice.

"I know I am genuinely sorry Alan," I sighed.

The waiter brought the dessert. One of the reasons I loved this cafe was the fast service. The boys working here were good friends. I'd explained to Jacob the urgency. Hence, he had brought my consoling prize early.

"Oh my God," Reed squealed. "You're such a cutie Rom-Com. I love you so much."

I fell of the chair trying to push his kissing face away. The guys started chuckling at us. They all had the look of oh-here-they-go-again. Reed broke into a love monologue and I sat there with my face flushed, rubbing my behind.

"You two should just marry now," Jacob stated and walked off before I could get up and punch him.

Suddenly there was complete silence. Someone tapped on a mike. I looked around trying to find the source.

"Yell-ow buddies!"

There was a moron with purple-streaked spikes announcing something on the mike. I was too busy trying to keep a licking Reed off me. It was too easy to make him forgive people sometimes. You just had to know the certain tricks that drove him wild.

My mind wavered off to the restricted area again. I wondered what she would be doing at this time. On a scale of ten how mad was she still with me. Either I could take her on a romantic getaway which will make her realize that it wasn't Reed but me who was recklessly in love with her or I could be the sweet guy and apologize normally such that she would keep me friend-zoned.

"Romance Winters."

Was it just me or had someone announced my name out loud. I broke off my Walker trance and looked around as pairs of expectant eyes looked at me. It had to be something this buffoon had done. Maybe they weren't open to public display of affections.

"I didn't know you were into creativity," Alan mumbled to me. "I think you should go now before people start booing you. We could get thrown out of the cafe. Apparently there is a poetry slam going on and you've been selected for improvisation."

What was he talking about? I looked at him dazed.

"Rom-com," he said unsure. I followed the gaze of his finger pointing. There she stood in her bright sundress with the yellow screaming all the shine I had been missing all this while. A smug look was splattered all across her face. I felt the punishment was well-deserved so I got up to serve it.

She stood up as well.

Her short-crop black hair curved around her perfect face and ended in straight levels right at her bare shoulders. I could glance at a part of the slender neck. My lips trembled to caress the marble. I sighed at my vampire-ish tendencies. Those lips could drive any man on the edge of planet. Why did she affect me so drastically?

She sauntered forward like poetry in motion. If only she was an angel every step of hers would make a flower blossom from the Earth. Her musical voice vibrated around.

"Before this man here," she blatantly pointed towards me in derision. "Before he starts to spew out some anti-feminist bull, I'd like to say a piece for him and chauvinists akin him. I suggest a slam. If he has the guts to take up a challenge as his sexist ego would instigate him now to, I'll be glad to do this."

I looked at her with a straight face. I didn't deserve such a hit but it was Summer. She was allowed anything.

Her kholed eyes bore into mine as if searching for the depths of anger. I retuned her look with as much remorse as possible. Just as my lips mouthed a sorry she ranted off.

She smiled towards the sun,
She followed wherever he went,
Never questioned any move, blindly trusting him.
So blind was she from the heat,

Little did she know what his real intentions were?
She stood there ecstatically gazing at his blaze,
Always bravely facing him,
He entranced her with his love.
Every night when he disappeared she wouldn't look anywhere
She'd droop and await his return loyally
Never once swayed by the handsome Sir Brown Grainy
Rejecting all the moves of the perverted Prince Peony
Even the moves of the ordinary Mari G. were blindsided
At the break of dawn, hope would rise in her as did her lover
Then again she would make her passionate trail
Then came the day he decided to show her his real title
To prove who was the stronger one
To shower her with condescension
instead of life as she deserved
He blazed
He glared
He forced her to burn
And she burnt
She blazed
She let him light her with his embers
But she made sure he knew
She'll be back
Then she'll avenge
And he'll burn
He'll burn.

She paused.

There was a deadly silence. If it's possible then everyone was breathing as one. It seemed only I was breathing different. My heart beat was taking the path not taken while they all were trotting the usual path. A bunch of eyes were looking at me with judgement. One pair that I cared for was throwing daggers of disappointment while the other was painting a picture of dangerous smugness.

It had been a long day. I was exhausted with being nice. I knew that Summer had the levy to everything in my life but that didn't mean I couldn't get annoyed or be upset. So I put up a poker face and marched towards the stage. There was nothing but determination in me. I had to let her know what I felt for once.

I paused ignoring everyone. I closed my eyes and pictured her face. It was smiling at me in the early morning where every line of her face was traceable into a map. I sailed across till the pirate in me was pleased with the instructions of the way to the treasure - her heart locked up in that box of ego I had to unlock with love.

Silly was she who misunderstood
Every moment she believed in him
She followed him all the way no matter what the problem
Without a grumble or a grimace
No thought of disloyalty
No sign of impatience
Little did she know it wasn't in his hands?
He tried his best to let go
Just for a few hours he would disappear so she would cease
He did it for her
He knew she would get hurt by his embers
He wanted her to go
He tried his best
But she stuck on their love trail diligently

He decided to give it a chance
He'd seen the vile creatures feed her with world-y beliefs
All lies
Before they could take away her innocence
He decided to announce his infatuation
The love made him blaze with passion
The heat was for warmth
The heat was for comfort
But she scrunched up, she grimaced
Her face broke into sadness that killed him
Made him fire more, now with helplessness
He watched her die slowly as he did everything to save her
She rejected him
Dejected his potion of life
And died
As did his love
But he blazed on, for her, waiting for her
Waiting to see that smile again
Even in anger she called out to his dead heart
Just waiting for
Her

I dropped the mike into the dead silence. The then judgemental looks were now giving me respect. People were so easy to sway sometimes. My eyes however had home for just one face.

She stood there like a cherry on my cake. I walked towards her slowly. I could see her breath increase with every footfall. I came as close to her pretty face as my ceasing anger allowed.

"Did you get what you wanted?"

She nodded her head.

"Did it make you feel different than usual?"

She nodded again.

"So, I win?"

Her pretty head bobbed. She tried speaking but all I heard was a let go off breath. I smiled and leaned forward kissing her cheek. I decided to head back as a proud Alan beckoned me forward. I brushed her shoulders lightly.

"And hey Summer," I said turning around and facing her flushed face. "I care about you and your baby more than I have ever cared about anyone my entire life. There might not be the obvious showing off that most humans subject the ones they care for too but believe me on this. There's no one on this god-forsaken planet that cares about anything related to you more than I."

With those words resounding in the atmosphere, I left satisfied. For once, I'd spoken my heart out and not just what my mind thought off.

The winter wasn't always the cold one. Sometimes, Summer days were too hot and they required the soft caress of the cold to be remain alive.

The Day Jamie Called Me a Pig

"Rome, you have to look at my stomach . . . it's huge."
I didn't want to reply to this. It had just been a week since the slam and the immense wrath of Summer that had been projected at me for a sexist comment. The words with which I had left her in the cafe had done the deed. The next day she'd climbed through my window, yes in her pregnant state and hugged my sleeping body. I'd got up scared out of my wits only to be greeted by the usual business Turkey had with me. It was while I was washing off the refuse that Summer had broken into a monologue about how much she cared for me and how she never meant to upset me in that way. Everything had worked out and we had decided to call it a truce by eating ice cream.

"I'm sorry but you are pregnant," I finally managed to say.

I convulsed as she gave me a furious look.

"Have you ever thought off a career in detective work? If you have then please don't! Your obvious statements will never solve the case. You don't understand the magnitude of the situation. I am fat! I should start boxing."

"What?" I chuckled despite trying my best to restrain. That made complete sense in no way whatsoever. But then Walker's definition was being a riddle constantly badgering to be solved. She looked extremely cute sitting in front of me, hammering about the usual feminine complaints.

"You are there with barely any fat. You're like a skeleton practically and then there's me. I'm a big blob of chubbiness."

"Walker you're being ridiculous." I said before thinking.

"Am I?" she squeaked dangerously. For a second, I feared for my life but then I mellowed down being accustomed to her usual bout of short tempers. My mind started processing things as everything happening at the moment looked fishy and then I realized something.

Jamie Summer Walker was pretending to be a woman because of my rant yesterday during coffee.

I sighed. This was exactly what I didn't plan on happening. I shouldn't have opened my mouth yesterday. I shouldn't have ever mentioned about how her pregnancy had no effect in changing her hormones wise.

"Romance," she squealed.

"Hey Walker, I really appreciated and respected the fact that you were indifferent to your hormones and remained who you are. This is not cool."

"You little piece of hypocrisy. Decide what you want in life and then yell it out to me. If I had my way I'd punch your head through the tree stump."

Thankfully, she was back.

"Pigeon is dead."

I tried hiding my glee. It was really difficult to keep a straight face as the joy was overwhelming. Thank god that annoying creature was gone. I'd become exhausted trying to clean his crap up, literally. Even though I was an animal lover, one creature less wouldn't hurt anyone.

"Rome, I have to do a burial and everything," she stressed. "I am so confused whether the theme should be black or red. Pigeon loved red."

Which animal has a favourite colour? Of course it had to be the abnormal, obnoxious, condescending pigeon.

". . . and then I skated to save the poor bird from being slaughtered. Why would you thank someone by cutting and roasting a bird is beyond me."

Since when were pigeons used to thank people in any way. I don't remember any American tradition being celebrated for . . .

Just as soon as the realization hit me so did the sharp beak that belonged to someone I dearly wished dead. How could I forget his presence that had graced me just minutes before and left me with a gift as well?

"Coo, coo," he sang innocently tilting its head right and left.

"You thought that . . . Jesus Rome! How could you even? Come here baby don't go to a monster like him."

"But I . . ."

"All this time Turkey serves you like his own master and this is what you wish for him?"

"Treat me like a master by crapping on me? Walker you are being . . ."

"I will not tolerate such behaviour. Apologize to my baby right now."

"Your hormones are going haywire . . ."

She threw a pillow at me and stormed off. Sometimes her mood swings were so arduous to handle. I wanted to follow and apologize but knowing Summer she needed some time to cool off.

I did what any man would do.

I fell into the clutches of my one true love.

Sleep.

*　*　*

"Did you even shop for the household?"

I ignored the voice as I placed the coke and chips on the billing counter. The whole day had been unproductive and that's not what a Sunday demanded. Therefore, I'd decided to binge watch some good series while eating junk. For once, I wanted to do what a normal teenager did and not some charity work as usual.

"Listen git, I am not the house wife that every time I shop for us. You walk right back there and scavenge for home."

I clenched my hand unto the counter to let the fury waves pass by. It was getting harder to deal with the way they'd become accustomed to treating me. I had some dignity. Ever since Summer had sauntered into my monotonous life the rigid principles of ignoring things had lessened while my awareness about certain things such as my reputation in front of others had heightened. It mattered to me if someone today witnessed me being derailed and went and gossiped about it with her. It would kill to think she considered me less of a man that I couldn't even defend myself.

Hence, with that thought revolving in mind I decided to be bold. Before I could even utter an insult Parsley pulled me close to his face by the collar. I struggled to back down but as usual failed. If one day I did decide to fight, they'd end up hurt which wasn't even an option on my list.

"If you think that I am requesting you in any way then please be clear with your facts. This is a direct order whose failure will lead to immediate termination of life," he snarled at me.

Then just like that I felt my body get rigid and follow the instructions blindly. I wanted to get back in control but something was stopping me. I had no idea what I was lifting or when I finished. Soon, I was queuing back to bill. This time the cart was loaded with items.

"That's like a good boy," Parsley smirked from behind his counter. We weren't financially all that well so all of us worked part time as much as we could balance with our school. A male infatuated house demands a lot of money after all. Luke was high maintenance to speak off. Even though we despised his spending on materialistic things it didn't change the fact that he was the youngest or the fact that we loved spoiling him. For me the love was obviously indirect because to his face I would never give in to the fact.

I felt akin a dog as Parse ruffled my hair and gestured me to get lost with the shopping. Someday I will show it to all of them what I was worth. One day I will avenge my rights.

I sounded like some gangster movie starring a poor guy who was done so much injustice in life that he had to resort to unfair means to win. I started picturing a typical Mexican fight. It was just as I was swinging my guns imagining

Parsley cowering in front of me that the bell rang. I ignored in hopes that someone would open the door while I didn't have to spoil my muse. It was in vain.

I grumbled as I dragged my feet downstairs. Who was insane enough to ring the bell at such an ungodly hour? I checked my watch. Seven freaking o'clock was no time for visiting. It wasn't as if I didn't have a life to care about. I swung open the door in full hopes of blasting the intruder but stopped short.

A silver circle was pointing right at my face.

There holding the instrument was a human much scarier than the gun itself. She glared at me. The fire in her eyes was blazing hot which pierced me before any bullet could.

"Hands up Winter," she spat.

I chuckled.

She shot me.

The bullet grazed my arm and swished away. It hurt a little. I could feel the sting and the wet liquid.

"I'm in no mood to joke with you. It's either listening to Walker here or getting shot. Now, hands up."

I wouldn't lie. I was scared. Somehow I had pissed Walker off so much that for once she had lost her sanity too such an extent that she had murder tendencies. I slowly raised my hands never taking my eyes off hers. Today, the pupil was brighter than usual. What had I said to make her this passionate?

"Now, where is my pet? What did you do with the pigeon?"

"What are you saying Walker? That turkey is dead."

She shot again. This time she put away the gun in time and I managed to leave unscathed.

"You are a liar. To even think that I trusted you with my life and this is how you repay me, you ungrateful swine."

I cringed at the word swine. Those pigs always managed to freak me out. First of all they were pink. When things are pink, you don't trust them. Second, when they make noises as if they are constantly constipated, you don't think twice before running away. The disease swine flu was hint enough how much pigs needed to be exterminated. Even as a kid '*The three little pigs*' was my despised story. Once I stumbled across flesh eating pigs on television. I was so done with those animals.

"Where is he?" she snarled. The gun poked me in the chest and my heart beat quickened.

"Listen, you only told me he passed away. I don't know what you are talking about?" I had never been so confused in my life. What was wrong with the women in the world?

"What are you talking about?" My pet pigeon Turkey is missing. What have you done to him?"

I will never be able to keep track of her pets in life.

"I haven't seen him since you've left," I mumbled.

"Lies!" she yelled. I heard the shrill voice vibrate around the house. My heart resounded with the voice. Fingers crossed, no one was home or else I would be brunt of some torture. Why did I always care about this? I wish for once my main concern would be the problem and not the after effects.

"Listen woman, I haven't seen your pet okay."

"I will shoot you Romance."

It was probably the first time she had named me like that. I did not like the tone at all. It raked my feelings.

"Okay. Shoot me."

"Pig, pig . . . pig!" she suddenly mumbled, her tone of surety wavering.

"You do whatever you want Summer. Just don't call me that."

"No, pig . . ."

"Jamie Summer Walker, what's your deal? I've done nothing with your pet. Stop calling me that. I hate it."

"Romance," she said pausing at every word. "There is a pig."

She took hold of my shoulders. I held my breath as the gun body hit my face. One click and I was history.

My eyes fell on the root of all bloody problems. Yes, if I ever had a pimple then I would do everything in my power to blame the worthless creature. He sat there clicking his head as usual. I stared at him annoyed as ever until my attention shifted to the animal he was sitting upon.

I screamed and pushed Walker forward. I held her shoulders as I tried hiding my face behind her back.

"What is that?" I squealed in my most feminine voice ever. I cleared my throat ashamed.

"Uh . . . it's a pig?"

"What are you silly? Get it out of my house. Where did it even come from?"

"It's your house, how will I know?"

The pig grunted as Turkey flew up and came to perch on my shoulder only to be scared away as I violently backed pulling Walker along.

"What are you doing Romance?" she gasped as she lost balance.

"The pig," I managed to mumble in my normal voice.

"Are you scared of that cute thing?" she chuckled.

Just what was she into? Her chuckled were blossoming into full blown laughter as I could feel the vibrations increase from her body. My eyes were fixed on the enemy in case it decided to exterminate me from this planet. The beady eyes sure gave the signal of a pig with a devious plan.

"It's such a darling," Walker giggled. She walked forward and bent low. I bit back a scream as she petted the head gently and cooed. I struggled to cease myself from running like a lunatic, spanking Walker's hand of the slime thing and pulling her away to safety. Far away into eternity where she couldn't possibly meet creatures like that. I had a terrible feeling about this.

"Aren't you the most adorable thing ever?"

No, please had she ever YouTube-d *kitten trying to open a door?*

"You're so perfect that I can totally fit you in a teacup and kiss you all day."

You could fit me into a tea cup and kiss me all day. I'll be way more appreciative than this pink fluff. Turkey was sitting on my shoulder. His claws bit into my skin. Looks like someone else had issues with a certain green eyed monster as well.

"You know what?"

Oh no.

"I'm going to keep you."

This was turning into a nightmare.

"I'll call you Rome because he absolutely adores you."

Wait, what? I adore what? I gave her an incredulous look as she grinned at me evilly. It seemed as if the pig was smirking right back at me. All my life I dedicate to loving animals except gross ones like swine and all I get as a consequence is one named after me. Life was unfair. Nightmare had kick-started with a beautifully ugly beginning.

"You do whatever you like Summer. I don't care anymore," I said furiously. Not only had she decided to force a new member in the group who I hated genuinely, she had also decided to shoot me for something I'd never committed without even a slight tremor of remorse. This wasn't how it worked every time. I had every right to be mad as well when she pulled out such selfish deeds without a single thought about the effect on me.

I turned my back to walk away. Without warning a whistle left my mouth and Turkey who was now atop my head flew down and clung onto my arm.

At least, I wasn't alone in the hate.

The Day Jamie
Quoted Mad Max

"Jasmine", she mumbled.

I lost my focus on ways to kill the pig as all of it shifted to her pink mouth. How did she even know the name?

"Aren't these Orchids the prettiest?"

I sighed in relief.

"Wasn't your girl the prettiest as well?"

My head started spinning again. I was controlling my urge to shake her up akin a rag doll. This was one aspect of life I didn't want explored by anyone, even the woman I would give my right limb for. Why was Walker such an intruder at times?

"Who was she, Romance?"

Indeed who was she?

*　　*　　*

The day after the horrendous creature had been adopted, Summer decided to as usual jump inside through my window. There was no point in telling her to be careful so I continued reading. I could feel her pacing the room waiting for some attention which I continuously decided to deny.

"I don't understand why you are so miffed."

I ignored her.

"It's just an animal Romance," she pleaded. "I really like it."

She was speaking as if she knew the pig from ages. It was irritating how blindly Walker started caring for anything in the world. For all I knew, tomorrow she would be ambling around with a snake slung around her neck calling it the 'best pet ever'.

"You have to give her a chance. She's adorable. Yesterday, she grunted every time I fed her," she blabbered on.

So, the pig had been given a gender. I wouldn't be surprised if it soon had a bonnet and a cute little frock adorning it. Knowing Summer, she'd even apply a dab of lipstick to make it look prettier.

"Okay, so here is how it goes. I've done something to make you and Turkey this mad at me. Hence, I shall make it up like you always do for me. I have even lost the count of times I've been mad at you – such a drama queen, sometimes."

I rolled my eyes at her. It was sad how rolling my eyes from being a bad habit had become a habit. Despite my loath for change, there was nothing I could do to stop the metamorphosis titled 'Jamie Summer Walker.'

"Dude, we gonna rock the shiz," Walker suddenly yelled and jumped on my bed. Her arms were open wide with a dangerous glint in those eyes.

"I don't understand what atrocity you are speaking off. Before addressing that I would like an immaculate command over your language. When you are capable of it please don't subject me to such nonsense. Now, speak if you can follow proper diction," I rambled on.

She gave me the cutest confused look ever. If I hadn't been spiffed, my heart would have melted right there and then. I tried my best not to peck her on the cheek.

"What do you say sometimes? Even if I was an Ivy League graduate, I would still get baffled. Okay, smarty pants I have decided we shall go witness."

It was my time to be confused.

"Did you ever get yourself checked by a professional neurologist? I'm telling you the good it will do the world will be higher than the happiness accumulated by the production of chocolate," I chuckled.

Her look changed to a despondent one. She sat down on the bed and looked at the floor.

"Hey Summer," I said after a while. There was something about the sad picture that disturbed me more than it should have. I scuttled over to her and kept my head on her lap. Her eyes met mine. They spoke thousand words her verbose mouth could never.

"I'm sorry," I mumbled.

She nodded.

I got up. I pulled out the last Toblerone bar from the drawer and handed it out to her.

"Romance, don't you love this chocolate? How can you share this when it's more important than an English dictionary to you?" she whispered sadly.

Dictionaries were the most essential instrument for anyone. I had a special place for them. There had been an instance when some thief had sneaked inside the house and I was sans anything to defend myself with. Therefore, I'd picked up the healthy book and walked outside the door with the same level of confidence that a metal or wooden bat would have brought for me. There was no one more surprised than the thief when the book hit him. It scared him so much that he ran outside as fast as possible. My only regret was he took the hard-bound with him. No amount of *Wanted* posters brought it back.

"Witness me blood bag, witness me." She yelled aloud in the room shaking her head like a lunatic.

I'd finally got her reference from before. My chest swelled with pride for I never thought I'd find a girl who was cool enough to watch Mad Max.

"Are you calling me a blood bag?" she asked with mock sternness.

"Maybe," I replied. "I think your blood would be the sweetest to suck on."

She blushed. I put my face closer to her neck till my lips were caressing her soft velvet skin. Heat waves were rolling on to my face.

"Romance, back off please," she whispered slowly.

"Or what will you do Walker?"

She moved aside. I'd been leaning towards her and thus without any support my body fell. I hit my face on the bed.

"The most epic face palm in the world," she announced giggling.

"Oh you didn't Walker," I yelled and leapt at her. She screamed while running around the room as I chased her trying to tickle her.

That's when Turkey decided to join the fun and do what he loved best.

Poop on my head.

Some liaisons never lasted for more than a day.

*   *   *

"What are you doing here?" I asked with gritted teeth.

His eyes widened a little in fear. "I can explain dude."

"No, I don't need any explanation. Give me a straight answer and get lost."

"Listen man, I and my woman have been going through a lot of problems. I really tried convincing your meat to go away but she was adamant."

"She's not my meat. What the hell happened to your diction by the way?" My attention wavered for as the once boorish riff raff was speaking like an educated loon.

"Well, I've been taking classes since a month to improve in conversations. I need a job to support the family."

There was something in the tone of his voice that touched my heart. I didn't want him to see I'd mellowed down so I kept trudging forward without a second glance.

"Hey bro, you're the only guy I trust the most. I really respect you man. Please don't be like this. Believe me I tried convincing her off it."

All these years of knowing him had made sure that he would have done what he said. Not only was Hunter a man of his words but he was unselfish as well. Memories flooded my mind one after another of how much he'd taken care of me when he had no such obligation. It was true. He was no less than a brother.

Nevertheless, I wanted him to know I wasn't still okay with what had been carried out without even informing me. Hence, I gave him a curt nod and walked faster to catch up with Walker.

"Romie," someone screeched.

That voice. I swear to God if someone had a gun right now I would have shot myself before I met the owner of the scream. This was turning out to be a nightmare.

A woman slung her arms around me as my face was rained down with smooches. It was the yuckiest feeling ever.

"Dora," my voice wavered trying to be excited but failing miserably. "Who called you here?"

She backed away. Her blonde hair was dyed with streaks of blue and green. Those brown eyes were still with that crazy look of being a serial killer. The teeth had rusted thanks to all the mind wavering substances she was into. Her breath stank of bad wine while her whole self was polluting the air with the cheap perfume. I sighed as her yellow nails held my arm.

"I'm so excited to see you again baby. It's been so long since we hung out together," she cooed.

I cringed in horror as the past hit me- all those drunken nights when she had been my muse. The difference was she used to be a pretty picture. Her one wink was worth doing everything to wipe her off her feet and do her all night. I had lost the count of boys who were behind her like leeches. Unfortunately, so was I. There hadn't been a day she'd turn me down. It was only when intoxicated would she let me in to please her. The way I was entangled in the magic of her beauty was not even funny.

Oh, how glad I was for the present.

"I have to go relieve myself. Excuse me!" I tried running away.

"Wait, I'll come along with you darling."

"No, you don't understand . . . I need to pee."

"I know," she winked at me. I'd never been more repulsed in my life or scared for that matter.

"Hunter," I mumbled looking back. He gave me a smirk. I rolled my eyes at him. His grin widened. I glared at him.

"Hey Dora, I just saw a beautiful pair of heels. Let's check them out yeah?" Hunter requested.

The mere mention of shopping brought the old Dora on her face. The way it used to shine when I got something she liked. Without a second glance at me, she bounded off towards Hunter now holding his arm.

"Do I want to ask?" Walker grinned.

I rolled my eyes shaking my head.

We were sitting in the theatre soon. There was a marathon of Mad Max with all the four movies running. I had seen the latest one with Walker some days back but we had decided to watch it again due to how enthralled we'd been. This marathon was the best way to bond. I managed to sit in between Walker and Hunter. Dora was sitting next to Walker. I was worried they would bond and some secrets that needed to be locked in Pandora's Box would be swung open.

My mind wavered off any crisis as the movie begun. There was nothing that would distract from watching such legendary scenes. Nothing at all!

*   *   *

"Why are you sniffling?" I asked Walker appalled as the fourth movie was about to finish. Though it had been so long inside the theatre, I couldn't get tired off the beauty we were watching. My eyes travelled towards Dora who was weeping as well.

"Guys, what's wrong?" I asked. I turned towards Hunter to make fun of the females only to get more astonished.

"What the hell is going on? Why is everyone bawling?" I asked frustrated. "Oye Hunter, what's up mate?"

"Why are you going Australian on us?" Walker asked sniffing.

"It's hot. He's hot," Dore whimpered.

"Okay, I need answers before I walk out because this is really uncomfortable."

"The topic of women empowerment in the movie," Summer mumbled.

"I want a baby," Dora wailed.

"And you?" I asked with impatience as Hunter was looking away. His eyes were swollen and he was trying his best to control the tears.

"You are mad at me," he said in a small voice.

"Are you serious? Are you kidding me? What? You've never cried before not even when a bullet hit you. Okay, who has mixed what in the drinks?" I looked at Dora with accusation. "Leave this. You girls get over whatever this is. Hunter, walk out with me now!"

"Out with it," I commanded Hunter. I looked directly into his red eyes. He had been trying so hard that even his face was flushed.

"I can't do this anymore Rome. Everyone wants me to be different. I don't feel like I am me anymore. The family wants me properly dressed, speaking well and with a formidable job. I work hard the whole day and come home to a grumpy wife. There's not a day she doesn't remind me of all the bull I've done in life. I swear Rome; I'm going to end up in therapy."

I cringed.

He looked at me with apology. I shrugged it off.

"Hey listen, I know it's tough okay? I warned you the day you were deciding to marry at seventeen that it won't be easy. You said you'll handle no matter what. It's just a matter of time and you'll be fine man."

He nodded unsure.

I hugged him. "Look I'll always be around to support you. If there's ever any money trouble you know exactly where to go."

His smile was back. It wasn't the same but still something.

"But seriously how can any sane man be with her?" I complained.

"I love her lot Romance. Even if she doesn't admit it I know she equally loves me back."

"But why does it have to be Dora?"

"Imagine your favourite ice cream flavour in your case favourite dish. Now think how you would feel when you can have it for free every day. It's the best feeling ever!"

I gave him a judgemental look. The Hunter I knew was back.

We were done talking so I started to walk back to the theatre. A hand held my shoulder ceasing my action.

"Do you know the feeling you get when you gaze at that Walker chick? If you do I don't have to answer why I love Dora. You should know that is one emotion that can never be described."

He left me with those words resounding in my head. They both fell in love early and decided to elope – the typical teen scene which I use to run away from. There life was such a movie scene where the bad boy tries his best to make something with his life so that the family can live in peace. I just hoped that it didn't end the way it usually does.

I saw both of them walking hand in hand. He was muttering something which was making Dora laugh. He kissed the top of her head and she gave him an adoring smile. Despite my fears I started smiling.

"Is this Romance Winters randomly smiling? How long have I been inside the theatre?"

I rolled my eyes at Walker.

"Hey Romance?"

I looked at her. She was looking down at the floor. She shuffled her feet and blushed.

"What's up?" I asked confused. Someday I should write down a book titled '*Hundred Ways Summer Looks Cute*'. It would be such a bestseller.

"Sorry."

"What?" I asked more confused.

"I shouldn't have adopted Rome knowing that you despise pigs. I shouldn't have blamed you for Turkey. I shouldn't have pointed a gun at you like that. It was silly. I'm sorry."

I gave her a hug. She melted in my arms. The gun as an instrument had failed. Walker as another was sure passing day by day.

* * *

Here we were with me staring at her with accusation.

"So, when will you tell me who this Jasmine is?"

I stood up.

"Romance, what's wrong? Did I make you mad again?"

I felt the golden tresses pass through my fingers, the soft pink lips that had caressed mine. Her aquamarine eyes I use to stare at for ages, the way her little body held mine close for comfort and the puckered nose that scrunched up when she would giggle. I missed her laughter chiming through the halls. She looked the best in the morning. I had never woken up to such a beautiful face before. How she used to sneak into my bedroom in the middle of the night thinking what a rebellion it was. The first kiss when my heart had felt like a bumble bee. The feel of those lips . . .

I felt my emotions closing up again.

"No," I muttered. "I have to go do some work yeah? I'll catch you later Walker."

"Okay," she said in a small voice.

I sighed. "I'm not mad Walker. Jasmine is just someone I don't like talking about. I loved her and she died. End of story."

Somehow memories never fade no matter how hard you try. It's difficult to let go of things but people are the worst. They have such thin fragments of attachments and yet the threads holding them are made of diamond. You try and try to let go but end up making the relation stronger.

I tucked close another top button hoping that Walker hadn't glanced at the tattoo that had been engraved on my heart ages ago.

My diamond thread was pierced right there.

The Day Jamie Cried

Who was this Perry character?

Even though Walker had mentioned him really casually it seemed as if there was something that was beckoning in finding him out. She even seemed enthralled by his charms. To say I was worried would be an understatement. I sat there colour coding my highlighters while Turkey pecked around the room. It had slipped my mind to feed the poor thing. Somehow, over the days I'd started appreciating the animal like never before.

"Oh for god sake you worthless creature," I grumbled as he refused on my head for the millionth time. He was going to cost me a lot of shampoo. Just when I was warming up to him he decided to show his true colours.

"I didn't really want to talk about him Romance."

Why wouldn't she? That only occurred when someone wanted to keep a secret. Summer was a girl who loved to blabber everything happening in her life out to me. This was like a hit on the ego.

Despite my resolution as to cease the usage of any sort of networking site due to its tendency to waste time, I couldn't help searching Perry's name once.

There were too many results for me to make sense. A guy in a fedora holding a Chihuahua, a woman smiling as if trying to hide someone pulling out her hair, uncountable profiles of the platypus from some popular Disney cartoon and what not. I couldn't help chuckling as I sifted through their profiles for some hint. What were humans into nowadays? What was wrong with our race? What was right with me?

Status: Interested in women

You're not the only one human.

About: She's a gangster. I'm a gangster. We are in love.

Are you serious? I hope the jail life is treating you both well. What even does love get people to do?

It went on and on. I couldn't stop my judgements as they wildly flew over the creative profiles. The worst part about wasting so much time had been the lack of recognition. There was not one person I found that seemed suitable for her.

My phone was vibrating.

I gasped.

There were fifteen missed calls from Walker. Usually people sent a message as well to inform the urgency. The absence of the same got me worried immediately. I dialled her number instantly.

"Romance," she mumbled.

My heart broke. She was sobbing over the phone. I tried deciphering what the problem was but the mystery continued. She couldn't talk. There was no point in asking about the location either. I felt the pain wave travel from the phone towards my body.

I rushed outside like the house was on fire.

There was no one on the street. The cafe she was sitting in wasn't walk able distance during emergencies. If I ran it would take around half an hour. Having Walker suffer for that long was out of question. The only plan I could devise was keep walking until someone was kind enough to lend me a ride. Even if they demanded for my left limb, I'd gladly cut and give it as payment.

It was the peak hours. Hardly, anyone habituated my area then. Most of them went to work while the ones at home usually didn't come out in the scorching summer sun. My area didn't receive rain till late September by which time the heat would have irritated everyone off. Every monsoon was like a gift from God. Though the Winter started by the end of October. We were happy and mostly used to with what we got.

"Hey," I shouted in frustration, kicking a stone at the car that passed by.

It was sad that humans weren't ready to help anyone in such distress. Clearly, if I was sprinting on the sidewalk while asking you for a ride, it was important. How inhumane could you get?

I heard the wheels of another car coming closer. Even though my hope was lost, I still put up my thumb as a universal gesture for a free ride.

The car screeched to a halt.

Great, there were some good humans alive.

"Can you take me to *'Misfits cafe'?*"

"Sure, hop right in."

We drove in silence. My mind was stuck with obsessing over Walker's health that I didn't notice the stranger at first. Slowly, my attention spun to him.

He seemed around nineteen years of age. The black hair was messily made as if he'd just got out of bed. The tanned skin stretched out on strong southern features. By the way the man was dressed I couldn't help being stereotypical. He had to be some sort of artist.

"Is something the matter?" he asked me politely. The voice was strong like leaders have but his lanky frame was a demerit to that quality.

"No," I said looking away embarrassed.

"I'm Jamal Ali. Let's start normal shall we?"

"Romance Winter," I replied.

One of the things that made me immediately comfortable with his company was he didn't throw a judgmental look on the name choice.

"What do you do Mr Winter?"

"I don't get your context?"

"Have you ever murdered someone?"

"Not in reality," I chuckled.

"Then we'll get along quite well," he grinned at me.

There was something genial about the man that made you immediately trust him.

"So are we having some girl problem?"

"How did you know?" I asked amazed.

"A guy running around like a maniac, hopping into a stranger's car without even asking anything and constantly distracted didn't help me realize at all. It's probably the name of some Jamie that you have been constantly chanting. Either that's your god or the woman you love. I doubt it's a boy's name seeing your physique but hey what do I know about homosexuality."

"You think you're smart eh?"

"I try Winter, it seems people think I am."

I laughed. Despite my worry, this character was quite amusing. The want to extract information from him was growing every minute.

"Yeah, Jamie is a friend. Just a few minutes back I received a call with her crying over the phone. It's just panic that's making me hyperventilate."

"I understand. Once you start caring for a woman, life is a roller coaster. I myself had a share of quite a few to know what it feels."

"So what do you do Ali?"

"I work in the cafe *Misfits.*"

Where had I heard the name before? Oh right, that's why he never asked for the proper address. I'd just presumed he knew the location when he didn't enquire further. What a coincidence this was?

"Don't you go to some school?"

He gave me a sad smile. "If only I was privileged enough. My parents are dead. I live in an apartment alone. The expense is too much already to handle an education as well."

The other thing I loved about the guy was how straightforward and honest he was. He'd accepted life the way it was gifted to him, whether it is that ugly sweater with a big initial of your name knitted by grandma or a handsome piece of dinner set. It was worth all the respect in the world.

"What is it like in the cafe?"

"Well, it's the best thing in my life. Old Mr. Peters owns the place. I have insomnia. He lets me paint the walls again every week. There's some psychological way I deal with problems and that's painting it out. He doesn't care if I doddle on the crockery as well. That man is a legend I tell you."

It was just minutes meeting this man and already I knew so much about him. The best part was it wasn't as if he'd been dying to tell all this to someone, he was just comfortable with whom he was.

"There's also this other guy. He's helped me through a lot of things in life. There's almost a brotherly affection with him. His name is Grover."

I gasped in shock. That was silly. It couldn't be one of the idiots I had for brothers. I tried to assure myself by relaxing.

"What is this Grover's surname?"

"Grover Winter . . . wait aren't you a Winter as well. Oh man! I never realized that. No wonder you look so familiar."

I couldn't believe this. It couldn't be such a huge coincidence. Grover couldn't really be working in some cafe called misfits out of all the words in the world with a guy as weird as this all the while caring for him like that. It definitely must be Grover's nice twin.

"Is he your brother or something?"

"Yeah, you can say that," I grumbled.

"He's a great guy."

I nodded. There was a funny feeling being born in my stomach after all this conversation. It was like some dark secret had been unveiled and I'd be paying for being a part of it later.

"Hey, I don't know what personal relationship you have with your brother but for me he's been that rock solid support who hasn't let anything defeat my will. That's one guy who's stood by me whether I was crying like a moron or puking my guts out after a drunken night. If there is anyone I would care to give even a little damn for he's one of the few. You should consider yourself really lucky."

"I'm glad he's been such an inspiration but let's leave the part connecting me out."

It didn't mean I wasn't straightforward with my feelings as well. There was a new found respect for the eldest Winter but that didn't change anything between the relationship we had. It was good to know at least Grover was being there for someone else.

We reached the cafe.

"Thanks Jamal. It was nice meeting you."

"You should hang around here sometime more. It'll be nice getting to know another Winter. Grover never speaks about his family. I didn't know he had a younger brother? I'm sorry I'm assuming from the looks."

"Yes, I am the younger. However there are four of us in total."

His eyes widened slightly. It was funny how much Grover and even me, knew about him while he was just clueless on our family. Maybe Grover didn't trust him after all.

"I'll catch you around later then," he said shaking my hand. "You should hurry."

I gave him a friendly nod while running inside the cafe.

It was a wooden cottage with everything made out of the same. I could smell the fresh timber mostly due to presence of so much green outside. The inside smelled deliciously off intermingled scents of food. The moment they hit my nose, I felt ravenous. The people were all merrily drinking or talking loudly. It was a friendly layout. There was a boy of around Luke's age running around trying to serve everyone properly. He had a smear of wheat on his face. Jamal gave me a wink as he started preparing the cash counter. I saw an old man, who I presumed Peters, waddling away to the back. Through the windows I could see that the sun had hid behind the clouds. The insides of the cafe started glowing as the dim light bulbs gained more power over the darkness.

A body crashed against mine making me take several steps backwards.

"Oh my God, Walker what is wrong with you? What happened? Are you sick? Is there some fool I need to beat up? I swear I'm going to kill the human who brought tears to your eyes." I professed passionately.

"He's dead."

Please let that pigeon be dead. I beg let it be the bird.

"Who is?"

"Morgan Flash . . . how could he die like that, so brutally? Make him alive again Romance."

I hope it was the Perry guy. This Morgan Flash whoever he was would be so much better dead if he was this Perry character.

"Look, is that one of your friends Walker or uh maybe an animal?"

She looked at me with tear stricken face. I felt what being extremely sad was.

"He's the man I fell in irrevocable love with. I didn't even get to drain him in fully and he died."

Thank God, this Perry was dead. It solved so many problems in the world. I hid my relief as I patted her comfortingly. It should have been obvious that Perry was a nickname rather than the real one.

"Who even keeps their name Perry you know? It's the dumbest name in the whole world."

"What would you like to have sir?" The boy that had been scurrying around before asked me with a slight blush.

"I'll order later uh . . . Perry."

I hid a gasp as my eyes read his name plate. That explained the blush.

Before I could apologize though Walker was back with talking to me like a lunatic. No matter whatever fortunate accident had happened, I had to maintain the demeanour of someone who cared. It was really tough being me these days.

"What are you talking about? I'm speaking about Morgan Flash. This guy . . . it's like *you're* in love with Perry rather than me."

She threw a book at me with the cover having the picture of a handsome boy smirking away to glory. *'The Unfortunate love Story of Fortunate lovers,'* read the title. If the whole name hadn't been a giveaway of how much nonsense this book contained, I don't know what was?

"Are you telling me that you're balling your eyes out for a fictional character that has died inside some imaginary story?"

She nodded her head.

"I wonder what's good around here, I'm famishing."

"You're such a loser. I'm crying over here and all you care about is food."

I massaged my arm where she'd hit me multiple times. "This should be reported as abuse . . . ouch okay, I'm sorry let's sit and cry? Some idiot made me panic and run half the way to this cafe. I'm exhausted. You must be tired too? It isn't easy sitting in a cosy cafe with delicious food and coffee while reading a book."

She glared at me.

"Okay, how did this Morgan dude die?"

Her body plummeted down on the sofa with a grunt. She crossed her limbs and looked away from me with another grunt of disapproval.

"Do you think the strawberry tart would be better or should I just stick with my apple pie?"

That yielded no response.

"How about I order the pie and just smell you once. We can work out a deal that way?"

Again, I was ignored.

"Hey Walker . . ." I leaned across the table to hold her hands. The wooden sofa creaked as I pulled it a little forward with my body weight. "Look, I just got really frightened for you. It just annoys me a little that it wasn't for a big deal. It isn't your fault. You didn't ask me to be that dramatic but you know how much I care. I'm sorry I shouldn't be mean with you. How did the Morgan guy die again?"

She sniffed.

"The apple pie is amazing here," she finally said. "He died by falling into a hole?"

"I'm sorry but did he by chance follow a white rabbit with a ticking clock? You should never do that. It's good if he died because of that, hallucinations are never a good thing. I should know well."

My fear was attaining a slap for such cockiness. However, Walker surprised me by bursting into peals of joyful laughter.

"What would you like to have sir? We have a wide variety of delicious specials . . ."

The brown orbs settled on to me with shock as recognition hit his face. His eyebrows scrunched up into a frown as his tongue darted out to lick the lips every two seconds. Grover was nervous as he fiddled with the pen in between his fingers. He opened his mouth to say something. Only a sigh escaped him.

"Perry," he yelled. "Would you take this order? I have to go cook in the kitchen with old Pete."

The boy tripped towards us. He threw me a nervous smile and took out a small pad out of his pockets. Even though he was a teen, puberty hadn't done its job properly yet. The voice was just about to crack. His cheeks though were the chubbiest I'd ever laid my eyes upon.

"What would you like to eat sir?"

"Uh, could I have some apple pie accompanied with lemon ice tea? That would be great, thanks."

He jotted it all down. Then with expectant eyes he looked at me again.

"What would your lady like to have?"

I wish she was my lady. My so called lady shook her head at me.

"That's all for now kid."

He nodded his head. "That will take around fifteen minutes to prepare sir. I hope you enjoy."

"I'm sorry about the Perry thing before. It's a cute name you got there."

He threw me a grateful smile.

"You think Perry is a cute name?" Walker chuckled. I rolled my eyes at her.

"It'll be nice if you cease sprinkling salt on my wounds woman. I uh . . . I need to use the washroom, I'll be right back okay?"

"What will I ever do without you Romance? I'll be so lost once you're gone." I shook my head at her in hopelessness. She grinned at me. Somewhere I knew she understood what I really was going to do. I appreciated the fact that she didn't fixate on it.

"Hey," I muttered reluctantly.

He ignored me.

"Look I'll go away if you listen."

"Jamal would you hand this out at table four? I'm almost done with the software problem. It just needed a scan."

"Grover, will you listen for once? It's not for my benefit."

He didn't respond so I took it an affirmative.

"Look, I'll not tell anyone about this. Don't worry your secret is safe with me. It's okay. That's all."

There was silence for a minute so I decided to leave. At least my message had been delivered.

"Your apple pie is ready sir. I hope you don't give it a chance to choke you."

I nodded at him. That meant he understood I wouldn't violate the privacy terms. That was the entire cue I need to walk back to the table where Walker sat with a despondent expression.

"I don't know why are you so affected? It's just a story."

"Did you ever think what if all the stories are somehow true? I mean maybe a writer could be penning down something which has happened, is happening or could occur in some other part of the world with someone. What if they're even writing destinies? I mean wouldn't it be so cool?"

"Whoa?" I said taken aback. "That is some deep thinking there Walker. How free are you in life?"

She groaned and stuck a spoon in my pie.

"Hey, who said I am sharing? Do you want Morgan to be mad at you . . .?" I flipped the book in search of the girl's name. "Be mad at . . . you Isabella?"

"First of all you can't be Morgan because he dies falling inside a hole. If that's how you plan to go, you're on your own from now. Second, that's not all I have been sharing with you. It's nice how you've let go of the obsession with immense hygiene for we both know just how dirty I am." She licked the spoon in a disgusting manner and stuck it back into the pie.

I groaned.

"Don't you know Romance? The Winter is coming?"

I stared at her in mock horror.

"What are you terrified about? It's just a story."

You felt just like some story too Walker, if only you knew.

The Day I Cried

Humans when poked with pain portray it through instruments which for ease they named 'tears'. Then they classify it into gender labelling the males to be the ones sans it. I was subjected to that theory with the absence of feminine company. Thus, when the need to bawl came into question I looked away and tried to hold them.

"He really loves me Romance."

I really love you.

"I know I'll be happy with him because I've never met someone who cares more."

Why are you so blind? All I've done since meeting you is give a damn.

"I know I'm breaking your heart but I'm telling you it's just an infatuation. You'll find someone you actually feel for. It's just not me. I just you know . . . love someone else."

That was simple and blunt. How do I tell you that I don't want to lose a second time? Her back was towards me. I could feel the wetness on my face now. It was more the imagination that someone else had the right to hold her, the fact that he could lay down a kiss on those lips anytime he wanted while I sat in the shadows and watched what was killing me.

Why did it always lead to a choice?

It always ended up with me being the loser. It was her fault. I was doing fine when she wasn't there. The walls were so high no one could wreck through. I could handle my emotions. Never would I let an ounce of pain be shown. There was nothing but neutrality. Now there was nothing.

"Did you know a worm has five hearts and no one to love? I'm telling you these random animal facts are the best to know. They are so cool," she blabbered on changing the topic. It was disheartening to see how easy it was for her.

I had one heart and no one to love. Maybe she should read up random facts about me and categorize me cooler enough to accept.

"Octopus hardly ever leaves their homes unless a tragedy."

I should leave mine for Antarctica. It would be nice to be a tragedy and not a participant as usual.

"Oh my god, are you okay?"

I saw a blurry face close to me. I tried to control my emotions but it had been too long. I couldn't hold everything in anymore, this was the last straw.

I started bawling.

Slender arms held me close. I could feel her warm body against my head. Her fingers were caressing me gently. "It's going to be okay Romance. Just let it go."

She wasn't the fake ones. Knowing Walker her main aim would be to let me cry and get over with it. She wouldn't stop me from emoting. Her arms were the only comfort that could muster me to cease. She held me and comforted me as long as it took. I appreciated that. Even when I broke away all I saw was that smile lighting up the cold in me.

How can someone be like that on this planet? I couldn't lose her. I needed her to know how serious I was.

I kissed her.

Her lips felt so good against mine. I couldn't think of anything but the way she made me feel. My stomach was in turmoil. It's the feeling you get when some roller coaster suddenly plummets down only kissing triples the motion. My head was spinning from inhaling her vanilla strawberry. The fact that she was kissing me back was a hint for hope enough until . . .

"No," she said.

She pushed me back suddenly. I hit the floor and gave her a look of astonishment. She was glaring at me.

"No, how dare you?"

"Walker?"

"How dare you manipulate me like that? Just because you have the power to handle me strongly doesn't mean you misuse it. You know very well that no matter what you still affect me but you also know that I believe in my principles. You're not the only one arduously willed about their morals. Loving someone else and kissing someone else is not something I follow and being the kind of guy you are, you should be aware of it. How dare you?"

I tried breathing in. It was so hard. Every inhalation was like a stab of knife.

"How dare you?"

I got up. I wiped away the water. My face was towards the floor. My lips were burning from the feel of hers. They weren't done. They wanted more fire but this sun was dying. The black hole that would form would suck my whole life into darkness. The tone with which she'd spoken to me had done the deed.

"Okay," I replied emotionless. "I'm sorry Jamie."

I looked into her eyes and she backed away. Her face changed colour from anger to panic. It was the first time I'd addressed with her first name.

"Romance, I . . ."

I walked out. In life there are times when you decide to go against your beliefs for the betterment of others. There's always the way where you need to be unselfish and walk out. You have no choice because defeat has already punched your gut rendering no return. This was that moment. There was nothing else I wanted to do but sleep in the hope that I'd never cease doing the same.

The last thing I heard was a faint call of my name. On an ordinary day I would happily turn back, take her in my arms and let her say whatever she desired. The pain in the voice would affect me badly enough to commit to anything she said.

Not today.

* * *

I hit the ball against the wall as hard as I could. Every time my mind would travel to how easily she'd pushed me away like it was the most natural thing in the world. It didn't take her seconds to break my heart. I would have let her go with more patience and thought.

Sometimes I wondered why I even tried to care for someone when it all ever led to was agony. I was doing so well being poker until one fine morning she decided to saunter in and shine like a warm summer day. It didn't take seconds for that to turn into a storm. Relationship in my definition was just a medium to end up depressed. The only way out was, to severe every bond and live secluded forever.

"Hey loser, have you seen my watch?"

"Don't disturb me Luke," I said patiently.

"Oh, is someone in a bad mood?" he taunted.

"Please go away."

"Why is your face splotched? Have you been crying? Oh my god! Did someone break your wee- . . ."

"Luke? Why are you still here?" Parsley entered with a stern expression flicking Luke's ear for almost saying a bad word.

"Someone made lil Romy-wormy cry." I could see both of them looking at me each with their own happiness.

"Maybe it was Kitty. She must have virtually broken up with him," Parsley sniggered.

I was used to the jibes on kitty. They found it their secret pleasure when I retaliated. Parsley out of all the people had the best time. Therefore to void them off their satisfaction I usually didn't react.

"Nah, it must have been that Walker chick. This guy couldn't even retain riff-raff like her. I knew from the beginning all she must have wanted was his body. Of course this bas- . . . I mean brother of ours is the girl in the relationship . . ."

I hit the ball as hard as I could on Luke's face. He screamed in agony clutching the top right hand corner of his face, right above the eyebrow. The impact of the ball had pushed him behind and his arm had dug inside the nail that had been poking out of the wall. It worsened the situation as he started crying. How could have I forgotten to take the nail out?

"What the hell Romance?" Parsley yelled at me. He gently removed a sobbing Luke's hands apart and cursed. The skin was dangerously swelling up.

"C'mon we need to go to a doctor," Parsley said urgently.

"No! Parse please," Luke wailed loudly. "I'm scared of needles. I don't want to. Please I am fine."

That imploring voice transported me into a flashback of a similar situation.

Luke was wailing.

I stopped dribbling the basket ball and ran inside. He was sitting on the floor while his hand was bleeding. A piece of glass was sticking out from the skin.

Being a seven year old the only voice of reason I had then was to try finding someone older. There was no one at home. Mom had given me the duty to take care of the baby. Even I knew then how badly in trouble I was.

Somehow I managed to carry him outside. He kept sobbing. I kept trying to soothe him. I sang the lullaby mom use to serenade every night to get him to sleep. I'd learnt in class that a doctor was the person who cured the sick. According to me Luke was sick. I saw a man in white walking ahead. I ran behind him.

"Excuse me mister," I requested. "Will you fix my brother? I've broken him."

The man turned around and gasped. "Holy cow, we need to rush to the hospital fast. Come on little kid."

"I need an id proof first mister. Are you legal? Dad says I should always see if a man has a proof that he is human."

Despite the situation he smiled at me. He quickly drew out his license and flashed it at me. I didn't get anything but I remembered dad showing me a similar thing while teaching about the outside world. I nodded and let the kind man take my brother.

"I love him a lot sir. If it was up to me I would never let him even get a scratch. He's the best baby brother ever. I'll always take care of him."

He kept nodding as we ran towards the nearby hospital which happened to be luckily a street down.

I was told to come inside the operation theatre as Luke wouldn't stop crying. The needle freaked me out as well but I went and stood in front of Luke.

"None of you monsters will touch my brother. Mum calls me superman. I love Batman but wait till I show you how hard I can hit."

One of the nurses held me in her arms. I tried struggling as hard as possible but failed.

"Can I please at least hold his hand," I begged finally.

There I stood doing my best not to cry as they poked him with needles. Tears dripped from my eyes as his screams grew louder. I promised myself that Luke would never be put through such pain again as long as I could help it.

"I'll take him," I said.

"What?" Parsley stopped and looked at me confused.

"I'll take Luke to the hospital."

I got up and walked towards them. I held Luke's arm.

"You will do no such thing," Parsley snarled. He held my shoulder and pushed me away.

I didn't budge. I looked at him and he backed off a little. "I'm in no mood for any bull Parse. I'll take the boy. Now go do whatever the hell you do at this time."

I started walking fast. My hand was holding Luke's arm and dragging him along. He was still sniffling. No matter how hard Luke portrayed himself as; he was as delicate as a dandelion.

We were sitting in the family doctor's room. He was frantically looking around. I wanted to hug him really hard. My mind was dying to mutter words of encouragement into his ears. All these years I'd always managed to take care of him and now I was the reason he was in so much pain.

Doctor Hugh Clint walked in. He threw both of us a smile. Luke moved slightly towards me. The moment the doctor moved forward, Luke whimpered and tried to run away.

"Hey son, it's alright. I'll just check okay?"

Luke shrugged. The doctor checked his head. He flinched but tried to put up a strong upfront. It was when Clint started examining the nail wound that the real panic started creeping in.

"We will have to boost tetanus to prevent any infection. The metal went inside the skin."

Luke paled.

Clint went outside and came back later with the nurse holding the injection.

"It's alright. I'll live with the infection. I mean how bad can it be? It won't kill me. Tell them Romance I'm already disabled, I can deal with a little infection."

His eyes were moving erratically. I could hear the brain working hard to devise a plan of escape.

"It's alright son. It won't hurt you a bit."

"That's what she said," Luke mumbled.

I bit back a laugh. He was such a sweetheart sometimes.

Clint moved towards his patient. He folded Luke's sleeve and held out his hand for the injection. I got up and sat next to Luke.

"Help me," he pleaded.

"I'm sorry brother," I mumbled sadly.

As soon as the needle poked him, he squeezed his eyes shut and held my hand. I put my second hand on his vice like grip and soothed circles. His eyes were tearing up again.

"Remember when you and I use to kick Grover's and Parsley's posterior in football?"

His eyes swung open. He looked at me excited.

"Yes, Parsley always managed to drop his shorts. He'd try showing off and down went the cloth," he chuckled. "You were so good at it. I was like three? They wouldn't want me but you'd always stick around . . ."

His voice wavered. The sternness crawled back on his face. All of a sudden he removed his hand.

"It's done," Clint smiled.

Luke nodded at him and walked out without a second glance at me.

Life throws circumstances at you which make your loved ones drift apart. The memories are the only medium of patching things back. It's not always the best needle that tries sewing things back but that doesn't mean every failed needle wouldn't get another. One day, I'd sew everything back together no matter how torn the rug was at present.

Today was the day that gave me hope after a long time. I wouldn't let it die like my summer days.

The Day I Quoted Mad Max

"You don't even trust me."

"Are you kidding me?" I rolled my eyes. This woman was delirious. How much more did she want from me? I was literally giving all of me on a platter with seasoning. Trust was a thing off the past. We were avoiding the topic of what had happened some time back for the good health that we both desired. It became such a stress caring for at times that it had seemed like another way to remain human, only it was backfiring in some other way.

She'd let go of the whole confession so I had nothing better to do then do the same. Staying away from her was not a choice anymore, being with her was a compulsion now.

"No. You haven't told me one thing about Jasmine."

It will always be a mystery how woman could ignore everything for example me barring my feelings out for her which would be the last thing I did with anyone but fixate on that one thing that isn't possible to talk about.

"Jasmine is dead, I told you."

"Yes, that's not enough. Aren't you like one bit affected by what happened?"

I stared at her as if some alien was sprouting nonsense about capturing my planet.

"The woman I love died and you're asking me if I was affected? Yes, Jamie I wasn't even a bit rattled. I got up, had my coffee, ate my food and went off to sleep. It was all the usual."

"I'm sorry," she pleaded holding my hand.

All I wanted to do was snatch away from the vice grip. Caring wasn't a joke to walk away from though. Patience was the key to solving everything.

"Hey, you did nothing. It's fine. This was something that had a huge impact on me. Naturally you want to know what's up. Thanks for looking out for me Walker. I appreciate it."

We weren't in a relationship yet every day felt like struggling through one. It was usually me trying to admit at being at fault. As long as she was happy it was okay. Her nervous smile wasn't what the aim was though. The usual worry started gnawing in my stomach.

"What's wrong?"

"I just wish I didn't make you sad like that all the time. It's like all I ever do is that you know."

I pulled her in for a hug. It was such a paradox. I kept thinking I was making her sad and doing everything to do the opposite then there was her doing the exact same thing with neither of us meeting at a middle point.

"The reason I started smiling is you Walker. What is all this new found sadness you talk about?"

She chuckled. I ruffled her hair in an affectionate way.

"It's probably the hormones. Being pregnant sure makes you emotional."

"You threatened to stab me yesterday. If that's not emotional I don't know what is?"

"Shut up," she hit my arm.

"Don't hit me."

"Did you just hit a girl?"

"Were you just sexist? You want a poetry slam to your name I see."

She started chasing me around. Jasmine was thankfully buried again. I knew someday would demand an explanation where memories would be raided like some lost ark. That time I'd be ready to tell her what she wanted to know. For now, the sole focus was finding the sensitive spots I could tickle.

"You're stupid," Jamie yelled joyfully as she went around the sofa.

"I'm not stupid . . . I'm just having trouble thinking as slow as you."

"I'm going to kill you when I catch you."

"Yes, death is some light years away."

"Light years is a measure of distance not time you idiot."

"I know that. You think you're the only one with . . ."

My face hit a human. The only hope was it wasn't one of the brothers for they'd start beating. Who would want to be thrown into a bad light in front of the only one you wanted to be held in high esteem?

The person was however the last one I expected to show up.

"What are you doing here?"

He ignored my rudeness.

"Who is that?"

"What are you doing here?" My eyes narrowed into his cold grey ones.

"Where is Parsley? I've some work with him."

"Can you see him here? I'd suggest you look upstairs, Mr. Winter."

"You're getting ruder by the day."

"This isn't being rude. I'm being polite Mr. Winter. If you don't mind I have much better work to do."

"Yes? I'm sure. There are more shags out there waiting for you to be the saviour and satiate their uh . . . primal hunger." He gave a judgemental look over of Walker.

Anger waves travelled through my body. I clenched my fists. When would this man stop assuming about everything that happened with his third so called son? Did he even believe that there were emotions in me as well? Just when things were fine he decided to barrel in to twist everything.

Jamie touched my hand. She applied force for me to open my fists. After a while, I let go. Her skin smoothed out the nail marks as she clutched my hand in hers.

"It's fine Romance. I didn't feel bad."

Sometimes, she knew how to make everything calm down at the right time. It seemed like time had slowed down into a waltz while playing an apologetic tune.

"Listen son . . ."

Time was back to slipping away like a sly devil.

"No, don't speak back. Just listen to what he wants Romance."

Sure Jamie why don't you tell him about the addressing terms though? Why should I cease my thoughts as always?

He was a grown man. There was nothing barring the maturity he'd gained from all these years.

"Tell the boys I paid them a visit as a good dad should. Unfortunately, the circumstances weren't well for me to wait."

Then again did he even know the definition of maturity? I nodded.

"Give me a proper response like humans do. You're not a cow."

"Just do it please," Jamie whispered.

"Yes, I'll them how unfortunately you found me here with my shag when all you needed was your lovely sons who care so much for you."

"That's more like it. Good night."

"Good night Mr. Winter"

The front door smashed. It was only when Walker's breathing calmed down that I unclenched my jaw.

"Are you okay?"

I shrugged. The stairs seemed never ending. The unfriendly words still vibrated in my head. I shot Parsley a quick text so there was nothing to deal with later. In the hurry to get away from reality, my mind had skipped Walker's presence.

*   *   *

It was three am. The sheets were drenched in sweat. What was wrong with the air conditioner in the house? The ceiling above shone with stars. Mom had wanted someone in the family to be an astronaut. She'd randomly stuck around stickers in house giving all of us hint. The only person who was close to being that was Luke though. The only reason being - Mars was red which was had been his favourite colour from what I remembered of the childhood. Grover wanted to be a professional football player. Parsley was a mystery to even his own self. My mind was set on law. There was too much injustice in the world for a human to deal with. The first thing that would go inside the jail was certain parents who forget their duties as a father or mother.

"You're up earlier than I planned."

"Walker? What are you doing here?"

She plonked down on my bed. "Well I wanted to admire your sleeping face for some time."

I stared at her waiting for some sign of cracking up. She didn't bat an eyelid. The creepiness level associated with Summer was cranking up a notch faster than the air conditioner was clearing away my sweat.

"C'mon, let's go."

Even though I was distracted, she had enough strength to pull me outside into the balcony. The sudden burst of cool air was quite refreshing. Then my eyes scavenged the scene.

"What's going on?"

There was a blanket flattened on the floor with lots of pillows around. The balcony was really small so Walker had shifted the few plants Grover kept inside the house. It was a risk being here for this wasn't attached to my room. However, it wasn't as if those guys didn't have girls over at all. The laptop was lying on top of the sheets as if it belonged there. There was an ice box and from what I could make out mountain of food items in one corner.

"I'm going to ask again, what's up Walker?"

"Well, I thought we'd skip school today and just chill around here, you know?"

"Uh, you want me to skip school?"

"It won't kill you if you do for once."

I laughed holding the side of the balcony door ledge to support my weight. The sleep was empowering. It was possible Walker was blabbering nonsense in my dream.

"Wait, you're serious?"

Her frown was a hint to stop taking things lightly.

"I just thought you've had a bad day. It would be nice to sit around in the wind; I checked the weather forecast for today, eat something while watching some comedy to lighten up the mood."

It was my time to frown.

"Look Summer, I really don't think this is a good idea. Let's just sleep please. I mean I've already missed a few classes. The risk of attaining detention or suspension is too high for any liking. Let's just do this some other day. I don't know what you were even thinking?"

"Yeah, what was I thinking?"

Why couldn't she concentrate on the fact that my father's visit had messed me up? All that was needed to extinguish the weariness was resting not some movie watching plan while whiling away precious time.

"I'll bunk down on the floor. Go sleep in the bed."

"I'll sleep right here."

"Jamie," I groaned. "Don't be difficult. I'm really not in the mood for all this. Please just listen to me once."

"Okay, I'll clean up and come."

I made a bed for myself on the floor beside the real one. There was an old mattress that would do. I'd probably wake up with a sore back. It would be the end of the planet if I let Walker sleep on the floor in her condition.

"I'll sleep there," she whispered.

"No, just lie down on the bed quietly. I'm comfortable."

"It's all because I'm pregnant right?"

I groaned inwardly. Why did she always blame everything right? "No, I'm trying to be a gentleman woman. Just sleep."

There was sound of padded feet walking towards the bed. A creak from the wood in the bed gave me assurance she had followed my wish. The silence of the night descended on us. My eyes fixed on the stars. Why did it feel like there was something that was my fault? It was like that bit of lyrics you know in the head but can't recall at the moment.

Then it hit me.

What an absolute douche I'd been.

"Walker, are you sleeping?"

"Yes," she mumbled.

I bit back a chuckle. That was exactly how people lost in the magic of sleep responded to questions. I let a few seconds slip by.

"What's the right way to Tango?"

"Are you still trying to be a gentleman? Stop, if you are. It doesn't suit you much."

Whatever did she mean? I was the perfect candidate to become a prince if some country desired one. Another plan floated into my brain making me smile with confidence.

"Witness me."

There was no response. I crossed my fingers. Just as it happens in movies with the main characters giving up hope yet somehow working it out in the end, she finally spoke.

"*I live, I die. I LIVE AGAIN* (Quote from Mad Max: Fury Road)."

I grinned.

There was no need of apology anymore. We both understood.

"I found this new place that sells ice cream. They have some new fifty flavours. I wanted to try the walnut-coffee, will you go with me?"

A soft sigh left her.

"Look I'm a dumb guy Jamie. You know my knowledge in matters of romance. Yes, the irony again. I didn't realize you were doing that as a sweet gesture for me. It seemed just like any other random plan."

"It's okay. Do they have bubblegum flavoured cream?"

"They also have cherry cola."

Suddenly she was beside me with her eyes twinkling. I chuckled.

"Can you tie a knot with cherries?"

"Uh . . . that's an awkward question. Jas . . . uh use to make me do that a lot and start clapping. What does it signify?"

"Nothing," she said innocently and snuggled beside me. I moved aside so as to give her more space. "I was sure you could."

It was way later that I checked what it meant. Basically, if you possessed the talent of tying a knot with your tongue of the stick the cherries had, you were suppose to be a really good kisser. Now that was some quality I loved bragging around after the discovery that fateful day.

It had been quite a while now. Walker had slept mumbling something in her sleep. I pulled my mouth closer to her ears to whisper gently –

"You know, hope is a mistake. If you can't fix what's broken you'll go insane. (Max Rockatansky, Mad Max: Fury Road)

The Day I Called Jamie A Pig

"We are out of juice," Grover said while reading the sports section in the newspaper. None of us cared to check anything else out. "Luke, get some after practise. You have to cycle there today. I've some extra hours to put in."

"Tell Parse to get. That shit works there anyway."

Grover threw a piece of apple at Luke. "Stop swearing. Romance will get it."

It wasn't even astonishing how everything ended with me. I finally found the orange in the fridge. An orange a day kept brothers away.

"Wait, I need to speak with you . . . alone."

Luke rolled his eyes at both of us and walked away. There was no sign of Parsley.

This was going to be a nightmare. I should just trudge upstairs to snuggle back with Walker. It wasn't a big deal to miss school if I could skip this talk as well.

"Jamal is sick. We don't have enough cash to take him to the hospital. I was thinking of putting in some from our funds. What do you think?"

Was he being real? The Grover Winter was asking for my opinion on such a grievous issue? It had to be a joke. From what Jamal had informed me, Grover really loved the cafe. It was a secret he'd been hiding from all of us. We knew he worked in a cafe but the name had always been a mystery.

"Don't pretend you don't know him. He's told me about meeting you."

I groaned.

"Yes, it's an invasion to my privacy. I'll let it slip. Now back to the important topic at hand – what do you think? The reason I ask you is solely because mum left some cash for you as well. Parse and Luke are good with letting me have some share. They didn't even ask for reasons."

He looked at me accusingly as if I'd demanded some thirty things in exchange.

"Have my entire share if that's what it takes," I said casually. Jamal was a good man. I wouldn't want anything happening to the kid.

"It's the insomnia. The body is reacting back now itself. The doctor said he can have some pills for sleep. We need the money for intensive check up and more medicine."

I gave him a curt nod.

"I also need a favour."

I raised my eyebrow at him. His cheeks tinged with colour. Any other day it would be worth making fun off.

"You're good with economics. We need someone to balance the prices as well as handle all the balance sheets. It's just till Jamal can get back on his feet. You don't work anyway and we could use some cash. It'll make you feel less like a free loader as well."

"Yeah, I'll do it."

It had become a habit to ignore the insults they threw at me. I'd started focusing on the work at hand.

"Dad showed up yesterday."

"Yeah, Parse told me."

We were done with conversation. Grover picked up the paper again. Within seconds he was immersed. I'd peeled off the outer layer of the orange so I moved to throw the refuse in the bin.

"I'll pick up the juice on my way back before work. Just show up from tomorrow."

"Okay."

I guessed it was Grover's way of saying thank you. It wasn't the right way but it was enough.

*   *   *

"Yes, it sounds good Romance. I mean you'll be earning for the family also. It'll be nice to pay off for some things."

I shrugged. Even though Walker wanted to work at my place, I'd forced us to hang out here. It was just the desire to attain knowledge of how she survived in such a dump. Every minute was regretful though. The dumb pig kept strolling in as if it belonged here.

Go back to your sty.

"Come here Rome I'll wash that off you."

It sounded weird until I realized the pig was being addressed. I'd almost moved myself next to her. First of all, that creature stank. Second, it was covered in god knows what germs. Third, it was a female. Why the hell had Walker named it Rome?

"How much will the job pay you?"

"I don't know." I swatted away some flies.

"Do you think you'll be able to cover up your expense with the salary?"

"I don't know Walker."

The flies were really pestering me now. I smacked one dead. Walker gasped.

"What did I kill some London, Paris, Japan, Delhi?"

The silence was uneasy. I couldn't help my irritation. It was that bloody pig bringing all its annoying friends along. Suddenly, she burst out laughing. I smiled back at her. We sat down munching on cherries.

"Do the knot again, please . . ." she asked me the seventh time.

I sighed. The stick felt dirty. There was no water to waste for washing the cherries properly. The thought of upsetting Walker was a scratch out. Hence, I was sitting on the floor tying knots in my mouth.

Every time a successful knot fell off, she'd start clapping like a lunatic.

"Oh the girl would be so lucky . . ."

The look of confusion was replaced by fury as her next words followed.

"Are . . . you happy with the salary?"

"Walker, shut up about the money will you? I understand I've to take care of personal expenses. Please will you stop interfering? I can handle this on my own."

"Okay, I'm sorry," she said in a small voice.

I sighed again. This was exhausting.

"Look, I know you mean well. Let's just call it a truce okay? I am thankful that you care enough to bother asking so much. It means a lot seriously. I just need my space at times you know."

She nodded.

"I'm an idiot, Walker. Sorry?"

She nodded again.

"Don't be like that. I don't like it. How about we go visit Pigeon?"

The look of excitement was enough to make the semi-darkness inside a little less intimidating. It had to be a rainy day. Thankfully, the clouds were still not giving up their water. We walked for a while in silence. She started humming an old classic and I joined her soon.

We walked through the cemetery to the end of the back gate where under the tree Walker had buried her second pet.

The stone had some words Jamie had jotted down engraved on it –

'Here lies the body of the bird,
It wanted to fly instead of being slaughtered,
That's how all of us are in the real world,
We only need a chance,
When we do get that it doesn't matter what we are called,
It doesn't matter if we are a Turkey or a Pigeon,
We just fly.'

She'd told me how Turkey had been killed under a vehicle because it had been trying to fly again with the broken wing. What I did learn from the bird was the real meaning of trying till death. I should have made that a little more realistic when I told her the same.

"What do you think your grave should have?" Walker asked me.

"Hopefully, it has my body."

She rolled her eyes at me. I winked at her.

"I want mine to say '*the darkness was so real she never realized to catch hold of the light until it was too late. He was the beat, she the heart.*' I hope it says that."

Where did this woman produce her intensity from? Every time she spoke in riddles it seemed as if it held so many secrets. The worst part was it always felt like she really cared for me but couldn't really because she really loved someone else to.

It didn't make much sense ever.

"I guess there could be words like *we close our eyes to kiss because beautiful things are meant to be felt not witnessed.*' Then I'll get out of my grave and kiss some woman to prove it."

"What nonsense," Jamie giggled. "Don't die Romance."

"Why would I? There's so much to do in life. I need to marry and have six kids. What even are you talking about?"

"Are you serious?" she asked appalled. "Won't six tire me off? This one is some work I tell you."

"This is you presuming we end up together after you've rejected me and made sure I know of your love limit?"

Sad lines appeared on the face again. It took so many muscles to scrunch up her pretty face into something prettier. I didn't like this side of beauty. However, she needed to feel the pain my body felt mentally and physically still sticking around her after everything.

"Hey, did you know I plan on proposing the woman I love with an onion."

"Why?" she slowly smiled.

Success

"Well, it's simple. There will be so many rings inside. She won't need to pretend she's crying when she peels of the rings . . . yes, she will. The real diamond will be somehow fit inside. Don't ask me how I will plan this miracle. I just know it's romantic."

She was giggling now. "How in the world do you find that remotely close to romantic?"

"They'll be uncountable rings, uncountable promises."

"I bet I could count the rings if I tried."

"That's why Jamie Summer Walker you'll get a potato."

Her laughter rang out. If someone passed us laughing in a corner surrounded by graves, I was pretty sure we'd be termed demented. They wouldn't even hesitate to kick us out. Just before we could get serious in paying respect to Pigeon, the water drops started falling down.

"What happened to these clouds now?" I asked annoyed.

"Their water broke," Walker giggled.

"What?"

"Oh c'mon Romance, it was a pregnant joke. Tell me it was a good one."

I shook my head at her in mock disappointment. She shook her head right back at me with a sly smirk. We clutched hands and ran outside.

"Promise me one thing Winter . . ."

"Anything but a cherry knot . . ."

She chuckled.

"Promise me whenever you enter a graveyard for someone close you won't go out upset. Make sure you come outside happy, preferring to delve into the better memories than the ones that upset."

What was she even asking me? Her face was full of so much expectation that I couldn't deny.

"I better get some food for Rome. The poor swine will be ravishing."

"You're a pig Walker. You're all pink and stout. You even like mud. Why don't you name the *female* swine Jams?"

"That's very mature of you Romance."

"You're weird Walker."

"I'm you're weird Winter."

*   *   *

"I'd like to add a fourth name to the shared account I own please."

"Yes Mr. Winter, what shall I put in?"

"Jamie Summer Walker."

The Day I Asked Jamie Out

Reed stuffed his mouth with marshmallows so he wouldn't get beaten. He was pretty annoying at the moment. Guarantee I didn't know anything about being romantic but instead of helping me out he was cracking up.

"You want to send her an egg and a chick with a note saying this egg would want to go out with you chick. Can't egg you more to chicken out?"

"Yes? Isn't that the perfect way?"

"Are you like even human anymore? Just pause and go over whatever you've just told me."

I thought about it. The plan seemed foolproof. I don't know what this boy had a problem with. It seemed like a good idea. The other one involved me sending her my boxers of superman asking if she'd like to be my super girl for the night. Reed had immediately scratched off the idea saying we didn't have to gross her out. We can do it sanely also. What was wrong with giving a girl that cloth was beyond my understanding? I didn't know whether I should worry he was deciding or feel relaxed. It would be just like asking her out officially.

I felt good as I thought of all that.

"You should take her out on a boat. Make her the typical scene where violins play some romance, flowers make a point and then you come off as caring when you have all her favourite dishes on a table in the centre. It'll be perfect way to ask her out."

"You do know this is for prom and not bloody marriage?"

"Fine, then take me out like that. It's never a bad idea to make your best friend happy now and then."

I stared at him in disbelief. "I just got you nearly a year supply of chocolates some days back. What are you talking about?"

"That's not romance."

"Oh I'm sorry I didn't realize we were in a relationship," I said sarcastically.

"I thought you said yes that day when I asked you out. Oh the horror! All this while I've been thinking we've been together. Now you break my heart."

"Stop," I hit his head. "You're too much drama for a man."

"So be my woman."

"Reed, will you stop it? We have some other task at hand."

He took hold of my phone and started messing around with it. I sighed. It looked like I was on my own to format a plan.

"Here, the work is done."

"What?" I asked him confused.

"That . . ." he said pointing at the device in my hand.

I looked at the screen in time to see the *message delivered* text disappear. A feeling of dread filled my stomach. Surely he hadn't said something silly to Walker.

I quickly tapped on the screen to find her contact. There was a text from Reed to her. I stared at it for a whole five minutes trying to make sense of the world.

If you want to me to keep you warm, say yes to go with me to prom.

Was this romantic in any way? Even I could make out how absolutely crass this was. I should've known better than to trust Reed. It was nice to be this simple though didn't girls like elaborate plans that made them feel special. Walker wouldn't mind either ways but wouldn't she be the happiest if I put in more efforts to prove how badly I wanted to go with her?

"Oh c'mon don't look as if the world ended. It wouldn't have done us any good to waste so much brain into formulating a plan just to ask her out for a silly dance. You know we can do that once you get serious about actually asking her out. I promise we'll fix a mind blowing scheme then."

He made sense. It was a sad fact but true.

"Romance, let's just maintain our calm now. There's no point feeling extreme of anything. As philosophy teaches us, be in the golden mean."

Now he was making no sense.

The feelings were exactly like the scenario in fifth grade. It was the first time I'd forced some guts to ask a girl out. I'd been so nervous that when her answer had finally been said I'd broken down into tears and fled the class. The jokes about that were still flying around in school mostly among the Winter clans.

My phone buzzed.

"Oh my god, what did she say?"

Alan took hold of my collar and started shaking me - so much for maintaining world peace.

"Will you let me check first?"

"What did she say tell me quickly . . .?"

Before he could strangle me to death, I clicked on the message Walker had sent me.

That was really sweet. Did you write this though, Romance? I mean it's really uncharacteristic knowing you. I don't want to beat around the bush anymore. Perry already asked me out. I said yes. If I'd known you'd defy the rules of friendship and ask me for prom I wouldn't have. You know it. I'm really sorry.

The message was followed by a trail of crying emoticons. At least someone could shed tears. Yet again my heart had been broken after all those years. I'd been fine maintaining my non belief in relationships until Jasmine. Now, Jamie was doing the same. It was clear who had the best luck in love in this world.

"Where are you going?" Alan held the back of my tee ceasing the process of storming out.

"There's a man I need to kill."

"You'll end up in jail."

"I don't care. I'd rather be in jail than outside in this world."

"No, don't say that. We've both watched so many shows involving American prisons. You don't want to end up there at all."

"Reed you know I can pull away. I don't want to hurt you. Let me go."

"No," he said adamantly and hugged me tightly. I tried walking away with his body around mine but that didn't work. We'd both lose balance and fall down.

"Okay, fine but if that Perry guy comes in front of me I'll kill him."

Alan let go off me. "Let's go watch that football match you wanted to."

Now I knew his hate for the sport. I really appreciated the fact that he'd go against something he despised for me. It would be a change of scene as well.

I hugged him in appreciation.

"I like what this Walker woman is doing to you. All these wild emotions are worth everything."

I scoffed pulling away. "Let's go now. There's enough emasculation for tonight."

"Hey, that's offensive," Alan said in mock anger as I ran away from his clutches. He chased me outside.

That's how we ended up in the bleachers hoarsely yelling for my team to win. The game didn't let me ponder on a certain someone who had broken my heart.

*   *   *

"What are you doing here?" I asked automatically as my room door swung open. I could smell that pigeon from miles away.

"I just wanted to talk to you," she said in a low tone.

I knew this would happen - the talk that everyone has after an awkward situation. My evening had been so much fun that I'd figured some sleep would remove the left over hurt feelings so that a fresh morning could be the stage for the talk. Walker was on a different chapter all together.

"What the hell is going on?"

I switched on the lights and the whole room was full of balloons. There were rainbow coloured with a few white ones floating around. Each one of them had one word splattered across it. Even if I wanted to ignore anything around the room there was no where I could look.

"I wrote the words down myself."

I gave her a mock impressed look and slowly clapped my hands as if no one had put as much efforts as she had today.

"You're the better person. I made Reed wrote down the text words. You take the trophy Walker. Didn't you get some confetti? I would have showered you with love."

"Romance, I know you're mad. I'm really sorry. Here," she pleaded.

"What the hell is this?"

"It's a teddy bear." She said as if it was the most normal thing in the world.

I gave her a demented look. A fluffy piece of toy with a red shirt and a fedora was holding a red heart with the words *I'm really sorry* just as the balloons had them engraved across the expanse of it.

"See, it says it's sorry. It's impossible that you not forgive such a cute thing?"

Why didn't she understand I wasn't in the right mind to discuss all this? If she kept forcing me the circumstances would be hurtful to both of us. I took hold of the teddy and threw it away.

"Hey, that cost me a lot."

Where did she even get the money from? I'd never thought about that before. There wasn't any financial source I was aware of that would be providing Walker. She didn't have many clothes. I could literally tick off on my fingers all the outfits she owned. The house rent, the food, her education . . . there were so many things.

Today wasn't the day I wanted to solve this mystery though.

"I'm really tired. Can you please let me sleep? We'll talk about this tomorrow. Actually there's nothing to say much. I made a mistake. I apologize for being a fool. Okay, good night."

I snuggled into my bed.

A sniff vibrated in my room. I put my face into the pillow and screamed mutely. All these girls needed were tears as weapon to make any guy squirm in uneasiness. There was no way I'd let her go without smiling.

"Hey Walker, where is that bloody teddy? I'd like a cuddle tonight. Who knows maybe some wishing star would fall making it come alive. I'd end up with a talking bear too. I don't know though if it would be happy with the weird heart thing it carries."

I was sitting on my bed. She was looking at me with deploring eyes.

"Oh god, you're annoying me now. It's enough that you cry but then you look adorable. What do you want me to do?"

"I don't look cute."

"Have you seen yourself cry?"

"You boys just say that to every girl. I've seen so many similar scenes."

If only she knew how much I was dying to laugh and hold her in my arms for being silly.

"Fine you're right. You look ugly. Jeez, go take your sob fest somewhere else."

I slammed back into my bed.

"You're so mean to me."

"Just come in the bed Walker. Quit the yapping. Let's go to sleep. It's the best feeling in the world. Come I'll take you on this ride of joy."

Even though my hopes were pointed towards her walking away I was quite surprised when she got in with me. I crouched up in one corner.

"Walker, are you sleeping?"

"Yes," she mumbled.

I chuckled. Sure that's exactly how people sleeping replied to questions.

"I kick in the night. You might end up on the floor."

"As long as it's not heaven I'm good," she whispered.

"You're quite confident you'll be going to heaven eh?"

"I have to follow you don't I?"

There was silence after that. There was no point being arrogant so I put my arms around her. She moved closer to my body. Her head rested on my chest. It felt really nice to just have her there without the feeling of wanting to do anything more. We just stayed there in silence. Her breaths slowed down after a while.

I pulled a little away to gaze at her face.

Turkey cooed gently beside me. He'd entered somewhere in the middle of our conversation before. He'd probably didn't like the arguments for he'd started flying around popping the balloons loudly. It had been tough talking to her when Turkey was causing so much disturbance but we'd both managed to ignore him.

"You think she should end up with me too right?"

He cooed again in response.

"Yeah, I hate you too."

Her arm went around my neck as she moved even closer. I shut my eyes before I lost control. That night I slept off to the best lullaby in the world.

'It was the beat of her heart against mine.'

The Day I Slammed Down Jamie

The bell rang.

    I had two down, three more to go.

I wiped the sweat away from my face. This was what adrenaline felt like. The smell of danger, the thirst to prove my strength and the feel of the muscles flexing was all that I had been missing. Blood was dripping from the side of my head. I smirked cockily at my next opponent.

Five minutes into the game and he was carried away on a stretcher.

They were all screaming my name.

It wasn't a dream. I could feel the soreness to keep me awake in reality. My knuckles were burning. I let out a roar of anticipation for the next prey. Everyone yelled aloud with me.

I saw a bulky man enter the arena. He gave me a malicious look of death. The whole stadium went quiet as the man trudged towards the ring. He stopped before the bars. I did not break eye contact. He flexed his muscles, they were triple the size I owned.

I rolled my eyes.

"Show off," I muttered.

A wave of anger splashed across his face. He stepped inside. He craned his neck from side to side and then brought his palms together with a smack indicating my dismissal.

I gave him an innocent smile.

He circled me. I stood still pretending not to care. It wasn't the first time someone like that had approached the rink. Their strategy was well but it had a loophole. It tires the body easily. While I'd stand there saving up energy, he being the condescending git that he wanted to prove himself to be, would waste it trying to pull amateur moves. The best part was it riled them how calm I would be in every situation.

It was easy to block every punch thrown at me.

We were in a head grip. He was spinning me around. The lack of body weight opposed to his wasn't letting me control the situation. For once, the possibility of losing was spinning in the head as an actual option.

A whiff of strawberry perfume teased my olfactory senses. I caught a glance of short black hair and the sheepish expression she carried around when planning something against life rules. There could be no mistaking the glint in those black eyes. With the purpose of proving my strength in front of her, a surge of energy rushed through my veins and I managed to pull out from the deathly grip. With a new purpose in life I put everything in the fight and managed to trick him into submission. The last I saw of him was a disbelieving look while he was limping out. I'd thrown him an apologizing smile. He'd saluted me out of respect.

One of the good opponents I'd always remember. He might have been death but then he should've known who Satan was.

Wasting no time, I looked at the spot I'd seen her. Jamie Summer Walker was nowhere to be found. There stood a girl who could easily be mistaken for her. They both had quite similar features not to mention the way they both lit up looking at me. One was a friend the other a fan. I gave her a curt nod making her squeal with excitement.

The last opponent and this competition was mine. The money would be enough to a few bills at home. I could also buy a birthday present for Parsley. Every year I would secretly place a gift in his room making it look as if dad had sent it from wherever the hell he was. A genuine smile would light that boy's face the whole day just because of some one piece of materialistic pleasure I'd manage to get for him. It didn't change the fact that I still loathed him though.

There was a round of hoots. My mind was whirling with so many things I didn't notice the third opponent enter the rink. The whole stadium was yelling now. The last match was always the best piece you saved on your dinner plate to devour later.

I wiped away the sweat and blood from my face.

A punch hit my face gently. I guess I'd taken too much time to think as usual. I took up my defence stance to analyze the enemy before I could attack. When boxing one of the most important thing to do was size up your foe. This way you can make a differential table on the pros and cons while the said foe tried to hit you and waste their precious energy.

He was lanky for one. A bandana was tied round the head. There were a lot of paint marks on the face which in my head could only be classified as a traditional thing. The hands that he held up were tiny, knuckles brittle and the skin looked velvety soft.

How did he even manage to cross all the rounds and end up here was a huge mystery for me?

We were circling each other. Somehow I didn't believe this man had ever boxed in his life so I threw him the easiest punch ever. To my surprise, he deflected it.

There was a sudden flash of movement and suddenly the man was near my body. He was holding my hands back and his head gently butted my face. I had a bad feeling about this. Maybe, Alan had decided to play a funny trick and dress up to fight me but I could see the idiot waving at me from behind.

"Hey," the man breathed in my ear in the lowest tone possible.

"What the hell . . . Walker?" I said horrified. I pushed back by breaking through the amateur grip and looked at her. The bright eyes could only belong to one person.

There was no option of losing for all the hard work to collect that money couldn't go down the drain. I had no option but to fight her. With some leg work I managed to pin her against the cage bars as gently as I could and put my face close to her ears.

"How did you manage to get inside? Are the guards so dense that they couldn't differentiate between a male and female? What the hell are you doing here anyways? You're not supposed to know about this. Alan can't do one work straight and no wonder he can't."

My fury was getting the better off me. It wasn't until I heard her yelp that I pulled away slightly. She was struggling to put up a show for the audience. They were all yelling my name by now.

"They call you Roar? Seriously you're named after a sound?" she giggled.

I rolled my eyes at her. Sweat and gore dribbled from my face onto her body. It was the most disgusting feeling ever.

"You're bleeding," she said concerned. Her body was facing mine now. The friction was driving me crazy. I felt her gloved fingers slowly move to caress my face in care.

I ducked and gave a light punch on her face just to keep the show going. I let out a loud roar so that everyone's attention would be back on me.

"You're pregnant," I mumbled. "I don't know when you will ever get that in your head."

I saw a flash of anger cross her face. It wasn't long before a rain of punches showered down on me. I don't know what instigated the madness but for once we had actually started fighting. I could feel the impact of every punch hard but I didn't want to retaliate. Never would I dare to even get a scratch on that masterpiece.

Her hand punched my jaw really hard and I started seeing stars.

She gasped slightly. Before she could give her identity away I shook my head to let the dizziness pass. My mouth was suddenly paining as if on fire. I spat out the blood. Her eyes widened. I knew she was at her breaking point and thus I had to finish the fight before the things got out of hand.

"I just want to talk to you."

"Summer, a boxing rink isn't a place to *talk*. You could've waited for me to come out," I told her furiously.

She whimpered. I really wanted to hug her for consolation. This wasn't the right time.

"You haven't been answering my calls."

"I wonder why?" I rolled my eyes in mock sarcasm. She gave me a glare. I chuckled.

"I'm sorry for what's going to happen now but you've left me with no choice. I have to win this game anyways," I muttered to her as a warning. Before she could reply I bent down and took hold of one of her legs. My other hand went to support her back so that I could pull her up with both my arms and swing her in the air. Keeping in mind her sensitive situation, I gently swung her around all the while making it look scary and then threw her down as lightly as I could. I fell on her body and picked up her leg in the usual win stance. She was playing the role as well.

"Would you stop over struggling? It looks like I fed you poison instead of pinning you down," I said quickly.

She heeded.

The whole crowd burst into a chant. They'd even written some anthem for me which was being bleated out along with the aid of certain instruments. I shouted and screamed to rile them up more. The referee took hold of my arm and punched it in the air symbolizing triumph. It hadn't been the best finish to a competition but even the silver linings of a cloud were appreciation worthy at times.

They gave me the cash cheque. One of the sponsors handed out the trophy while the other tied up the champions' belt around my waist. I took a lap of the rink waving at everyone before going into the changing room where she was sitting with a clean face now.

"Congratulations," she said smiling. "Here let me help you."

She took the trophy from me. I kept ignoring her as I went around doing my business. She kept blabbering about how beautiful the day was or what colour of shade would suit me best.

"I didn't know you boxed," she asked cheerfully. I was sitting on the bench taking off my shoes. The stench of sweat was so dominant that I was surprised she was still standing ground. "Damn you Winter, you have so many injuries. Let me fix it."

She disappeared for a while and then skipped back inside holding the first aid kit. She sat down in front of me as I pulled out the last sock and threw it away.

She dabbed the cotton with antiseptic liquid and brought it near my head. My hand automatically took hold of her wrist in a vice-like grip.

"Don't," I said gritting my teeth in anger. "I don't need you to *fix* me."

"But I just want to . . ."

"I said no. Doesn't that word ever get through your thick head because you sure do have a habit of saying that word a lot? It should be common for you to understand?"

Her face fell. She dropped the cotton swab as I pushed her hand away violently.

"Okay, I'll go," she said in a small voice.

She was near the door when I got up, strode towards her, took hold of her hand and twisted it making her turn. I pinned her against the lockers making them bang loudly as her body hit the metal. My head was bent to meet her eye level. She looked at me with fear.

"What do you want?"

"I just wanted to talk about to you."

"Talk about what Walker? I don't think we have any bloody topic left. You've scavenged my life enough. Aren't you happy first taping the chart together and then tearing it apart much worse than what it was? Isn't that enough for your vile schemes or will you literally now want me dead?"

She flinched. All the fighting hadn't quenched my thirst for violence yet. I wanted to harm something really bad.

"I want you dead?" she chuckled. "If only you knew."

"Then tell me," I said pushing myself more against her.

"You're hurting me," she cowered. It was then that I saw the purple rings forming on her hand due to my grip. I felt ashamed. What was happening to me? I wasn't a monster. Tears were forming in those eyes. Hadn't I made a promise with myself that not a tear would ever form in those eyes with me being the reason?

I let her go. One of my fingers gently caressed her face. She thought I was going to punch her and flinched. Soon her features relaxed and the eyelashes started fluttering again. I backed off. I walked towards the bench pulling her along. I gently pushed her to sit on the bench, picked up the cotton with the dab of liquid and handed it out to her.

"Help me Walker. I need you," I said looking away.

Moments of silence passed between us. I waited patiently in hopes that she would take care of me. Every passing second was breaking my heart more and more until I felt the surge of pain from the liquid on my wound.

"Ouch," I shuddered.

"Sorry," she grinned at me.

I was so happy to see that smile that nothing else mattered then. I didn't even care if she rejected me a million times now. I'd do anything to get that smile permanent even if it meant letting go off my feelings.

"Darling baby," someone yelled loudly in the locker room.

We both turned to gaze at a frantic Alan. He ran towards me as fast as his legs could carry him. His arms engulfed my body as he threw his whole weight on me and we both fell on the other side of the bench.

"I almost thought I lost my boyfriend," he wailed into my ears kissing my face everywhere. I hoped he wouldn't get the lips because that would be the last straw. It had happened once and I couldn't take the disgust again no matter how much I loved this boy.

"Get off you oaf," I shouted. "You're hurting my back."

He apologized. We both got up. I fell on the bench now sorer than ever. I was glaring at Alan so much that he quickly snatched the cotton swab from Walker and started trying to treat me. Walker was trying her best not to laugh.

"Hey beautiful, I didn't notice you there," Alan said giving her a friendly nod. Since that day of her accusations, they hadn't really spoken with each other. I could feel the waves of awkward hitting me hard.

"Alan," she said in a small voice after a long time. "Sorry for being such a dramatic bitch."

"Ale," Reed tinkled. "Don't ever call yourself that honey. You're no less than an angel. I'd take personal offence if you insult yourself like that. Talking of drama . . . I know better than anyone just how much trouble it can get you into."

I couldn't agree more to that. This Reed man had so many times taken me down with his silly tantrums.

"I still am really sorry. It was unfair to you. You were such a good friend to me and I was such a mean fool."

I couldn't help holding Walker's hand. She instantly looked at me and I gave her an encouraging smile. She seemed to feel better.

"Did I ever tell you Reed never quits being a friend unless you murder my boyfriend here? Then I'll get my curler irons to show you exactly what a *good* friend is. I love you Jay-Jay. You can do all the drama you want but I'll be stuck on you like a leech. If you think that I'm a creep who loves too much then might as well picture me as your husband. Reed is never quitting your shadow."

The words held so much meaning that even I shuddered at the truth outlining it. Alan could sure scare a person in broad daylights with just mere words.

"C'mon, let's get you and the bundle of joy inside some ice cream."

With that both of them left not even glancing once at me. So much for all the love showered on me. I guess I'll fix my own wounds now. The world sure made a point of giving you love but making sure you sat and watched it walk away to get some ice cream. I scanned the floor to get that infected piece of cotton so as to throw it away. It was good at least my initial love OCD stayed loyal to me.

"I love you loads," Walker whispered. She kissed my cheek, winked at me and ran away again.

Three words that were meant to impact anyone like a bullet to the heart. It wasn't always the love between lovers that should be placed on a pedestal and cherished but the other kinds; the richer kind of love was what mattered. Even if I gave up on love, I will never give up on us.

It was the most clichéd thing to do but I did it anyways.

Years later when some idiot like me would be sitting on this bench, he would come across some words engraved on the narrow side of the seat.

'Summer will always shine for Winter to come and Winter will always snow in anticipation of Summer.'

The Day I Stabbed Jamie

Curiosity is an unhealthy desire for things that should be kept a secret at times. However, if it wasn't for this one emotion, we wouldn't have cared to learn or know more about anything. There wouldn't be any invention and the humans would still be nomads running around wild with no respect to the high intellect otherwise present in each. Presently, it had forced me to follow Walker to wherever the heck she was planning to take me. The prospect of finally knowing something different about her had me up and going. Even though every day I felt I'd moved a step ahead in figuring her out, she'd throw me right back to the start in anticipation of another mystery to solve.

We were strolling in those muddy streets again where I'd skated some days ago. Then Walker had appeared out of nowhere and scared the living daylights out of me by stabbing.

The point of a friendship was equal to sharing. Recently I'd told her things about my past which I didn't like grazing out. Therefore naturally I expected some information which she'd blatantly denied. This was the only moment I felt close to her for she seemed eager to share.

The road switched to rubble and rocks for houses as the area was associated with. It smelt of a nasty cookout of drugs. It had been a couple of weeks now that I'd worked for my charity here. For quite a while my energy had been concentrated on the better off organisations in the city. My charity here was planning on re-establishing in the area I lived in. I'd been really hyper about the situation due to the prospect of being able to give in more hours.

"No matter what happens today I don't want you to judge or make insensitive comments okay?" Walker requested nervously.

I gave her assurance by holding her hand firmly in mine and squeezing it. After all this time she should know I wasn't the one who jumped to conclusions or based my relationship on anyone's past. I understood her insecurity though. She seemed satisfied for she kept walking ahead.

"I remember playing basket ball here," she said nostalgically pointing towards a sad looking net hoop hanging with the support of an old broken streetlight. It wasn't the actual net that finished the touch but the cobwebs that some eight legged creature had spun. There wasn't anything special in it but it was special in its own way. This was where Walker had her childhood which unlike mine hadn't been that colourful. The brown, grey, yellow hues around were a proof enough.

"How come you've never told me about basketball before? We could have had a duet challenge in school," I replied trying to keep the conversation flowing in order to extract more random facts.

"It's never too late," she mumbled. "You would have beaten me with the rusty skills I have."

"That doesn't mean playing continuously wouldn't improve your rust. I'll pair you with Alan. That man plays a mean game."

"I'll pair you with a star hoping you shine but from a distance and when you're done with your expectancy you become a black hole to suck in life like you always do."

"Touché mademoiselle," I said bowing my head in submission.

We hopped over a broken tyre. Some kids were sitting outside discussing in their wild language about which game to play. My mind was so distracted with watching them that I missed following Summer.

"Excuse mister . . ."

I looked down at the voice calling me along with the tug of my shorts. A boy of around five with dirt smeared all across his face looked at me with a concerned face. I could tell by his gestures that something was really upsetting him.

"Why girl so tough?" he asked me in a serious tone.

"They eat a lot of veggies. Milk is also one of the components that help them in keeping tough," I answered with similar gravity. Mom had told me that no matter what a child's curiosity shouldn't be left parched.

"Don't be a ninny. Why she no listen?"

"I'm sorry, I don't follow," I asked him confused. He sure knew how to intimidate a young man who was trying nothing but his best to help.

"Heidi is the cute one but I chose Linda cause she play good. Heidi is a mad cow now. I try say sorry but she remain a cow. Even ma be shout at pa when he no eat food. Why girls be so mad?"

"I've been asking the same question all my life kiddo. How do I answer you? This should be taken as a warning. Even if you're fifty with all the knowledge in the world, you'll still not figure out women. On one hand they claim to not have feelings but go around kissing you nevertheless. They say they don't care and the next thing you know they do. If they say yes to something it is highly likely it was a no and you doing anything to carry out whatever action from that anything will result in them being mad at you. Do you follow?"

He gave me a curt nod. That boy understood nil.

"Women are mad. We can't live without them though so go make that Heidi of yours the happiest girl. Also, I advice don't call a woman *cow*."

"Okay mister. You talk but I come to the end that you are no use. I do not know what you say. Heidi is my girlfriend. How you make your girlfriend happy?" he blabbered pointing towards the disappearing back of Walker.

There was so much genuine desire to make his girl smile that it melted my heart. He seemed mature in so many ways that it amused me. After Walker, this was probably the next most adorable thing I'd come across. .

"You know what works best on women? Get her a bunch of flowers and say some beautiful lines dedicated to her. They have a tendency to get swayed by words if you truly mean them. She'll be really happy if you can show her you actually care. They don't want much in life. On the other hand please don't show! You should always mean it."

He gazed at me for quite a while, pondering on the words that I'd just spewed. The brown eyes were shining as he was processing the idea. Gradually, he gave me a satisfied nod of consent. With a quick salute he jogged away. In order to parch the thirst of my curiosity monster as well, I stayed rooted to my spot.

Five minutes later the boy came back with something hidden behind his back. I grinned at him as he approached a cute little girl with pigtails. She was sitting on a rock with her face downcast and flushed with sadness. The blonde hairs were tied up in blue ribbons. Her blue frock with huge white dahlia print was complimenting her beautiful eyes. Boy was she going to break some hearts later in life.

The boy started off with his words. I was so enthralled by the simplicity and love that I stood there with my mouth hanging open like a lunatic. I would have never been able to be so smooth. This was way more than what I had expected. I could make out even while standing facing her back that Heidi was a goner. He ruffled his hair with one hand out of nervousness. I gave him an encouraging smile egging him to go on.

He brought his hand forward. Betsy giggled. I laughed out loudly as my eyes fell on the scene. He looked at both of us confused but kept his confidence up. Walker was calling out to me now. I jogged to catch up with her sitting on a step of some random shack.

"Where have you been? Who have I been chatting with all this while? Do you even care to observe how nervous I am? Do you even measure how scary this is? I'm here with my nerves on an overdrive trying to explain why all this means a lot to me and what do you do? You stand there with a bunch of random children making your own scenes. Am I making any sense in that dense head of yours?" she asked in one breath.

Was it my imagination or was she actually turning blue?

"Hey Walker, calm down. I'm sorry but I really had to help the kid back there. He had made a girl sad and how can I walk away when a female is left like that?"

"Do you even hear yourself? You are ready to make another woman sad for other? What are you saying? What am I saying? This is so confusing. Promise me you won't ditch me again."

I sat next to her slinging my arm around her shoulder. "I saw a girl sitting with a sad smile and it reminded me of a younger version of you . . . there must have been a time when you would have felt like that as well. There was no one then to give you a cheer. I didn't want the same with Heidi as well Walker. For me a girl's smile was a priority today than you."

She pecked me on the cheek. "Thank you for being honest."

Words well meant always worked magic on women, as I said before.

We sat there for a while listening to the chatter of the local kids. Now and then someone would pass by throwing us various mixed expressions. We ignored them lost in our own world.

"Let's go," Walker said finally. I gave her a hand as she pulled herself up.

I was thinking about how everything was different when you were a kid and how things got complicated as you started growing up. Most of my childhood was the best memory ever. I wouldn't change even one second of it. Then came the adulthood kicking me so hard it was difficult to limp ahead at times.

I hit my face on Walker's back head. "Ouch," I yelped rubbing my nose.

"Will you please return to my home planet," Walker said rolling her eyes at me. "There, that's my home."

I followed her finger. There was a huge broken down building. Some of the window panes were shattered. The paint had peeled off from most of the walls. There were a number of weeds growing around in the garden. The door was almost coming out of its hinges. There were random pieces of clothes along with shattered glass decorating the floor area around the house. There was not one sound coming out from the house, as if no one stayed there.

"You live here?" I asked her baffled.

"Yeah," she said in a monotone.

"Isn't this like an orphanage?" I remembered one of the ladies from charity talking about the silent house that was across the street. This fit her description perfectly. The picture she'd painted had been gruesome enough to discourage me from visiting the place ever. Yet, as usual destiny had its own plan.

"It's not my fault that you never wondered where I came from or who my parents are. It's so easy to get lost in your own life sometimes, eh?" she spoke in the same emotionless tone.

That was a lie. Most of my life revolved around solving everything related to her. It wasn't even funny how much I thought about everything related to her. Though, it was true that I didn't ever inquire about her origins or think about anything other than how she was feeling towards me.

The more I thought about it the more truth her words seemed though. It was usually all about why she was miffed with me or why she wasn't happy around me today or why she wasn't accepting how much I loved her.

There was so much of me that the main point of Jamie Summer Walker was lost.

I didn't realize we had started walking inside. She was knocking at the door as I looked away shamefaced.

An old lady appeared at the wooden door. I bet this building was there when the Puritans came to habitat this country. That's how old the surroundings felt. The woman in front of me was as wrinkled as a cloth left in water for too long. Her eyes could barely open due to the sagging skin. She was a haunch back with her remaining white hair tied up on both sides in pigtails. Her face lit up like a Christmas tree as her eyes fell on Jamie Summer. She engulfed the girl in a hug.

"Willow, how have you been?"

The woman nodded her head with a roll of her eyes. She seemed to be saying from what I could gather was '*same old, same old*'.

"I'm going to show my friend inside okay? Are *Parents* here?"

The woman gave a stern look. She reluctantly shook her head.

"Will, it's okay. I trust him alright? I promise nothing will happen."

She thought for a while before nodding her consent. Before we could leave though, Willow started poking Walker incessantly.

"Yes, yes I remember the warning signals. I'll be careful," Walker whispered and kissed the old lady on the cheek.

It was a surprise to look at the inside of the house. Everything was spick and span. My OCD was feeling so satisfied it wasn't natural. Every picture hanging was perfectly positioned. I couldn't feel any speck of dust no matter where I placed my hand. It smelt of lemon and fresh mint which was refreshing. The silence was still disturbing though. The place was huge. It had been quite a while since we had been walking. Every piece of furniture was shining from the polish. There was no sign of untidiness.

"It's rest time. Everyone would be in their rooms. I'll take you to mine."

We started trudging up a flight of stairs. There were two pair of stairs from each side meeting up at the top in a common area and then bifurcating away in separate directions.

A picture of some men and a stern looking woman was hanging in the common area. They all looked sophisticated. One of them even had the old reading glasses. All of them adorned the same kind of archaic styling of clothes. The picture in itself was black and white. My head was aching due to the need to blast Walker with questions.

I didn't.

"Those are our *Parents*," she said finally.

I was worried about the current lack of emotions in her. It was awkward having her behave like me. I could see how she used to exactly feel when I had the same behaviour on.

This situation was a proof of how much I'd changed over time.

"Our? Wait, you have so many parents?"

"We as in all of us living here Romance. It isn't just me who would be habituating in such a huge mansion now? We are supposed to *call* them *Parents*."

"Where are you real parents?"

"They're dead . . . at least for me. They left me here when I was baby. I have no idea where they are."

I lifted my hand to place on her shoulder but she turned and started walking away. I despised how she was acting. This had been the worst idea yet.

"We can leave if you want," I said silently.

"No."

I followed her. We passed some hallways until she turned into one and started walking inside. The narrow aisle had various doors on the side with a polished gold plank, each having a name engraved on it neatly. We stopped at the door with the number '077' and the inscription *J.S. Walker*. She held the knob and twisted it

There wasn't much inside. A bed was kept in the corner neatly made up. There was not a crease on the extremely white bed sheet. A small cupboard was on the other end with not even a piece of cloth peeking out. The study table had a couple of books lined up in shelves. There was a case with the stationary kept inside. The curtains were neatly aligned at the end of each pane. The window was so clean I could see my face on the glass. There was an absence of mirror. Now that I thought of it, I hadn't ever seen Walker look into one. A pair of white sports shoes was kept lining against the wall. There was nothing else around.

"This is paradise," I sighed.

She gave me a look of ridicule and almost rolled her eyes. I felt better that at least all of her wasn't lost. I'd fix her once we left. Two scoops of choc chip ice cream and Summer would be shining again.

She sat on her bed. There was something intimate about being in the room. It seemed to whisper so many secrets to me which were so encrypted I found it frustrating to concentrate on anything else. I wondered what she did all day when she wasn't around me. I wanted to know more about this weird place with its immaculate policies. There was so much to ask and so little time.

"Amie?" someone yelled excited. "Oh my god it's finally you. I thought I wouldn't ever see you again. I'm going to call everyone."

Before I could make sense of anything, a bundle of hyper humans entered the room and attacked Walker. Even in this over dose of emotion I could make out how fake Summer was being with her smiles and laughter. I could see she genuinely loved all these whoever they were but she wasn't in any mood to rejoice. Another question was badgering me. Why had the girl said it had been so long when every day Walker came back to this place?

Then the round of introductions started.

Poppy was her immediate neighbour. She had her hair oiled back properly making her forehead look huge. Her front teeth were a little longer giving her the typical bunny look. She had brown eyes that shone with warmth. She was chubby.

Jenna was a mystery. She naturally had a poker face. She didn't even look excited to meet Summer though she'd given her a hug longer than usual. Her hair was straight and cut short right till her chin. She had kholed eyes.

Zen had an aura of beauty around her. I was mesmerized by how pretty she was. The marble white skin shone with care. I could smell an appealing cocoa scent wafting from her. The golden braid reached up to her waist. She was giving me the cutest smile any girl could muster.

The girls had no make-up on them. They all wore the same dress or what seemed more like the uniform now that I observed carefully. They all inculcated polite mannerism for all I received were just gentlemanly handshakes in this generation of hugs as Walker had made me start to believe. I gave them a friendly smile. The best part was the absence of urges to wash my hands off germs. This was one place I could let myself be wild. Other than around Walker, I was hardly careless.

The boys were almost similar except in their features and personalities of course.

Joshua was Walker's childhood best friend. He had sand papery hair with a buff body. All the guys I'd seen had muscular bodies though as if they exercised strenuously every day. His hair was properly combed. He could give me tough competition in wearing non-creased clothes.

Shelter seemed like the only human around. He had his arms slung around me and was blabbering about all the people standing around. He had a genuine smile that stretched up to his eyes. His hair was even a little ruffled and I could see one side of his shirt popping out of the pants. There was even a button missing in the shirt. He was Walker's other best friend.

The last was a guy named Yulius. He just gave me a friendly look and disappeared into his own thoughts. According to Poppy he was disturbed. Shelter though claimed him to be a smart, intense man who lived in a world weaved by himself or in his words - *An intricate web of creativity and imagination which was as close to magic as possible.*

They were all amused with my name though. All of them discussed about it for quite a while before I interrupted them.

"So do you guys have any story for me about Walker?"

"Oh no," Walker groaned after being unusually quiet for so long. "Just go on about how silly his name is please." She looked at me with imploring eyes and then mild anger. She mouthed, "You shouldn't have."

Then started a whole string of all the crazy narrations they could come up with. They had warmed up to me by now. There were fights, debates, blabbers and what not just for me to know all the things I'd been missing all this while.

"She used to purr like a cat whenever she wanted milk so Shelter would sneak in the kitchen and get her some."

"Once she dressed up as Willow and tricked the old darling into believing she had gone mad."

"Remember as a baby she used to pull her own hair once a day saying they'll grow back stronger?"

"I think she pulled Josh's more. They fought like a cat and dog."

"She was so naughty . . . she put a mice in Annabeth's bra drawer. I'd never heard that bully scream louder."

The stories kept pouring in. I was enjoying so much while Walker kept trying to shut them up. She gave up after a while and went into her own trance.

A bell rang loudly.

"What?" Poppy looked surprised. "It's already supper time?"

"Time passes by like a saviour on a white horse. It's up to you whether you get trampled or aided," Yulius finally said something.

"Ah my Words with Worth," Shelter smirked, hooking his arm around Yulius. "Let's go before they beat us up."

I looked at her. She waved me away. I nodded and let Joshua pull me along. Zen stayed back with Walker.

The dining table was laid out properly. I could make out around fifty more kids. This place held a lot of people. I sat down gazing at the perfectly kept crockery. Why was this place insanely sophisticated?

There was a bowl of soup on my plate. It looked disgusting.

"What is this?" I asked Joshua. The boys were sitting separately.

"Pea and coriander soup which looks disgusting but isn't the same unlike Shelter here."

Shelter hit Josh's head but continued slurping his soup.

"Don't you guys ever get stuff like pork or you know pizza?" I asked nonchalantly.

They both looked at me with excitement. Then began a series of questions on all the wide varieties of food I'd consumed. According to their *Parent's* rule no one was allowed any kind of junk and thus they were all subjected to healthy products like the soup all the time. They both had had a slice of pizza in their lifetime from what Summer had been able to sneak inside.

"What are you guys even living for," I asked them horribly disturbed. "This place feels like it doesn't belong on this planet like you guys are some vampire cult or something."

That made them both laugh. I saw Shelter open his mouth to answer the biggest mystery but Walker appeared suddenly. She was frantic about something and literally pulled me out of the chair.

"What's wrong," I yelped.

"*Parents* are here. We need to get out before they see either of us or believe me the trouble will be real."

I heard the urgency in her voice and so did the other two. They both helped us jump out of the window to run away from the backside. I could see Willow ushering Walker away and breathing a sigh of relief when we skipped over the back fence.

We were back to walking in silence.

"Hey, you okay?" I asked her concerned. "This was really fun, yeah? I loved meeting all of them."

She nodded.

"Walker, it'll be fine. I'm there for you."

She nodded again. "I'll be fine."

We crossed over to the city after a while. The traffic with the noise was a sudden hit from all that peace before. Suddenly I had an idea.

"Wait here," I told Walker holding her shoulders firmly. "I'll be right back."

She didn't respond but stood at the spot I had stopped her. I ran, got the thing I wanted and sprinted back to her.

I stood in front of her until she looked into my eyes. Her browns seemed to have ceased burning with passion. I didn't like the dead look at all but I still inhaled deeply and began with what I'd planned to do.

> *"Walker, Twinkle Twinkle you're my star,*
> *I never want you from me far,*
> *Up above or down you stay,*
> *Shine like the diamond every day,*
> *Twinkle Twinkle you're my star*
> *Please I'm sorry, here's a flower."*

Little kiddo had inspired me to do this. Even before I brought the gift to give her, I knew she was going to fall for it.

She burst out laughing. Her giggles vibrated around my empty head filling it up with the best sound ever. She clutched the cauliflower and howled more. It took her some time to calm down in which I enjoyed gazing at her beautiful face finally back to normal.

"Someone really named you wrong because you don't even know the R of romance," she chuckled kissing my cheek. "Oh what would I do without you silly?"

"Did I manage to make it better?"

"You've stabbed my heart fool. It's all pierced and bleeding with laughter now."

A sudden surge of joy spread through my blood as well. This was the day I'd lived for. She ruffled my hair still vibrating with happiness. Her eyes trained towards the ice cream truck and I grinned as she started walking towards it. She looked back and beckoned me to follow her. I nodded happily as my eyes took her back profile skipping away to glory.

That's when I noticed she was wearing a blue frock with big dahlias printed all around.

The Day I hugged Jamie

I was sitting in the school bleachers thinking about yesterday. We'd gone to the institute after school where I'd finally had a gaze at her past. There were mixed feelings about it. There was something about the whole foundation that seemed fishy to me.

"Romance, I need some choc-chip ice cream."

"I'm thinking right now Walker. We'll go in a while."

It wasn't easy slinking away from her. She usually sniffed me out wherever I was. Maybe there was a tracker in my phone that helped always extract me out.

"I need the ice cream," she yelled at me.

I looked at her in horror. There were a couple of boys passing us that started sniggering. Walker was getting impatient.

"Okay, let's go get your sweet woman."

"Can we visit your orphanage?" she asked shyly.

I peeked at her realizing that entire tantrum had never been about a bloody dessert. The thing with Jamie was whenever she couldn't express herself, she would start getting annoyed. It was frustrating when things weren't clear in the head so that the jumbled words would push the irritation further.

"Of course we can. You don't have to worry about asking such things," I replied throwing her a quick smile.

She slung her arm into mine.

"I can't wait to meet all those kids again. Do you think we should take some candies for them? I mean they'd love that, right?"

At that moment, I couldn't have loved someone more than I loved her.

We always walked around. The town wasn't that big nor were the places I frequented far away. It was a good exercise along with maintaining my lost physical regime. Ever since two years I hadn't set foot in any field. Sometimes life just decided to pull you off your passion without any reason. Then there were times when you decided to stop because there was no other option. I was stuck in the middle.

"Did you know about the Andrew kid?"

My attention spun back to her. "No?"

"He has dyslexia."

Everything made sense now. In the beginning, I use to be patient when Andrew threw arrogant tantrums about not understanding matter. Slowly I started switching to snapping at him at times and even punishing. How could have I been this foolish?

"He was reading the book reverse last time. I asked him to read me something and he did. The back cover of the book spoke about some Huang and he kept on talking about Richie. As far as I could make out there was nothing about America included in the book. Then when you started teaching them for a while, he couldn't write on the sheet of the paper. He couldn't form numbers. I went to the library and checked up the book he was reading. There was no Richie."

I could have never guessed all this that fast. I squeezed her hand gratefully. It helped me understand the kid much better than I ever had. No wonder he never wrote down letters to Santa Claus or the tooth fairy. All those times he denied orders to come and solve sums on the board was because he couldn't understand how to write. I always took it as a rebellion.

Walker taught me a life lesson at that moment. I should stop jumping to conclusions about anyone without knowing the whole story.

"Romance you're back. Thank God! Teresa has come home. She's a mess right now."

I gasped as Ms. Roxanne looked at me sadly. How could that be possible? Teresa was one of the girls who had been sent off to live in a good family as a foster kid. She was the most adorable kid I'd ever come across. I still remembered how jealous Giselle used to be whenever I gave more attention to Teresa.

Giselle . . . how was I going to handle this situation now?

"I'll go take care of the kids. You handle this one, okay?"

I hugged her tightly. She'd saved the day.

"Teresa is upstairs in my room. She's been asking for you since a while now. I'd tried contacting you yesterday but your cell was coming switched off."

I bade both of them farewell and rushed upstairs.

The girl was sitting near the window looking outside. There weren't many changes except the face had drained more. The plumpness decrease was a worrisome matter. As usual she was staring into space. There weren't any new marks on her skin.

Good, she'd not been hurting herself.

"Tessie, hey there," I whispered.

"Romance, is that you? Come sit beside me."

We both sat in silence. She looked wearied out as if the world's pressure was on her shoulders. I wanted to pull her in for a hug but I waited patiently.

"Who is the girl?"

"She's a friend."

"Do you love her?"

"Yes."

"Have you told her?"

"Yes."

"Does she love you back?"

"Not really."

"Then don't waste your time. You're better than that."

"Okay."

"Love is but that genre of music that you fall for. It doesn't mean you can't switch when it doesn't satisfy or give you the same result. You have every right to chose another."

"I agree."

That's when her little body wrapped around me tightly.

"I've missed you so much," she said in a babyish voice. "Did you get my letters?"

I nodded patting her hair. The letters were written as complicated as she was. Sometimes they would talk about nothing in general, sometimes they'd talk about her day and the rest of the times there'd be a random thoughts she'd have various opinions on. For a seven year old she sure was smart.

"They took my Hugsie away. I got upset. That's why I came over here for a while."

Hugsie was this soft toy of a polar bear that Teresa always carried around. It was common knowledge never to snatch the toy away.

"Do you want me to go beat them?"

"No, Teresa was a bad girl. She had annoyed mother. Hugsie didn't deserve such a naughty girl."

"But Teresa apologized right?"

"I said sorry so many times. I even ate my cereal Romance. They didn't give me a boo-boo for being bad."

She was sniffling rubbing her pudgy nose. I held her tiny hands in mine.

"Then Teresa isn't a bad girl. She did what she should have."

"Really, you think so?"

I gave her a reassuring nod.

"Can we go meet her?" she asked me shyly. I was worried about this. It wasn't more how Teresa would behave but the impact on Jamie. I couldn't say no to this girl though. That would lead to far worse circumstances. As far as I knew, I was confident enough in Walker's skills with kids.

We strolled downstairs. She was holding my hand tightly. I didn't let go.

We entered the study room. Everyone was huddled in the toy corner. Jamie was sitting with Paulo in her lap. There was unison of gasps as she narrated something. Andrew was sitting beside her struggling between amazement and maintaining his usual uncaring demeanour. I felt my heart fill with joy as she told all of them a story. She made sure there was eye contact with every kid so that none of them felt left out. Giselle sat on her other side clutching the sleeve of tee-shirt. It looked like Elle had a new favourite.

She was the first one who noticed me.

"Romance, I thought you hadn't come. Look Jamie is telling us a story about some pirate. You have to listen to it."

"Tessie, you want to hear the story?"

She nodded shyly. Her feet stepped back until she was hiding behind my legs looking at Walker with a timid expression. Her thumb was in her mouth.

"Jamie, this is Teresa. Teresa, meet Jamie Walker."

"Hello there angel, you're such a cutie."

Teresa slowly walked away from me towards Jamie. The moment she was touching distance she stopped. They stared at each other. Suddenly Teresa giggled, poked Walker's cheek and ran towards me hiding behind my legs again. Walker chuckled.

"Romance, Jamie taught me the first five letters of the *alphatical* series."

I realized I'd been ignoring Giselle so I pulled Teresa with me towards the circle. I requested Samantha to shift so I could plonk down next to Giselle. She threw Teresa a look but didn't say anything. Her fingers slipped off Jamie's cloth and held mine.

Walker started narrating her story again.

It had been a while, everyone was hearing her enthralled. It was in the middle of a sea adventure that Teresa suddenly became frigid. She'd been sitting in my lap. I knew a fit was coming next. However by the time my reflexes could react Teresa yelled and ran towards Jamie.

"Get out of my house. I told you Teresa don't come inside the house ever again. Why don't you take your selfish self and get the fuck out."

"Teresa, calm down please," I said.

All the kids were getting scared. I couldn't go forward. Giselle was hugging me in fright. She wasn't letting me leave her. Teresa on the other hand was beating up Jamie while yelling obscene insults at her.

Andrew ran to get Ms. Roxanne.

"You think you can come take my Romance away from me bitch? You don't love him, go away. It's your fucking loss . . ."

"Teresa, please stop it . . ." I pleaded. I couldn't shout at Giselle as she was so frightened. What was taking Andrew so long?

"Shh Tess . . . it's all going to be fine. You want me to leave? I'll walk right out."

Walker had clutched the girl's fists in her hand. She had handed Paulo to Flint who was old enough to handle the baby. There was a gentle expression on her face. I could see the nail marks on her neck and cheeks. My body tensed with anger and helplessness.

"What happened on your neck?" Teresa asked Jamie shyly. She stretched her hands slowly and caressed the wounds. "Does it hurt?"

It was the right time. I signalled Ms. Roxanne to pull Tess back so that I could handle the situation.

"Tess I need help with making brownies. Would you mind?"

Thankfully Teresa was distracted with the name of her favourite eatable. She waddled over to Ms. Roxanne eagerly and held her finger.

"Let's get everyone back in a circle. It's alright now. Jamie, can you wait outside? I'll settle them and come right there."

She nodded at me.

"Okay, I want you all to start writing the tables till five. I'll come back and check each one."

"Can we copy Mr. Winter?"

"No, Enrique you cannot unless you're a monkey." I retaliated patiently. Under my breath I whispered, "Which you out of everyone here certainly can."

"Hey," I said ruffling my hair nervously. There was no way I could apologize to her.

"It's okay Romance. I don't need any sort of explanation. I get it. Doesn't she have split personality disorder?"

I stared at her in amazement.

"I lived in an orphanage too Romance. I understand these kids a lot. There problems aren't new to me. It's not the first time someone has attacked me like that. I'm not traumatized. You should go check up on Teresa. Make sure she's fine."

For the second time today, I pulled Walker in for a hug.

"You're amazing," I whispered in her hair.

"Not more than you," she mumbled back.

"Romance . . . can I stay with you for a while? I'm really scared."

I looked down at Giselle. Her face was tear-stricken and she was clutching Enrique's hand. I glared at the boy.

"Giselle, can you give me five minutes? I need to speak with Enrique here about y . . . his addition skills."

She nodded. Jamie started talking to her gently. We hadn't even left the hall when I heard Giselle giggle. That woman had some magical powers over people.

"Do you like Elle?" I asked Enrique sternly.

He stopped digging his nose. "Yeah, I do."

"How much do you like her?"

"She shares crayons with me. I like her that much."

He made no sense. I needed to dig further.

"How much do you earn?"

He looked at me confused. I hit myself in the head. It was difficult to maintain a straight train of thoughts at times.

"Will you ever hurt my Elle?" I grumbled.

"No sir. I wouldn't dare to. She is one mean scratcher."

"That she is," I said proudly. "I approve of you. Just remember if you even bring a tear in her eye I swear to God I'll stran . . . take away your chocolate privileges."

He nodded. Then he extended his hand out for a formal handshake. I shook hands with a stern expression making sure he understood I'd keep a constant check on him.

We both went back in the hall. I decided to split my time between Giselle and Teresa for today. The rest of them could be handled some other day. Jamie assured me she'd check the tables properly. I had half a mind to request her to tell me the tables till five but I decided to blindly trust her with it. Right now there were much more important things at hand.

* * *

"I had a great time," Walker smiled at me.

I'm glad you did. Sorry about Tess though."

"It's okay Winter. Things like that happen. I told you I don't need anything from that incidence."

That's when I decided to do something for far longer than I'd got to today.

I gave her hug number three.

The Day I Bit Jamie

We were sitting on a bridge throwing bread crumbs for the ducks waddling below. It wasn't the same kind of friendship but whatever remained was still precious to me. Walker was swinging her legs in tune with the hum coming out of her mouth. The tone was soothing enough to calm my nerves.

Her rejection for the prom date was still a pain in the chest though.

"Romance, let's do something," she groaned bored.

"Let's see who can throw the piece at the longest distance?"

"You're so boring," she rolled her eyes at me.

"Oh am I Walker? Tell me what interests the great Jamie Summer Walker," I asked sarcastically giving her an intense look. I could make out she was nervous. She backed off as my gaze lingered. I brought my face closer to hers. Her breaths increased.

"You continuously try to establish the fact that I don't affect you and yet these symptoms. What do you want me to do Walker?" I asked her sadly.

"For one, get away from me," she whispered slowly.

"What if I answer the way you do . . . *no*."

"Then I'll do what you do . . . be irrational."

I looked at her confused just as her hands put pressure on my chest. I was unaware and thus couldn't stop the fall. I yelled as my body hit the water with a splash. The cold water was a relief from all the heat. Summer was laughing aloud. Thus, a plan to attain revenge was in order.

"Help," I yelled spluttering. My arms swayed up in mock action of drowning. "I can't swim."

"Oh God, are you serious? What should I do? What do I do?" she yelled back panicking. It had been a half a minute but there had been no response for aid from her side, so I went underwater.

"Romance . . . Rome . . . Jesus, where are you? Please answer me . . . Oh leave this . . ."

There was a splash of some more water and suddenly there she was underwater staring at me. Her face had pure panic written on it.

"I can't swim," she blabbered as we broke for air.

If there was an award for the stupidest decision to be handed out there was a perfect candidate available for it, not before thinking of a prize for the most failed plan of the decade though.

With as much strength as I could, I grabbed her arm and pushed her upward. Pulling my body close to hers, I wrapped my arm in such a way that I could drag her. With strong strokes, I managed to drag both of us towards the shore.

"What were you thinking?" I spat as soon as she was lying safely on the shore breathing heavily.

"What were you?"

"Clearly, I wasn't," I murmured. "I hope you learnt your lesson though."

"Life is like a river. You don't know how to swim and it keeps drowning you until some idiot who helped life gets his senses and saves you. Also, diving is like flying for mere seconds. It's the best feeling ever."

Silence followed. We kept staring at each other. Both of us were drenched. My eyes were fixated on to hers lest they gaze down and see something I should avoid gazing at no matter what may come. A minute later I was guffawing. She joined in.

"I have an idea," Walker said enthusiastically. The shore was an end to a slanted land full of green grass. It stretched on along with the stream. The sun rays bounced off the water making it sparkle. The ducks were waddling in peace now. The slope end from the other side had rows of trees popping up to make the place greener. This was a scene worth the time of a painter to be put down on an easel and hung around some rich man's home. Once I'd crossed Alan sitting some way up pretending to be a French artist painting a scene. He'd been trying to impress this man who used to come jogging every evening around this area. I'd slyly sneaked away in case he made me a part of such an atrocious plan. Reed was an amazing painter though. I had enough of his work in my room to prove the same.

"Let's go to your home and play some video."

I rolled my eyes. She was fascinated by racing. She'd played so much of it now that no one could defeat her. Once Parsley had randomly challenged her for he was the champ of racing at our place. Needless to say his loath for her had increased tenfold. It didn't help that every time he now played the high scores would all scream her name at his face. If anything it had made me more cautious for Walker when he was around.

Hence, we ended up sprawled on the couch with controls in our hands. I was on the edge of my seat praying to win. No matter how sexist it sounded I felt emasculated every time the screen on my side flashed you've lost.

It was the tenth time I had lost. In the process I'd slid down from the couch and was almost on the point of crying.

"I'm bored of winning easily," she grumbled.

Ouch, male ego terminated from this planet, time to pick another identity. She slid down next to me and was soon lying on the floor with her head on my lap.

Maybe the prospect of losing the eleventh time wouldn't be such a bad idea.

"I like to watch people sneeze especially babies. They look adorable. Your turn, say something I don't know about you."

I sighed. There we went being random Walker again. Sadly, I had no choice but to participate. All the times I'd denied her hadn't ended well what with dogs chasing, broken limbs and so on.

"I'm a cannibal. I eat the skin of my lips and like it . . . ouch what?"

"Don't be gross. Tell me something worth."

"That is worth knowing. What if I kiss you one day and eat your lips?" I chuckled as her delicate fists hit me again. "I uh secretly nanny this kid that lives down the lane. The parents call me when they go out. It's easy money plus the baby is a good kid. Therefore, it's a win situation for all." I blushed. Summer was staring at me in disbelief which quickly changed to the kind of joy I breathe every day for.

She pinched my cheeks cooing some obscene sentences I couldn't understand until the numbness on my face made me gently pull her into a hug.

"I like to eat an apple right before I'm about to shower," she said.

"I sleep with Turkey's feather under my pillow . . . no, please don't ask me a question."

She giggled nodding as if she completely knew the reason. No, I wasn't in irrevocable love with that monster. The feather had fallen on my bed in one of the days she'd climbed in through the window. It was the first time I'd actually woken up in the morning to see a beautiful scene of brown eyes and a cute little nose of freckles with those lips I wanted to devour calling out my name perfectly. The feather reminded me of how fresh she looked.

"My left hand moves when I write with my right. It's like that even when I scratch. I don't know what the science involved is but it's really weird."

"I have a birth mark on the side of my stomach shaped like a sun which reminds me of you."

For some reason I was spluttering things that were never meant to be said. She wasn't giving me information worth this value. There had been a day at the hospital when Reed had tried to pull up my shirt and show that to her but thankfully he'd tugged at the wrong side. I'd gone on about how it was a sign from the universe that Summer was in my life. Unfortunately that part of cheesiness I desired to keep low had slipped out today. Thankfully, Walker ignored it not before giving her feelings away by blushing though.

For some reason she was thinking on the same lines for the next thing threw me off balance.

"I smoke a cigarette now and then because like everyone I have complaints with life that don't get sorted. It's a weakness. I feel like a failure but there's nothing I can do. I sleep in a shack in the same area that institute is in. The reason all of my friends were glad to see me was due to me staying outside. If I go in there and get detected with nicotine in my system, I can get royally screwed. I don't have enough money to feed myself forget having a decent live in."

She was holding my hand. Somehow we had ended up walking. She kept talking about her times with smoking while my mind was making assumptions of its own.

One of the worst things to do when someone is talking is make assumptions instead of listen to their reasoning. Out of all the people in the world, I should understand that the most being on the brunt of every assumption possible. Hence, I quit thinking and starting hearing.

She had a point. I'd hardly seen Summer smile the way she should. It never reached her eyes. It never stretched her cheeks. One of the rare memories I could collect was when I'd given her the promise ring.

For the third time in such a short while I was back in that area. We had been walking for quite a while now. She finally pointed towards a sorry looking place that was covered with a cloth. There was hardly anything in it for it to be termed as shelter.

"Why didn't you tell me this before," I asked furiously. I pushed aside the flap in anger to enter the broken place. There was literally nothing but a piece of brick and a cloth strewn on the floor.

"I come back in the night. I'm not here mostly," she said blankly.

"Walker . . ."

"No! I don't want your pity. I haven't brought you here so that you can flaunt your riches on my face and ask me to stay with you because then Winter you don't know me at all."

Even though my heart was against it, her rationality was spot on. Silence preceded this for me to contemplate on things. She'd shown me the extremes of how much she trusted me. I had to do the same.

That's how any bond grew stronger. It was my turn.

"I'm Dark Joker. It isn't Hunter," I whispered. The words echoed in the silence and even after as she gasped slightly. "I didn't want you to have a different impression of me then what it was. Before I became a law-abiding, obsessed with perfection, idealistic man, I was someone who was the complete opposite of what I believe in now."

I had to tell her. There was no point in keeping this away as well.

"My dad use to smoke up a lot when we were kids. Work had him tied down really hard. He was stressing so much that drugs was the way out. The day mom had the accident and I was sick, she didn't get distracted because I ended up puking. The hospital had called her. They said dad had overdosed and was in a critical condition. In her hurry to reach him we had the accident."

Walker squeezed my hand hard. Silence followed as tears streamed down her face. She struggled to speak. I held on.

"Why don't you tell your brothers who blame you for all this?"

"You think I haven't," I said sadly. "Who are they going to believe? Their father who they idolized or me who is nothing but a sibling? We were all young to even make out rationality then. Forget them. I blamed myself for years until I made sense of the situation. It's not like I still don't but the feelings aren't that . . . strong. I can . . ."

She slung her arm around me. I snuggled closer. For once I wasn't worried that someone was watching me be weak and needy. The pain was clouding my vision so much that I resorted to my old habit of biting skin so that the physical pain didn't let me burst into tears. I was not fine with being an emotional wreck. The only thing I didn't realize was I bit Walker's hand instead.

"I'm sor- . . ."

"Will you go talk to them now?" she asked ignoring the teeth marks on her velvety skin. I clutched her hand in mine to smother out the wounds. Tears were slowly welling up in my eyes. I never planned on hurting her in anyway. That's the day I realized how unselfish a woman could be. I had bitten hard enough for blood to spill out but all she cared about was focusing on my misery and sorting it out. The books had told me how strong females could be but today I'd witnessed it well enough to always respect a woman in terms of strength or even unselfishness.

"No."

"Romance you don't deserve all this hate. Just go sort this out like a good kid."

"No," I said more adamantly.

"Will you stop being a guy and listen to me," Walker said exasperated.

"Will you stop being a girl and make this sound easy by just talking? They haven't cared for all these years to find out the truth and go around believing some bull like a seven year old kid causing an accident. You think they wouldn't have sense or what?"

She became silent.

"Look, it's not that I don't want things fixed but they have been like this for so long I won't cave in to something I didn't even commit. I don't deserve such a harsh treatment. They can punish me and get over with it. They can't torture me. I've learnt to not get affected by things. You make me weak. I can't make them my weakness too. I'll break."

"There was the ink that gained arrogance. He had just the pen as his family. He didn't get appreciated by the pen for he was different. The pen blamed him for every mishap written. Even a small mistake was a big deal. He was worthless, he was shunned. The pen didn't realize the importance he held until one day he fell. Out poured all of him, sucked off life while the pen waited to see the change of his destiny. It landed the pen in a scene much worse than imagined as he saw the last shred of hope turn into disaster. His body lay wasted in dustbin with no rope for escape. Then he knew how much the ink meant, and then he knew the importance of family. But like in most moral stories for lessons to be learnt properly . . . it was too late, it was too late."

She left.

Her words swam in my head. Although I got what she wanted to say, my stubbornness wasn't letting me win rationality. I fought for as long as I could but my heart was set on never sorting this problem out.

Selfish could be my new middle name for all I cared. If the ink had to perish along with the pen then so be it. It wasn't the ink's fault the pen didn't realize its importance.

It was later that I realized I wasn't the ink but the pen.
The Day I Ended up Fractured

All those times I blamed Walker for ending up in hospital was nothing compared to me being here. I despised looking at the white walls or the face of Hugh Clint for that matter. He'd been an inspiring man but frankly I was getting sick of the orders. Reed was sitting outside frantically apologizing through the glass mirror for what occurred. It wasn't anyone's fault. Yesterday hadn't been the best for. None of my brothers had cared to text and ask where I was.

The events relayed in my mind.

*   *   *

"That's not how you make cupcakes, love?"

"How do you then, lover?"

"Well for one, you do them separately."

They both giggled. I ignored them. The math class was really challenging today. My mind was set on finishing all the sums the teacher had handed out. It was good to feel that normal again. Then there were these fools chuckling while watching some video and giving their own subtitles.

Unlike my obsession with numbers the two of them despised anything revolving around the same.

"Do you even know what's it like to sleep on a cactus?"

"Yes, I've slept on the expanse of your chest. Do you shave off your hair or what?" Jamie giggled giving voice to some Spanish woman in the video.

"Ouch, your words sting me. I'll have my goat execute you."

"You goat to be kidding me!"

I'd given up on trying making sense of their stories a long while back. They'd gotten used to the ignorance and yet continued to annoy me incessantly. The worst part was yet to come. Every video didn't end before a very special appearance of your one and lonely Romance Winter.

This time I was made into the nosy neighbour.

"Why is everyone shouting here? I was curling my hair by rolling it in chopsticks."

The neighbour was Chinese. My friends were stereotypes.

"Do you want the goatess to shower you with brayssings?" Walker chortled.

The magnitude of lameness in them was increasing day by day. It wouldn't be late when I'd get so immersed in books that I'd forget their presence.

"Now I'll go and make my goatee," Walker said with a straight face. Reed started giggling.

Luke was having some trouble in school. Yesterday night he'd come home with a black eye. He'd figured everyone was asleep or out without noticing me in the kitchen. He'd slyly slunk in towards his room. In the morning there had been no sign of Luke. I'd hoped one of the others would notice and interrogate him.

Who could be troubling him so much?

As if to answer my question Luke came into view of our class window. From what I could see the whole corridor was deserted. He leaned against the lockers. There was a fresh cut on his lip. I clenched my fists in anger.

He gazed around casually but I could sense the nervousness till here. The teacher inside was droning about some trigonometry formula. For the first time, I couldn't concentrate on numbers.

A group of senior boys suddenly crowded around my little brother. They said some obscene things to him for his face paled. Before I could retaliate, Jeffery Smith had punched my brother's stomach. Luke doubled over coughing. I got up. That very moment Luke's eyes met mine. The pain clenched my heart. He looked so helpless. I was about to walk towards him when he shook his head. His demeanour changed back to the usual cool and he grinned at me. Just because I couldn't do anything sitting in the class, he flipped me the finger and walked away. I shook my head in disappointment. Some things never changed.

"Mr Winter, is there anything you have to say or are you so enthralled by the formula that I'm receiving a standing ovation?"

"Sorry Mr. Hart. I didn't mean to disrupt."

He waved his hand away.

Reed and Walker were staring at me for some explanation. I knew my face was scrunched up in fury. They both had analyzed me enough to decipher each emotion, unfortunately. I couldn't hold back the reality from any of them.

"It's nothing major. I'll handle it," I murmured.

They both shrugged and started the video again.

"Why can't you tell what went wrong Romance?" Reed said.

"How should have I know there is a certain time limit to keep the curlers in the hair? Now it looks like a cuckoo's nest."

"The trick is to remove the rod once it starts feeling too hot. Don't let the device get to you."

They both stared at me. I rolled my eyes and got up to move some other place. They both chuckled at me. I immersed myself into the sums so that there were no stray thoughts on either Walker or Luke.

*   *   *

They were standing there near the water fountain gazing at females with lucrative eyes. It was time for some action. It was exhausting just watching everything go down. I needed to do something to satiate the helplessness.

"What do we have here?"

They all stared at me as I stood with a stern expression glaring at them.

"Isn't he Grover's younger brother? Another Winter wants to get beaten up I think," Jeffery Smith smirked at me. The other boys agreed in mumbles.

"What do you want kid? I'll give you a deal. How about you get out of the way and I'll leave your bones intact?"

I kept my gaze steady.

"How about we make a deal," I said calmly. "You come alone and fight me. I'll leave the bones of your friends here intact?"

"Do you think you can outsmart me?" He threw me a lazy smile.

I shrugged. "There's nothing up in your brain to outsmart. I do however believe that I can beat you into a pulp."

The other seniors chuckled. That riled him up. His face stressed into angry expressions. I didn't move a step back. He literally had no power over my emotions. Right now the image of Luke groaning in pain was enough to make me fight the whole school if possible. I didn't even care if they suspended me today.

"Are you chickening out Smith? Scared that a junior will beat you up?"

"You're on."

He took off the school team jacket and stretched out his limbs. I dropped my bag. There was no need to show off. The adrenaline rushed in my muscles. He sprinted towards me and threw a punch. It had been so sudden that I wasn't aware. My reflexes however were still fast. I held his punch in my palm. He glared at me with fury. I gave him a calm nod.

"You think you can beat me?" He pulled away his hand.

"I know I can beat you."

He threw a couple of punches. I deflected them easily. He was an amateur at this. I wanted to laugh at the expressions that were forming on his face.

"Are you done?" I asked coolly.

He landed a kick on my side.

"I guess not."

He'd tried so much that he was huffing with loss of energy now. I didn't even feel an ounce of weariness.

"I think it's my time to show now?" He looked at me in confusion. It took three punches and two kicks to land him a corner crouching in pain. I walked towards him and bent down.

"Next time you try to hit one of my brothers, just remember me. You'll learn to be a compassionate human."

I gazed at my masterpiece for the last time, satisfied. His nose was bleeding. There were bruises already forming on the face. He was clutching his stomach where one of my kicks had laid its impact.

I'd planned it out well. It was after school. I'd made sure no one was around to witness any of this. It wouldn't do well on my clean reputation. Knowing Smith he wouldn't blabber about his defeat nor would his croons unless they wanted out from his group.

"Where were you?" Grover growled. I placed my hands into my pockets. He wouldn't appreciate my red knuckles. "I should have left a long while."

I got inside the jeep without a word.

"Crystal had been looking for you," Parsley told Grover.

They started their usual banter about school. Luke and I stared out lost in our own thoughts.

"Did you see the Smith kid come out some time back?"

Suddenly the air behind was electric. Both of us were frowning at the back of the front seats trying to hide our own secrets.

"Yeah, what happened to him? He looked so beaten up," Parsley replied.

"He was calling for it. If someone hadn't wounded him like that I was right on the edge off. He was getting on my nerves with that jerk attitude."

"Do you know who did it to him?"

"I've been with you inside the jeep all the while. Of course I don't know. Maybe this Romance would know."

This Romance was quite an appropriate way to be addressed after a good fight.

"No, I didn't see anything," I mumbled.

They started talking about some other random things. I could feel Luke's eyes on me. I sighed and turned towards him. We stared at each other for a while. His expressions changed until he looked at me confused. His frown turned neutral. He gave me a curt nod with a little smile.

That was as good as thanks for me.

* * *

I woke up in the evening with my phone ringing loudly. My vision was blurred so I couldn't make out who the caller was.

"Romance," Reed yelled on the phone. "You have to come here as soon as possible. Jamie is in pain . . ."

The world suddenly way clearer than ever. My senses were on high alert. The panic in Reed's voice was making me rattled.

"What's wrong will you tell me?"

"She's having contractions I think? I don't know. You have to get here as soon as possible. Maybe I should . . ."

I cut the call.

The room was steaming hot. I'd forgotten to switch on the fan in my hurry to nap. Last night had been tough to get some sleep. I kept thinking off what Walker had told me yesterday. I should go talk to my brothers. It wouldn't do any of us any good though. It was better if I carried on like today.

Within the next ten minutes I was ready and running outside towards Alan's home. There was no time to ask for a ride or pick up my skateboard.

The moment I was at his door I banged on it like a maniac. No one was opening the door, I lost patience.

I backed off and looked towards Reed's window. No amount of calling out heeded result. I decided to climb with the help of the pipe.

"What are you doing?" Jamie's face appeared on the window.

Her sudden appearance freaked me out. I'd been jumping on the pipe in my hurry and suddenly hearing her voice made me lose my balance. I'd managed three fourth of the climb so the impact of falling down was really hard. Unluckily I fell on my head which blurred out the world in seconds. The last thing I saw was Reed's panicked face before I blacked out.

*   *   *

"Jamie can you keep a secret?"

"What is it?" She asked me curiously.

"You have to know if I tell you this my life could be at risk. It's important this stays between us."

She gave me a curt nod. Even if those almond shaped eyes had gazed at me for mere three seconds, the words would have spilled out. There was that blind faith I had on her which beckoned trouble all the time.

I'd gained consciousness sometime back. Walker and Reed had run towards me like I'd been dying or something. They cried about some prank and how sorry they were. My head was aching so I waved them away. There was no use being mad at them. It was a friendly prank. They didn't expect me to panic so much. Lately I'd been in too much of a care mode so everything was going overboard. The doctors had been running around the whole day. Just a few minutes back the nurse had given me some medicine saying that the dizziness would reduce.

"These people here in this white institution deal with drugs. I want you to secretly go and inform the police. I love all this but even so much of cleanliness while giving such things seem suspicious."

Her giggles made me smile at her. "All this laughing is cute Jamie but you need to report them though okay?"

A nod satisfied one part of the hunger. The problem was I'd been dying to spill things. The hospital seemed woozy. That's what I had meant to call it but my world was a little slow. Everything seemed funny.

"Jamal isn't doing well. His body has started rejecting food now. I'm sad he can't do the jungle rumble now."

Her hand was caressing mine slowly. There were tears falling down from the visage. I leaned forward and kissed them away.

The events of a while back were a blur. In fact lately life had been a big blot of doubt. I needed to start some sort of medication just so memories retained. Times like these required attention on bifurcating actions so that it never happened again.

Every time my fingers would fidget with the tubes Walker would handle the situation.

"Listen your right hand is fractured. It's minor so the plaster will be off in fifteen days. The medicine is for your head okay? You hit it really hard. I didn't know the dose was so strong . . ."

I nodded at her seriously. My index finger automatically came in contact with her cheek skin and traced it as if the line was a brook bubbling away to glory. The warmth spread to my heart. What was the magic of that physical touch from someone you loved that made things ten times better?

What if Grover or Parsley or even Luke had been around as well? Wouldn't it be much easier to deal with situations if they backed me up like I did to them sometimes? There wasn't even a message asking where I was from either. Death could have snatched me in its jaws but they wouldn't give a damn.

It was tiresome being the good guy.

"Did you know I love my brothers?"

"Yes, of course the awareness is there. You have their backs most of the time."

I nodded frantically.

"There's a cliff some distance away. Romance is falling from it but no one saves him. Everyone stands back and watches as he falls into his doom. Luke even hides a scoff. Jamie is relieved like a whole burden has been eradicated. Parsley moves towards the . . ."

"Romance can you try sleep please? These medicines aren't treating you well."

"You know I earn money for them? It's not easy working all night. Then they call me a free loader. I earn and transfer to their accounts. The amount of strings I've had to pull for that one."

She was looking at me with sudden interest now. The tension was electric in the air. There was a frown which beckoned to be straightened. There shouldn't be any problem with such smooth features. Creases were meant for old gits like me. We'd been flowing like rivers since forever. These brooks like Jamie had a lot to learn. Instead of wanting to flow straight all the time, they should take curves."

"What are you talking about? You work in the night?"

"Yes, how else do you think there's an account from which mother gives money to everyone?"

"I don't understand?"

"Oh you are so cute Jamie . . . there's this blog work I do. It gives me enough earn for now. The boxing matches also provide me well at times but you know about that already."

"You mean you earn money already?"

I nodded.

"Which site is this?"

Her eyes were staring into mine with ultimate focus. I smiled as her lips moved. What would it take to kiss them all I wanted, whenever I wanted to? The restrictions were really annoying now.

"What are you doing?" she asked repulsed. Her fingers were touching her lips. Had I tried to do something silly? By the way my lips were tingling, I dreaded the worse.

"I'm sorry, I can't make sense," I whispered trying to shake my head.

"It's alright Romance. You didn't do anything wrong. I just got shocked."

The sleep was starting to fill my head. I shook my head again trying to clear everything. There were black spots everywhere. The nurse had probably given me poison for being so rude the whole time.

"I think you should sleep. I'll come back later."

"Hey Walker, don't tell anyone whatever I've told you. I don't remember what I am blabbering."

"Your secrets are always safe with me Winter. Trust me."

Your name will always be safely locked in my heart.

The Day I Ate Half of Jamie's Toblerone

Someone screamed loudly. I got up clutching my phone as if it was a gun. I yelled for whoever it was to put their hands up lest I end up in prison for murdering in defence.

"I've got it Romance. I finally have it."

"What a baby?" I asked stupidly. "Shouldn't you be at the hospital then?"

I was getting concerned now.

"What?" she giggled.

As the words that I'd spoken sunk in I asked what indeed was I asking. The safest way out was to blame lack of sleep. Walker had usually made it a point to wake me up as early as a cock rose to cackle. Even though I slept at dot eleven just to manage a good amount of rest, her insistence on being abnormal had pushed the time to ten. Walker aided the process by exhausting me in all ways during the day.

"What did you get?"

"Look," she said excited. "It's a pimple."

285

I couldn't help but burst out laughing at that. Memories of a few weeks back flooded in.

"What are you looking at?" I asked Walker. It had been around fifteen minutes since she'd been staring at the mirror. With my stalker feelings on high alert, I had been gazing at her shamelessly.

"Why don't I have a pimple?"

"Err, what?" I asked her confused for I thought I hadn't heard her properly.

"Pimples, where are the pimples?"

Now normal girls would be crying aloud in misery about how disfiguringly gross their faces seemed after those monsters popped out. They would make a huge scene nothing that Shakespeare could even think the likes off.

Then there was Walker.

"Why would you want one?" I asked her ridiculously.

"My skin is too perfect. I want to feel normal.

"Okay," I said carefully. This was a dicey situation. I wasn't sure if Walker was genuinely upset or there was an underlying motive to it. I didn't want to pity and end up with bruises as well. There was only one decision that looked plausible at the moment. I turned around and went back to sleep.

Soon, she jumped on me.

"Uff, what do you want woman."

"I want . . . to be a normal human."

"Go wish on a wishing star Pinocchio," I chuckled at my own joke.

"I'm way too perfect. I need some imperfections."

"I love the modesty Walker."

My mind was distracted from sympathizing with her as she was sitting on my stomach. The position felt so intimate that I was worried I'd pull her down for a kiss any moment. She looked adorable trying to pout for me to comfort her in this dire situation of need

Thankfully the situation was 'dire' for she rushed back to check whether all the crying had worked.

There she was jumping around as if someone had awarded her the Oscar. I rolled my eyes. She did a weird dance which despite my horror at the show had me laughing. I didn't realize the attention would pull me to be a part of the act.

"It all worked. I didn't drink lots of water, stressed about everything in the world, walked around in woollens to feel the summer heat and ate junk," she exclaimed excitedly.

What had this woman even gone through? I gave her a look of mild horror. If only scientists decided to work on the level of craziness possible in humans, she'd make a perfect sample to experiment on. I took off my jacket. There was something about the comfort it's confinement had that always tempted me to have it on. Walker despised the habit. All this heat talk was fidgeting with my system though.

"How does Marley sound to you?"

"Alright," I played on with no intention of finding out more appalling information.

"I'll call you Marley then," she squealed petting the pimple. "No one will ever pop you Marl. Don't worry you'll never leave my face."

I looked at her scandalized. I thought she was joking but then she actually went towards the mirror and started fidgeting with her skin. Somehow I managed to run away. The disgust of the germs I'd have to endure had me fleeing like Luke from injections.

What if she made me touch Marley? Why was I calling it by name? I rushed to the bathroom to puke.

"Oh God, I'm sorry," I yelled shutting the door.

Maybe watching your elder brother make out with his girlfriend's hand in his pants was what should have scared me . . .

Walker still won the race though.

Before Parse could come out to beat me up, I started walking out of the mad hole. My phone vibrated. There was a reminder. How could this day slip out of my mind? It had been ages since I'd been planning everything. It was time to implement the action . . .

*   *   *

"What in the name of good lord are you fools doing here?" Walker asked astonished. She was clutching her chest.

"Ola amigo," Shelter smirked. "We decided to travel the Earth finally. As aliens, it is an honour to meet one among us who has achieved such closeness to an earthling. Pleasure my lady."

Josh and I started chuckling as he bent low in mock respect.

"What are you doing here idiot?" she asked pausing at each word and smacking his head in the silence.

"I might have a haemorrhage. I told you people we shouldn't have come to meet the Undertaker," Shelter shrieked.

"Josh," Walker turned to him. He stopped chuckling at once.

"Don't worry Jams, we've made sure the plan is foolproof. We spoke to Willow. The girls stayed back just in case *Parents* decide to have a surprise visit. Poppy was losing her head though so . . ."

"Wazz happenin bros?"

All the boys rolled their eyes. We had to endure Poppy the whole way trying to talk in what she called a '*cool*' language. She said she'd seen enough movies to know how the teenagers behaved in America. Hence, clad in a hoodie with everything baggy, she'd been rapping the whole way back. More than anyone, she was happy to be outside.

"Are you sure?" Walker asked glaring. "The amount of trouble you'll be in is unimaginable. You do know how bad it can go. Remember Tin . . ."

For a second a look of panic crossed on each face. I opened my mouth to ask but kept it shut. There was no point intruding.

"We know Jams. I just . . . we miss you," Joshua said sadly. "I'd be Tin a hundred times just because I get to meet you."

"Me as well," Poppy agreed slinging her arm around Walker.

"A man who doesn't stand by comrades is a man said no one ever. United like the river to ocean I'll be with you fair lady."

Yulius sure knew how to make situations grave. Shelter was biting his lower lip so he wouldn't burst out laughing. All of us were looking at him.

"Look, I wouldn't give my life and all now. That is too much. Sure, I'd peek out of the window to see you if it comes to that. I have a beautiful life to fulfil. Imagine the amount of hotness girls would be missing if I go away . . . ouch, I love you Jams . . . ouch, ow not there I'm delic- ow!"

She was hugging him hard. Shelter petted her back. He snuggled his face into her hair and whispered in her ears. I smiled and walked off to give them some privacy. We had to leave in an hour. There was no way I would risk their lives from what Tin's story seemed, I was concerned. Just for safety, I kept a reminder.

I watched some random football match for a while. Luke was sitting next to me munching on chips. Neither of us said a word to each other.

"Romance . . . Romance, please get up." Someone was shaking me. I swat their hand out of the way and snuggled closer. I could smell a familiar scent.

"They need to reach back soon . . . please get up." The hissing voice finally made sense. Somebody fell from the couch as I got up like lightening. Luke was sitting rubbing his head in sleep. He groaned and went back to sleep. I'd been hugging my brother. No wonder the smell had been known.

"Right, I'll drop them off and come," I said groggily. They were waiting outside having a heavy discussion about why burger was more beneficial than pea soup. I chuckled as none of them were making sense anymore.

"They all pulled up their hoods as we entered the area. We'd made sure no one would recognize them. There had been a worry with the *Parents* who might have sighted them while we were walking back but that we'd find later. Walker had sent Turkey along so that Shelter could send back in an hour or so if things were fine.

"Listen . . ."

I stopped in my tracks. We were standing at the back door. Willow was waving everyone in. Shelter and I stayed back.

"Jamie is a messed up kid. She's not going to let you see anything. You should know that she really cares for you. I'm glad you're in her life buddy. She needed someone like you to help her out through everything. We've just been brought up in a way that normal things seem abnormal to us. There are some ideals we all believe in. It's sad at times. However, I appreciate your care for her," he said nodding his head with gratefulness.

"I promise I'll be her ribcage."

"Now you're being dramatic," he smirked before ruffling my hair in farewell. "Oh and lover boy . . . don't try breaking her heart because I'll break your ribcage then. See you soon!"

The whole way back all I could think of was how much the absence of these people from Walker's life should be affecting her. The amazing thing about that woman was that she didn't let anything affecting her let be a burden on others. She hardly ever let me see how sad she was. I was inspired by her strength yet again. With determination of taking her out for ice cream I stepped inside the house.

"Hey," someone whistled at me. I groaned. I knew this was going to happen but this soon?

"I swear I won't tell anyone."

"I don't care even if you do," Parsley rolled his eyes at me. "You think I'd stop you from bragging about my conquests? I wanted to warn you Kitty."

I stared at him with narrowed eyes. There was something dicey about the way his tone was. It gave me goose bumps.

A warning from Parsley could as well be a death note from Satan.

"I know everything now. You better watch your every step or believe me I will rat out to the authorities. There'll be trouble you'd never see the likes off."

How could he have possibly found out about the institution was beyond me. From here I had to approach cautiously lest I trigger the alarm.

"What are you saying?"

"Just tell that Walker girl of yours to be careful. She's already hit all my nerves. Just because I haven't done anything yet doesn't mean I can't ruin her life. One hit and she'll be out of that place."

"What do you mean?"

"Oh don't act so innocent! Why do you think she doesn't go back over there? They made a mistake of letting her attend school. She's discovered there's more to life. That's where she belongs."

We had to be careful from now on. Parsley knew way more than he should and that already meant a lot of trouble. I took off my hoodie. Why was it so hot? The sweat was icky and gross. I needed a shower. Would anyone find out if I slyly poisoned Parsley? I mean how bad could a prison life be? It wouldn't be the first time I'd end there anyways.

"I can't tell you how much I love you."

Someone was hugging my body tightly. The strawberry scent of hers was driving me wild. Before I could push her away to a safe distance, her lips were on mine. Her fingers were entwining in my hairs applying pressure so that face could bend down for her reach. She was tiptoeing as well which pushed our bodies precariously together. I could feel her heartbeat racing like a formula car. Suddenly, her tongue was in my mouth and that's where I drew the line. My strength was coming back after all this craziness. I pushed her away.

"We're not supposed to be doing this," I scowled at her.

She stared at me for quite a while as I moved around the room fixing things. Anger waves were making their way over my body. It took all the will power to not start shattering things around. In my peripheral vision I could see Walker sitting on my bed hugging that vile teddy bear.

"Mum, what are you cooking?"

I came in my striped night suit dragging a teddy bear along. Even though my teacher at school had said big boys don't roam with such teddies I couldn't let go of the one mum gave. The sole reason it belonged to her.

"Stop playing games with me Walker. I am not someone you can mess around with," I stressed without looking at her in case I went weak again. There were some limits that were meant to be set and not crossed for the benefit of both parties.

"I couldn't believe when you said you're Dark Joker but it makes sense now."

I took off my shirt ignoring her. The heat was really getting to me. It was making me dizzy. There had been a lot of stress these past few hours. All that was required was a cold shower.

"Is that a *J* engraved on your chest?"

Crap

My gaze fixed on hers in the mirror. She was frowning at the initial as if coming across something like that for the first time.

"Romance, why is there a *J* on your chest?"

"Why don't you tell me if you're that smart Walker?"

The silence was deafening. For once I didn't care.

"Okay, I'm sorry."

I sighed. That tone was defeating the purpose of being mad. What she needed to understand was every time things couldn't be carried out the way she wanted. I was a human as well. For once maybe she should see things through my side of view. However when a woman gets that sad voice which can't be left until it's switched to original, the mind remains a mess.

"Hey," I said kindly. I plonked down beside her. "This was for Jasmine."

She nodded sadly. I patted her head.

"Why did you decide to become Dark Joker?"

I was grateful there weren't any nagging questions revolving around an old dead lover therefore answering about another tabooed topic didn't seem so tough.

"After Jas uh . . . well I didn't really know how to channelize my anger. Thus, I went into narcotics and situations which landed me in trouble. Obviously my real identity would let me create havoc for a limited amount but if I put on a mask people would recognize less. The adrenaline had become like a drug. I did things I'm not proud off. I won't deny that some of them were worth it all though. The smiles I gained are much more than tears shed."

My voice was dipping as memories were flooding my head. The regrets were there which no matter what wouldn't diminish. I had to live through the guilt of causing hurt to so many nevertheless.

"I thought you were really cool. In that lovely home of mine, you were a ray of hope for humanity."

And just like that everything was fixed.

I patted her head again. "Thanks."

"I'm very sad."

"Why?" I chuckled.

"Marley popped already."

I don't know what she did with her words but they always managed to make my day brighter. I walked up to my drawer and took out a new bar of toblerone.

"Here," I handed out to her.

Immediately her face lit up. She took hold of one end but I didn't let go. I snatched the chocolate back and broke it in half.

"Hey," Walker grumbled.

"Revenge is a dish best served cold darling," I winked walking towards the washroom. My face slammed against the closed door.

"So is the aftermath Winter, so is the aftermath."

The Day I Was
Difficult To Please

She'd caught me again.

This time it wasn't in the best of places or with the right people for me to make excuses. The worst part was she gave me a look and walked away. That one look of judgement was enough to twist life into horror.

It was with extreme despondence that I admitted to smoking being the escape from all the troubles. It had taken quite a while to not crave that hit of serenity. Lately, the lack of peace was driving me insane. I didn't want to start being lunatic enough to be sent back to those dark days.

Everything sounded so dramatic. Why was I picturing my life as a sad deal when so many were in far worse trouble?

"Walker," I yelled as I caught up to her. "I can explain."

"Why don't you get that stench off yourself first?"

My hand was clutching on her shoulder lest she walked away. Her brown eyes were scrutinizing mine with as much accusation as possible. I cringed.

"Look, I really . . ."

"Everyone deals with their emotions. I thought you're brave enough to handle as well. Clearly, I was wrong."

"You don't understand the gravity. If I don't calm myself I'd go around doing stuff that would be . . ."

"That in itself is a whole lot of bull. Romance for God's sake you're not a loser who needs intoxications to make decisions to live by. What stuff will you do eh? You're talking as if you'd murder someone."

"If Perry comes in my way - sure," I muttered under my breath.

The brown orbs disappeared from their position for a while. That second was enough to break the concentration I'd been gathering to tell her everything. It was true. I was a coward when it came to dealing with some things. Love was one of them.

"You know what? Leave all of this. Do whatever the hell you want. Go smoke, get cancer for all I care go right ahead and die. I won't even be surprised if you end up in therapy. Seeing the way you have been, I won't be astonished if you already have anyways."

It wasn't the words that hit me hard but what she did next. She fumbled with her fingers while saying all that. The tone of fury kept rising until the words were coming out in bunches due to all the messing around with her fingers. Finally, she threw the ring at my face and started walking away.

The promise ring . . .

For some reason my anger stayed low. I started finding the situation darkly humorous which was never good. It was probably the term 'therapy'. That one word had the capability of wiping off any emotion that should be expressed.

"I went cuckoo," I said laughing emotionlessly.

"You mean you were actually sent for therapy?" Walker asked, ironically with disbelief. She looked at me like a person who didn't believe in life anymore.

I couldn't help chuckle.

"You can't help a man who falls in love unless you're a professional psychiatrist apparently," I said scornfully.

"What are you talking about?"

"Jasmine..."

They were all sitting in a circle. I rolled my eyes. My fingers were twitching again. They'd reduced from the time I'd come though. It had been two weeks of hell now. I was close to a breaking point. Instead of wanting to make me love a new life, these people were forcing suicidal thoughts into my head. There wasn't a day I searched around for something to kill myself with. Apparently, they had enough lunatics akin me to be clever enough to secure the pace off pointy things.

"Now Rick, how do you feel about drugs again?"

I sighed. I was the latest specimen they were treating their bull on. All these human guinea pigs had been accustomed to replying as they wanted. I prayed the next month would end soon and I'd be released before it was too late.

"I gave up on drugs quite a while back. They are bad for health. They harm the people around. I don't know if I am high still. I had a long drag before I got admitted."

He had been in this hole for ten years. I knew the electric shocks had demented his brain. Sometimes when I demanded for stuff they sent me through the pain as well. There was nothing I would want in this world if I had to go through all that.

"That's beautiful," the idiot sitting on the chair assured Rick. I was pretty sure he was entertaining the man so that he could scoot off to home early.

Home

I wondered what that was like anymore.

"Now Romance . . ."

"It's Xerkis," I snapped. I despised Romance. There was nothing in it that represented me. It brought memories I wanted to bury deep where they couldn't be extracted out.

"Yes dear. So Romance, what are your thoughts on this so called escapes from life?"

That it's the best way to be rather than hurt people. Maybe even you should try some considering how boring your life seems put together with how annoying you make life living. The world would do a lot well if you went into those things. Images of him jumping on his own chair as if he was flying on some clouds made me chuckle.

"Would you like to share some of that humour?"

"Fuck off!"

Everyone gasped around me. These people were very strict with insults. They let us pass in the beginning but as the time passed by the punishments got strict.

This wasn't all therapy. They considered us mad humans with no feelings.

"Off to the E-room."

My heart stopped. There could be some way to repent. I'd do anything to escape that. Before I could react though, the officials came with a stretcher.

Not the electric shocks, just not the electric shocks.

*　　*　　*

I was shivering.

"Jas, come back," I sobbed. It had been a week since I'd remembered her. This afternoon had been so traumatic that all I needed was someone I knew to hug me.

"I'm right here with you my baby."

I looked up so fast that my neck strained. There she stood looking as perfect as she'd always been. Her blond hair waving gently as the black eyes gave me a loving look. She sat beside me as her warmth engulfed my cold.

"Are you real?" I whispered when my trance broke.

"Why don't you touch and see?"

There was not a bit of that skin that could have been surreal. The velvet feel brought tears into my eyes. The water falling from her eyes traced my scars as if healing them mentally.

"What have you gotten yourself into?" she murmured sadly. "What have I gotten you into?"

It wasn't just her but a million other reasons. Something held me back from explaining though. It was enough that her head fit in the crook of my neck perfectly. I could feel her brittle body next to mine.

"Have you ceased eating again?" I asked concerned. The ribs were well hidden behind the baggy tee-shirt. That didn't stop them from being traceable. Constantly I'd been going through emotions trying to handle her anorexia, hoping she'd get sense in that pretty head. It never worked no matter how much the love.

"Shh," her voice caressed my panic. "It'll all be fine."

I stayed silent.

*　　*　　*

"*He's doing well. There hasn't been any complaints on food, any protests, in fact we haven't punished in a month now. He's lost weight and colour though. Also, he's become quite mute for some reason. There are a couple of other things I'll discuss with you tomorrow when you come to collect him.*"

This was music to my ears.

"*Pain is like sunset. It is an essential part of life but it drowns into the ocean of hope. It'll come every day in some form whether orange or pink or even neutral. Remember Romance, no matter what don't let your ocean dry out.*"

I pulled her close to me. "*As long as you're with me there's nothing that will go wrong love.*"

"*Then we might be as well be together forever.*"

She was my sunset.

Walker was looking at me with mixed expressions.

"They diagnosed me with having hallucinations. Apparently, my only coping mechanism had been to imagine the problem itself as a solution. The Kitty these idiots keep teasing me with is just that. She's a mere illusion."

The tone of void emotions was troubling Jamie. No matter how much I tried I couldn't let go of the fact that she'd upset me. The only way was to be indifferent. Share situations that were intense as if they didn't affect me anymore. Being weak was a good thing, not for me. It wasn't easy to let go all the time.

"She hasn't disappeared yet. I realized she wasn't real a long time back. Whenever I am troubled though, she returns. The ghost stays around becoming more and more of my consciousness than how she was. Now, that Kitty is probably whatever perfection I keep demanding in life."

"Do you still love her?"

"No, how can I? She's gone. It tells me one thing though that I didn't truly love. Her death shouldn't mean that I cease the emotion nor does it mean that I should be correcting her imperfections. Those are the things you initially fall for anyways because they make a human exactly that . . . a human."

"How did she pass away?"

"Anorexia finally took the better of her. It had become such a bad obsession that no amount of cajoling could get her out of the fact that she was fat. Every five minutes I would tell her how pretty she was but to what avail was it for deaf ears? All the days seemed like a countdown. It was a nightmare watching her lose weight until her body gave up. I couldn't force food down her throat. I should have done more. I could have saved her."

Jamie touched my shoulder. I pushed her hand away.

"So if you don't care to whatever happens to I then so be it. I will, however always give a damn for you."

"Romance, I'm sorry I didn't . . ."

I walked away.

That night was full of twists and turns. The memories of the asylum were driving me mad. I ran downstairs to have some milk and cookies.

"Can't sleep?"

That was perfectly what I needed right now.

"How much will you ignore me Kitty," he chuckled.

I held the glass together. Not today, please not today.

"Whatever. There's Luke's football match tomorrow. He might not say it but it would be great if you drop by."

"What?" I asked surprised. "You want me there?"

He rolled his eyes at me.

They probably had planned to hit the ball at my head. For all I cared he could take a knife and stab me right now. The cold milk helped reduced the tension. Mom always chucked it at me whenever I threw tantrums. She'd throw in cookies for free sugar as she called it. Instantly, the anger would dissipate.

I was staring outside letting the cool wind evaporate the sweat when I caught a glance of the all familiar back. What had been she doing here this late?

*   *   *

"Ouch . . . stop it! I swear Turkey I'll strangle you one day."

As usual his royal highness was there to wake me up for school. Maybe instead of alarms people should buy pigeons. If you don't comply, you can't put them to snooze or throw anything at them accurately. They'll ultimately poop on you. Best way to wake up.

"It's Sunday for god sake, leave me alone," I yelled pulling the blanket over my head.

He pulled the cover off.

"What the hell is your problem you stupid bird." I got up giving it a crazed look. Taking hold of my slipper, I started running behind with Turkey flying all around. I chased the bird all over the room. I couldn't even hurt a feather.

"No, that's against the rules; you can't poop on me twice."

He sat on my other shoulder cooing happily. That's when I noticed the note tied to its leg. The temptation to crumple the paper and throw it away was much higher than curiosity to read it. However for her sake I took the paper.

'Blue is Romance, Jamie is yellow,
Please, Please be mellow,
Look inside the sheet of your pillow.'

She couldn't get more childish then this. The claws gently poking my skin were hint enough that I had no choice but to do as she had wished.

After molesting the pillow I finally achieved the second piece of paper.

'Butterflies red, blue, green look cool,
Not in my stomach you fool,
First time I saw you drool.'

This was brilliant! A treasure hunt! Of course, Jamie Summer Walker didn't believe I had a life. This was an easy one. The first time I'd seen her was at school. Did she expect me to search the whole institute for one bloody piece of paper? That wasn't enough. An orange was lying on the side table. How did she know I loved oranges? Then I remembered telling her yesterday about the orange fest we use to have at home with all the brothers competing to win the ultimate prize – a whole box of oranges. It was lame but it was an archaic family tradition.

I brushed my teeth furiously.

"Coo!"

"Oh shush your owner. It isn't like she didn't do anything."

"Coo!"

"Yeah, yeah fine. I'm going. Don't worry. *I won't do anything to hurt your master.*"

Then Turkey did something that I never expected. He flew towards my shoulder, ruffled his wings and then caressed his head against my cheek as if showing affection.

Maybe the bird wasn't all that bad.

Thirty minutes later I was scratching my head as to where the paper could be. Turkey was flying above not giving a damn about the world. Sometimes, I loved that bird.

Where would Walker's stubborn head hide the clue? That's what she must have been doing in my room yesterday that sly creature. The only thing I could do standing was look around while whirring my mind back to the first day. Where had I first seen her?

It struck me. The Math class where we had fought for the seat I had claimed as mine. I sprinted towards the spot. Sure enough a paper was stuck under the desk. A Toblerone bar was lying on top of the table.

"That doesn't help your case Walker," I scowled at the sweet weakness imagining it to be her face. The temptations just never left me once I became addicted.

'Biology was lose, Chemistry funny,
Why still so gloomy?
Take a happy pill from Old Amy...'

I sighed. This was getting more time consuming. Even if fun was present, I couldn't push myself to appreciate her effort. It wasn't the same as digging out the past just to satisfy someone else's accusations.

"C'mon Turkey, We have a long way to walk."

Amy hadn't changed. She swung the door open with a grump and the next thing I knew I was in a tight grip. The only flaw with the plan was where she'd sent me.

"How have you been honey?"

"I've been good."

It was so easy to lie to strangers.

"And how much have you been troubling my little princess?"

It was even easier to get away with lying. The real answer would have earned house arrest probably. Old Amy was one character I didn't want to be on the wrong side off.

"All well. She's been happy."

Her face was getting blotched. I felt scared.

"I'll give you a thrashing . . . I'm joking ha, here you go son."

She handed me the next clue. Her hand was five inches off the target. That's when I looked carefully. The woman was high for life. It was a good opportunity.

"Hey Amy, can I look around. I might have left my watch in somewhere."

"Whenever you are down-y, howl out for Amy!"

I took that as a positive consent and walked in.

'Happy, happy as a lark,
Whether the emotions light or dark,
All you got to do is visit the park'

It would take a fool not to realize she was taking me to all the places we'd haunted, all the venues that held precious memories. I wanted to puke at the nonsense. I still didn't want to appreciate all the effort she was making me put.

"Oh also here," Amy waddled towards me as I was leaving. She handed out an apple pie.

"It's clean," she chuckled at my accusatory glance.

So with every place I was given something I liked as well? Wow, so creative.

The park was deserted. I sat down on the swing to ponder on things. Clearly, I wasn't in a hurry to finish this never ending hunt. Was Walker even worth everything? What if I broke down like when Jasmine had left? I couldn't handle another period of depression.

Maybe I should walk away.

It will make things a lot easier.

"Elf, oh my god . . . you're actually here."

I gazed at the little toddler running towards me. Despite my want to frown, a smile spread across my face. Children were gift from God after all.

"She said you won't. She was crying. I said of course he's elf. You've been a good girl, he'll come. You came. She is a good girl."

"She sure is," I replied smiling.

"Here," he said extending both his hand. One hand held the next clue, the other a little picture of both of us laughing. I didn't know where it was taken or when. It was beautiful.

No matter how far I walk away I would run back at triple speed the moment she called back.

"Have I been a good boy?"

The little boy looked down shyly. I chuckled.

"Yes, Santa is really proud of you kid. You shouldn't worry at all. Here, for now go have some ice cream from me okay?"

"Oh you're the best Elf," he yelled jovially. His little body hugged me. It topped the list of best feeling after everything revolving around Walker.

"You're my hero."

Just like that I was Dark Joker again but without the mask or the unnecessary nonsense.

> *'Home is where the heart stays,*
> *Mine belonging to you love lays,*
> *Some institution with my sadness pays.'*

Ah! That place again. The only thing that would make me go to that hateful hole was her friends. Somehow, they'd become close to me especially Shelter. I'd sneaked in a phone for him. He made calls occasionally for the benefit of Walker. It was one of the things she looked forward to. After her usual *how are you* she would ask if Shelter called.

"I was expecting you."

"What the hell?" I jumped back clutching my chest. "Can you be less creepy man?"

"You don't know about me yet Romance. I might be eating human flesh."

"Sure, I could be Batman."

"Wasn't Dark Joker a rip off?"

We both laughed. Reed was an amazing best friend but with him sometimes things took a well feminine side. I loved him to bits but hanging out with Shelter brought the lunacy I'd been missing in life.

"How are you faring fair sailor?"

I appreciated the fact that he didn't ask about her first.

"Better," I smiled.

"Well, you look handsomer. Have you been having sex?"

"Just because you don't get action doesn't mean I won't either," I smirked.

"Touché," he grinned at me. "Jamie came crying over here yesterday. She scared me out of my wits. How could one manage to climb all the way up to third floor and remember my window is a wonder? She explained everything. Thank God that woman came here. If she'd roamed the bloody city crying I would have killed her."

"Not me?"

"It wasn't your fault mate."

That's why this guy was an amazing human.

"Here then."

I took hold of the next clue and a book. *'I never promised you a Rose Garden'* had been one of the books on my to-be read list. I'd kept it aside for they were never in stock. It was a miracle she'd found this copy. I stared at it with joy surging. I started appreciating a little whatever she'd done the whole night for me.

> *'Come back where you belong sailor,*
> *Home abound where you'll surrender,*
> *Forgive me finally as a failure.'*

Who could explain to her how far away from a failure she was? I needed to go back to my room. There was no brainer in this one at all.

Turkey was sitting on my shoulder. He was tired as well. The sun was setting now. I felt a cool breeze wash away the exhaustion. I waved farewell to Shelter promising to tell him what happened ahead. He gave me a glorious smile and patted my back. There was no sign of sadness in that man. He was an inspiration.

"Oh Joshua also sends his love. He had some work so couldn't make it. Yulius says *'faint heart never won the fair lady'* whatever that meant. I'll see you soon boy. Keep her smiling."

I waved again.

*   *   *

The room was in darkness. I felt my way towards the bed. The moment I sat down the lights came on. There was no one around. An eerie silence maintained. Turkey had snuggled on the pillow.

Suddenly there were loud noises of horns and wild feisty music. Confetti flew around in the room. Turkey was excited again. The next thing I knew a clown appeared from the bathroom. It fell on its own feet and started rubbing its bum.

As a kid I loved circus. More than that clowns made me jovial. No matter how sad I was clowns always got the giggles. The one in front of me was doing a great job. The whole act was hilarious. It lasted for quite a while till I was in a fit of laughter.

"Can I poke your nose?"

"No!"

"Please, I've always wanted to, please."

"No!"

"Just let me poke once, please."

"Okay!"

I poked her nose and started giggling. I couldn't help it.

"Winter, you idiot," she chuckled.

"You didn't have to become a clown you know. You're already one in general life."

"Hey," she said in mock fury. She hit me with the pillow. "Romance, I uh . . . please accept this."

"What? I don't want to marry you!"

"Don't be silly it's a promise ring."

"Do you see boobs on me to care?"

"That's so sexist," she hit me, accompanied with every word. I chuckled.

"Okay woman, put it there."

"That's what she said."

"Do you want to get there?"

She replied by burrowing in the sheets. Dawn was fast approaching. We'd been talking the whole night. It was one of those peaceful times. I wanted to forge this memory for permanency.

"Look, I'm really sorry."

"Shh, don't," I whispered turning towards her. The rays were falling on her face. The freckles were looking like peppered magic powder. Her eyes were the brownest ever. The skin was looking as if diamonds were embedded in each cell. A picture she was, which was worth painting and preserving for eternity.

"Did you know its sunrise already?" she said surprised. She got up a little, her hair falling like curtain on my face. The strawberry scent threw me off track on all sane thoughts.

The ocean was hope but so was sky. If the pain drowned into the oceans making sunsets, something to cherish from afar then the euphoria rose every morning as well. No matter orange, pink or a neutral colour I wouldn't let either end or die out.

Jasmine had been my sunset.

Jamie Summer Walker was my sunrise.

The Day I Slapped Jamie

"Romance is the straw to my berry," Reed defended in a whisper.

"He's the captain of my ship," Walker retaliated back.

"That boy is roots to my tree."

"This *man* here is the laces to my shoes."

"Guys," I rolled my eyes. They both looked at me with affection. Frankly this was scary. "Shut up!"

"Such modesty demands to be worshipped."

I spanked Reed on the head. It had been all well when they'd been concentrating on each other. It seemed annoying me was much more fun for I could detect occasional mischievous grins and lucrative winks. The teacher was droning about some crisis that had occurred hundred years ago which nobody cared about now especially when there was so much trouble burning your mind right in front of your face.

Yesterday had been a real difficult deal for me. It seemed like I'd let go off Jasmine unknowingly. The thing bothering me was I was spiralling the same way I had before with Walker. It was history being repeated again. If World War could happen again, why could not the war within myself?

"Can I talk to you Rom-com?"

"No Reed. I don't know who you are? Why would I care to?"

"Cut down the sarcasm, will you?"

The serious look was enough to make me acquire a pass for the washroom. He nodded as I walked out from the front door.

"Listen, I know what you're doing. Stop it before it's too late."

"What do you mean?" I asked baffled.

We were looking at each other's reflection through the washroom mirror. The message of disappointment was chalk clear in those brown eyes.

"Romance I care for you. I need you to stop what your intake is. If things don't become normal again I'm afraid I'll have to tell your brothers again."

My eyes narrowed at him. He'd done the same thing last time. If it hadn't been that one moment of weakness when the complaint was filed, I'd still be living a better life. They didn't understand my need for all these addictions. At least I wasn't doing the lunacy Dark Joker was famed for.

"Don't give me such empty threats. You have no right to tell me anything regarding the betterment or reverse of my life. Go date some guy. Spend your time behind others than in front of me."

He pushed past me. I knew the words had been hurtful. There was nothing I could do to control my anger except . . .

*   *   *

It had been two weeks since I'd been last caught. Things had cooled down to another level. Hence, the path was safe to be trodden upon again. All day the only thing rotating in my mind was the smell and desire of that vice. Countless times I'd passed by trying to stop myself. However today was exceptionally tough. Reed and I had the worst fight ever. He'd avoided me all day and stormed off to home without even speaking with Jamie. She'd given me a suspicious look but eventually shrugged it off. Instead, Walker had constantly spoken about Perry. That woman understood like no one had but then she did things that showed like she didn't care at all. This insensitive side rendered me helpless to world's vileness.

The knock was like a cannon blast.

In the time the door flung open my decisions had changed constantly. The moment I was going to walk away God opened the door of opportunity. When you're this close from what you really want whether good or bad, nothing make sense anymore.

"Hello there young one, I thought you wouldn't be coming around. It's been what . . . two weeks?"

The longest time period I'd stayed away from this place. It was the saddest achievement of my life.

"So do you have anything I could use today?"

"You're my favourite customer. There's no way I wouldn't have anything for you sweetie."

I nodded. The last stash she'd given me during the treasure hunt had already been long consumed. The next two times I'd come over here. Then Walker had caught me. Thankfully the joint hadn't hit me yet to do something regretful.

There was nothing more regretful than this. I never supported drinking or drugs after the therapy. This was killing me slowly. I shouldn't do something that was against my principles. It made a fool out of me otherwise. These things aren't any good escapes from the reality. They just postpone.

"I have some work so err . . . see you later," I muttered.

"Are you okay honey? You're sweating."

I nodded.

The path away felt heated up. My skin started tingling. Why was the sun so harsh today? No matter how hard I looked for that ball of fire, it was nowhere to be found. My heart was going to kill me at the rate it was beating. Nothing felt normal.

"Have you kissed this Perry boy yet?"

"Oh Romance, it's so good. I like kissing him."

Your kisses are like touch of hot fudge on chocolate ice cream. It won't be a surprise if I ever got third degree burns. I love kissing you.

"Perry does this crazy thing where he picks me up in bridal style. He keeps saying the giggles are worth it."

I'd carry you till the end of the galaxy if it meant that the best sound in the world would vibrate around.

"He's the funniest ever. I can't stop being happy around him. He's so understanding, Romance. The best part of that is we don't argue as much. He's the best human around."

Right, I was a piece of furniture who didn't want anything but your tears.

I burst through the door. It wasn't locked or I would have knocked the thing down. The smell immediately calmed my senses a little.

"You're back darling?"

"Do you have cigarettes?"

This was the safer way out. I wouldn't lose my sobriety. There was no chance of being caught doing illegal substances.

The nicotine hit me like water to a parched throat. All the thoughts vanished leaving my mind completely blank. I sighed in relief. What were problems? They all had solutions. It was right when I was smoking the fourth cigarette leaning against the counter as if some superstar that my eyes fell on her.

At first I thought the hallucinations had started again. Just before panic attack could violate me though, she crossed my vision again. I stubbed the cig and cautiously walked towards the door.

"So what was is it like being in school?" Old Amy was asking.

"Oh brilliant, there is so much to learn Amsie. I really wish you could sit in one of the classes. I never knew I'd love the life other people led. I've made so many new friends."

"Speaking of friends, the one standing outside seems troubled. How are things with you and him?"

All of a sudden the glow on her face diminished. The twinkle left her eyes. Even though she hadn't said anything, it hit me hard. I started backing off, scowling.

"I love him so much it hurts."

Wait, what?

"But we can't be together Amsie. I care for Perry you know."

Oh God, it was about that fool Perry again. If only murder was legal. I started walking away slowly with my back towards her.

"Romance, where are you going?"

I shrugged.

"Amy told me you're not feeling well? Is everything okay?"

I nodded.

"You're being silly. How do you feel?"

I glared at her. That idiotic question was the last deal. She didn't leave eye contact though. It wasn't her fault. I had to control my temper. The only way was the worst possible but better than yelling irrationally at Walker.

"Stop that Romance," she said annoyed.

I ignored lighting up the stick.

"Don't be ignorant. You know I don't like it. Please stop it. The smoke is irritating. You do realize it would affect me as well."

"Why don't you realize things you say affect me adversely too? Why should it always be me being sensitive towards your feelings?"

"Are you saying I am insensitive? What are these things?"

I rolled my eyes. I puffed out a smoke.

"Stop it," she said patiently. "Will you talk properly? I'm getting confused."

"Aren't you always?"

"Don't be like that please. We can talk things out . . . will you quit it!"

She whipped the cigarette from my mouth.

"What the hell is your problem Walker?" I yelled at her. "Can you just leave me alone? Get out of my sight, get out of my mind and get out of my life . . . just get out."

She looked at me furiously as I lit another one.

"That's exactly how I feel when you talk about Perry again and again despite me showing how I feel about you."

"Is that all the problem you have? I'll stop. It's not that difficult."

"Will you also stop seeing him?"

"That . . . is not possible for me to carry out."

"Then we are done here. See you later."

Instead of hammering the fury down, the nicotine had riled me more to retaliate. I couldn't think straight anymore except for the fact that someone was trying to order me around which wasn't acceptable in any terms. Even Walker had no right to tell me what to do in my life and what not.

Silence followed us. I had my back turned towards her. I couldn't care less.

"You know what? You're right."

I chuckled emotionlessly.

"I have no right to stop you from killing yourself."

Harsh but that was bang on. It was nice she could understand the situation for once.

"Instead of telling you to quit, I'm going to suffer with you."

What?

The next thing I knew was she was lighting a smoke for herself.

"What the hell do you think you're doing?" I asked incredulously. I gripped her wrist before the vice touched her innocent lips.

319

"Doing what you were?"

"No."

"You have no right to tell me what to do," she said arrogantly. She pulled her hand away from my grip.

"Walker, don't you dare put that thing in your mouth."

"Relax it's just a paper rolled with some herbs inside. I want to know why you do it anyways. What is this pleasure that occurs which normally life can't provide you."

Why couldn't this woman understand how serious I was? The gravity of the situation itself was flying above her head. I'd never forgive myself if she smoked. There was nothing Walker was against more than this ever since she'd been pregnant. 'it wasn't just about the effect on us anymore.

"Jamie, I'm getting really mad. Drop that thing away. I don't want to hurt you."

At the mention of her name, she paused. I got distracted feeling confident she wouldn't, knowing how much it was troubling me. However, things aren't predictable. The thing touched her mouth at lightning speed and she inhaled.

I lost my nerve.

I took hold of the stick and crushed it in my hand. I threw the remains away and before I could control my actions, I'd slapped her.

She looked at me shocked.

I couldn't breathe. What had I done? Before her expression could switch I made a run for it.

*   *   *

"Alan," I yelled the hundredth time, banging on his door. "Please let me in."

"I'm sorry but I'm busy being behind someone else."

I put my hand up as a shield from the sun while looking up at him. He was peeking down from his room window with the expression of the least interested person on the planet.

"You know I never meant to hurt you. Let me explain."

"Yawn, maybe I should take a nap with somebody."

"We both know there is no one. I'm climbing if you don't open this thing. I'd break the door but I'm currently low on cash. I'll give you three minutes. You decide which way is better."

This was one thing that needed fixing no matter what happened with life. Reed had been my best friend since forever. There was no way I would let him be mad for more than a day. We'd had loads of fights before. The trick was to shower him with all the affection. Even if today he didn't forgive me, all I wanted was to make sure he was okay and not binge watching or eating.

"Two minutes Al, open up."

The last time he'd remotely come near depression had been bad. It was generally a horrible situation. Reed was weird. He'd gone around dressed up as an elf handing out candies in school. There was even a jingle and a whole new language attached with the persona.

What nightmare those days had been . . . the nights being worse! He cried himself to sleep every single day. It had come to this that I had to bunk inside his room in case he tried to do something inhuman.

"A minute Reed, get your handsome self down before I break my bones."

The last time I'd tried climbing the pipe, the plan had given away. I'd landed up with a fracture in the hospital with a frantic Walker and a weeping Reed. Some memories were just meant to be laughed at later. If the door wasn't unlocked my only option was the other pipe on the other end. Well, with the way things were today fracture would be the highlight of the day.

"Ten seconds Al," I yelled. Even though the insides were trembling, I didn't let my exterior confident self waver.

The countdown was quickly dying away. The options were being slaughtered every other second. From arranging a heart attack to prank calling a fire engine, I realized the output productivity was higher under pressure.

"One . . . that's it I'm climbing upstairs. Take me to church if I die."

I held the pipe tightly and heaved myself. It would require around twelve or so more heaves for reaching the top.

"Oh for god sake, get down wanna-be stunt-man. You don't have cash for fixing a bloody door but there's all the money for bones eh?"

"Was the sun too late to tell you're my shining star?"

"What?" he asked horrified.

"When I see in the mirror I see your soul."

"You're being creepy now."

"If Reed was a weed, you'd be sold in billions."

"Wow, goodbye"

"I'm sorry. I have been having these latent feelings towards you. It's like sometimes my heart would come popping right out of my chest."

He was staring at me as if I was insane.

"Are you high?"

"For your love, I'm always high. Will you let me be your hero?"

"Romance are you trying to flirt with me?" he chuckled. There was no tone of unkindness which egged me on.

"If you take the answer positively then yes I might be?"

He shook his head.

"Can I hug you Reed?"

He avoided answering.

"You know you want me to," I teased.

He looked away.

"I won't stop from kissing you baby," I cooed. The looks of disbelief were actually becoming fun to watch. I moved forward making kissing sounds until a small smile lit his face. Suddenly, he was hugging me tightly.

"I love you Rom-com."

"Now you're just going overboard . . . kidding ouch, I love you too . . . sort of."

He pinned me down to the ground. It was adorable when he considered his strength to be far greater than mine. The laughs were worth every insult though.

"I'll completely forgive you if you do one thing . . ."

"What is that one thing? It depends."

"Oh don't worry I won't ask you to quit on anything. You know the impact on yourself and others very well by now. How you chose to use that is your wish."

"Okay, I'll do your thing."

*   *   *

That is how I ended up outside Walker's shack knocking on the flap. She didn't respond for the first minute. Reed kept badgering me on.

"Romance . . . is that err you?"

"Hello fellow earthling. Here is a creation fresh out of Alan Reed's latest fashion models for a prom gown. He would like it very much if you adorned this and went to the high school ball with your idiotic, annoying date. Lots of love, Reed . . . and Winter."

"Are you wearing the dress?" Jamie asked biting her lower lip.

If only she would stop insinuating me further. It was moments away before someone would lean in for a kiss and she would regret it.

"No, this is what I usually wear and roam around."

"You look so cute," Jamie squealed. I shut off my ears as she started laughing out loud all the while managing to squeal something that excited her. Finally, she hugged me.

"I'm so sorry Walker. I never should have slapped you."

"Apologies should only be meant for things that don't deserve adverse actions. You did nothing wrong."

If only she'd seen the dandelion flowers suddenly get blown away by the wind she'd know how hard I was wishing for the moment to freeze.

Just for the two of us to remain frozen in this self written historical moment.

The Day I Bit My Lower Lip

I clenched the vessel of the glass harder.

The woman I loved was swaying right in front of my eyes with another man whose face I couldn't decipher in the dark. There had been just one moment when she'd glanced at me and sheepishly looked away. I leaned against the wall still trying to fight the rejection of a few days prior.

"Would you uh . . . never mind," a voice said meekly.

I gazed down to come across a pretty girl with downcast eyes supporting blushing cheeks. Her pink gown was cut at the sharp shoulders while the lower half flowed sinuously. There was hardly any make up on the fresh face. There was something about the features, the way she blushed, the way she was nervous that pulled me in. Her aquamarine eyes reminded me of open-wide oceans, a memory I'd tried drowning so much.

"Hey," I called after her in a hoarse voice. "Do you want to dance?"

She looked at me with high expectations. Her colour deepened. I took hold of her slender hand and pulled her towards the floor. We started swaying to the music. A part of me wanted to immerse in some other girl's aura for a while but the other part, the dominant one, was dying to make Summer envious as she had me struggling with the same.

"I'm Jasmine. What's your name?"

I gave her a startled look. The features weren't that similar in whatsoever ways but I knew there was something behind those eyes that had compelled my heart to beat a tad bit faster. I could feel my hands clench. Sweat started to form on my forehead. Even after all this time . . . my attention went back to Summer. Was it possible to love two women at the same time?

I stayed silent for the guy holding her was pulling her closer.

"Hey, are you here with me?"

I saw her eyes looking at me with accusations. There was no remorse. What fun life had with you when it decided to play one of its popular games? Love; just when I'd given myself to another woman past came knocking right through my door. Yet, my heart knew what it wanted.

"Listen, I don't know what's your deal but you could at least tell me your name."

He pulled her away from the floor. As the lights switched on and off I could make out their shadow caricatures strolling out towards the balcony. I clenched my hands as I saw them with their fingers entangled in each other's hands.

"Ouch!"

I jumped a little as she grumbled in my ears. Realizing that I had been squishing her fingers, I apologized gruffly.

She gave me a demented look before walking away. I stood there for some time, trying to recollect composure as humans around struck me with their flailing limbs.

I shouldn't have handled the situation so lightly for now I was suffering in misery. I blankly looked at the two people making out in front of me. There held no secret bond of love. I felt no sense of connection. What was wrong with relationships today?

I walked towards the bar. If only school had the decency to provide alcohol there would be nothing better. It was my last year after all.

I plonked down on one of the plush sofas they'd decorated as atrociously as Crystal's mind could plan for the prom. The softness of the cushions led to comfort and soon I was contemplating my life by segregating all the beauty that entailed with it.

The sky from the glass windows above gazed back at me as if searching for the stars on my visage. The only thing it would probably find would be darkness though. My mind was not yet ready to accept reality so I let it tread on the path much taken before – the past.

For some reason I decided to ponder about my so called father. It had been a decade exactly since I'd even spoken to him properly. It had always been a formal meet. If my brothers hated me, it was nothing compared to how much he loathed. At first it used to hurt for that accident had taken away every bit of relation I had. Slowly as poison works its magic, I let the connections die. Mr. Winter could keep providing me whatever he desired out of duty but he would never be a father for me. My father was as good as dead. It was still a mystery why he'd decided to show up all of a sudden at our doorstep some days back. There was surely another twisted plot of his that he had wanted fulfilled. I just had to wait for it to unfurl.

"Hey, are you okay?"

"What are you doing here Jas . . . Jamie?"

I hoped she didn't notice my slip.

"You just looked like something was suffocating you. I just wanted to check . . ."

"Cut the crap."

We sat in silence. Just a few days back she'd been stressing over none of the prom gown fitting her due to the stomach bulge. She went on and on about how her thin figure had been violated for anything to look beautiful.

If only she could see herself through my eyes.

The velvet shimmering cloth hugged her curves right where they should. Her face was glowing as it always did only today the glitter magnified the effect. It was even crazy for me to admit this but for once make-up looked amazing on someone. The right side of the cloth had a shoulder cut making the velvety skin on her neck stretch further. Her lips were plump and pink.

When would she ever stop giving me side effects?

Her face was however downcast. I felt ashamed for making such a beautiful woman feel sad on the night she'd always dreamt off.

"Would you like to dance with me?" I requested gently as I slid on the floor to kneel. Her eyes fluttered to mine in confusion.

"I might not have the opportunity to be your date but at least can I be lucky for one dance with you my lady?"

She smiled.

"Plus you should also get the privilege to dance with the smartest boy in this area," I winked.

She giggled.

We walked towards the dance floor. Our fingers entwined symbolized so much more to me than it would ever do to her. The music slowed down. I scoffed at my luck. Of course, universe has to make fun of me. Look son, gaze at the Cinderella you'll never have because even after twelve o'clock she'll be someone else's, glass slipper or not.

I tried my best to keep the bodies at distance but there were too many people around. Jamie was literally hugging me. At one point we both looked at each other and started laughing. She wound her arms around my neck. I encircled her waist with mine. Her head lay gently on my shoulder.

If only time knew the right moments to pause.

"It's nice slow dancing with you," she murmured into my ears.

"Just like it is with Perry?"

There was no response. I didn't want to ruin it like that.

"Did you happen to pass by Alan?"

She started giggling. "He looks adorable in that pink tux. If there was only a way to adopt him, he'd be mine before the clock chimes twelve."

"Hold your horses Cinderella I haven't quit the race yet."

"Are you saying you love Reed, Romance?"

"What the big surprise in that?"

"Is Romance Winter really admitting to having feelings for another human? I should be writing this date down in history."

"It isn't like I haven't admitted stuff to you woman. You baffle me," I scoffed.

She pulled back a little with her hands balled on the waist. A stern expression forced the right eyebrow to lift up in question. "You better start apologizing or the consequences would be adverse."

"Yeah, will it now?" I chuckled lifting my hands up in surrender. "Do whatever you want with me mistress, I'm your prisoner."

She blushed until an evil smirk crept on the innocent face. One shouldn't worry when a devil makes schemes to overthrow; it's when the angels start plotting against your destiny that one should agonize.

"Alan," she screamed over the music. "Romance just confessed he loves you."

Before I could hold my breath Alan was holding me.

"I'm not dancing with you like that," I said appalled, pushing myself away from his body.

"But you love me?"

"That doesn't mean I slow dance with you."

"So you do love me?"

"Whatever," I rolled my eyes at him. He smirked.

Another angel was dying to break my serenity, it seemed.

"I'll tell Jams about the time you kissed Ms. Pan by mistake if you don't dance with me."

"You do know Walker has seen worse, right?"

"Walker you should know that Romance used to wet his . . ."

"Stop, I'll dance with you," I snubbed him immediately. Telling something to Walker was one thing but announcing it on the prom dance floor was downright outrageous.

Suffice to say, it was the most awkward dance of my life. At least Alan enjoyed every second.

"I'm scared."

"Why?" I frowned at him.

"George, the exchange student from London, he's asked me out for the after party. There was nothing innocent in the gestures he made."

"You're over analyzing things man," I replied nonchalantly.

All of a sudden Reed pulled me towards his body and squeezed my behind. "That in no way is normal."

"You don't have to give me a demo." The horror in my tone was real.

"What if he wants to you know . . . take my flower."

"What?" I started guffawing. This man had some sense of humour. Why did he find the last person on this Earth who would know what to do or even be remotely interested in all this? Where was Walker when you required her skills?

"Romance, be serious. I'm a young man. I don't want to be violated."

"Look, you'll be fine. You have the right to say no. Guys understand if the girl . . . guy in your case isn't ready for it. Just say no and walk away if things get too intense," I advised patiently.

He nodded frantically. "What if it's say second base? I think I'm good with that."

"Yeah, set your limit."

"Can I call you if anything goes wrong?"

Right now the only thing right was the music. There wasn't one part of this night that seemed otherwise.

"Sure, I'll save you."

"What if he makes me pregnant?"

That was it. It wasn't as if all the patience accumulated into an abyss was stored inside my body. There was a line of pushing me, I was done.

"I'll still call you if anything happens."

I waved my hand in agreement as I walked towards the punch table. Why didn't anyone decide to get alcohol? What was wrong with the feel of today's generation in parties? That Crystal Meth woman had also been useless.

"Romance . . ."

"Reed, you are a full-grown man. Even if you have feelings towards other I'm sorry to say biology won't permit anything even remotely close to you getting pregnant to happen. So stop worrying will you?" I said through gritted teeth.

"Uh, I got you some alcohol. It's under the table behind the store room door there."

Trust Alan to come to my rescue. I gave him a half brother hug and ran towards the closet only to be stopped by a stymie.

"I'm sorry about before."

I gazed at her. The more I tried to differentiate the more she looked like her.

"I'm sorry, are you really Jasmine?"

She nodded to my question. There was that tilt of the head Jasmine was characterized to have. I moved closer cautiously, my eyes digging into her aquamarines. The nose crinkled up. How could someone come alive after death?

"I'm just jealous Romance. You have another woman now. It's not fair. You promised you wouldn't stop loving me."

"I do still love you."

"Then why do you keep telling that woman you love her? It's not possible to be equally infatuated with both."

"I have always loved you Jasmine."

They were announcing the names of the Prom King and Queen on the stage. Everyone was breathing excitedly for that one piece of information that would change someone's world for a little while.

"Do you really? Are you sure?"

If I said it I meant it. Why would there be a doubt in that?

"The Prom King for tonight is . . . Parsley Winter."

The whole crowd yelled in appreciation. They'd gone crazy in the house. Parsley kept yelling about some lost brooch that he'd brought for Yasmine. Grover couldn't find his bow tie. It turns out they'd ended up with Luke in his family box. There had been quite a lot of yelling. I'd got ready quietly hoping no one would care. Obviously, they dragged me into the fight and turned the whole blame on to me.

"I love you very much that it hurts," she whispered moving closer. Her sinewy fingers traced my skin until the thumb was slowly leaving a hot trail of passion across the expanse of my lips. It couldn't be true.

This was so real. It felt so real.

"The Prom Queen for the night is . . . Jamie Summer Walker."

Of course, there shouldn't be any doubt in that. That woman looked similar to some glittering inhuman beauty that was out of reach. She deserved all the happiness.

"Will you go away with me Romance?"

So did me.

I pulled her towards me till out bodies were close enough. My fingers traced her back. The spine was jutting out. As my face closed on her neck, the collar bones became more prominent then they should. The bones of her ribs were poking my chest now.

It was Jasmine. My Jasmine had returned. I knew it was good idea to skip the funeral. No one believed when I said she was alive, everyone turned away their faces titling me as a retard.

Now, I'd prove them all.

Her lips tasted mine hungrily. All those years of loss had to be compensated. I pulled her body up so that it became easy. It was like feeling the first drop of rain after a parching summer. It was like a cool balm on a mosquito bite that had been burning. How could I ever forget the feeling of being this happy?

"Romance, what are you doing?"

I blinked.

Walker was staring at me with a mixture of confusion and fury. There was a slight tinge of disbelief in those eyes.

"Stop this! It's not only you who can gain happiness Walker. I have every right too. Whatever this act is, get away. Let me be with Jasmine."

"That's not Jasmine. It's Erica Showalter from your chemistry class. What are you even saying? Are you okay?"

She was eyeing me suspiciously. I didn't deserve less after all the stunts yet it annoyed me. Why was she calling my Jasmine her Erica? This Walker was a damn selfish girl. Then I looked on the side to prove myself.

It was Erica Showalter.

"Where is Jasmine?" I asked her confused.

"Who is that dude? You just pulled me in for a kiss randomly. Here I was clapping like a normal teen around and the next thing I know someone is showering the best kiss of my life. I don't know what you're talking about."

I didn't either.

"Thanks for making this the best high school night."

I shrugged. That wasn't the same for all.

"Hey are you okay? You look really pale."

"She's back Jasmine . . . I mean Jamie. Jasmine is back."

"What are you blabbering? I can't hear you over the music."

"It's happening again. You have to make it stop."

"Romance, you're scaring me. Hold my hand, please calm down. What's happening again? Who is back? Your words are incorrigible. Are you running a fever? Why are you sweating?"

My body pulled hers in for a hug. The hallucinations were back. Kitty was back. There had to be a way of fixing this mess.

"I'm fine."

"Are you sure?" she asked pulling back. Her face splotched with confusion. One second I'd been going lunatic and the next I was the calmest person around.

"Yes Jamie, I'm all right. You can see yourself, right? You better go. Perry will be looking out for you."

She looked at me unsure.

"That crown makes you look like some Tinker Bell. You should totally keep it on more, princess. You look beautiful with it."

"Are you saying I don't look beautiful sans the crown?"

"It's not me saying that," I replied innocently.

Her hand hit my arm playfully as she giggled. Reluctantly, she walked away though. Every few steps her head would turn back to containing the expression saying *I really think you're going to drop dead any second*. Every time I'd throw her a reassuring smile. Just like Jasmine, Walker disappeared into the crowd.

It was time for me to settle down.

There are problems in life that rattle everyone. Then there are ways they deal with them. It could be a good path or the bad path.

For me it was the worst path that had neither rain nor sun.

All it had was unreal happiness, the kind I was living in without Walker in my world.

The Day I Wanted a
Piggy Back Ride

I was singing loudly. My heart was thumping with the beat.
The music was loud enough to burst my ear drums but I
didn't care. As long as my happiness lived, I did.

"Romance, we need to leave," Jamie was insisting. Her
pretty fingers adorned with one silver ring which was my
promise ring were holding the sleeve of my arm.

"What was god thinking when he created you beautiful?
He must have forgotten he needs to keep you in heaven not
send you to earth," I rambled on. I pulled her body close to
mine. My fingers pulled back her curls that were falling on
the oval face.

"You coloured your hair?" I asked intrigued. Her hair
shone bright red. It made her look akin some Greek goddess.
I was enthralled enough to bow down and bask in the glory.
How hadn't I managed to notice that the whole night?

"My hair uh . . . it's always been red. I use to colour it
black."

More lies.

It seemed as if the Summer I knew was dead and there was a better version of her only much upgraded standing in front of me. I didn't know whether I liked this one though.

"Romance please I don't want you to get hurt. Let's go home?"

I did like the new her after all.

"You smell like strawberries," I sniffed. I moved closer till my face was in her hair. "It's more intoxicating than any alcohol on this planet. I declare it."

She giggled as I stumbled with my finger pointing upwards to indicate the number one.

"Can we go now? Perry must be . . ."

"Kill him. He's such a bee. He keeps coming in between to sting my heart and then the worst thing is . . . do you know what the worst thing is?"

She shook her head sadly.

I stretched her lips with the help of my hands trying to make her smile. "Why are you feeling sad? He never dies after stinging. Keep that smile on. It keeps me warm in these snowy days Walker."

She held my hand trying to pull me down.

"Okay, before we leave can we at least sing one song? That's all I ask."

She looked at me for a long time. I used the same to trace patterns on her skin. If she was the universe her freckles were the constellations. They made her exotically bliss to get lost into. I would free fall any day.

"Fine, one song is all we'll sing." She held the mike. I took hold of the other.

Just Give Me a Reason by *Pink* started to play.

We started singing. It felt like her voice was killing me softly. I started feeling dizzier but I continued to sing.

It was a summer day. The blue bird I'd been eyeing had come and sat on my shoulder. It looked so familiar. She suddenly tiptoed inside the scene wearing a red frock with a red bow tying up her hair. Her laughter echoed around making the sun rays spread harder. The sky was azure. Her eyes twinkled with hidden mischief as she pulled out a cloth. Before I could figure out anything she tied up my eyes.

"I want you to shut up. Just listen to me today." Her breath tickled my neck, the friction making the miniscule hairs stand up with Goosebumps. The strawberry scent was as strong as ever.

She took hold of my hand and placed it on her heart. I felt the beating go erratic as she moved closer to me.

Her lips touched my skin lighting up a trail of passion. Her fingers left my hand and encircled around my neck. She kept mumbling she loved me as she kissed my whole face. It felt like a feather touch only the feather was on fire. I didn't realize I'd stopped breathing till my head really started spinning. My insides were going wild. I wanted to talk, I desired to touch but I held back.

"Do you have a heart?" She asked me.

"Not that I know off . . ."

"Good because my heart belongs to you."

Her lips kissed me frantically. They weren't soft but yearning. I'd never seen her so hungry for passion. Jamie was driving me crazy with her scent and kisses.

"I love you so much Winter," she whispered into my ears. "I have to go. I can't be with you for you love. Believe me if I had a say in life I would stay but I can't. I have to leave . . ."

"Why, don't leave me. I need you," I muttered in a broken voice. "I love you too Summer. Don't go."

"I have to."

"Why?"

"That's because I love somebody else too."

My heart stopped.

"His heart is stopping."

"Shit, I have to take him to the hospital."

Both the voices were panicking. I couldn't make out who it was.

"Please do something," she pleaded.

No, don't be sad love. I'm okay.

"Calm down Jay, he'll be fine love I won't let anything happen to him."

Whoever you are, you deserve a hug. I swear if I was in any condition I would kiss your cheeks. Then I'd punch you black and blue for calling her *love*.

"He's saying something," she suddenly said. "Listen, his lips are moving."

Who was this new someone now? I was already confused with the voices when a new one was added. It sounded very low. I tried to decipher the words.

"Can you understand what he's saying Jay?"

"Uh I'm trying," she muttered. I understood what he was saying. The guy wanted a piggy back. I tried to speak out loud so that I could clear up their doubt. The real mystery though was why was a random guy asking them for a back ride?

"He's asking for a piggy back."

You go girl. No one but Jamie could have understood my emotions perfectly like that.

Suddenly I felt the ground slip from beneath my feet. I heard a grunt close to my ears. My cheeks felt the soft velvet touch of someone's hair. I could smell an amalgamation of cologne and alcohol.

Oh, I was the voice that wanted the piggy back. It felt better.

"Can you check his heart beat? He's up so I'm guessing everything will be back to normal otherwise we'll walk to the hospital."

I couldn't recognize voices in this trance. The only thing clear was the tone that helped me distinguish the gender. Knowing that one person had been Jamie didn't create much of a challenge when the tone was a little nasal and high. I'd been trying to figure out whom the guy was or if I'd heard this voice before.

He didn't sound familiar.

All I could make out was he was really caring and kind. Who else would pick the heavy weight that I am and carry me around?

"He's normal," she breathed in relief.

Right, it would be the guy who was in love with Jamie Summer Walker.

We walked on for what seemed like forever. Now and then either of them would talk. I kept slipping in and out of sleep. My whole body was sore. Jasmine was spinning in my head as well. After going through so much I'd been able to get her out of my life but these random circumstances were messing up everything again.

"I miss you Jas," I whispered.

The person carrying me stopped. I could feel his muscles tense up. I wanted to open my eyes really badly. The absence of movement in my limbs was annoying me. There was nothing worse than losing control.

"It's going to be fine Romance."

How did he know my name? Why would Walker tell my name to him? That voice soothed me down though. Things felt better after that. I let sleep take over me again.

It seemed like hours when I felt my body slid down. Someone held me from the side. I slung my arm around the neck.

"I'm going to let you sit here for a while okay? Try staying straight please . . ."

I nodded enthusiastically.

The moment the support left me, I felt myself falling on to something soft. It smelt like mud. I curled up trying to feel warm. My hand found a stick. It was like holding a *tesseract*. Suddenly all the power in the world belonged with me. I got up feeling renewed. Asgard was mine to rule. The dimensions of the things around were blurring. Where were my loyal followers? Who was going to dust the floor I was treading on?

It was just around the corner stood *Drameon,* the pet monster that my immortal enemy had recently brought, who upon seeing me looked away. I glared at him. No one dared to ignore me. That was last straw of patience.

"You shall pay for the disobedience sly creature."

The monster gave me a lazy look and kept its head back on the paws.

That riled the temperatures higher. I held the *tesseract* in the air and moved forward in a pose ready to attack.

Three steps away from the monster had him staring at me with curiosity.

"What are you doing Romance for god sake? Get away now." Someone yelled.

I ignored.

"This is not cool brother. Let's go inside."

I could hear footsteps approaching me. There was no time left. So, I did what any drunken man would with all the power of the world would have done then.

I poked the monster.

I heard the person walking towards me curse loudly. A slender hand slid in mine.

Jamie Summer Walker.

She was pulling me towards some direction. I started running without any questions. Even being the most powerful man made me vulnerable to her magical powers.

This felt like déjà vu. It wasn't the first time we were running away from a dog that had been purposely provoked. My head was clearing up. I could at least feel control of my limbs.

"Well, in my defence I was checking what riles up women. If men are dogs then women should be bitches. Apparently, poking the private parts is still a no."

I heard Walker laugh out really loud. We had stopped. Her face was clear now. There was so much joy splattered there. Being the reason for such a phenomenon was way better than being God itself. She sat down on the floor. We'd managed to leave the dog behind. If I tried recalling, Parsley had butted in the picture and shooed the dog away.

"Oh Rome, what will I ever do with you," she said chuckling.

"Spread chocolate on me and take a bite. I'd be better than any product Willy Wonka produced."

Everything went silent. I splattered down next to her. Her head landed on my shoulder. The night was a curious mystery waiting to be unravelled. It was my imagination or it had started to snow. Every unique flake was as different as Walker's thoughts. The cold was diminished as her warm body snuggled up to me.

"Are you still drunk?" she asked.

"This whole world my girl is a bottle of alcohol. It depends on you how much you drink. The more the amount, the more the problems you face due to your intoxicated silliness. But isn't that how you learn?"

"Ah! I can never tell. A sober Romance would answer the same," she giggled.

"Did I ever tell you how amusing your laughter is?"

"Stop it!" She hit my arm lightly. "So, I have a confession to make. It feels as if you won't remember anything I say today. It'll be nice to get this burden off my head finally."

"It's alright. I know Santa Claus does exist. I've been a really bad boy in life that's why he doesn't give me presents anymore. Dad told me this when I was nine and mom died. He said the reason she went was because how bad I was . . ."

"Hey, let it go for now okay?" Walker pecked my cheek. "That's not what I wanted to talk about with you though. Jeez Romance, seriously you think Santa Claus is real?"

I shrugged.

"Do you remember the first time we . . . kissed?"

I tried racking my brain. It was difficult at the moment so I shook my head.

"I'd never been kissed like that. It was enough to render me useless to think for a long while. It was like this day. There was snow, a lot of it. You had been drunk. We'd gone bowling and you had too many shots in excitement. Imagine my surprise when I saw you rolling glasses down the bowling alley rather than the balls. You even challenged a group of girls to a battle calling them midgets. We were eventually thrown out. You were pretty much sick. Then you kissed me."

I could remember snippets of this. As she continued describing my mind suddenly put two and two together. That hadn't been a dream? Even then I'd felt the realism. How could I forget the first kiss? It was irritating me to no ends. I didn't know what to say anymore.

"Hey," she pulled my face to gaze at hers. "It's okay Romance. You were drunk. You can't possibly remember. That's why I can do this as well."

I felt her breath mingle with mine. Seconds later her lips were slowly dancing with mine. I turned a little cupping her face in my hands. It was heating up. We weren't in any hurry. There was no pain. My dizziness was increasing every second.

"Romance, I uh . . . err"

We broke apart. It took me a while to clear my mind. I felt astonished as my eyes fell on my brother shifting uncomfortably. He was wearing his boxers probably that's why. He ruffled his hair with his right hand and sighed. Why was Parsley nervous?

"I heard some commotion so ran outside. I saw you poking the dog. When I tried stop it from running behind you guys it retaliated back . . . tore my clothes up."

"Sorry about that," I mumbled still woozy.

"Uh . . . do you want me to help you inside or what?" he asked with a little authority back in the tone.

"Okay"

He held out his hand. I took his support. Jamie also got up trying to handle my weight.

"You are not going anywhere," Parsley snarled at her. "Go back to wherever you came from. I'll handle this."

Jamie nodded and walked away.

I was tired to argue. I'd handle this with Parsley later. The exhaustion wasn't letting me think properly anyways. It didn't take me time to fall down on the bed and pass out.

Before being dead to the world, I noticed an earring on the floor. It was in the shape of a snowflake. My eyes were fixated on the piece of jewellery. Something about it was disturbing me greatly. What was it doing in my room?

Just as sleep hit me so did the realization.

It was mom's earring. Someone had been ruffling through my drawers. Only the morning will tell now what secrets the night held.

For the knight in his shining armour had won the war but lost the lady.

The Day I Broke Jamie's Finger

I didn't remember anything that happened last night. My head was already aching but I had much more trouble ahead which made me oblivious to whatever occurred yesterday.

Whenever you feel like pregnant woman are always a piece of cake to handle maybe you should take a step back and think again of all the sins you've committed in life to have believed in that.

She was scratching my face as the screams vibrated in the house.

"Get this thing out of me," she yelled into my ears.

I'd dialled for the paramedics but there was still no sign. It wasn't possible for her to be having the baby this soon.

"It's eating my stomach. I'm telling you it's going to gobble up every bit of organ it can find. Save my heart, Romance."

"Why would I save your heart?" I asked surprised.

"It's the thing that lets me live you idiot. Don't you know how biology works?"

Just how ironic could the situation get?

"Romance, it's coming out."

"Hey, it's not like I got you knocked up. Will you stop damaging me?"

"You're useless. I need Batman to save me."

I glared at her. Her fingers were clutching my collar and pulling me towards her face every time she had a contraction. I'd been trying to wipe away the sweat but it annoyed her further. There was no way I could win in this situation.

"Can you see stars? I can see stars. I'm never going to sing a bloody twinkle rhyme to this it."

"Her you mean?"

"If you don't stop this pain I'll *it* the '*her*' out of your vocabulary."

She made the word *it* sound like eat just so that the sentence became more intellect according to her. By my accord, it was the dumbest thing I've ever faced.

"I'm dying. That's it, I'm dying."

I rolled my eyes at her. All the past months she'd been so calm I'd almost forgotten she was pregnant. There were no complaints or demands. I should have known all that would break on me one day at once. Walker did know how to control her pain though so I gave her enough credit to deal with all this. The priority list at the instant contained of getting immediate help. Thus, I managed to pull myself away and run outside to look if the ambulance was around.

"Oh if it isn't little Popsicle, long time no see?"

I spun around and came face to face with a clean shaven man wearing a well-ironed grey suit. A pair of Ray bans was slung down from his pocket. His tie was a little loose as the working hours were over. His hair was combed properly making the whole aura spick and span.

Why was such a stranger smirking at me?

"I would really like to catch up mister but I have an emergency."

"You've grown so much," he said in a fake whimper wiping away imaginary tears.

I frowned at him as he ruffled my hair. Strangers these days didn't know their limit. I'd no ounce of idea about the identity of this man and he was this close to hugging me to death.

"It's me Dustin Higgins."

Right, that just helped me solve the whole mystery. I stared at him as clueless as before. There was no way I knew a man that refined.

"Don't you remember your little friend beat us up in that alley some months back? I'm Shark!"

I kept repeating that name in my head. I'd definitely heard it somewhere. Walker had beaten them up? Then it hit me. The day I'd walked into the thug street and found the woman lurking around there as if she belonged with the blood and gore. The street urchins had decided to tackle us but to everybody's surprise a short bomb had diffused upon them.

My eyes raked up Shark's profile again. The long hair was army cut short. The beard and moustache had been shaved away to reveal a sharp jaw of a sophisticated man. The bulging stomach had been replaced by a non-existent one. There was no tell-tale of who he used to be except the tattoo still peeking out from under the top half of his shirt.

"How is the little angel faring?" he asked jovially.

"The little angel . . . oh no," I groaned. I'd completely forgotten the purpose of rushing around like a manic. "She's sick. I've called the hospital. The ambulance hasn't arrived yet."

"What's wrong with her?" he took hold of my collar and pulled me up. I was around six feet tall but Shark was another story. My feet were thankfully still touching the ground. His breath fanned my face. The only person who had been helping the whole day was me. Why in the world was I the one getting beaten up? If this kept happening I'd be the one in hospital and not Walker.

"She's inside."

The moment I pointed towards the house he left me and ran inside. Before I could dust myself up properly he was carrying a very astonished Walker outside.

"When I said I wanted Batman to help me I didn't literally mean it," she whispered to me as he passed.

She was so surprised with what was happening that she'd forgotten to scream. She lay in the front seat of the Ferrari staring at the stranger in suit. There was almost a tinge of marvel hiding behind those pain ridden eyes. It was safe to say I was jealous.

What had this Shark looted to end up with such wealth? It was beyond my sanity to think.

"Are you coming or not?" he growled at me. I slunk in from the back door.

"Who is this handsome?" Jamie turned back and mouthed to me. She brought her index finger and thumb together gesturing me how perfect he was. I rolled my eyes at her. She fanned herself frantically with her left hand showing as if his *hotness* was too much to take.

"Maybe you should crank up the air conditioner," I mumbled to no one in particular.

"Maybe you should remember what's more important in life than waste time looking like a ruffian on the street. The first thing that should have come out of the mouth was I need help," Shark retaliated back at me.

That made sense. I should have run out and asked whoever random stranger passing by for help without taking the factor of danger or probably being a serial killer in hand. Of course, how could I be so dumb?

My phone vibrated.

Jamie: Where the hell did you find this hot fudge? My hormones are already wild. You're not helping me Romance.

I gave my phone an incredulous look. She was tapping her fingers on the side handle impatiently. We were speeding by pretty quickly.

My phone vibrated again.

Jamie: Can you believe he actually picked me up? How cool is that? I swear Romance I'm going to faint. Did you see how smouldering his eyes are?

Yes, that's exactly what was left to do. Reed would be one joyful human the day I noticed some man's features. God forbid he faints the day I tell him I found a guy's eyes *smouldering*.

Jamie: Are you even like on this planet anymore?

Me: I've not even a mild interest in anything which revolves around yours.

Jamie: That's not true. You really delve deep into my life as if it's the most interesting thing in the world.

Me: Look back.

The moment her pretty face gazed at mine I poked my tongue out at her. That was the moment Shark decided to screech to a halt and I fell face forward hitting the back of his seat.

Jamie giggled.

The door on her left swung open and Shark stood there with a grave expression. He held out both his hands which Walker took hold off eagerly. She slid out and slyly pretended to trip. He bent down to hold her in his arms again. She winked at my incredulous look.

Women

I rushed in behind Shark. It didn't take much time for Walker to be on a bed being examined by a doctor while the two of us hovered around.

"I'll take her in for a thorough examination just in case. May I know your relation to her?"

"Friend," I said.

"Friend," Shark mumbled.

The doctor gave us a suspicious look. Guaranteed none of us looked even remotely close to being known by her but that wasn't my present concern.

"Her baby seems to be fine so that's nothing to be worried about."

"She's pregnant?" Shark asked astonished.

What did he think the bulge instead of her normal stomach was a store room or what?

"You little punk got her shacked up." Before I could anticipate any threat towards my life he'd already punched my eye. There was a commotion around as I clutched my eye in pain. It wasn't as if I didn't deserve all the hate for I could have stopped all this fiasco, being a little more alert.

That's how I ended up next to a smirking Walker. Shark had been temporarily thrown of the premises for being violent. They gave him an ultimatum of an hour before getting permission to enter again. The only relief I was currently feeling was for the fact that everything was normal with Jamie. It had been some minor medical term involving gases or something I couldn't understand.

"Will you ever tell me who that dark haired stranger was?"

I didn't like the smitten look on her.

"Shark," I mumbled reluctantly.

"Dolphin," she replied.

I sighed. When would this woman stop getting on my nerves? It took a while for her to understand but when she did the result was hilarious.

"I've been flirting with a thug all this while?" Her breath hitched in disbelief. "I've been making all these gestures for a man who has survived in jail?"

I shook my head at her in disbelief.

"My mind has been a pig rolling in mud for a man who didn't use to have good intentions once upon a time."

"Do you even listen to yourself?" I asked her.

"Oh right, sorry no offence."

She was impossible.

"You," someone yelled. "How dare you put your filthy hands on her?"

I jumped out of my seat. Had it been an hour already? I'd planned on escaping before he decided to come back. My eye was already sore from the impact of his hard fists earlier. I didn't want to go blind.

"It wasn't me," I moaned. It wasn't like I couldn't fight him, I definitely could. There was no lack of confidence as well that I'd lose. However, there lay no point in retorting to actions that result in regret later. "Walker, will you tell him I didn't get you pregnant?"

"I don't know anything about this."

I looked at her incredulously. He ran towards me so I sprinted to the other side of her bed.

"Do you want him to blast my other eye as well? Please, stop being difficult."

"Do you even have good enough salary to support both of them boy?"

"Listen, even though that baby isn't my responsibility I'd support them through a tornado if it comes to that."

"How can I believe your word when here lays the result of your carelessness?"

I groaned.

"I can assure you this isn't my art work."

"Do you have any proof?"

"Jamie, please help," I pleaded.

Shark was gaining distance on me. There was an injection lying on the side table which seemed like the only weapon I could defend myself with. There wasn't the need to hurt anyone. Jamie was chuckling at the scene. He was constantly fuming insults at my direction. The pressure was getting to me.

"I couldn't have done this because I'm still a virgin."

Deafening silence followed the confession. I looked from one to another. Suddenly both of them burst out laughing. I sat down blushing. They couldn't stop guffawing. What was so funny was beyond me.

"Well, it was you who knocked sense into me," Shark said proudly.

It had been a while since they'd calm down. Thankfully, they were focusing on the metamorphosis that Shark went through instead of the sadness that my life was.

"I think you're the one who actually understood how we felt instead of punishing us. You made me realize how fragile life was. It was kids like you who we wanted to raise not people like us. If we wanted that to happen we had to finish ourselves and instead work on the potential we have. All I wanted with life was revenge for the way it had treated me. You taught me the importance was neither fighting it nor loosing from it."

"So what is it?" Jamie asked confused.

Was it just me or did she look adorable baffled at what she'd taught such a grown man.

"Well, living it. It wasn't easy at first obviously. I decided to be someone who wasn't there when I needed them in my time of injustice - a lawyer. I understand the victim's point of view better without the need of education as such. It's not like I haven't gone through books though. I'm smart."

"You're also quite handsome. Who would have though what that beard hid?" Walker chuckled.

I hit my hand on my forehead. Could this get more ridiculous?

"So any lady lucks yet?"

"I'll go get some coffee. The doctor said your reports will be out in another ten minutes. We'll leave soon. See you Shark."

He smirked at me. "Take good care of my angel. Also, get some."

"Whatever," I mumbled.

*   *   *

"What is this?"

She was sitting with her legs perched on the futon. A bowl of popcorn was on her stomach as she flipped through something on the television.

"I think you should go away Romance. This isn't for you. Only people with strength can watch this."

I could see her face was pale. That didn't mean my ego was less hurt. "I can endure anything. Bring it on."

"Don't say I didn't warn you."

After five minutes I was sitting with my eyes wide open.

"Is this . . . are you watching porn?" I asked aghast.

"Keep watching."

After half an hour I was done with life. She was cracking jokes about how useful the bulge was for keeping plates and bowls when eating while I couldn't take my eyes off the screen. What the hell was happening? I was so glad for once in my life that I wasn't a woman.

"Ah . . ." The woman on the screen screamed. I yelled in fright to as the camera shifted focus to unwanted areas.

My hands automatically clutched Walker's in a need to be comforted. This was the scariest movie ever.

"What are you watching?" I stuttered.

"How babies are born? Isn't it obvious?"

I was on the verge of fainting. This was disgusting. How could I let Jamie go through all the process?

Suddenly, the woman shouted so loudly I squeezed Walker's hand hard making her squeal in pain.

"Are you okay?" I said in worry.

"Look what you did?" she sobbed. She pulled her index finger back. I lost all colour.

I'd broken her finger.

I ran towards the landline and frantically redialled. The hospital was probably going to sue me for harming a woman so much. That's when I realized how much like an idiot I'd been dialling for the institution that was in another state. No wonder, the ambulance never came. I'd cut the call immediately after giving the address in a hurry to make sure she was fine. The ringtone was so low that I would have never heard if they did call back.

I called the right place and gave the perfect address.

"Why are you laughing?" I asked confused.

"You're so cute."

"What?"

"Didn't you ever notice I'm double jointed? All my fingers can bend see."

That's when I rushed to the bathroom sick.

The hospital should know about harm towards men as well.

"Now you'll know what morning sickness feels like," Jamie giggled.

"Go away," I groaned.

She patted me till I was fine. Then she wiped away my sweat lovingly. She held my hand and pulled me towards the couch. Gently, she placed my head on her belly, switched the channel so that it started showing off some action movie and then caressed my hair as if for once we were an actual couple.

And just like that Jamie Summer Walker managed to turn a horrible day into one of the best days of my life.

The Day I Rolled My Eyes at Jamie

I hadn't seen Jamie since a month now. I'd visited her for a week after the hospital fiasco but I was back to my own defects. The fairness lay in not subjecting the baby and my love to all this or what I became after all this. Thus, I quit hanging about her.

It seemed my life had gone into hibernation in wait of that ray of sunshine. Somehow the darkness left seemed never ending, as if falling into an abyss. I missed gazing at her sweet face shamelessly as it lit up like the fourth of July. The silence from the absence of the constant blabber was deafening.

"Listen, useless burden, will you drop Luke to . . ."

I ignored the dead silence.

"You're smoking."

"Yeah, are you sure? Thank you for the resourceful information Sherlock," I answered annoyed.

He didn't speak for a while. I almost thought he'd walked off. My happiness was short lived however.

"It isn't the right thing to do. I don't want you to smoke. You can do whatever bull you want to do in your worthless life, end up in prison for all I care. Just don't go around burning your insides whatever the reason maybe. I don't care."

I hid my astonishment. Was it just my hallucination or was Parsley actually trying to be my older brother? I pulled out the cigarette from my mouth and stubbed it.

"Thank you."

Two simple words and yet the impact was hard. I never in my wildest dreams imagined Parsley of all the people to ever thank me. Before I could react further there was a loud bang of the front door and whatever moment had been created was extinguished in seconds.

My mind was screaming at me to light another medium of pleasure. I ignored the requests. It was stressful not to be able to see the woman I loved beyond comprehension but it was not a reason to while away my life in a smoke. I was a better man than that.

My phone vibrated. I gazed at the caller id. Ah! The nostalgic feeling of desires, of the lost pleasure and all those times I'd found life worth living for, hit me. I tried my best to fight the temptations. It was worthless. If any of my brothers found me with them again, they would flip. Deep down even I knew it wasn't worth anyone's anger. I shouldn't be indulging in this. I should sit at home and finish my English essay so as to maintain my strict principles of punctuality.

*   *   *

The world was my plate and I would devour every morsel of grain on it. Was it even possible in reality for a human to feel the rotating movements of the Earth? If the answer was in negation, it meant I'd finally become celestial. The feeling was exotic.

She strolled like snowfall, not the heavy kinds though. The moment the soft flake hit my cold skin, it burnt. This fire was a reminiscence of one being. The one girl I would currently give up my limbs to see. The lights were dimming in and out. I could feel my heart beat increase as the flames hit me again. These were the embers I'd desired to feel for so long on my constantly freezing skin.

I wanted to stand up tall and spew out poetry like a nineteenth century lover for my flame. However, something was pinning me down. I forced myself to put up a fight but it seemed useless as opposed to their strength. It was probably my limbs which had decided to give up because otherwise pushing me down against my will was a difficult task.

There was a voice calling out to me. I could sense even in my daze state that it was her. My body screamed out in protest as I tried my best to relax so that I could get out of my trance. The whole world was becoming a big blot of blur. Suddenly, I felt some brutal force and I was pulled up. There were so many rainbows around. I wanted to skip and squeal like a five year old but the restraint was still there. My emotions were taking a downturn slowly. I was afraid of falling into depression.

I did fall. It felt really soft, the surface. So, I let my senses switch off and everything blacked out.

*   *   *

"Are you glad now?"

"I want food," I grumbled dazed. I ignored the voice. My head felt really heavy.

"I thought you knew better than this. As always, it was wrong to trust you."

I reached out for the glass of water on the side table. The liquid burnt a satisfying feel down my parching throat. There were so many sore spots on my body as if I'd just faced a thrashing. There was no definition of sense at the moment.

"Rome, I warned you not to get into these things. Don't you understand what you've put us all through, yet again? Every time I decide to give you one more chance, you do everything in your power to screw things up. After all that . . . what mom faced, you still have the guts to do something this horrendous. I applaud your insensitivity. I really wanted to start fresh with you, forgive you for all that you've done but you . . ."

I threw my glass at the wall in anger. The broken pieces felt like all the words he'd just thrown at my direction.

"Don't try to act as if you care now. You want to start fresh with me? What kind of bull is that now? Please, why don't you go back to licking Grover's posterior? You can even think that I would believe in a word you say is a joke for me. After all these years, without even providing a valid reason you still blame me then please, be my guest. It won't kill me now. As a matter of fact – I blame you! I blame all of you for what I've become. I don't have to deal with this."

I started storming off. He held my arm tightly. I tried shrugging it off but as opposed to his built, Parsley was a strong man.

"Rome," he said in a poker voice. "Just remember this. Next time I will not save you."

He let go. I walked out but the gravity of his tone unsettled me. What had happened at the hub? My intuition told me that somehow I had to be grateful that Parsley had arrived there for some really bad stuff had gone down. I felt foolish. Never had I lost my senses so badly. However, admitting that would be a big deal. Ego sure is a man's worst enemy.

"Parse, was Summer there?"

The most important thing had slipped out of my mind. He was aware of the importance of the question for me and hence I was sure he would put me through a struggle to get an answer. There would be a subjection of harassment rendering me embarrassed just for a simple piece of information.

"First of all," he started off with that tone of authority. I despised him yet again having the upper hand. "I need a sincere apology. You need to make me ecstatic for saving your worthless life. Fixate on the fact of how useless you were and how I was your hero. In case I ever need a favour you won't think twice before fulfilling it for me."

There is was. The anticipated guilt trip he wanted out of me.

"No," I muttered, gritting my teeth in defiance.

"It's too late to apologize, I said it's too late . . ." he started singing.

I rolled my eyes. If Summer hadn't been so important to me or had it been anyone else I needed to find out about, I would have walked off. "Fine, I apologize."

"I'm holding on the rope got me ten feet of the ground . . ."

"Parse," I threatened him. It was humiliating enough to admit him being the bigger guy. Now, he was literally egging me to beg.

"Oh look, I'm late for practise. I'll see you later loser."

"I'm really sorry Parse. You saved my life, you're my hero. If there's anything you'd ever need, I'll do my best to fulfil."

"Yes she was there. The police almost found you but we both managed to distract them successfully. She's fine and I made sure she went back safe not that I give a damn."

I wanted to know more. That would mean another set of pleas which I wasn't ready for. The only factor that let me go peacefully was that she was safe. How does she even manage to track me down half the times was a mystery. Maybe Walker was a stalker. She must be working for FBI or someone just so to find out secrets about my family.

I needed to eat something before I lost more sense.

There wasn't any cooked dish in the fridge so I decided to make a sauté vegetable salad. I could later go and pick up some food from the deli. My mind wandered off to the night at prom when I'd been drunk. There must be some hint as to who that Perry character was. I'd seen Walker with him just once but it had been so fleeting that I couldn't make out who he was.

Then it struck me.

Paris Pulaski, the guy Walker had hung out with since she joined school. It all made sense now. He'd been smitten by her. I'd watched her laugh along to all the lame jokes he cracked. When she wasn't with me she'd be hanging out with that Tiara woman and this riff-raff.

What if my not visiting the school and ignoring Walker had brought them together? I paled. It wasn't like she'd cared to come visit me anyways. I didn't even know how her pregnancy was ailing. The fury made me start chopping faster until the inevitable occurred and the blade cut a patch of my skin off the finger.

Pain cruised through my body.

I was staring at my finger in fascination. Gone were the days when blood would rattle me. After the rehab it had become a source of unwanted memories but currently there was so much I wanted to forget that trying to cope up with the past was laughable. The knife I'd been cutting the vegetables with had dropped to the floor. What if I could lick the blood? The prospect of cannibalism had always been fascinating.

Someone dropped a band-aid on the table. I looked up to see Turkey flying in circles over my head. I ignored him.

He perched on my shoulder and poked me with his beak. When I still didn't heed to what he desired he poked me again, incessantly.

"Alright," I groaned. "I'll put this . . . happy?"

It cooed and flew to feed from the bowl I'd placed especially for his visits. Even though my loath for the bird had reduced a ton from the first day we met, it still didn't imply I was in irrevocable love with it. Turkey somehow felt like a human though. For a bird, he sure was smart.

"I thought you'd never listen."

I froze.

"Oh my God, what have you done with yourself?"

The school hadn't seen my face for almost a month now. They had probably sent notices ranging from detention to expulsion but no one really cared. I didn't complaint. Even if I had managed to drag myself to school hoping I wouldn't see her face, the authorities would have kicked me out. I hadn't shaved since a month or groomed myself properly. If anybody else saw Xerkis Moon they wouldn't recognize me. It felt like I was Romance Winter now, someone very few knew.

"Will you stop pretending like I'm not present?"

If you only know Walker how impossible it was to assume your absence in life. I gave her a sideway look which to my astonishment made her blush.

"So?" I smirked. "What's happening with you Walker?"

Her colour deepened.

"I err . . . you"

"Look, I have a lot of work to accomplish in life than sit here and hear you stutter. Catch up with you later."

"Your rugged looks are making my heart beat wild which it shouldn't be because I'm suppose to dislike you in that way not that I do in general. You have got to stop looking sexy, it's not healthy."

I chuckled. How I had missed this same old Jamie Summer Walker. I still didn't want much with any girl but this one was completely different. It was like someone who didn't appreciate chocolates but when it came to Nutella, the story was another to narrate.

"I have to show you something," she said looking towards the floor.

"Okay."

We hadn't hung out all this while so I wouldn't ever let this golden opportunity slip away.

"Are you for real now?" I asked with my eyebrow raised at her.

Her body crouched up as she clutched her palms together behind her back. She was looking anywhere but at me.

"Walker you are pregnant."

"Oh are you serious? I never realized," she said rolling her eyes at me.

"You can't ride this."

I pointed towards the tandem with an exhausted sigh. This was a losing battle but I had to try for the sake of her health.

"Are you calling me fat Romance Winter," she asked narrowing her eyes at me as a threat.

"Err . . . obviously not?"

"So you are calling me too thin to have the energy for this even after knowing I'm pregnant and cannot be titled *thin?*"

This was so confusing. How could I ever win this?

"You know what let's just go where you wanted to take me. You're perfect the way you are."

The blue cycle gleamed in the sun. Whoever was free enough to polish this thing must be given a reward. I wouldn't spend a second on trying to make this shine. Walker was humming a tune in a low tone. My mind was still rattled with the discovery of who Perry was. For some reason, I didn't want to let Walker know that I was aware.

"Why did you quit smoking?"

I'd seen her smoke once when I'd had a terrible outburst. In fact it had been the very day we'd ridden this same tandem to Old Amy's cottage. That day I'd yelled at her not to smoke and as far as I knew she hadn't witnessed her, whatever she told me about continuing it.

"You asked me not to."

I gave her an appalled look.

"That doesn't mean you listen. I wasn't thinking straight."

"You don't like it. I won't do it."

There was such finality in her tone that I couldn't say further. I peeked into the side mirror to see her face. She had a determined look etched on to her features. We had been pedalling for quite a while now. The city was switching into countryside. The trees were increasing in number and there was more twittering of birds than horns of cars echoing in the atmosphere. We cycled in silence.

"Walker, where are you taking me?" I asked her gently.

There was no response.

"Jamie, are you there?"

She cleared her throat. Minutes passed by but I didn't hear the melodious jingle of her voice.

"Take your time. It's alright."

Suddenly she stopped pedalling. We would have lost balance if I hadn't been keeping alert. My legs immediately landed on the ground to act as brakes. Her body fell on me slightly but she straightened up. Somehow I was aware she wasn't ready to face me yet so I kept staring ahead at the winding road disappearing between the trees.

"It's them," she said in almost a non-audible whisper.

"Uh . . . who are you talking about?"

She got down from the cycle. Her body was still as the wind gently blew her blue frock and hair in one direction.

My mind was still not used to the redness. I stood next to her gazing right ahead.

There was a red brick house after the spread of farms a long way ahead. There were two huge trees surrounding the little man made structure which provided shade. It was a neat scene with the sun hitting off the crops. The silence was broken now and then by the sound of farm animals. There was a little red bicycle gleaming against the wall of the cottage. The door opened and a small kid ran out while shouting something happily to whoever was inside.

"That's my family," she frowned. "That's where my real parents live. I found the details in the administration office."

She was back to the emotionless tone I despised. The look of helplessness never suited her.

"Why did you come here?" I asked kindly. "You knew it'll have an adverse effect on you."

"I need to face fears," she mumbled.

"Who told you that?"

"You know people say it."

I sighed. "Walker, you don't always have to follow the world rules. Just be selfish why you don't?"

"I just want . . ."

She was caressing her belly now. The look of sadness was enough to break my heart. I knew what she wanted though. She wanted to see what she was missing.

"It's just that this baby should not face what I did."

I was completely off the mark. I should have known this woman wouldn't do anything that revolved around the word selfish.

"Listen," I said holding her hands. She looked at me as if whatever I said would change the world. The pressure to make my point had never been this stringent. "I've known Hunter for years. He's a fool who makes decision that never turn up right, there's always something that goes wrong with his life, he's served in juvenile for quite a while . . ."

"Romance?" she giggled.

"Right sorry," I smirked. "He'll love that kid more than his life which is saying something. I wouldn't have let you give the baby to him otherwise."

"She'll be fine, you promise?"

I cupped her cheek and wiped away the single tear falling like a dew drop. She . . . Walker was having a baby girl. I didn't even want to imagine what else I'd missed this month other than her finding out the gender.

"Yes, I promise. Otherwise I'll go get the baby myself to you, okay?"

She nodded. Her eyes travelled back to the cottage.

"Do you really have to do this? If you do then I'll walk in right there with you Jamie. I'll make sure they know what a wonderful human they've let go off. They're idiots who don't deserve someone as perfect as you."

"Perfect?" she scoffed. "I live in an institution that is abnormal. There are so many things I've to hide from you that I can't be me half the time. I am fat right now. My hair is a mess. I don't have my best friends near me. I live in a dump. I'm the weakest human on this planet. I can't even be with the guy I love because my life sucks!"

I pulled her towards me and glared into her eyes.

"Your institution can suck it up because once school ends I'll make sure you have an apartment and that you're petitioned to live on your own as a minor. Secrets we all have and you tell me whatever you can which is fine for me so you shouldn't worry about anything. Secrets are like weapons that shouldn't always be used for the bullets can cause wounds that will not always heal. You're fat because you're going to be giving life to someone which in my mind matters more than some insecurity. Your hair is shining in the sun rays and all I want to do is run my fingers through the glorious waterfall all day. Your best friends will be with you forever whatever the distance because that's how friendship works."

Her eyes were shining again with water. I didn't care for she needed to know what I felt. It was high time Walker realized how important her presence was.

"Weak? I'll really laugh at that if this wasn't that serious. You quit smoking the instant I told you. How many times you've made sure off your dislike towards the same and if I get a cigarette in my hand right now, I'd still smoke it. You're the strongest person I know. You're ready to go through nine months of pain for someone else. For God sake woman, what strength do you want? Most of all you still love that Perry boy even after he's hurt you so much. I salute you."

She hugged me. I held her close making sure my passionate speech had reached the silly woman. I didn't even care if it were the hormones anymore. The fact that I could make her smile was enough to make me last a lifetime.

We both pulled apart and looked at the cottage again. Time passed by. Her palm became sweaty as it held mine tighter. I chuckled.

"Sweat?" she asked blushing. Walker had an issue with perspiring. She hated anyone touching her if there was sweat on her body. Whenever I held her hand, it always became sweaty which for some reason she found annoying and I amusing. I clutched her hand tighter as she tried pulling away.

"So?" I asked distracting her. "Shall we?"

"No," she said determined.

"What?"

"There's some bits of past that shouldn't be scavenged more for that just leads to pain. They were a secret and they'll remain that. Someone told me after all - secrets are like weapons that shouldn't always be used for the bullets can cause wounds that will not always heal."

I shook my head at her. "You're something Walker."

"You're everything Winter."

"Yuck, so much romance . . ."

"You're such an irony."

"What do you want to do?" I asked her desperately wanting to switch the topic.

"Let's go eat choc-chip ice cream."

That's when involuntarily I rolled my eyes at her. No matter how long we didn't speak to each other there would always be that one day when Walker would cycle on a tandem right in front of my front door and then with her stupid pets take me some place as if nothing had ever happened to cause upset to either of us.

Life wasn't a Disney movie but when Jamie Summer Walker was around, every moment was much more worth than a movie's.

The Day I Winked At Jamie

All of them looked at me. I gulped. What had happened now? Trouble should be my girlfriend with the way things had been working lately between us yet it still demanded to remain the affair you don't talk about. This reminded me of an older situation where once before they all had gathered similarly with the same concentrated looks of judgements painting their faces. That time Mr. Winter who had finally got off from work to unfortunately come meet his sons, had been present as well. Things had taken the wrong turn making my fate end up in a twisted journey circling around rehab and therapies. My nerves were probably wrecked due to that reason.

Lately, I'd been indulging in a lot of things that were intervention worthy. I was afraid this was what it was. If the thought was true then I was prepared to walk out. There was no question of me being a minor anymore and listening to any order. They could all kill me for all I cared but no way was I ever ending up in that hell house again.

It was sad to notice though how much Jamie had changed me. It had taken a year to practise being immaculate with methods, to build an empire of stringent beliefs and live a life robotically. She'd brought colour to it, life, joy and all those things I'd been desperately running from. Love had once ended me. I couldn't let it win again.

So, I behaved casually.

"What's up boys?" I tried in a confident voice. It didn't work for the looks didn't waver from their sternness.

I threw a glare at Parsley. It had been a week since that incident but I was pretty sure he'd ratted out on me. If there was one thing I least appreciated in life, it was complaints.

"So . . . I'm going to go get some orange juice. Anyone would like to have a glass? It's healthy what with the whole citrus vitamin story going . . ."

"Sorry"

I looked abashedly at Grover. They were just moments away from breaking down and starting off with the snide comments. He walked towards me. I bit my lip in anticipation of the beating that would now occur. I shut my eyes when he was at an arm's length.

I felt someone engulf my body. He had more width than me so I immediately got the feeling of someone protecting me. He was holding me tightly as if his life depended on it. It was the best hug I'd ever received in my life. The fact that it was from my brother after all these years pushed out the air from my body.

"I'm so sorry," he mumbled into my ears.

My eyes were wide open in shock. Either they would pop out or my heart would stop in an attack. I gazed at Parsley who was leaning against the wall, looking sadly at the floor. There were creases on his face that painted a picture of remorse. As I didn't receive any explanation from there so I turned towards Luke who was sniffling.

"What the hell is going on?"

Tears always made me uncomfortable. I wanted to dearly walk away before things took a crazier turn but something told me things were already worse.

Hope grew in me.

"Is it Mr. Winter? Did he pass away?" I asked casually.

"I wish he did," Grover muttered.

I pushed him off. His face was scrunched up like he was trying his best to hold on. I knew when he was ceasing his emotions; his eyes and nose would go red. The effort rang warning bells in my mind. Then the words he had said some seconds ago sank in.

"Hey, what's wrong?" My concern was rising every second.

"All these years we've treated you like a stranger. I don't even know how to begin. No matter how much I apologize, it will never make up for anything," he was talking sadly.

I was too shocked to speak.

"Romance, I know I've never been the older brother to you but you should know . . ."

He looked into my eyes. There is something different when two pair of eyes actually meets. The meaning is much deeper. It had been years since I'd been able to look into my brother's eyes. I'd forgotten how warm they had been.

"I love you."

Those three words

It had been ages since I'd heard those words from them. There was so much genuine that the years off coldness vanished. Grover was tearing up now. I'd known my brother to be a strong man. He'd inspired me to be the same. He'd held me sobbing like a lunatic at mom's birthday. He'd been the backbone for the whole family. Tears falling from his eyes just magnified how strong he was.

He was brave enough to admit what he felt.

Jamie had been telling me the same thing all this while. This was the moment it made sense.

"I love you too brother."

I pulled him in for a hug. He sobbed into my shoulders. For once, it wasn't about controlling as a *man* should but breaking down as every man should have the courage to. Bonds were an emotional talk after all.

"I want a hug too," Luke wailed. He ran towards us and tried to encircle whatever his lanky arms could cover.

I pulled him in for a hug as well.

"I love you guys," Luke yelled out loud. "I promise I won't swear for shit."

We both hit his head from the back.

He giggled.

"So," Grover said pulling away. "This calls for a celebration. I'll get us all some orange juice."

"What about some beer. I feel like my manliness has gone down so many notches with all the tears," Luke said.

"Orange juice had citrus. You heard Romance before. Let's have something on his request for once," Grover said with finality in his voice.

Luke opened his mouth to rebel. Grover pulled him into his arms and slung his arm around his neck. He pulled the boy into the kitchen. I smiled as their banter reduced in volume. It wasn't until I heard footsteps that I remembered I had one more sibling.

My eyes met a pair of browns. It was only Parsley who had inherited mother's features. He had the soft velvety skin mom had. It had roughened and tanned in all these years of playing football in the blazing sun.

He had his arms folded. He opened his mouth to say something but shut it again. A moment of silence followed between us. He finally broke the gaze and gave me a curt nod without looking into my eyes. I gave him a small smile quite aware of the fact that he couldn't see me. He turned to walk away but stopped and looked at me again.

"You should thank that Summer chick. She came and knocked sense into us as well as father. Dad got weird. He cleared out some serious accusations. Believe me Romance, I don't like him anymore. It wasn't as if I did anyways. That man was always fishy about everything. This doesn't imply that I've fallen in . . . *irrevocable* love with you. I just care for you enough to see you breathe."

All of that coming from Parsley was like rain on a hot summer day. My smile widened. I patted his shoulder. His frown relaxed. There was a hint of smile on his face.

I watched his back as it disappeared into the hallways to get into the kitchen. I took out my phone and texted that one person who had again brought sunshine to my life. I'd left her in a mess yesterday. I should've taken her a little more seriously.

It didn't mean things changed with my situation. I needed those addictions. It wasn't a question of choosing anymore.

Me: *Knock knock!*

I smiled at her profile picture. She was poking her tongue sideways giving her flirtiest wink. Radiance of the phone seemed less than what shone on that face.

Jamie: *What is the use of this exaggeration when I don't know who you are?*

Memories flooded my mind. I chuckled.

Me: *I see you have learnt the art to be cocky? Is that Miss Walker a copy of the original edition of the perfect question I'd thrown at you some time.*

Grover was yelling out my name.
"I'll be there in five," I yelled back.
He shouted in agreement. My phone buzzed and I looked down.

Jamie: *I see you have learnt the art of living life casually. It's nice to see some break from the lifeless puppet you'd been.*

I couldn't agree more. My blood flowed better. There was lightness in my head though if that was truly due to *art of living* was a tricky question.

Me: *Come here Walker. I'll show you just how much a lifeless puppet I am with the best hug of your life.*

"Show it to me then."
I jumped.

"You've got to stop creeping from behind me. I really need to shut off that window," I chuckled as my heart picked back the normal speed. I looked around for the obnoxious pet of hers. Actually, for her pets that pig still sticking around. It baffled me how no one had yet made bacon out of that fat meat.

"How do you feel?" Jamie asked concerned.

I groaned. All this time and she still stuck with that annoying question.

"Let's go have some dinner. I *feel* hungry like never before."

"Wait," she stretched her voice holding my arm. "Aren't you forgetting something?"

She let go of my hand and opened her arms. I chuckled.

"Aw come here sunshine," I cooed.

Just like so many times before I couldn't help thinking how much her body fit with mine. We were the two pieces of jigsaw puzzles that would always fit. Then there was that other unknown piece which tried its best and managed to fit with her. That though never completes the picture the way it was suppose to be - just one of those let-it-go-because-it-works in life.

"Done?" I pulled away quickly before my feelings got the better of me. "Let's go."

She followed me quietly. I felt a tad bit guilty but the smell of steak vanquished all thoughts.

The kitchen was full of utensils being banged. I saw Parsley swerving the sauce in the pan. Grover was laying out the table while Luke was standing next to him with a knife held tightly in his hand. He was spewing out some dialogues like a pirate. A white napkin was tied up in a way that it was covering one of his eyes.

"Ar! Ar! Matey, come join 'ere the feast we hold. Where my parrot be now?"

"You better sit down properly mate or I'll tell you what a parrot is capable off," Grover scolded him. "Let go off the knife as well for I'm pretty sure you'll stab me soon. That will be the end of the handsome legacy of the Winter Empire."

"You're forgetting the sexy one is still alive," I guffawed. For a second I forgot that we had reconciled as my body automatically convulsed in defence of any attack such as wild knives or fruits but to my surprise the room burst into laughter.

"That's bang on Winter humour right there. Learn something Lukey. You've been missing so much."

I sighed. This was something that would take a lot of time to get over. It felt artificial that I was suddenly a part of them. It annoyed me suddenly that they heard a stranger's words over mine when all these years I'd tried to fix everything.

But then again, Walker could hardly be called a stranger. Many a time she just entered the house like it belonged to her. She'd keep her legs on the table and demand me to get some ice cream.

"I made your favourite dessert – tiramisu . . . that is if you still like it," Grover said ruffling his hair with trepidation.

"Fine," I snapped.

"Are you okay?" His face fell. I saw a tinge of disappointment and guilt lining his face. "Did I do something wrong?"

"No, no big brother," I began sarcastically. I was trying my best to keep the tone soothing but it wasn't working. The blood was rushing into the ears and face. "This is all perfect. After ten years I would still love the same dessert because all this time I knew one day you'd just forgive me for whatever god forsaken punishment you were putting me through and then I can sit and eat some bloody tiramisu."

Silence followed us. Luke was looking from me towards Grover and back. Jamie placed her hand on my shoulder but I shrugged it off.

"He's just trying to be nice Romance. Cut him some slack. He's been working all day just to make it special for you," Parsley said calmly.

"But Romance has gone through a lot with you guys. He isn't use to all this you know. It'll take him time. Every change does."

"Did I ask you?" Parsley snapped at Jamie. She flinched beside me.

"I'm just trying to help," she whispered.

"Haven't you done enough? There's some meddling an outsider can do. Please stay out of the family business freaking intruder."

She whimpered. I really wanted to snap at Parsley but my anger was taking over all the senses. I tried to calm down for fury was never the answer to any problem.

"You're being really rude. Is this how you talk to women?" Jamie bashed out at him finally.

"I'll talk exactly the way I desire. There's nothing your fat mouth will change. Get a grip on your own life before you try fixing someone else's."

"I'll fix your brain for you loser. This is the same fat mouth that has kissed . . ."

"Guys," I yelled. "Shut up all of you. I'm so done over here."

I stormed off. Even in my head I knew what a sissy fit this had been. As soon as I reached my room, I calmed down. The feeling of guilt was worse than ever. I sat down on the bed. Jamie walked in but didn't say a word. She sat down next to me. In half an hour she fell asleep. I pulled back some scarlet tresses lovingly. She smiled in her sleep. I'd taken all this time to concentrate and get my head straight. What had happened tonight on my part was the worst I could show off myself.

Such innocence and goodness should never be put through the mask of sadness. It ruined the laws of nature. She deserved only affection just as some few others I could think off. Her head was in my lap so I gently lifted it and placed a pillow under it.

"Hey," I said softly.

Grover's face hit the table. He had been sleeping with his hands cupping his face. I had tried my best to be gentle.

"Don't hurt me for my knuckles will be ten times worse."

"I'd take that warning real seriously," I chuckled backing off with my hands in the air.

"Hey, it's you. Come sit down, I'll heat up some food for you."

In that moment I saw my brother grow ten years older. I didn't like the lines on his young face or the way his eyes were crinkled up in sadness.

"I just hate the fact that this family can never be together. It's always broken up. There are so many bonds to tape that we might as well give up and let the vase remain broken," Grover mumbled sadly.

"You know what mum always told me?"

His eyes sought mine. They were trying to console me but it wasn't me who needed that right now. He put down the hot dish with the steak in it. It still smelled heaven. I took hold of his hand. He gave me a smile and sat down gratefully.

"She said that there are times when storms hit hard. They destroy everything in their sight blindly. The impact shatters everything but there's something that can't be touched. It's nature's way of yelling doom but its nature's way of teaching you. Love can survive anything. I love you guys and hence we shall outlive all miseries."

I felt exhausted with hunger. Grover petted my head as I began shovelling the food down. We spoke about what had been happening in school. At one moment he looked at me with concern and I knew what was coming next so I meticulously switched the topic. It had been an amazing night. I kept the dish in the sink.

"Goodnight brother, I'll see you tomorrow," he yawned tiredly.

"Hey bro, aren't you forgetting something?"

He looked at me with confusion.

"Someone made some delicious tiramisu. This stomach is going wild for it. Give me my love so I can devour it passionately."

He grinned at me. He took it out and placed it in front of me. "I'm going to go before you start making love. I really don't want to intrude in this scene."

"Learn from the expert brother. There are tricks that will drive your girlfriend wild."

He chuckled but waved his hand. I ravenously consumed the delicacy. Grover sure had some talent behind that cool male exterior he strutted around with.

"What are you doing here?"

I looked as Jamie walked in cutely rubbing her eyes off the sleep.

"Just you know fixing things."

"You took up a job of the plumber?" Jamie chuckled.

"You're damn lame in life."

"I make better jokes than you."

"I flirt better than you."

"Prove it," she teased her tongue poking out at me. This wasn't healthy for me and therefore I pulled her hand down making her fall on the chair.

"I've finally discovered what love means?" I whispered close to her face.

She smiled nervously. I could see I already had her caught in my charm. "What?"

"Jamie Summer Walker"

With a confident smirk I winked at her making her flush bright red.

"Looks like Summer is being affected by its own heat eh?"

With those words hanging in the air, I threw the spoon in the bowl with vigour, put my hands in my pocket and walked out whistling.

This was the cherry on my perfectly baked chocolate (preferably Toblerone) cake.

The Day I Pinched
Jamie s Cheeks

It was still the same school routine. No matter what we'd gone through, she'd still be there at the gate every morning waiting for me in her car. There would still be those obscene beats to which she rapped loudly. The constancy of at least something kept me sane. We'd finished the day's course so I was sprawled across the couch doing nothing. My mind however was thinking about a lot of things.

"Romance . . ."

I didn't respond until he hit me gently on the head.

"Eh, you're calling me?"

"I don't remember naming any furniture around Romance. Get out of the summer world."

By his grin I could easily make out the meaning wasn't that direct. I shrugged pretending to not care. The biggest issue was Walker was around in the house. We were at a point where no one spoke about the so called love feelings anymore.

"What is this rumour I receive little brother?"

I groaned. Every time he said that I regretted listening to the next words. His grin widened.

"You've started dating this not so riff-raff Stalker girl?"

Lately, my anger issues had been resurfacing. If Grover said anything against her I couldn't promise a clean scene.

"You know I don't like being ignored Romance," Grover said grave.

This respect of naming me properly would take so much time to adjust. I opened my mouth to retaliate when he ruffled my hair lovingly.

"Hey, you are doing okay?" The concern in his voice had me off track again.

Changes were one thing when not constant led to indecisions in my life. They were one thing I avoided as much as possible. This sudden brotherly love was the biggest challenge I was facing to adjust with. It was as if any second they'd burst through with guns showing how foolish I'd been to fall in their trap.

"Romance . . .?" He was shaking me.

"Yeah, no everything is fine."

He looked at me with disbelief but nodded after a while. We started discussing strategies about the upcoming football match. The happiness that surged through me due to the normalcy of the situation was immeasurable. Even when we argued about two players, the brotherly factor didn't diminish.

I couldn't believe how much I'd missed this.

"Oh no, I had to pick Lukey from practise. I'll catch up with you later."

He patted my shoulder. I nodded throwing him a smile.

"Hey," he said scratching his head. I knew instantly he was nervous. "I don't know much about these love feelings but I'm telling you to not give up on anything. Even if you don't score once, it's not like you can't again or quit playing the game. Just keep the diligence and passion you'll fare."

Even though it wasn't required, this was the best thing Grover had ever told me. The main point was feeling less burdened about problems. It felt as if Grover had reduced the heaviness of having unrequited love. I gave him thumbs up sign.

Just as he closed the door, Jamie walked in with a tub of choc-chip ice cream. I stifled a groan.

"Did you know the father penguins take care of the eggs, keeping them warm and not the mother?"

I laughed. "Why are you so random in life Walker?"

"I'm telling you it's a miracle. Imagine if in the future I leave the eggs at home so that I can go for a job and you can stay home keeping them warm. Women empowerment would be at its best height."

"What?" I asked in disbelief. I had started laughing so hard that no more words were making sense to be said aloud. I took hold of both the ends of her cheeks and pulled. She complained but how could I resist such extreme level of cuteness without rewarding it. Her skin felt soft beneath my fingers. I couldn't get over the charm or the want of her skin. Colour flooded my cheeks as images flashed in my head. I pulled back my hand.

"You are so silly. You don't know any facts at all. What even is this boring life Hunter . . .?"

She stopped looking at me scared.

Hunter

Not only was my best friend's name that, it also included some wonderful personality. How I would love to scratch that name out of my birth certificate the minute I got my hands on it. Mr. Winter had constantly failed to impress me all these years. He didn't deserve any form of recognition.

I moved closer to her face so that the freckles were visible. Her eyes looked down but I pulled her chin up so that she was staring at me again.

"Every time that a male penguin falls in love with the female, it goes all around its area to find that one perfect stone. Once, he makes sure the stone is as perfect as you are Walker; he places it in front of the female's legs. If she kicks it away he never proposes any other woman and stays heartbroken but if she accepts, they stay together forever."

Her pupil widened a little.

They also said if people look at you with widened pupils they really love you.

She was staring at me holding her breath. Her hand was gently caressing the bulge that her belly was now. The school was approaching to an end and so was her pregnancy. It would be a month or so and Hunter's spawn would be roaming this planet. The way we were gazing into each other's eyes was lethal and hence I decided to change the topic to something that had been bothering me since ages.

"You never explained properly how you knew my actual name?"

"Well, I told you. I found you on Facebook."

"So show me this fake id which informed you such bull. I'll go punch Parsley then."

"It wasn't all Parsley you know."

I looked at her confused. How would she know who it was?

"I saw them take your picture once. Luke had placed his foot in front of your path as a stymie which you didn't notice and fell. They made a video and posted it online."

Some questions these brothers would have to answer soon.

My phone vibrated. It was kept beside Walker so I stretched my body across hers to reach it.

"If you don't mind I really don't . . ."

"Don't . . . like people crossing your personal space? Yes, I remember love."

Her face had mixed emotions of pride and despondence on it. She was stout and short, the perfect girl anyone could be lucky to have.

"So, show me this famous Facebook profile," I badgered her.

She seemed hesitant but my determination was pretty clear. I waited with bated breath as the screen loaded. This was the moment I'd have to control my anger. Someone had publically ruined my reputation, crossed boundaries which weren't the best ones to play with and posted pictures which could land them in trouble if I reported. However, family was always a different case.

"It's not that bad," Jamie murmured.

I glared at her. "Your face is not that bad, this is just horrible. Let me go find these brothers of mine."

"I err . . . have to go. I'll meet you later tonight for dinner."

I nodded distracted as my head concentrating on finding Parsley. Luke and Grover wouldn't be back for another hour or so. I searched downstairs before heading up.

"Parse," I called out to him.

There was no reply. I checked Luke's room. He wasn't there. I went towards his room. I knocked. No response. I was pretty sure he was inside the house for I'd been constantly sitting downstairs straight after school. The door to get out was right in front of my face all evening.

"Parse, I need to talk to you." When no one responded, I turned the knob and walked in. "there you are, I've been finding you since a while now. Obviously my brain didn't think of checking in your own room. I don't know why I've become so careless lately. Wait, are you feeling okay?"

He hadn't even peeked out from the blankets to acknowledge me even.

"Parse," I asked concerned. I walked forward till his face was in view. It was blotched red.

Speaking of red, why was he under a comforter in this blazing heat? I'd been sweating downstairs without air condition and Parsley had a habit of feeling hotter than normal. I caressed his forehead gently. It was blazing hot.

"Oh God, you have a crazy fever. I'm going to call a doctor and Grover."

He didn't say anything. The worry started multiplying in my head. My phone network was out. I ran downstairs but there was nothing again. I had to call them but first the important part was to neutralize his fever. I ran in the kitchen and filled up a bowl with cold water. Soon, I was sitting beside him dabbing a wet towel on his head.

"What are you doing," he grumbled. "I feel so pathetic."

"Parse, you are sick! Why didn't you call m- Grover or someone eh?"

"I tried calling you," he groaned. "You didn't pick up."

I'd never checked properly after picking the phone from across Walker. Damn it!

"I'm so sorry. Don't worry, I'll get help."

His hand clamped on my palm. The heat travelled all through me as well. What was wrong with him? I really needed to get a professional to look at him.

"I'm fine. Don't call anyone."

"Are you kidding me? You're hotter than the summer sun right now. I need to call someone."

"Don't mention anything with that girl in it. You know I don't like her. I don't want help. I don't want arguments."

I had to comply. He was stressing more which was making his face scrunch up in pain. It was only when his eyes were closed that I meticulously managed to shoot Grover a text.

"It's just stress," he spoke finally. "I've been worrying too much about things."

"What is wrong Parse?" I frowned.

"Just some illegal wars . . ."

"What?" I asked confused. He shrugged me off.

"I haven't slept in a week or eaten anything. How about if you really want to help, get me something to eat from downstairs."

I changed the towel from his forehead and ran downstairs. I knew he loved salads so I decided to fix him a Russian one, the way mom use to. I also remembered his affinity to hot chocolate when things weren't working out.

By the time I rushed back up though he'd passed out. I didn't disturb him for the sake of completing sleep.

The moment I stepped down from the last step, the door banged open and Grover rushed in yelling.

"Where is he? How is he? What is happening? Romance, where are you?"

"Hey, calm down. You'll wake him up. He's just having some wild fever along with extreme exhaustion. I think all he needs is rest. He'll be okay."

Grover plonked down on the sofa. "I've been telling him to take it easy but once that boy sets his mind on something, he just doesn't listen. That girl is also not helping with his health."

"What girl?"

Grover looked at me startled. He moved his eyes towards the television screen and mumbled something that sounded like toddler.

"Are you talking about Yasmine Yondler?"

He nodded his head slowly. "Yeah, she's sick. He's been trying to get her to have treatment but she's not listening to him. She's adamant she can go back to normal without chemo. How is that even possible? Everyone has tried telling her off, even me but she doesn't listen."

"Okay, do you think she'll listen to me?"

"Forget it Romance. You have enough to deal with already. It's not like you're running around in a full green football field."

"But . . ."

"I'll handle it. All I need is your support. I'll knock sense into Parsley once he's a little better."

I nodded. Luke had been staring at us quietly. He was sliding away when I caught up with him.

"So what is this fake id that's been circulating around this annoying social site about me eh? Do you have a clue?"

He looked at me innocently. "I've no clue what you're talking about bro."

"Really," I asked rolling my eyes. I took out my phone and opened the site again. "Ring any bells?"

"Uh . . . I've never seen this. You hate social media, don't you? Why would you have an id on the most social site ever?"

"What?" He was annoying me now. There was something with people not accepting guilt even after the same was literally smashing your face. I didn't want to burst out at my little brother unnecessarily. "I'm making some fresh juice. Do you want some?"

He nodded his features still genuinely confused. There was no knowing if he was faking it though. I hadn't stayed around him much to fathom his expressions. Knowing Luke as I knew him though, he would be lying to get safe from a beating.

This wasn't the biggest concern right now. Parsley was. I let it go.

*   *   *

"You know Angelique is hotter than Crystal. Have you seen her size?" Luke said cheerfully.

"Now wait a minute little one, don't hold your horses so high. My Crystal is way more perfect than your girl could ever be."

Nothing beat Jamie Summer Walker though.

"Please, all Crystal does is meth . . . I mean math."

"Not one more word or we shall fight young squire," my brother threatened mockingly pulling out an imaginary sword.

"Let's have it," Luke yelled enthusiastically pulling out another.

Both I and Parsley gave each other amused looks. It was one of the rare bonding moments I ever shared with him.

"Grover we all know you'd lose even if there was a needle sword fight," Parsley smirked. "With muscles like those all you're good for is picking Meth's books."

"Wait there sire, I shall deal with you after my conquest on this one."

Parsley chuckled.

He was looking better. The colour was getting normal on his face. The fact that Parsley could pass taunts about any of us was proof enough.

"Hey lover boy, pass me my phone," Grover yelled from across the room as he and Luke were still struggling in a combat.

"Amateurs," Parsley shouted. "You bet me and Romance can beat either of you anytime."

I picked up Grover's phone but stopped as the message sender's name registered in my brain. I pretended to bend down to tie my lace as my fingers swiftly pressed the message on the mobile screen. The best thing with Grover was he didn't have anything to hide nor was he scared of anyone finding anything related to him.

'How is he doing? I wanted to visit but you know how he has been lately. Romance also found out about the Facebook id. I didn't think he'd mention it ever so I said you and Luke have

made it. Please tell him you guys have, I'll owe you G-man. I spent the dinner time with Romance so couldn't come meet you. I will do that tomorrow. Goodnight!'

"Hey, that was unfair. You distracted me," Luke yelled.

"You don't concentrate on what's happening in present and try questioning my moves, this is what would happen," Grover replied back coolly. He was taking a fake bow. I

"Such a betrayal, such a betrayal must be written down in history," Parsley laughed.

Such a betrayal should be forged down on my skin, with my blood.

The Day I Last Met Jamie

I'd ignored her for weeks now. I'd lost count. My window was wedged down shut. Every time I even felt her presence in the house, I'd walk away. At first she'd tried her best to make me talk but soon she understood it was of no use.

I was so done with Jamie Summer Walker and her rucksack of lies.

Here I was wasting away my life yet again for another girl and another lost love. My heart, it felt dead. There were no emotions as I downed another bottle. All my hopes of not ending up like a loser again had been just that, hopes - the kind of hopes that were written down to be weak for fulfilment.

I tried stopping a long while back. That seemed like a dream now. My whole world was spinning. It was sad that the reality was the same.

That beautiful face appeared. I raced her tears as we do in monsoon with the raindrops on the vehicle's glass window. Her face was coming in and out of focus which was making it difficult for me to race. I was getting annoyed. Then her eyes fixed my irritation as they glowed with love. All the fake love I kept imagining all along. The freckles were like threads jumbled up into the best masterpiece possible on this planet.

She was hitting me with her brittle wrists. I was numb.

"I told you to be responsible but you never care to listen," she yelled at me.

Jamie Summer Walker had finally regained some of her shape. Baby girl was currently doing well in some charitable brought home of the Hunter family. I regretted not being there during the birth, when she actually needed me. However, there was no one to save me from myself. My illegal intake had me twirling in a different realm of pleasure where there exited no sense of emotions. It had been around two weeks possibly after which I was meeting her.

"You look beautiful," I mumbled slowly. The world seemed to be flying up as my head tore through clouds.

"You look foolish," she growled back.

"I missed your voice."

"Shut up Romance."

I started giggling. "I missed the way you scolded me over little things."

"Will you get a grip? I can't hold your body weight."

I tried making sense of those words but nothing held meaning. Where was the hug I'd been craving for since forever? Where were the lips that would satiate my months of contained hunger?

"Romance, please . . ."

That imploring voice hit my senses finally. The happiness started fading as I felt the grip of darkness. Everything seemed to fall now. I felt myself hurtle towards the Earth at an insane speed. No voice left my mouth. Everything was passing past in a blur. Before I could hold on to anything, my head hit something hard and the next thing more darkness engulfed me as everything went completely numb.

*   *   * * *

"It had to happen."

The voice faded out again. I tried to open eyes to look at the familiar face.

"Should we take him to hospital?"

My mind reeled with denial. I couldn't speak a word.

"The doctor said if his body doesn't secrete it out, they'll need to pump him. He was close to overdose."

I felt a hand clench mine hard. It was calloused and warm but smaller in size.

"Will he be okay?"

I heard a voice on the verge of breaking. My elder brother's instincts kicked in as I struggled to get up and take Luke in my arms. Luke had never sounded so weak and lately I'd been making my brothers suffer a lot.

"Hey buddy, he'll be fine. Look he is even regaining his colour. Give it some time and he'll be beating you for making his room untidy."

I gasped at the thought. Luke always had to do something to misbalance the picture!

"I lost my key."

I groaned inwardly. Luke had a secret trunk which he kept under his bed. Its location was such that only he could scramble in and get it out. This was probably the only childish thing left in him after mom's death. We all knew the box had little things Luke collected over time which mattered to him. Grover's favourite comic, Parsley's lucky sock, my favourite ball, dad's broken wrist watch, mom's necklace and so on. Even though they technically belonged to us, we let him keep for the sake of whatever *family love* remained.

"Do you err . . . think it's his, you know?"

Silence followed. Parsley was here? I thought he had claimed to never see me again. The mouthful I'd received some weeks back rang in my head.

"Where is Jamie?"

Finally someone asked the most important question.

"She's been admitted in the hospital just in case," Parsley said in a small voice. I felt my heart clench. "If it was up to me I would have killed each one of them. How can they take anyone against their will? Believe me if Romance wakes up to this bull, he's going to lose his cool."

"Frankly speaking Parse, it is in her will . . ."

Parsley   grunted in annoyance. I was rattled. The dizziness was capturing my mind again. It was difficult to keep fighting to keep in conscious. I had to somehow tell them to get Jamie Walker out of the hospital. In fact I had to first find out who hurt her enough so that she landed up there.

"Parse, look he's convulsing."

"Rome? Rome?"

I felt someone shaking me. The pain was making my head swirl. What had happened at the place for Jamie to be stuck in that white building of hell yet again? The guilt was eating my insides as I tried my best to stay conscious. There was the exhaustion with its two horns smirking at me. The last thing I saw before passing out was her smiling face.

* * *

The blur was coming into focus. For some rationale I was aware of being in the hospital. The sad part was I knew the reason as well. My memory didn't fail me again as flashes of what had happened some time played in my head. I shouldn't have crossed my limit. There was nothing but remorse left as the enemy.

"Romance, are you awake?"

My eyes swung open as the gruff voice entered into my sense. I could feel the raw emotions cutting through my heart. How could I put them through more emotional turmoil? This wasn't even a situation I couldn't have controlled.

"Are you okay? Please tell me you're fine." His voice was breaking down. The past few days had been witnesses of my two brothers breaking down. I didn't want the same with the third. Not with this one.

"I'm good," I said in a hoarse voice. "I'm top of the world."

The focus was clear now. I saw his face with the tears streaming down continuously. I'd never seen a person more broken than that. My arms automatically moved to take him in a hug but something was barring me.

"Stop moving idiot," he grumbled. "You'll get your tubes mingled."

"I'm sorry," I said with as much emotions as I could.

His hand hit the side of my face. It wasn't a complete slap but the impact was just as strong.

"You big loaf of all the dumbness in the world, do you have any idea what these past days have been like? We all worried ourselves retarded for you. Why the hell can't you listen to me?"

"I'm really sorry.'

He hid his face behind his palms. I heard him mumbling something but there was no clarity.

"I love you so much brother," he finally said seriously. There were no more tears adorning his rough features. He was back to the original Parsley. "There's been a lot of mess though past few days. You've missed quite a lot. You've been out for like two weeks now. There's no saying how much more you'll suffer."

I gasped. Just how long did it take to pump out the poison?

"Of course adding the operation days makes it almost a third week. You missed Grover's presidential speech for senior year and Luke's football game. That kid plays a mean game. We're through for the season."

Despite the gravity of the situation I whopped weakly. Parsley threw me a quick smile but switched back to the bossy, mature Parse. There was a glint in his eyes that of an adult that had made a final decision and would hear no out for it.

I was scared. Worry ate my veins as his mouth opened to speak again.

"I'll have to send you back to rehab now Romance. All the damage you've done to yourself. I can't let you harm yourself anymore. It's crucial you get out of this habit because the next month . . ."

I looked at him in horror as his voice started fading out after rehab. I would rather die than go back. The amount of mental and physical torture they'd put me through was enough for a lifetime. I didn't want to come back lifeless again.

I started to defend when he put up his hand.

"We shall discuss this later okay?"

My head had started spinning again. I couldn't handle the white walls where everything seemed squeezed into the nutshell. The echoes of the screams at night were still a nightmare. The voices of the mental patients who were trying to commit suicide some way or the other made me cringe in fear. The counsellor speaking as if he had bitten the forbidden apple and now possessed all the worldly knowledge which gave him the authority to dictate mine was another scenario I never desired to witness again. The medicines that made me think of situations worth killing yourself for. I'd gone into major depression there. Instead of instigating my emotions they had killed it through their various means of torture. It wasn't just the hallucinations they had to remove but my constant want of intoxications. I still remember being tied up in chains without control of the limbs so that I didn't scratch out my skin in frustration. The marks were still prominent. There was no space for another.

"Rome . . . Romance calm down. Hey . . . it's okay. I won't send you anywhere. I'm sorry I suggested that without thinking. It's just the stress of trying to fix a problem. I swear no one is going anywhere. Calm down please," he said panicking.

My heart was beating really loudly. The food had tasted like someone mixed water with vegetables. I'd seen people puke in their bowls and eat it back. They'd sent me to a mental asylum more than a rehab. I felt sweat splattered on my face.

"Romance please, I'm so sorry. Please calm down. Doctor! Listen I'll keep you close to me. All three of us will take care of you."

They'd given me electric shocks when I'd defied them. Their insistence on reminding me that Kitty was dead and I should stop imagining her around had worsened the situation. All I did was talk to her every day to keep my sanity but that was also unacceptable to them. She was my only key out of the cage they'd bound me like an animal.

Parsley's affectionate voice was loosening my nerves. His hand was clutching mine. The words he kept repeating finally made sense and I felt the heaviness vanish away.

After ten minutes everything was back to normal. The doctor whispered something in Parsley's ears and went away. I was asked to sleep so I let the darkness win over me again. The whole time that sense still prevailed, I could sense Parsley's uneasiness along with his strength.

The next time that I gained consciousness again, Grover and Parsley were having a heated conversation. I cleared my throat making both of them jump. For some reason they both started talking to me in a flowery tone which immediately raised my suspicion.

"What's happening guys?" I asked them seriously. My voice came off as really weak.

"The day is fantastic brother. Luke will be here soon. He wanted to get you cupcakes. That idiot hasn't been listening to the doctor. He just wants to see you happy. Yesterday, he brought this huge basket of Toblerone . . ."

"Grover, what's happening? Please I can't keep asking. It makes me tired," I whispered.

They both sighed.

"I have a right to know," I encouraged them bravely.

"Your stomach is fine. The weakness will stay for a while but the doctor said fortunately you haven't been drinking or smoking for that long that the effects are adverse on the body. They still need to run some tests though to make sure they can operate."

The words were making sense slowly. I gazed at them for quite a while with the other set of questions ready. Parsley was looking worse than before. There were dark circles under his eyes. His hair looked as if it hadn't been combed in ages. There were lines drooping from around his lips as if there had been no sign of life since ages now. It was tough on me to see them like that. That's when I made a strict promise with myself. I would never touch those intoxications, no matter what, again.

"That's all; we just need to make sure you stay out of worry."

I frowned at him. There was something he was hiding. I had to know.

"Where is Summer?"

They both looked at me alarmed. The moment that happened I knew there was definitely something amiss.

"What is it guys?"

I could see them looking at each other silently deciding what to tell me.

"Look, either one of you start talking or . . ."

The monitor started beeping loudly. Their eyes went to the screen in unison and widened.

"She's in the hospital as well . . . recovering from her injuries. You both were caught by some hoodlums wherever you'd been. She tried to protect you as you were already down and well she got hit. Parsley arrived in time with a couple of other guys from the team and beat the ruffians. The police have them. That's all that happened."

My heart sank. This was worse than I had thought.

"Romance, it's okay. We're taking care of Walker alright?"

I nodded. I knew Grover cared about her from that text I'd read. It was still a fresh wound that none of them had cared to tell me they were friends. It was as if no one trusted me enough. Jamie had been closer to me than them. They couldn't share her like this without even informing me.

The best way to while away time till discharge now was reading. I'd already finished two novels when Luke walked in. He'd decided to stay over for the night.

"What's wrong?" I asked Luke as his pale face gave me the usual look over.

"You won't believe what just happened."

"Well, by your tone I think there's something revolving around Parsley covered in a white blanket trying to pass off as a ghost in order to scare you?"

He shook his head seriously. I chuckled.

"I just proposed Meadow," he whispered in disbelief.

"Uh . . . okay?"

"No, you don't understand. She's not my kind of girl you know. She's like you."

"Are you saying I'm not your type of girl?"

He gave me an incredulous look. I smirked.

"No that's not what I meant. She's verbose with immaculate vocabulary along with that air of condescension like she's some royalty. She reads so much that her intellect is higher than my expectations of winning games."

"She sounds perfect. I do see how she's not your type though," I said thinking carefully. "Then why did you propose her?"

"It was in the moment. She slipped, I caught hold of her and then suddenly I felt queasy in the stomach. It's like every time I look at her my eyes can't get away. She has this little mole right next to her eyes that makes her eyes so appealingly pretty . . . I don't know, I lose sense and breaths around her. It was the proximity of those lips near mine that the adrenaline rushed in and I asked her out."

I couldn't help laughing after that. The innocence with which he was speaking so clueless was adorable. It was fun watching Luke struggle as a fifteen year old teenager with emotions he'd never felt before.

"You're in love Lukey," I cooed.

"I'm . . . so not, yeah right," he scoffed waving his hand. No matter how much denial he could act out, the hint of the pink tinge on his cheeks was a giveaway.

"Okay, you're not in love," I agreed slyly.

"You're in love," he accused me.

I nodded which made him roll his eyes. The truth was no good denying so why not accept it when it's been thrown at my face like that.

"So what did Meadow say?"

"She didn't believe me. There were tears in her eyes. She said something about me playing with her feelings," he shrugged.

"Did you clarify?"

"What did I have to clarify? She said that and ran away so I started walking towards the hospital again. I mean if she didn't say yes, what else can I do?"

"Luke you didn't follow her? Did you even try to comfort her?"

"For what did that woman need comfort? I asked her out not threatened to kill her family."

I sighed. This boy had so much to learn.

"Luke she didn't believe you because of the way you are around with girls. To her it seemed like she was one of your toys which you just said stuff to for a reaction. You broke her heart. Didn't the tears falling from her face tell you anything or make you want to follow her and clear things up?"

I was losing energy with all this exertion. However, it was important to teach my little brother humanity.

"It all makes sense now," he said horrified. "Oh my God, I'm such an idiot. No wonder I was feeling so horrible till now. I couldn't point a finger at what was wrong."

I threw him a smile. All this talk about young love was making me miss mine.

"Did you see Jamie lately?"

"Did you know I qualified for the final game championship?" Luke said excited.

I frowned at him. It was blatantly clear he'd switched the topic on purpose.

"Yes, Parsley told me. Will you answer my question now?"

"This one day I tried making pasta so I could get some for you. It got fuc . . . messed up really bad. I almost set the whole kitchen on fire. Grover was mad. How should have I known that I've to time everything."

"Luke quit it. I know what happened with Jamie okay? I'm pretty sure this is how you're keeping up the secret by completely avoiding her but Grover and Parse told me. It's fine you can answer my question."

The relief on his face came so strongly that I was astonished. I should've known how much of a burden it must have been for the little guy to keep it all in. He was the kind of person who couldn't help blabber everything without realizing he was giving someone else's secret away.

"I thought they'd never tell you about the heart situation," he said sadly. "I told them you were strong enough to take it."

My senses were on alert. No one had told me anything about the heart situation whatever it was. Now I was worried. Was Walker having a heart surgery or something that I should've known about?

"Parsley has been fighting the illegality since so long now. He's almost there. They're saying she can be saved. Would you have ever guessed Jamie was such an angel trapped in this horrible web of deceit? You won't believe how hard Grover and Parsley have been working just so Walker could be saved."

I kept quiet. Luke was a talkative boy, the less I interrupted him, the more he'd reveal.

"You don't know how hard I was hit when Jamie walked in that day and explained everything. We confronted dad and then the reality was just crazy Rome. It's so weird that none of us even had a clue of your heart or the fact that Jamie had to give you hers for transplant."

My focus shifted on him immediately. I'd never been more focused in my life than at this moment. Every word Luke was speaking was hitting my brain sharply.

"That fu . . . nonsense institute of hers makes me so mad I could light it on fire but I want those horrible people to get punished like they deserved. How could they keep so many children locked up like that just so they could play with their lives the way they wanted to."

My head was spinning. I could feel the blood rushing through my brain. My heart beats were getting louder as anger was seeping into my system. How could no one care to tell me all this serious issues instead of pouring in about beautiful weather when I didn't give a damn about it? Here I was whiling away my whole life as if everything was perfect when it had all been this intense. What was the whole deal with this Jamie Summer Walker that she couldn't have told me all this? I deserved to know. It was my right. How could all of them play with me as if I was a puppet?

"It's fine now though. The law suit against them is being worked upon. We need to get you operated fast. The day mom was coming back from the hospital; the day of the accident was actually there when the reports came about your heart being weak. Then you indulged in all that so dad had to send you to therapy without letting anyone know anything. The doctor says that the rehab place made some electric conduction weaker. The fact that you were again doing so much of intoxication has made it difficult for them to determine whether they can operate you or not. They've assured us though that there's enough time for your body to secrete out everything and then carry on the transplant.

We've been trying to find the organ that would match your blood type and we're quite close Romance."

I'd stopped breathing properly now.

Luke seemed to be really on a rampage. It was as if all the secrets in the world had to be told to me today.

"Jamie has named the kid Jasmine. God Romance, she really loves you that woman. Jasmine is the cutest thing ever. If I could I would lock it in the family box under my bed. Did you know Jamie calls Parsley Perry? I laughed so much when I found that out.

My head was bursting with knowledge. I didn't have the energy to ask Luke to shut up.

All my life looked like a big fat lie. Grover and Parsley walked in casually. They both seemed as if they'd had a good time. Their faces lit up as they saw me clutching the half eaten Toblerone bar until their eyes landed on mine and things changed.

"Are you okay?" Grover rushed forward with Parsley following pursuit.

"You idiots couldn't tell me you've told him everything? I just had a whole rant here. It feels so good to have finally informed Romance. I told you he's strong enough to take it."

Their faces paled. All three of us knew me, that I wasn't ready at all to have known all that. I could feel the effect of the truths hitting my health one by one.

"Luke what did you tell him?" Parsley asked urgently.

I could feel my hands shaking. How could have they lied to me? The guilt of what I'd put Jamie through had been eating my insides all day and now this? It was annoying that I couldn't even scream.

"Everything, I mean you guys have already. I just wanted to get it off my . . . what's wrong?"

"Luke you idiot, he didn't know," Parsley groaned. "We haven't told him anything except some cock bull story."

Luke paled.

My vision was blurring yet again. The whole left side of my body was aching. The place they'd inserted the IV was burning as if on fire. I could feel my eyes rolling back. The anger was making me crazier.

"Parsley you are her secret lover?" I managed to mumble. "How could neither of you ever tell me?"

"I wanted to Romance. I really did. She was scared. She needed time."

"How could you do this to me?" I felt my fists clenching. I wanted to punch Parsley.

"I love you Romance. Please, calm down. She loves you more than she ever did me. She's ready to give her heart to you. None of ours match. I would have given mine to save her for you."

I should have appreciated that but my mind couldn't hold down the anger. The fury was directed at me though. The helplessness was just fuelling the fire.

"Crap, we need the doctor. Luke press for help. Grover, he's heating up get the wet towels. The nurse said this might happen."

All this while she'd been there like a secret agent on mission. Is that why she couldn't be with me? How could she believe playing with my feelings like that was right? I love her so much; there was nothing more I wanted then but to have her around.

"He's calling for Jamie. We have to get her here somehow. Luke . . ."

"I'm on it."

It was a dark tunnel with a small hole ahead from which white light was pouring in. The more I tried to move towards the light, the more the darkness pulled me in. This was probably how death felt like. There was a sound of constant beeping that was going wild. It was making my head ache. All of a sudden I heard my name being called out. It was her. I had to reach her. My body was hurled through the darkness and the opening of the tunnel grew wider. The white light engulfed me as the sound of beeps and my name in her voice vibrated all around until there was nothing.

Just complete silence.

Epilogue

Son,

   This letter in no way is to celebrate the cheesiness that every letter carries with it. I wrote this down because these are actually going to be my last few words to you.

   You should never be the kind of father I was towards you. I don't even believe you will ever take lessons out from my life because frankly it was worthless. I don't need that much sense as well to make out how much of a non inspiration I have been to you.

   If you think I will tape down an apology here then that's a negation. I don't have the patience to say sorry for all the million ways I've disappointed you. You know what they are anyways.

   I've given you something that always belonged to you no matter if it never managed to show you all the love you deserved. Hence now, it will. You'll be able to live a lot longer and feel all the emotions that my heart should have showered on yours.

What's the best way to sort that out but give you my heart so that it directly gives you love?

Take care of my baby Luke. The only reason it is fairly easier to go is because I managed to make you boys hate me. Humans are gullible like that. It's easier to mould them into believing that which you want at times. Truth is especially that one target which always gets acceptance. It's easier to shoot away lies even if it is difficult to accept the truth. Your brothers should have had sense enough not to blame you without even a valid reason. I know being the father I corrupted their minds easily. I wish things had been different but then wishes are just that – plain old impossible desires which will never be fulfilled unless you put your heart and mind to it.

It's important that each of you stand up for another now. I know Grover is mature enough to take care of all of you but you've always been the sensible one. You need to take part in the decisions and not just blindly follow your elder brothers. Take care of them. They need you.

Redemption is one of the worst enemies for a soul and yet it is so important for the peace of mind. It will put you through emotions you don't desire but son don't ever be selfish when you know your actions will yield betterment for other.

There are trees that stay evergreen and then there are those that shed away for a while to grow back again into a new being. I'll do the same son. I'm shedding away for a while but I will mature back into a new being and this time I will make sure I stay evergreen more than barren.

Take care of Jamie as well. She loves you. I appreciate her presence in your life and would beg you to make sure you never bring tears into those pretty eyes. You both remind me of myself and your mum. Love is sacred son. Don't let it remain as a heart shaped chocolate, locked up in a box being sold off at a confectionary store.

> *You are the beat of my heart.*
> *Long deserved love,*
> *Dad*

I held my hand up to shield myself from the sun. The walk had been really tiresome. Jasmine was waiting for me outside in the car. Luke was having a baby today. He was a seventy year something old man. There was nothing I could do to cease his playboy skills anymore. Grover had left us on our own to embark on his own journey alone.

"How the bloody hell did you survive eighty more years with me eh?" I chuckled as I placed the orchids on the ground.

She smiled at me.

Even today the sun felt less bright as compared to her beauty. Her eyes were shining with tears as memories flooded both our minds. I walked forward till my hand was clutching hers.

"You really love me?"

She nodded her head gently. Even after all these years I couldn't get over the fact that Parsley had her before me.

"Parsley really loves that Yasmine woman. Even after all these years of amnesia, he still sticks around with her. Can you believe it?"

She smiled at me.

"Well, I wouldn't leave you even if death especially came and asked me."

She chuckled.

"You are life's beautiful surprise who knew my name belonged with hers and thus you gave me a lot of firsts. Your winks were lethal, your sniffs broke my heart and that's why I winked back every time to make you smile. You were so sweetly sour that every time I walked away from you, I got pulled right back in. Broken, my heart always belonged to you. *'You wouldn't have ever'* . . . was an expectation I shouldn't have. Perry or not, who cared who he was?"

I took a deep breath. My eyes kept locked into hers.

"You bit me, loved me against time -the two faced devil. Your fingers entwined with mine were symbolic to what destiny had kept entangled for me. Not even you, Jamie Summer Walker could figure out that Summer days were sometimes too hot and needed the soft caress of the cold to remain alive. I was never alone in the hate or the love. My diamond thread was pierced right through yours as if you were some story strung, only to be read. There was no death of hope like summer days every year, with you, even though hope was a mistake. Jamie Summer Walker, your beat of the heart against mine will always shine in the darkness beckoning Winter to come and vice versa. Even if you wear that blue frock with big dahlias printed, I'd give you shameless hugs. I am the pen, you're the ink. Your name will be safely locked in my heart. No amount of aftermaths will steal your title of sunrise. The two of us will remain frozen in this self written historical moment. Without you my world will have unreal happiness and it would be a war won for this knight but without you my lady. You turn every horrible day of mine into one of the best days. Every moment with you was much more worth than a movie's. You are the cherry on my perfectly baked chocolate cake. Every betrayal was forged down on my skin with my blood until there was nothing but complete silence. And yet, I love you and always will."

Her eyebrow raised in question.

"I guess I can be romantic after all."

She laughed throwing back her head. The red hair shone in the sun. The age had done no injustice to her beauty. She still looked like an angel from heaven.

"Dad, are you ready to go?"

"Give me a second Walker."

The boy nodded kindly. He gave me an encouraging smile. The features were so striking. I was glad he got none of mine. We just shared the same built of body. Otherwise the boy was just like his mother.

"Reed is coming over for dinner tonight with Smith. Could you even have believed that jock would end up with our Alan? They're a perfect couple though."

I strolled towards her. The light shone brighter.

"I also found you this, though a little late . . ."

I bent down and placed a perfectly round rock on the ground. Some years back I'd done the same with the wedding ring. She'd laughed till her stomach ache. Then she'd murmured the golden words to me. I could never forget that day.

I took in my last glance at her for a while. She waved me away.

"How will I do this without you?"

She rolled her eyes and egged me on. Her mouth made the words *I love you too*. I took hold of my walking stick and made a move back. On the way I scattered some crumbs for the local pigeons. There was Turkey junior back home that Walker took care off.

"Who were you talking to?" Walker asked, looking behind me with curiosity. "I saw you doing hand gestures."

"Well, you know I was never good with romance so I go practise it inside. That way I face fear along with doing something to cheer me up."

"But in a place like this?"

"There's no place like this to come outside happy when everything in your life was that."

He threw me a strange look. I envisioned her pretty face beaming at me as she gazed at both of us proudly. I slung my arm around our son as we both walked back home.

The sun started hiding behind the clouds. The words on the tomb of Jamie Summer Walker dimmed as the darkness floated in.

'The sun might extinguish someday being a star but the warmth it gives will linger forever even in the stormiest winter day. The darkness was so real she realized it was better to catch hold off the light until it was too late. He was the beat, she the heart'